THE
LAST
WATCH

THE LAST WATCH

J. S. DEWES

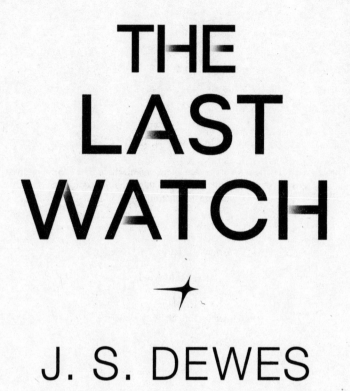

TOR

A TOM DOHERTY ASSOCIATES BOOK

NEW YORK

THE LAST WATCH

Copyright © 2021 by J. S. Dewes

A Tor Book
Published by Tom Doherty Associates
120 Broadway
New York, NY 10271

www.tor-forge.com

Tor® is a registered trademark of Macmillan Publishing Group, LLC.

The Library of Congress Cataloging-in-Publication Data is available upon request.

ISBN 978-1-250-23634-0 (trade paperback)
ISBN 978-1-250-23633-3 (ebook)

Our books may be purchased in bulk for promotional, educational, or business use. Please contact your local bookseller or the Macmillan Corporate and Premium Sales Department at 1–800-221-7945, extension 5442, or by email at MacmillanSpecialMarkets@macmillan.com.

First Edition: April 2021

Printed in the United States of America

0 9 8 7 6

For Robert Joseph MacCready,
who inspired me to write with the safety off.

THE
LAST
WATCH

CHAPTER ONE

"Spread your legs and bend over."

Cavalon's face flushed. Actually flushed. Embarrassing Cavalon Mercer was a feat few could boast. He was a little impressed.

He looked over his shoulder to grin at the guard, but the sour-faced man narrowed his eyes and jabbed Cavalon's hip with his shock baton. A jolt of electricity shot along the nerves of his leg.

"Spread 'em, soldier."

Cavalon's smirk faded into a scowl. He complied, spreading his legs and leaning against the wall in front of him. He flinched at the snap of a rubber glove. "If we're gonna do this—agh!"

Apparently they were going to do it, right-the-fuck now.

Cavalon squirmed, pressing his cheek into the cold aerasteel wall as the guard reached higher.

"I mean, if we're going to be *intimate*," he managed, "you could at least tell me your name."

"Bray."

"Pleased to—ugh—meet you, Bray."

"Does talking make this better for you?" Bray jeered.

Another guard snickered from behind a terminal in the corner of the room.

Cavalon pressed his forehead against the wall and closed his eyes. "No."

Twenty hellishly uncomfortable seconds later, Bray removed his fingers and pulled off the glove. "He's clear, Rivas."

"Was that strictly necessary?" Cavalon grumbled.

Rivas stepped out from behind the intake desk, Cavalon's underwear in hand. "We like to be thorough."

"Clearly." Cavalon snatched his boxers from the smug man's grip and pulled them on. If this was what life aboard the SCS *Argus* was going to be like, he was already over it.

Rivas returned to his terminal in the corner of the cramped intake chamber, lit only by a few narrow strips of recessed lights running vertically up the aerasteel walls. The holographic displays above the desk cast a dim blue aura across Rivas as he flicked through files. He stopped on a glowing icon and swept it open. "Full name Cavalon Augustus Mercer the Second. Confirm."

"That's me."

"Service number sigma 6454–19. Confirm."

Cavalon thumbed the pair of newly minted, absurdly antiquated, etched metal and glass identification tags around his neck. "Uh, sounds right."

"Your bioscan determined a biological age of thirty-four standard years. Confirm."

Cavalon narrowed his eyes. "I'm twenty-seven."

"Soldier is advised that biological age factors in degradation of physical form due to environmental factors including injury, wear-and-tear, use of narcotics—"

"Yeah, I get it," Cavalon sighed. "Sure, confirmed."

"Offenses listed as . . ." Rivas exchanged a quick look with Bray, then raised an eyebrow at Cavalon. "Redacted?"

A wave of relief washed over him, and he forced a grin. "Definitely confirmed."

Rivas shook his head and swiped the screen.

It flashed green, then a shrill, artificial female voice rang from speakers. "Identity confirmed. Please proceed to the next intake chamber."

A door in the sleek silver wall slid open, and Bray invited Cavalon forward with a condescending smile and a sweep of his arm. Cavalon drew back his shoulders and marched toward the door.

"Hold up." Bray grabbed Cavalon by the shoulder and pulled him back. "You've got Imprints."

Cavalon twisted his right arm to angle his tricep at Bray. The gold and bronze squares of the Imprint tattoos running from shoulder to wrist rearranged with the flexing of muscle, glinting as they caught the light.

"Just noticed that, huh?" Cavalon said. "You were too busy checking out my—"

"Shut it." Bray turned to Rivas. "Rivas—Imprints."

"Yeah, yeah. I heard you." Rivas detached a tablet from the top of the console and walked around the desk. He swiped the screen and a flood of neon-blue text poured into the air above it, the lines blurring together as the words sped by. He took a deep breath. "The System Collective Legion acknowledges that preexisting Imprints cannot be removed at risk of death. However, measures will be taken to counteract inappropriate use of preexisting Imprints, by whatever means deemed necessary by your commanding officer or the excubitor."

The holographic display above the tablet disappeared, and the outline of a small box materialized alongside a rather unfortunate mugshot of Cavalon.

"Do you understand?" Rivas asked.

Cavalon scratched the back of his neck. "Uh, yeah? I guess."

"Sign to acknowledge."

Cavalon pressed his thumb to the tablet. The screen flashed and his fingerprint faded away as more blue text flooded the air above the tablet, disappearing off the top too quickly to be read.

Rivas cleared his throat and continued. "You will be receiving a second set of Imprints per your intake aboard the SCS *Argus*. The System Collective Legion is not responsible for any adverse reaction you may have to an additional installation of Imprints. For the soldier's comfort and safety, it is advised that the soldier not attempt to utilize the functions of preexisting Imprints, at risk of volatile interfacing, which may include injury or death."

Cavalon eyed the waiver warily. "That sounds . . . bad." He'd only ever heard of half-breeds getting more than one set of Imprints, and never with any kind of stable outcome.

"Do you understand?" Rivas prompted.

"What would you do if I said no?" Cavalon asked. "Do I get to go home?"

Rivas's jaw flexed, and from the corner of his eye, Cavalon caught a glimpse of Bray's hand hovering over his shock baton.

Cavalon sighed. It wasn't worth it. Not yet, at least. "Okay, fine. I understand—no unsanctioned Imprint shenanigans."

"Sign to acknowledge."

He pressed his thumb against the screen again and the tablet accepted it. Bray grabbed Cavalon's arm and dragged him into the next room.

In stark contrast to the mood lighting in the *violation chamber*, this room seemed to be made of light. Walls of frosted glass showcased banks of white that bathed the entire chamber in an otherworldly glow.

Cavalon shielded his eyes with his free hand as the door whizzed shut behind them. In the center of the room sat a narrow counter, glowing from within, much like the walls. A silver box was suspended from the ceiling above the counter, and a series of articulated arms hung lifelessly beneath it.

An icy chill ran over Cavalon's bare skin and he shuddered. He'd always found Viator tech wholly unnerving. There was something off-putting about utilizing technology created by a species that had all but wiped out your own, even if the war had ended centuries ago.

Though clearly a secondhand appropriation of the original tech, this apparatus too closely resembled the real thing—like the one from which Cavalon had received his current Imprints on his eighteenth birthday. The same day he'd been forced to acknowledge his role as the Mercer heir, and the same day he'd vowed to find a way to escape his fate. He supposed getting shipped off to the Sentinels qualified as success in that regard, though certainly not the outcome he'd hoped for.

He glanced at Bray, who swept his hand toward the machine in invitation. Cavalon ground his teeth. His first Imprint experience had been borderline-blackout painful.

Wringing his hands, he shuffled forward, sucking in a long breath and letting it out through his teeth. He sat on the stool in front of the machine and a panel slid open, revealing a clamp recessed beneath the glowing glass counter.

The computer's voice returned. "Please place arm in the Imprint chamber."

Cavalon eyed the gold and bronze squares on his right arm, then shifted and laid his left into the clamp. Cold metal closed around his forearm and the machine whirred to life, buzzing and clicking. A series of thin red beams shone from each of the articulated limbs, and they positioned themselves noisily until the lasers lined up with their reference points.

"Please hold still during the Imprint process," the computer said.

White-hot beams shot into Cavalon's arm and searing pain engulfed his senses. He gritted his teeth and withheld a groan as the lasers danced across his skin, burning and smoldering until his arm felt like it'd caught fire.

Just as he started to think it might be a good time to pass out, the heat from the lasers dissipated along with the radiating light. His jaw slackened, teeth aching from prolonged clenching.

Dozens of polished obsidian squares lay across the irritated, bright pink skin on his forearm. He opened and closed his fist as the new Imprint tattoos folded and unfolded of their own accord. They hummed as they streamed past his elbow and up his bicep.

He twisted his arm to glance at his first set of Imprints. The gold and bronze squares lay dormant in their default arrangement—a tidy series of lines that ran from wrist to shoulder. These new Imprints crawled up his skin and fell into formation in a latticed grid on his left tricep, with a single dotted line of black squares trailing to his wrist.

"Imprint application complete," the computer chirped. "Control protocols updated."

Cavalon gulped. Control protocols? He ran his fingers along the new markings, then took a breath and tried to access them, call out to them and command them like he could his royal Imprints. But they didn't stir. They might have looked similar in appearance, but they were something else entirely.

His stomach knotted. Having a set of Imprints he couldn't control disconcerted him, to say the least. Who knew what these things could do to him?

"Come on, tough guy." Bray gripped Cavalon's shoulder and lifted him from the stool. Cavalon followed numbly, flexing his sore arm and scratching the irritated skin.

Inside the next small room, Bray pressed his thumb into a screen and a panel in the wall opened, revealing a pile of navy-blue clothing and a pair of black boots.

Bray grabbed the stack and shoved it at Cavalon. "Suit up. Boss is incoming." A door on the opposite wall slid open, and Bray left.

Cavalon called after him, "I thought we'd already moved past respecting each other's privacy . . ." The door slid shut, leaving him alone in the changing room.

He eyed the pile of clothes in his arms—standard, Legion-issue, dull navy blue layered with more navy blue. The centerpiece was a hooded, double-breasted vest which fastened high across the chest with two long straps. A single, narrow sandy-brown bar pinned to the left arm of the long-sleeved shirt indicated his rank of oculus.

His palms began to sweat as he pulled the clothing on piece by piece, trying and failing to not think about what stood on the other side of that door. Like every other kid in the System Collective, Cavalon had played the game of Sentinel at the Divide, but never during his opulent childhood did he think it a fate that would actually befall him.

The door opened and Bray stuck his head inside. "Soldier." It was a single-word command. Cavalon wiped his sweaty palms down the front of his vest and took a deep breath.

He entered another cramped, steel gray box. A simple narrow table and two straight-backed metal chairs sat in the center of the room. Clean, white light poured through one of the slatted aerasteel walls—an illusion meant to simulate the light of a nearby star. But there were no stars this far out, no celestial bodies of any kind this close to the edge of the universe. No planets or moons, no asteroids or comets or black holes or intergalactic dust. Not even space junk. Just nothing, just black. Just like the nursery rhyme. Cavalon would more than likely never see the light of a real star again.

He licked his lips as he walked to the table and pulled a chair out.

"No," Bray chided.

Cavalon stopped mid-sit and pushed the chair back, standing awkwardly at the edge of the table. He rubbed his new Imprints, pain still sparking along the nerves in his left arm, then drummed his fingers across the cold metal table. After a minute of silence, he turned to raise a questioning eyebrow at Bray.

The door across the room slid open. Bray snapped to attention— shoulders drawn back, fist to chest. A woman stepped in, back straight but head hung low, her olive skin taking on a cool tinge in the fake sunlight. She wore what looked like the undershirt of a flight suit—navy-blue tank top over a short-sleeved gray shirt, with a set of dog tags tucked between the layers. The glittering orange and yellow badges of her rank, meant to be displayed proudly across her shoulders, were obscured among the folds of the navy-blue jacket tied around her waist. She looked for all the universe like a ship mechanic, mid-repair.

She strode up to the table across from Cavalon, nodding at Bray. "At ease."

Bray turned on his heel and marched to stand beside the doorway she'd come through.

"Rake." She reached her hand across the table. Cavalon shook it, surprised at the firmness of her grip.

"Mercer." Cavalon responded on instinct, but immediately wished he could suck the surname back in. "Er—Cavalon. Cav's fine." He let out a heavy sigh. Like she didn't already know exactly who he was.

Rake sat as Bray stepped forward to lay a tablet down in front of her.

Cavalon eyed his chair, then gave Bray a sidelong look. The guard maintained his composure, but rolled his eyes, which Cavalon took as permission. He pulled the chair out and sat.

Rake stared at the tablet, scanning through pages of text. Her long, brown hair had been pulled up haphazardly, and she pushed some loose pieces out of her tired eyes, revealing a smudge of black grease across her cheekbone.

Cavalon raised an eyebrow. This was the "boss," huh?

"You got a little . . ." He flicked his fingers in front of his own cheek.

She sighed and wiped it with the back of her hand. Though it smeared into a soft gray, the smudge remained.

The corner of his mouth tugged up. "You got it."

Her expression remained impassive as she appraised him, then she lowered her gaze to the tablet again.

"You high brass?" He craned his neck to get a better look at the set of badges on the jacket around her waist. "Gramps made sure I got the special treatment, didn't he?"

"I don't think so," she mumbled as her fingers slid along the tablet's surface. "Your titles have been stripped. From the look of it, you're lucky he let you keep your given name."

Cavalon leaned forward and smirked. "What's it say? I'm intensely curious."

"I'm sure you are."

He shifted in his seat as she continued to sift through his file. He couldn't tolerate the silence for long. "So, you really take the time to tête-à-tête with every new soldier that comes aboard?"

Rake lifted her eyes from the tablet and stared at him. "I like to know who someone is before I ask them to risk their life under my command."

"Well," he scoffed. "That's a special kind of martyrdom. I think I'd prefer the blind-eye approach myself. Wouldn't that be easier?"

"Easier? Yes." She held his gaze, not wavering in the slightest. She was dead serious.

Cavalon bit the inside of his lip. He didn't know what to make of that kind of adamancy. For possibly the first time ever, he couldn't think of anything snarky to say.

He tugged on the suddenly too-tight collar of his vest. "Are you the warden?"

"This isn't a prison."

"With that cavity search, you could have fooled me." He smiled. She did not smile. "I'm the EX."

His humor faded, eyebrows raising in honest surprise. "Excubitor?"

Rake didn't respond.

"That's a pretty high rank for babysitting delinquent soldiers, no?"

She shoved the tablet away and leaned back in her chair. "I'm inclined to cut you some slack, Mercer. This isn't a normal situation. We don't usually take civilians into our ranks—"

"Are royalty 'civilians'?"

"—but you're not making it easy on me."

"Not up for a challenge?"

"If you think living at the Divide's not a challenge, you're in for a rude awakening."

"Right." Cavalon laughed. "You guys are the stuff of *legends*. How's that nursery rhyme go again? *Sentinel, Sentinel at the black—*"

Rake sighed and crossed her arms.

"*—do not blink or turn your back,*" he continued. "*You must stand ready to stem the tide, lest Viators come to cross the Divide.*"

Her decidedly unamused glare sharpened.

Cavalon shrugged. "There's another couple of verses. I'm sure you know them by heart."

"You think this is a game?"

"No, no. It's important. I get it. We're protecting mankind from another Viator incident." He leaned forward. "Except they died out *two hundred years ago.*" He sat back and crossed his arms. "Had to clean a few up during that little Resurgence War skirmish, but I guess that's a matter of course when it comes to xenocide. Bound to miss a few, here or there."

Rake's eyes narrowed. "You're really calling a nine-year war a *skirmish*?"

"Don't get me wrong. It's good the Legion is keeping an eye on things out here. And they're certainly putting all their best people on it—shuttling in every court-martialed and troublesome soldier they don't know what else to do with."

With a grating screech, her chair slid back against the floor. The table groaned as she leaned on clenched fists. She hovered over him, amber eyes alight. His breath caught in his throat, but on instinct he swallowed the feeling down. If nothing else, his grandfather had taught him how to counter intimidation. She was merely a discarded soldier, another one of these outcasts. He had no reason to fear her.

"This attitude is going to get you in trouble," she growled.

A soft mechanical buzzing drew his attention to Rake's right arm as it tensed, pressing into the metal table. Shimmering silver and copper squares folded and unfolded as they slid down her bicep and rearranged themselves onto her forearm.

"And I'm pretty much the most even-tempered one in this place," she continued. "I'd keep my head down if I were you, little prince. If your fellow soldiers find out who you are, you're going to have issues."

Cavalon scratched his left arm and looked down at his new tattoos, then back at Rake. Hers weren't black like his new Sentinel Imprints. And though they weren't gold and bronze like his royal ones, the effortless, perfectly geometric formation they took up as they slid down her arms told him they definitely weren't the black-market kind either.

Not just any Legion soldier had *real* Viator Imprints. In fact, he'd only heard of that combination of colors once before.

"Wait—Rake? Adequin Rake?"

Her impressively flat, stony glare persisted.

"I've heard of you." He couldn't hide the fascination in his tone as he leaned forward. "You were spec ops. A Titan under Praetor Lugen, right?"

"No one here is who they used to be. Not you, not me. You need to get used to that."

He had to consciously force his gaping mouth closed. "You're a goddamn war hero. How'd you end up at the Divide?"

For what seemed like the first time since she stepped in the room, Rake blinked. But she recovered instantly. "You should do your best to forget who you used to be. You can have a fresh start if you're willing to take it."

"That's just . . ." He scoffed. "Sorry, I was trying to think of a nice word. Delusional. It's delusional."

A fire lit in Cavalon's stomach as Rake reached across the narrow table and grabbed him by the front of his hooded vest. His eyes went wide as hers narrowed.

"You might be a big deal back on Elyseia," she said, her quiet tone disturbingly level, "but this isn't Elyseia. This isn't the Core, this isn't even System Collective territory. You're no one on the *Argus* except a soldier. An oculus. And you're lucky we even let you be that. No one here gives a shit about you. If anything, they'll despise you because of who you were."

Heat flared in his chest. "I'm not my grandfather," he growled.

His chair tipped onto the back legs as she shoved him, then released her hold. "Prove it."

Rake marched toward the door and it slid open, but she hesitated in the doorway. She took a deep breath before looking back at him. The anger in her eyes had softened, replaced with the same look of tired defeat she'd walked in with.

"Life on the *Argus* doesn't have to be hard," she said. "But we're Legion, you have to remember that. Your comrades are not going to respond well to this entitled-prince attitude. Do yourself a favor and cut the shit." She turned and disappeared around the corner before calling back, "Bray, give this one a psych eval."

"Oh, come on," Cavalon groaned as the door shut behind her.

The "good soldier" stick lodged in Bray's ass seemed to slide away, and he relaxed his shoulders, grinning at Cavalon. "Great first impression, princeps. Nice job."

Cavalon let out a breath and smoothed the front of his rumpled vest. That's what he'd always been best at. Great first impressions.

CHAPTER TWO

Adequin Rake sat on the bridge of the *Argus* in a captain's chair she had no right sitting in. She'd trained as a fighter pilot, a tactician, a marksman. But she did not have the skills of a dreadnought captain. Even for an immobile dreadnought.

Though, she might have felt more comfortable if it *were* in active service. She couldn't fly the thing if her life depended on it, but at least there'd be some tactics involved. Some kind of strategy, a way to utilize her training and expertise.

She wiped at the grease still smudged across her cheek. She'd had the chief mechanic teach her some basic life-systems maintenance so she could feel more useful, and got a whole load of feeling useful this morning when one of the thermal control units in Novem Sector decided to fail. Despite the inconvenience of waking at zero two hundred to fix it, she'd enjoyed the manual labor. At least she'd accomplished something.

She picked at the edge of the navy-blue padding on the armrest of the stiff chair, made of lightweight, durable aerasteel like basically every other thing on the ship. The bare-bones bridge crew milled about around her, attending to their daily tasks.

Her imposter's chair sat at the top level of the half-circle room. The decks of the bridge fell away in three staggered tiers, landing at the foot of an enormous viewscreen which showcased an outward view of the universe. Which was to say, the Divide. Which was to say, fucking nothing. The giant black screen was always black, always had been, and always would be.

Her second-in-command's master terminal and the primary

systems stations sat a tier down, and the bottom level contained the weapons and piloting terminals that would in all likelihood never be manned again. She'd even turned off the ship's dour virtual aid, because who needed a dreadnought-class battle intelligence to keep a glorified watchtower aloft?

Adequin looked up to see herself ascending the stairs from the middle tier toward the system overview console.

"Eh, void," she cursed. She held up a finger to halt her doppel-gänger. Its edges quivered, and it seemed to jitter backward and forward along its path before it came to a stop. "Hold on." Adequin turned to her second-in-command. "Uh, Jack?"

"Yeah, boss." A tier down, Jackin North hovered over his terminal's display, the bright orange glow of the holographic screens warming his light brown skin. He didn't look up as he continued to swipe through data.

"Have we drifted?" she asked.

Jackin's dark brown eyes shot up in alarm to meet hers. "Have we?"

Adequin tilted her head to indicate the copy of herself standing beside her.

"Shit . . ." Jackin buried his face in the screen again.

Adequin's future-self crossed its arms. "This has been happening more and more frequently, Optio," it said. "What's going on?"

"Come on, don't get involved," Adequin grumbled, standing from the captain's chair to face her duplicate.

"Jack *just* asked me to check—"

"Shh, you." Adequin took it by the shoulders and ushered it to the door of the bridge. "Just stay put, you'll be gone in—"

Her doppelgänger flickered and wavered, then disappeared from existence.

"Well," Adequin said, "looks like the thrusters are working." She descended the steps to stand over Jackin's shoulder.

He shook his head. "We aren't getting any errors, but something must be off with the stabilizers. There's no reason we should be drifting; there's nothing out here to pull us one way or the other."

"Could that new recruit's transport have caused it when it left earlier?"

"That's like asking if a mosquito could move a pile of elephants."

She shrugged. "I have to rely on you for this stuff, Jack. I'm no ship captain."

He looked up long enough to flash a grin. "I know, boss. Check the systems console, read me back a number."

She ascended the stairs to the system overview console, and a terrifying sense of déjà vu washed over her. She'd started to take the actions her doppelgänger had just a minute ago.

She shook off her unease and approached the console. She swept open the interface and a holographic display of the kilometer-long ship unfolded, each sector labeled with dozens of numbers.

"Top left," Jackin said. She read the numbers back, and Jackin grumbled. "I don't get it. It reads like we drifted outward over fifty meters. Maybe the sensors are just malfunctioning."

Adequin closed the interface and returned to stand beside the captain's chair. "This has been happening more and more frequently, Optio. What's—" She cut herself off as she realized she'd fully caught up with the actions of the time ripple. She hated when this happened.

Jackin shot her an amused glance as she trudged down the steps to stand next to him.

"How can we fix it?" she asked.

"I dunno." He scratched his short beard and gestured to the main screen, still showcasing a panoramic, perpetual view of the nothingness before them. "It's not like I have anything to anchor us to, or from."

"What about a buoy? Would that help?"

"Only if it'll stay put itself."

"I'll put in a request."

"Great, so we'll see *that* on the other side of never."

She smiled. "I'll label it priority."

"I won't hold my breath."

"EX, sir?" the crew foreman, Kamara, called from her terminal across the stairway. She turned in her stool as she tucked a strand of dark brown curls back into her prim bun. "It's almost twelve hundred, sir."

Adequin glanced at the chronometer above the viewscreen. "Right. Thanks, Kamara." She gave Jackin a pat on the back. "The *Tempus*'s incoming. I'll go meet them."

Adequin left the bridge and headed for Quince Sector, swiping her clearance to steal a shortcut through a narrow maintenance passage. When she arrived at the hangar, the service access door slid open, bringing forth a waft of warm air, tinged with the dense aroma of grease and rubber.

She stepped onto the second-level catwalk encircling the hangar and glanced over the railing to the operations deck below. The once-polished aerasteel decking had long ago lost its sheen, marred over decades of service from when the *Argus* had been the SCS *Rivolus* over two centuries ago—one of the most formidable ships in the System Collective fleet at the end of the Viator War. What would have once been bustling with pilots, deckhands, starfighters, and support crews, now sat empty, save for the large repair platform, home to a half dozen workbenches.

On Adequin's right sat the entrance to the port docking bay, where warning lamps oscillated between red and yellow to indicate the still-open air lock on the other side. On the opposing wall, a massive central bulkhead loomed, beyond which lay a mirror image of the same setup on the starboard side of the ship. The hangar had been split during the retrofit two hundred years ago, when the dreadnought had been repurposed for the Sentinels after the Viator War.

But the second hangar hadn't been used since budget "reallocations" forced them to discontinue charting and exploration missions. In Adequin's early days on the *Argus*, those missions had made her day-to-day far more tolerable. Sure, they literally never found anything, but the possibility alone worked to combat the stagnancy. She'd had to cancel them after less than a year, and though regrettable, she just as often wondered if another four years of vacant star charts and unfruitful element probes would have only served as another unneeded reminder of how truly on the edge of nowhere they were.

The echoing squeal of an impact driver cut through the dense quiet, and Adequin's gaze lowered to the operations deck.

The chief mechanic, Circitor Josslyn Lace, hung from the truss halfway up the side of a seven-meter-tall mobile service gantry. Two oculi stood below her, one whose arms and hands and pockets were completely full of wiring, parts, and tools, and another who stared up intently, arms hovered as if ready to catch the circitor should she suddenly lose her grip.

Adequin descended the long access ladder to the bottom deck and headed toward them. The unburdened oculus snapped a smart salute, and Adequin waved off the other as they fumbled with their armful of tools in an effort to do the same.

Lace's gaze drifted down, and she holstered the impact driver into her tool harness. One of the oculi hissed a gasp as Lace unhooked her arm from the truss, then slid down two meters before hopping the rest of the way off.

She faced Adequin and saluted, fist to chest. "Sir."

"Circitor." Adequin greeted her with a nod, eyeing the pair of protective goggles nestled in Lace's short silver hair, flecked with white ringlets. "Those go on your eyes," Adequin said. "Last I checked."

"Oh, that's right." Lace flashed a good-natured smile, her warm voice gravelly with age. "Hey, at least I had them on my person this time. Baby steps, sir."

"Consider stepping a little faster. This ship'll fall apart if you go blind."

Lace nodded. "Yessir."

Adequin eyed the partly dismantled service gantry. "That same gantry giving you trouble again?"

"Never not." Lace grimaced, pulling off her grease-stained work gloves and tucking them under one arm. "Good to see you not at the ass-crack of dawn for once. Thanks for helping me out, by the way. Woulda taken me twice as long on my own. Though I'm still not sure how I feel about givin' the EX orders."

Adequin smiled. "Glad to help."

"Did ya need somethin', sir?"

"Just here to greet the *Tempus*."

Lace glanced at the docking bay, its air-lock alarms still flashing. "They should nearly be done pressurizing; I'll need to clear them for egress."

"I'll take care of it," Adequin offered. "I know you're probably chomping at the bit to get back to repairs . . ."

Lace's faded brown eyes glinted with humor. "Thrilled, sir. Tell Bach he owes me a beer."

"Will do."

Lace returned to the gantry, and Adequin left, crossing the barren deck toward the bay entrance. She unlocked the controls beside the massive hatch doors just as the readout ticked down to the last percent. The screen flashed green, and she tapped in her clearance code.

The massive doors let out a hissing exhale, then bisected, pushing out a waft of cool, dry air. No matter what they did to try and fix it, the docking areas always remained a dozen or so degrees cooler than the rest of the ship.

Across the now-equalized bay sat the newly arrived, fifty-meter-long scouting frigate: the SCS *Tempus*, its polished aerasteel frame glinting silver in the harsh overhead lights. The blue glow of the quad ion engines faded, and the heat vents released a long, shrill purr before falling silent.

Adequin crossed the expanse of diamond-plated decking to the landing pad, one of six docking areas outlined with tattered, reflective demarcation tape. Crimson beacons lit on the underside of the ship and the hatch ramp lowered.

One by one, fifteen crew members disembarked, rucksacks thrown over their shoulders. Each one stopped to salute Adequin as they passed before disappearing into the main hangar. A few seconds after the last had left, Griffith Bach finally emerged.

Too tall to clear the squat door frame, the thick-muscled centurion ducked through the hatch and stepped off the *Tempus*. He hefted his pack onto his shoulder, and his silver and copper Imprint tattoos glinted along his bicep. His eyes landed on her and he smiled, his teeth a flash of white against his warm brown skin. Shades of gray sprinkled his trimmed beard, but he didn't look a day older than when he'd left.

As the most centrally located Sentinel vessel, the *Argus* acted as home base for the crew responsible for maintaining the network of buoys comprising the Sentinel alert system. For the last six months, the *Tempus* had patrolled the "downward" expanse of the Legion-occupied section of the Divide, stopping along the way to make any needed repairs. However, the closer one got to the Divide, the faster one moved through time. The same phenomenon caused the unnerving flashes of the future when vessels drifted too close, like the *Argus* had earlier.

So even though to Adequin, Griffith had been gone six months, it'd only been two weeks for him and his crew. This had been his assignment for the last three years—three years to her, three months to him.

Griffith dropped his pack off his shoulder and descended the ramp.

"Aevitas fortis, Titan," she said.

"Aevitas fortis," he echoed, pausing long enough to press his fist to his chest in a proper salute before continuing toward her.

"I'm gonna catch up with you soon, Centurion." She threw her arms around the burly man's neck.

He pulled her close, then let go to look her over. "You haven't aged a day either, Mo'acair."

"Yeah, right. If you keep this post, it'll only be ten years before I'm older than you."

His dark brown eyes flickered with unease. "You mean ten *months?*"

She shook her head. "Lace says you owe her a beer."

Griffith's jaw firmed, but a smile tugged at his lips. "Goddamn, she's relentless."

"About what?"

He rubbed a hand down the side of his face. "Nothin' important. After twenty years, you'd think I'd learn not to bet against her."

"One would think," Adequin agreed. "How'd it go?"

"Nothing to report. Buoys are all clear, no signs of activity. A few minor repairs, but we got it all squared away."

"Did you dock at the *Accora*?"

"We did. They're doing well. Being good Sentinels, as always."

"They heard from HQ lately?"

Griffith's brow creased. "They didn't mention if they had or hadn't. Why?"

"Nothing." She blew out a short breath. "They keep delaying meetings. Haven't had a true status update in five months. I think they're bored with us."

He gave her a warm grin. "They just trust you, Quin. They know you have your shit in order here."

"Yeah, I guess."

Adequin's nexus beeped, and she glanced at the interface—it was signaling an incoming call from Bray. She tapped the black band on her wrist to open the comm link. "Go for Rake."

"Sir, Oculus Bray." Bray's voice came crackled and staticky over the line. "I have the results of the psych eval you ordered."

Adequin sighed, exasperated by the reminder of the snarky, entitled bastard. "I'm in the hangar, meet me there."

"On my way, sir."

Adequin closed the comm link and offered Griffith a weary grin. "Duty calls."

He nodded over his shoulder at the *Tempus*. "I have to do my final report anyway. Drinks tonight?"

"I shouldn't. I have a ton of paperwork."

He raised his thick eyebrows.

"Just some reqs and other boring EX stuff."

He frowned and stuck out his lip. "But I've only got thirty-six hours."

She grinned. "Like I'm gonna let your shore leave lapse without seeing you. We'll make something work, promise."

"All right," he said as he backed toward the ship. "I'm holding you to that." He turned away and jogged up the ramp, ducking into the *Tempus*.

Adequin started toward the operations deck, but found Bray had already arrived, marching a brisk pace across the bay toward her.

He stopped and saluted, tablet gripped in his other hand. "Sir."

She nodded, and Bray unlocked his tablet, then opened the secure data-transfer menu. She tapped her nexus and a small holographic interface opened above her forearm. Holding the inside of the black band to the face of Bray's tablet, the transfer initiated, popping the encrypted file up on her screen.

Though antiquated, the proximity served as an intentional security precaution—the only arguably more secure method being actual physical paper, which could then be destroyed. Adequin hadn't yet encountered a need for that level of security in her time aboard the *Argus*. In fact, she couldn't remember the last time she'd seen a piece of paper.

Bray saluted and began to walk away.

"Bray?" she called after him.

He about-faced. "Yes, sir?"

"Do me a favor—don't tell anyone who he is?"

"Of course, sir," he said, his gray eyes steady with their usual resolute firmness, and she knew she didn't have to worry. He'd keep his word; he always did. Bray had always been one of her most reliable oculi, and well-overdue for a bump up to circitor. But she'd technically expended the number of promotions she could hand out given their current population, and had to wait on approval from Legion HQ before advancing anyone else. Which was another reminder message she needed to send tonight.

She gave Bray a grateful nod. "Thanks. Dismissed."

He marched away, and Adequin glanced around. The twangs

of Bray's retreating boots echoed in the empty launch bay, and the muffled sounds of Lace's repairs floated in from the main hangar, but otherwise she was alone.

She opened the encrypted file and a bank of text appeared in the air over her forearm. She read the first paragraph, then scrolled down, skimming the rest for the broad strokes.

Unfocused intelligence. Shrewd. Insolent. Complex issues with authority. Lethargy. Self-medication. Depression.

The last line read, "Caution and close observation recommended."

She let out a hard breath as she pinched the file closed. She hated this programmed psychological bullshit. Even with advanced AI, machines couldn't really read a person, really tell what they were like, what they were thinking. Or what they were capable of. She'd only ordered the evaluation out of spite, an attempt to assert dominance over the unwieldy recruit. Which deviated from her customary approach, but he'd proven to be a whole new breed of disrespectful.

Every Sentinel was a delinquent, of a sort, soldiers who had been court-martialed for some offense or another—insubordination, theft, perjury, fraternization, desertion, treason. But they were all soldiers, and they regarded her with at least a modicum, if not a great deal, of respect. Maybe because they knew who she was, knew she'd been a Titan. They also knew she must have done something to end up here, and that endeared her to them. They could empathize with that.

But not Cavalon Mercer. He'd been forced aboard the *Argus* and into her charge by machinations and politics, the motivations of which she'd likely never understand, and didn't care to. The bottom line was: He wasn't one of them, and he would need to be managed differently than a soldier. What that management entailed, she didn't know. For now, she'd just have to keep a close eye on him.

CHAPTER THREE

Cavalon hadn't grown up in space. He'd spent his formative years firmly planted on the terra of Elyseia until his thirteenth birthday brought him to the ritual coronation grounds on the planet's only moon. So he well-remembered what it'd been like to meet the universe for the first time.

"*You're looking into the past,*" his father had told him. "*By the time the light reaches you, those stars could be dust.*" It'd been awe-inspiring and humbling. He'd never felt so small.

That is, until now, as he stood in front of an observation window on the *Argus*—though "observation" was generous. He squinted and pressed his face closer to the glass to get a better look at . . . nothing.

But not the nothing of a moonless night or the barren space between solar systems or galaxies. This was the nothing of the Divide, of the edge of the universe. An invisible barrier formed millions of years ago when the collective mass of the cosmos finally balanced out the dark energy, slowing and eventually halting the previously ever-expanding universe. A border that separated all matter from the void that lay beyond—the literal edge of nowhere.

He'd never seen anything so . . . *dark*. Yet it was a blackness that somehow went beyond dark, beyond vacuum or abyss or void, or any word that could even begin to aptly describe it. There were no twinkling stars, hundreds or thousands or millions of light-years away, unreachable by practical means, but still present, still proof of something millennia gone. There was just . . . nothing. And there never had been, and there never would be. It was terrifying.

A hand patted him on the back, jarring him from his reverie.

A tall man with bronze skin and a shaved head stood next to him, grinning out at the vast emptiness.

"View's better inward," the man said. "In my humble opinion." He tapped the black band on his wrist, activating a small holographic screen above his forearm. "My nexus says . . . Cavalon? No last name?"

"Just the one." Cavalon breathed a sigh of relief, grateful that despite how poorly his meeting with the EX had gone, she'd still not put his surname into the system.

"I'm Puck." The man took Cavalon's hand in a firm grip. "Circitor Amaeus Puck. Pleased to meet you."

"Likewise." Cavalon eyed him warily. He didn't want to be paranoid, but he felt like the man was being too nice. "Sorry, did you say inward?"

"Yep. There's pretty much exactly two directions out here." Puck jutted his narrow chin toward the window. "Outward—toward, you know, literally nothing." He pointed a lanky finger the opposite direction. "And inward, the general direction of, well, everything. Like civilization and our galaxy and actual matter."

Cavalon swallowed. "Right . . ." Legionnaires loved their jargon. He'd add that to the list of terms he'd probably forget.

"Upward and downward too, I guess," Puck added, pointing either direction with the opposite hand. "Along the plane of the spiral arms, as one does. You remember that from back home, surely."

Cavalon sighed. "The spiral arms which are a hundred million light-years away?"

Puck grinned broadly. "Those're the ones."

"So you're my, uh, commanding officer?" Cavalon asked.

"Sure am. Walk and talk with me. I'll show you around."

Puck took off down the hallway, and Cavalon hurried to fall in line behind his long strides.

"How was the trip?" Puck asked, leading them through a narrow doorway and into a main corridor.

"Perfect. Traveling to the edge of the universe was exactly how I wanted to spend three months of my life."

"Oh, they slow-boated ya, huh?"

"Can you get here any quicker?"

"There's an Apollo Gate run from Legion HQ that takes about six weeks, but it depends where you're coming from, I suppose. Where were you stationed?"

"Nowhere."

Puck laughed. "No, *now* you're nowhere."

"Right . . . I mean, I'm not Legion." Cavalon scratched under the metal chain of his dog tags, already chafing the skin at the back of his neck. "I *wasn't* Legion."

"Oh. Huh." Puck glanced at his nexus screen. "Don't get many of those." He continued to scroll through the holographic display as they walked, expertly sidestepping oncoming soldiers. "Damn, that's a lot of degrees. How long'd you go to school for?"

Cavalon paused to dodge an approaching soldier, then jogged a few steps to catch back up. "Ten years."

"Damn," he said with a laugh, flicking through more pages. "Astrophysics with a minor in 'gravitational tempology'? What even is that?"

"A way to stay at university another year."

"Ahh." Puck chuckled and closed his nexus. "Well, shit, recruit. Other than Mesa, you're probably the smartest one here."

"Mesa?"

"She runs the Viator tech research lab."

"You've got a research lab?"

Puck nodded. "Oh yeah, they love to ship us every piece of random tech they don't understand and see if it'll kill us. Gives us somethin' to do, I guess."

They came to the end of the hall, which culminated in a wide, circular corridor. Cavalon followed Puck toward a railing overlooking an open atrium, four deep stories descending below them.

"Welcome to the amidship vestibule." Puck leaned on the rail with both elbows. "There's one aft and forward as well, but they don't really bother maintaining the lifts on those. I suggest you frequent these central ones if you don't wanna get stuck in an elevator for half a day."

"Uh, good to know . . ."

Puck gestured over his shoulder. "That was Novem Sector, crew quarters, if you couldn't tell. Right below us are Octo and Septem—weapons control and the armory, sensors, shields, ECM suites. All the shit we don't use anymore."

Cavalon gripped the metal railing, leaning over to peer down the circular atrium as a draft of cool air wafted from below.

"Bottom deck's Quince," Puck continued, "home to the hangar where the *Tempus* docks—that's the ship that rides the Divide."

Cavalon quirked a brow. "*Ride* it? You mean travel along it?"

"Yep."

"And they're doing what exactly?"

"Ya know, keepin' an eye out for all those Viator ships trying to cross over from the *other side*." Puck flashed a toothy grin.

Cavalon sighed. Despite things like logic and reason, the colloquial myth persisted that the Viators had "come from" the other side of the Divide when they arrived in humanity's sector of space thousands of years ago. But the idea that anything lay beyond had been disproved centuries ago when the System Collective commissioned a series of exploration missions "beyond the edge." Suffice it to say, the contractors were never heard from again. So either there was something really great on the other side and no one had felt like coming back, or, far more likely, they all died.

However, when one of the lucky crews chickened out at the last minute, they discovered that if you flew parallel with it instead of perpendicular, the concentrated gravity comprising the invisible barrier acted like a runway of sorts. They realized it could be "traveled on"—almost like falling into an orbit, albeit a strangely linear orbit that created its own momentum, involving gravity so dense it bent space-time. The phenomenon must have been what this ship of theirs utilized in order to "ride" the Divide.

That anecdote comprised pretty much the entirety of Cavalon's knowledge on the topic—his formal education had barely touched on that bit of theoretical physics. Back home, back at the Core, the Divide acted as more a vague concept than any kind of reality. People rarely spoke of it in any tangible way—maybe a passing mention during a drunken philosophical debate, or in a threat from an angry parent to an unruly child. Not a real place, where real people lived. So, despite being here, physically, for many painful and humiliating hours, it all still felt like some kind of hazy dream.

"But really," Puck went on, "the *Tempus* goes out to maintain the alert system. There's a whole network of ancient alert buoys hanging out along the upward and downward stretches. They make sure it all stays shipshape."

"And one crew takes care of all that?" Cavalon asked.

Puck gave a grim nod. "Yep, just the one. Only other ships we even have aboard are a couple Hermes-class vessels we ran charting missions with, years back."

"Hermes-class? Isn't that a civilian make?"

Puck chuffed. "Yeah, brass spends the big bucks on us out here. And even then—no warp cores. Only sublights."

"What about jump drives?"

"Definitely not. No stars out here to charge 'em anyway."

"So no FTLs?"

"Not one."

"So, you have nothing faster than an ion engine?" Cavalon asked, raising his eyebrows. "Why?"

"'Cause then we could leave."

"They think you're all just gonna run off?"

Puck smiled. "Try saying that with a straight face in a month."

Cavalon frowned, then looked out over the atrium as Puck gestured to the bottom floor.

"Quattuor's mostly research and development," he continued. "Tres at the ventral bow has all the fun stuff—mess, hydroponics, brig, medical, psych ward."

"You have a psych ward?"

Puck shrugged. "Something about living on the edge of reality gets people anxious, I guess. Never bothered me. Just another empty place in this mostly empty universe, ya know?"

Cavalon nodded. "Sure . . ."

Puck gestured across the vestibule to the middle level. "That guy's Duo Sector, which houses all the comms systems."

"A whole sector just for comms?"

"Communication near the Divide gets tricky. We actually don't have direct contact with the Core or Legion HQ out here. We have to bounce our comms off the closest Apollo Gate, and to accomplish even that, they had to retrofit the shit out of the whole system—half the hull on the starboard quarter is covered in comms arrays. Something about boosting the signal enough to overcome the interference. And even then, it only works half the time."

Cavalon bit his lip. They were millions of light-years from anything that could even be remotely likened to civilization, so it really shouldn't surprise him, but the idea of being so vastly out of touch with the rest of humanity still unnerved him.

"And last but not least . . ." Puck pointed across the atrium to another corridor on their level. "Unum leads to the bridge, brass quarters, and the EX's office. That's it."

"Well, I won't remember any of that," Cavalon said, leaning against the railing next to Puck.

"Luckily they've posted helpful signage." Puck smiled, then his eyes flitted to the new Imprints on Cavalon's left arm. "You a lefty?"

Cavalon pulled his sleeves over his wrists to cover as much of both sets of tattoos as possible. "Nah, just . . . felt better on the left." His gaze drifted to Puck's arms. His sleeves were pushed up, and a single trail of obsidian squares ran down his right forearm from the elbow to the wrist. Cavalon cleared his throat. "What are they for, anyway?"

"I've not had the pleasure of experiencing what they feel like," Puck admitted, "but it's, uh . . . punitive in nature. Correctional. Or what the Legion likes to call a 'vital peacekeeping safeguard.'"

Cavalon wet his lips, reflexively ironing the anxiety from his expression. "Everyone has them?"

"Only those who came aboard at the rank of oculus, or who've been demoted to oculus since. Which happens, like, a lot, honestly." He shook his head. "Anyone higher than that gets a free pass.

The excubitor, obviously, and our fearless second-in-command, Optio North . . . a couple of the animus, and the centurion that captains the *Tempus*. That's really it, that I know of."

Puck's back straightened as a thin, wisp of a woman approached. She wore the proper Legion navy blue, but in the form of a dress made of silk folds accented with glimmering threads of silver. An embroidered silk hood had been drawn up over her black hair, shadowing her warm beige skin. It was certainly no uniform.

Puck rubbed his hands together. "Oculus Cavalon no-last-name, meet Animus Mesa Darox, our resident Viator expert."

The woman's withdrawn face and sharp, overlarge eyes swept over Cavalon. From afar, her irises had seemed almost black, but up close they shone a deep brown, dappled with tiny flecks of metallic blue-green. "Pleased to meet you, soldier," she said.

"You're a Savant," Cavalon said.

"You are observant," she replied flatly, her humorless gaze unimpressed.

"I didn't know Savants enlisted."

"They do not."

Cavalon rubbed the back of his neck. "So . . . Puck said you run the research lab?"

"Correct. I am an animus," she said, as if that alone explained everything. Cavalon looked to Puck for help.

"A science officer," Puck explained. "Often contracted, not enlisted."

"Ah." Cavalon looked back to Mesa. "What kinds of things are you studying?"

"Most of what we do is classified," she said curtly.

"I heard the System Collective finally released the salvage from the exosphere of Paxus to the Legion. Did you guys get any of that?"

Mesa opened her mouth to respond before cutting herself short. She narrowed her large eyes at him, clearly surprised at his knowledge on the topic. "Well, yes. We received all of it, in fact. Or *will*." She let out a small huff. "They are sending it slowly, crate by crate. It is infuriating."

"Get anything good?"

She regarded him placidly, and he wasn't entirely sure she intended to respond. Finally her shoulders slid down and she drew her neck up straight, then gave a curt nod. "We did recently begin study on a very interesting weapon. I have not completed my final assessment, as yet, but it appears to be fusion-powered."

Cavalon quirked a brow. "Fusion? What kind of weapon?"

"It might best be described as a pistol."

"A fusion-powered *pistol*?"

"Yes," she said, then cleared her throat. "Its design is quite fascinating. Despite the nature of the power source, the time required to prime the weapon is surprisingly short. It is very unlike the typical plasma and electromagnetic weapons their standard troops carried during the Viator War. This must have been a weapon reserved for elite units, or possibly an advancement developed while they were in hiding for two hundred years. I think we may have initially underestimated their understanding of microfusion . . ."

Mesa clearly attempted to remain formal, but her passion leaked through in her eager tone. Cavalon found it a little infectious, and he couldn't stop from smiling. He'd always been impressed by the Savant capacity for knowledge. Of the two attempts Viator geneticists had made at crossing themselves with humans, he'd always thought Savants had received the far better end of the bargain. Sure, Drudgers were freakishly strong with an impervious constitution, but they'd been stuck with the worst of the Viator looks. Though as far as interspecies hybrids went, he supposed it could have turned out worse. Either way, Drudgers definitely had *none* of the intellect or ethereal grace Savants exhibited. Also, they smelled.

"So, all this tech . . ." Cavalon said. "Is the goal to reverse engineer it? So you can make dupes yourself?"

"Crude way of putting it, but yes," she said. "Also, we glean whatever we can from the engineering. Even after a millennium of access, Viator technology still eludes us, on the whole."

He smiled. "Crack that whole 'crossed over from the Divide' thing yet?"

Mesa narrowed her eyes at him in disgust. "That is a child's tale, soldier. It is well known Viators did not actually cross *over* from the Divide. They simply used it just as the *Tempus* does, to achieve increased relative speed to travel the edge of the universe."

"Then, sneak attack!" Puck flashed a grin, crimping his hands and pouncing toward her.

Mesa rolled her eyes, though a hint of a smile played at her lips. "I should leave you to your duties." She inclined her head, then sauntered away, silk folds drifting behind her.

"Bye, Mes!" Puck called after her. He tilted his head as he watched her go, letting out a wistful sigh.

"So . . ." Cavalon turned to Puck.

With an effort, Puck pulled his gaze from watching Mesa's withdrawal. "She's great, huh?" He beamed.

Cavalon laughed. "Yeah, she seems nice."

"Anyway, I guess we should get you to your first post." Puck opened his nexus, swiping back and forth a few times before shrugging. "Or not. Nothing's in the system yet."

Nothing, huh? Cavalon didn't know whether to consider that good or bad.

Puck shrugged. "EX determines it, so be nice to her."

Great. He would probably be mopping floors the rest of his life.

"For now, I'll have you help out in the mess," Puck said. "It'll be a good way for you to meet some of the crew, ingratiate yourself. They won't bite the hand that feeds, and all that."

Cavalon sighed. He wanted to believe that.

CHAPTER FOUR

—✦—

Cavalon followed Puck to the crowded mess hall in Tres Sector, where he received an apron, an unfortunate hairnet, and a comically large serving spoon.

Puck led him to an archaic food-service kiosk along the inside wall of the dining quarters—an open room with expansive ceilings that could easily seat a crew twice the size of the *Argus*. Two other aproned and hairnetted soldiers stood behind the kiosk, dropping food onto their comrades' plates as they shuffled through the line.

Cavalon turned to gape at Puck. "I'm sorry, I know you guys have issues with time relativity out here, but we haven't actually traveled back in time, right?"

Puck laughed. "No."

"How old's this dreadnought?" He'd only heard of food service like this at shelters in the slums of Outer Core planets.

"EX had all the fancy, automated food-service stuff removed." Puck waved a hand dismissively. "I guess this builds character and shit."

"This really is a prison," Cavalon grumbled.

Puck gave him a sideways grin and a pat on the shoulder. "That mashed protein is calling your name."

Cavalon blew out a steadying breath. He could do this. He could serve food to his fellow soldiers. Right?

Puck grabbed a tray and got in line. Cavalon turned the enormous spoon over in his hand, then steeled his resolve and pushed up his sleeves.

"Void . . ." Someone let out a low whistle. "Look at those tats."

Cavalon spun to find three soldiers behind him, empty food

trays in hand. The light-skinned, brutish man in the front smiled. Cavalon groaned inwardly, sliding his sleeves back down. Rookie mistake.

"Where'd you get those, pretty boy?" The man waggled his eyebrows. "Black market?"

"Nah," the stocky man beside him said. "Look, Barrow—gold and shit? That's *royalty*."

"Dammit," Cavalon cursed under his breath. That took them all of about six seconds. He glanced over his shoulder to find Puck, but his CO had disappeared into the crowd.

"Tell me it's true," the brutish man, apparently Barrow, said. "We've really got our very own royalty to play with?"

His friends laughed.

Barrow looked Cavalon up and down, his deep-set eyes sharpening with a glint of realization. "Shit, I recognize you. You're the Mercer heir, aren't you? How the hell'd you end up on Sentinel duty? Didn't think your likes enlisted."

Cavalon ground his teeth. Even with as dumb as this lot looked, he had to assume that if they read the news, they'd have put two and two together. However, it had taken him three months to get here, so they could have forgotten about it. Though, headlines like "Mercers Begin Tradition of Sacrificing Heirs to Legion Service" were the kind that took a while to fizzle down. Though a more accurate headline would have been "Mercers Find Socially Acceptable Way to Ditch Defective Heir in Favor of Obedient Shithead Second Cousin."

A knot tightened in Cavalon's stomach with a realization. The more likely scenario wasn't that these idiots hadn't paid attention, but that it'd never been included in the galactic-wide vids to begin with. It was Living with Augustus Mercer 101 to wake up and find major news events either skewed beyond all recognition, or simply eradicated from the headlines.

It gave him a small solace to know that what he'd done had been too much even for his grandfather to fully cover up—too loud, too flashy, and way too expensive. Just as Cavalon had intended. But it wouldn't have been hard at all for Augustus to throttle the news and stop it from spreading beyond the Core.

Bile rose up his throat at that, because it was specifically those people—the colonists in the Outer Core, the expatriates in the Lateral Reach, all the exiles all over the galaxy trying to build new lives . . . they were the ones who'd really needed to hear that news.

He'd been stupid for not realizing it sooner. Stupid, and blinded by that same damn irrational optimism that'd landed him here in the first place.

Cavalon cleared his throat, refocusing on Barrow's stone-faced glower. "Don't get much news out this way, do you?"

"We try not to concern ourselves with the Allied Monarchies." Barrow cracked his knuckles. "That is, until you start trying to replace us all with robo-Drudgers."

Cavalon sighed. Well, shit. Of course *that* would be the bit of news Augustus had made sure to spread far and wide.

The gathering lunch crowd began to murmur, glancing over as the conversation heated.

The stockier man chuffed. "Nah, Barrow, they're *clones*, remember?"

A palpable hush fell over the crowd, more and more resentful glares focusing on Cavalon. He flexed his jaw as he strove to keep the heat from rising to his cheeks.

"Clones?" Barrow shook his head, face scrunching with disgust. "All clones are abominations—even Drudgers." Barrow took an oafish step forward. "Just 'cause your great-great-great-times-ten or whatever fuckin' grandparents did decent shit back during the Viator War, that doesn't mean y'all have the right to fuck with the laws of nature."

"*Decent* shit?" Cavalon growled. "If they hadn't figured out how to counter the mutagen and turned it against them, not a damn one of you would even be here to give me such a fuckin' hard time. Besides—they're just Drudgers. Who cares?"

Only at the swell of gasps and honing of glowers through the crowd did Cavalon realize what a dumbass thing that'd been to say. He hadn't meant it to sound so defensive, to sound like he could possibly even for a second agree with a single thing his grandfather did.

But the jerk was being so *accusatory*. If he'd been cordial, maybe Cavalon would have told him that he wholeheartedly agreed. Despite their propensity to launch into wars at the mere sight of one another, cloning as a moral no-no was one thing everyone, across all the species, saw eye to eye on. Even near the end of the Viator War, when populations on both sides had dipped to dangerously low levels, neither resorted to cloning to bolster their numbers.

So, yes, his grandfather's approach to cloning and eugenics might have been borderline supervillain, but why did everyone have to assume he was in on it as well? Guilty by association was bullshit. Although "association" implied some degree of freedom. Maybe guilty by lamentable, shared DNA.

Regardless, Cavalon was the only one in the room who'd had enough balls to do anything about any of it. That's how he'd ended up in this shitshow, after all.

But instead of explaining his laboratory-exploding heroics to his new comrades-in-arms, Cavalon did what he did best. Pissed everyone off.

"You're right. I'm not sure a Drudger, cloned or not, would be as well-suited as you clearly are to babysitting the ass-edge of the universe."

Barrow's eyes sharpened, and he took another step forward. "What are you trying to say?"

"I'm saying you're dumber than a Drudger." Cavalon looked up and feigned contemplation. "Oh, and uglier too."

Barrow tossed his tray away while covering the remaining ground between them in two giant steps. He growled, then slammed his fist into the side of Cavalon's face. His vision danced as he hit the floor hard.

Impressive—he'd truly not expected that approach. He'd pegged the guy as more of a brute strangler.

Cavalon struggled to regain his senses as feet shuffled toward him. Barrow's friends picked Cavalon up by either arm, dragging him to his knees and holding him in place.

Barrow stalked forward, making a show of clenching each of his fists. Cavalon snorted out a bitter chuckle at the smug look on the burly man's face. Like he'd never before had some jerk's buddies try to hold him down so they could beat on him. It'd almost be pitiable, if it weren't going to be so damn gratifying to show Barrow what a terrible fucking idea starting this fight had been.

Cavalon drew in a deep breath, a surge of adrenaline slicing through him. With the tide came the taste of copper and the buzzing of his royal Imprint tattoos. They prickled the skin of his arm as they folded and unfolded, charging and priming.

With a grunt of Imprint-fueled force, Cavalon wrenched his arms from the grips of both men. He leapt to his feet and cracked the spoon across the head of one, then grabbed the other and threw him into a rack of dirty trays. Barrow threw another punch.

The Imprint squares slid up Cavalon's neck as he dodged the strike. With Barrow's flank exposed, Cavalon pummeled a fist into his ribcage. Winded by the blow, the man gasped, faltering long enough for Cavalon to punt him away with a kick to the stomach. Barrow hit the ground and slid into the gathering crowd.

Cavalon didn't realize he'd registered the presence of another attacker until he leaned back to dodge the punch. He caught the soldier's arm mid-strike, twisting to flip the man—nope, woman— onto her back on the ground.

A handful of onlookers rushed to join the fight. Cavalon ducked another punch, turning into a sweeping kick to knock the legs out from under another soldier.

The roar of the crowd escalated until he could no longer hear his own ragged breathing. The taste of copper overwhelmed his senses, and he spat a mouthful of bloody saliva onto the ground, grinning as he ran his tongue over his split lip. After three months confined to quarters on that tiny-ass Mercer Guard ship, he'd almost forgotten how much he missed this.

The Imprint squares whirred up the side of his neck and onto his cheek, solidifying as a fist came out of the commotion and struck him. His shielded skin barely noticed the impact, but another strike came on its heels. The Imprints were still moving into formation when the fist hit him, and pain fired through his jaw.

Cavalon grabbed the offender by the front of his shirt and threw him into a group of nearby soldiers. A few sidestepped and others attempted to catch the man as he crashed into them.

But instead of surging past to enact revenge, the men and women froze briefly, then rushed to attention, fists to chests. Those nearest him groaned in pain and keeled over as they gripped the black Imprints on their arms. A hush fell over the room along with a wave of uncertainty.

A narrow but unusually strong forearm locked around Cavalon's neck, choking off his air supply. Silver and copper squares buzzed furiously across the intruder's olive skin.

Cavalon gripped the arm with both hands, his royal Imprints rushing to help. But even in this short fight, he'd already managed to overexert them, and he couldn't match the strength. Cavalon growled as he blindly cursed the unknown assailant.

Though he already had a pretty good idea of who it was. Which was fucking perfect.

His vision danced as his air supply dwindled. He focused on slowing his pulse, then willed his Imprints to reset. They abided, returning to their default formation, and his adrenaline receded.

The arm released its hold, and Cavalon fell to the ground. He landed on all fours, hacking painfully as he regained full access to his respiratory functions. After a few steadying breaths, he looked up at the soldiers.

They stood in perfect formation, backs rigid, gazes straight. Even the ones who'd been hurt in the fight stood upright, sweat and blood glistening on their faces. Though their black Sentinel Imprints no longer appeared active, the pain they'd caused seemed to linger, and the soldiers fought back grimaces while cradling their right arms.

Cavalon turned over to look up at exactly who he expected to find—Excubitor Rake, glaring down at him with amber-eyed fire. She lifted her scowl to sweep it across the rest of the men and women in the hall. Each and every one of them looked guilty as shit, but they didn't say a word.

Despite the epically foreboding circumstances, Cavalon couldn't help but be a little impressed. Rake could walk into a room and command a degree of respect his grandfather would kill for. Probably *did* kill for. And not a respect born of fear, but of . . . something else. Humility? Admiration, maybe.

After a few heated moments, Rake's look returned to Cavalon. "My office."

She turned and marched toward the exit, and the crowd peeled away before her.

With a squeak of boots, two bronze-skinned hands tucked under Cavalon's armpits and lifted him off the ground. Puck gave a distressed grimace, then nodded toward the marching EX. Cavalon regained his balance, pulled the apron off, tossed it on the ground, then followed.

He trailed Rake through the halls in dejected silence. Though he kept his attention focused on the heels of her worn, black boots, he could feel the heat of the soldiers' glares as they passed.

After a painfully awkward lift ride up to the top deck, Rake turned down a short hallway and a door slid open before her. Cavalon followed her into a clean, formal office, similar in style to the intake room where he'd met her earlier that morning, though about three times the size. Rake rounded the wide, aerasteel desk at the center and sat on the cushioned high-back chair behind it.

Cavalon eyed the two rigid chairs in front of the desk, unsure whether sitting or standing would be considered proper protocol for getting reamed out.

"Sit." Rake opened the display on the holographic terminal above her desk.

Cavalon shuffled sideways and sat. Rake flicked through files in silence. He ran his thumb back and forth across the edge of his badges of rank, eyes drifting around the austere room—barren walls, a golden astrolabe the only item atop the desk. The intricately etched, revolving spheres and rings were stationary. A brushed gold plaque sat recessed into the top of the desk, EXCUBITOR A. J. RAKE etched into the metal.

"AJ?" He smiled and looked up from the plaque to find her staring at him.

If looks could kill. Cavalon had heard the turn of phrase before, but never had he seen it so aptly manifested. She returned her aggravated glare to her terminal and said nothing.

Cavalon palmed the hairnet off his head and balled it up as he slumped in the chair, trying not to feel like a teenager about to be reprimanded by the headmaster. He wiped blood from the corner of his mouth with the back of his left hand, then blinked down at the silent and stationary obsidian Imprints lining his arm. He'd completely forgotten about the warning his best friends the intake guards had given him about utilizing his Imprint tattoos now that he had two sets. Using them had not, in fact, resulted in any "volatile interfacing, injury, or death." This time, at least.

He held up his left arm. "You used these against the others, didn't you?"

Rake didn't respond, eyes remaining focused on her screen.

"But not me. Why?"

"I probably should have, but you were already using your other set. I didn't want you to end up in the morgue on your first day."

Cavalon swallowed hard.

"Just a lot of paperwork," she added quietly, still not looking away from her terminal.

He squinted at her. Was that . . . a joke?

After a few moments of silence, she said, "I'll start you in janitorial."

"Uh, aren't we gonna talk about what happened?"

She didn't look up from the display. "I don't like repeating myself."

"What?"

"We already had that conversation."

"We did?"

"Yes, would you like a summary? You, cut, shit."

Cavalon slid farther down in his chair. "Right. I cut the shit."

"That wasn't you cutting the shit. But I think you know that."

"It wasn't my—"

She slammed her fist onto the desk. The astrolabe's rings wavered from the vibration. "Do you think I want your excuses?"

Cavalon diverted his gaze. He felt like he knew the right answer, but he couldn't stop his natural tendency to make everything fucking worse. "Is that rhetorical?"

She stood, menacing in her slow purposefulness. She dragged the knuckles of one hand along the top of the desk as she skirted around it. A few silver and copper Imprint squares unfolded onto the top of her hand, and she stopped, hovering over him.

He looked up. "Seems like I'm not the only one whose Imprints react on instinct."

She grabbed him by the front of his vest. His feet slid out from under him as she lifted him out of his chair with an ease that implied Imprint-assisted strength.

That same fire lit in his stomach, the one that he couldn't quite place the origin of. Not the painful kind of fear he'd grown up with, but some other kind of angst. Maybe a fear of authority he hadn't been properly desensitized to. He imagined it a healthy reverence, generally beaten into soldiers early on in their careers. But he'd never been made to respect anyone except his grandfather, and even that only outwardly so.

Something told him Rake didn't give two shits that he was unschooled in deference. She expected him to have it anyway.

She cleared her throat. "How do you think infractions are handled on a ship full of criminals?"

"Um . . . throw them in jail?" he said, wincing as the edge of his voice squeaked. "Er, the brig?"

"Sure," she said, giving a receptive nod. "That'd be reasonable, in another division, anywhere else in the Legion. But keep in mind, every soldier I get . . . they already feel pretty at home locked in a brig. Confinement's not always the most effective deterrent. Part of my job—a part I don't hate, if I'm being honest—is coming up with . . . let's call them *creative* punishments, to ensure everyone's adequately reprimanded."

He swallowed hard, discovering the back of his throat had gone bone-dry.

She kept her unblinking eyes locked on his. "Do you want to find out on your first day how *very* creative I can be?"

He raised an eyebrow. "No?"

Rake regarded him placidly for a few moments, then dropped him to his feet. "So you *are* capable of self-preservation."

He scratched the back of his neck.

She sat on the edge of her desk and folded her arms. "Say it with me, though."

"What?"

"No . . . *sir.*"

Cavalon licked his dry lips. "No, sir."

"No, Excubitor Rake, sir."

"No, Excubitor Rake, sir."

"All right. Good job, soldier."

"All right. Good job—"

She cut him off with an effusive sigh. She buried her face in her hands, then took a sharp breath in before looking back at him, eyes almost . . . amused. "You obviously need to be babysat."

He lifted his shoulders in a poor attempt at a shrug. She wasn't wrong. He didn't know what the hell was wrong with him.

She rounded the desk and sat, reopening her terminal interface. "I'm assigning you to bridge duty so I can keep an eye on you myself."

"Uh, what about janitorial? Sir?"

"Janitorial bridge duty," she confirmed. "And a homework assignment. Are you ready for it?"

"Yes, sir."

"Try to learn some fucking humility? And learn to respect what we do here."

"Yes, sir."

"Extra credit? Maybe go five seconds without causing a major uproar."

"You got it."

Rake blinked, her stare level.

". . . sir."

She refocused on her terminal and silently slid through files. After a few minutes, she landed on one and quirked an eyebrow. "You've got quite a list of credentials."

Cavalon scratched his chin, unsure of what could possibly be in *his* file that Rake would consider a "credential."

"Sir?"

"Three degrees?"

"Oh." *That.* He nodded. "Yes, sir."

"Astrophysics, astromechanical engineering, and . . . genetic engineering. No surprise there."

"That one was forced on me."

"Top of your class, high marks in everything?"

"My fraternity also voted me most likely to die before graduation. Is that in there?"

Her eyes narrowed.

He shifted his feet. "Joke's on them, I guess."

"How can you be at once highly intelligent and utterly idiotic?"

"I know, right? You'd think all the selective breeding would have created a nice, clean crop of Mercers by now."

"Well," she said, leaning back in her chair, "I'm glad to see proof that human nature's fighting eugenics."

He laughed, despite himself.

He prepared himself for another glare, but her scowl had faded and she shook her head. "You seem like a lot of work, but we're in short supply of educated soldiers right now."

Cavalon blinked. "Uh, sir?"

"I'm willing to *consider* advancement," she clarified, then added quietly, almost to herself, "You might make a better animus than a soldier."

He opened his mouth to respond, but nothing came out. He had no idea what to say.

Rake continued, oblivious to his dumbfounded state. "But you have to fall in line," she said, tone low and serious. "Get your shit in order. Earn the promotion."

He shifted uncomfortably. He still felt like he was in trouble, but she was . . . He wasn't sure. Valuing what he might be able to contribute? She seemed to think he could, and maybe more oddly, *would* change. It wasn't a feeling he was familiar with.

Yet something about it sat right—clicked into place in the back of his mind. He'd just started a fight with a guy twice his size, in a room full of trained soldiers, many of whom probably had legitimate cause for wanting to kick the shit out of a Mercer. He'd fought them out of anger, out of spite—really for no reason other than to try and prove who he wasn't. Maybe it'd be more effective to focus on trying to prove who he *was*.

"Uh, okay, sir," he managed.

"Report to the bridge at zero five hundred. Remember your assignments?"

He nodded. "Cut the shit, learn fucking humility, respect what we do, no uproarious behavior. Sir."

"Get out of my sight."

He bid his legs to move, but they proved somewhat undependable, wobbling beneath him. With a deep breath, he regained his composure and strode toward the exit.

"Oculus?" Rake called after him.

He turned back to face her. "Yeah?"

She raised one eyebrow.

He cleared his throat. "Uh, yes, Excubitor Rake, sir?"

"Bring a mop and bucket . . . and a toothbrush."

CHAPTER FIVE

Once again, Adequin found herself sitting in that awful chair.

The half dozen bridge crew worked at their stations, the silence cut only by the occasional console beep or muted cough. At the foot of the tiered levels, the main viewscreen still showcased the inevitably vacant outward view.

A tier down, Jackin stood at his terminal, arms crossed, eyes trained on his holographic screen. His boot tapped out a slow rhythm on the metal floor as he scratched his short black beard and released a long, slow yawn.

Adequin shifted in her seat, resisting the urge to mimic him. It wouldn't be particularly motivating for the crew to see their EX as bored senseless as they were.

A damp sloshing passed behind her as that pain-in-the-ass new recruit pushed his mop across the floor. She prepared a judgmental glare, but Cavalon's eyes stayed focused on his work. He'd been mopping the upper deck all damn morning, and though she generally appreciated attention to detail, it'd started to feel suspiciously like stalling. He was probably afraid to find out what chore she'd come up with next.

But only because he didn't know any better yet. Giving him *something* to do—even if menial—was really just doing him a favor.

Jackin's terminal beeped and Adequin sat up.

"Boss, it's done," he called over his shoulder.

"Finally." She pushed up out of the rigid captain's chair and descended the short set of steps toward him. "Report?"

Jackin flicked through a few screens, then shook his head. "Nothing."

"Nothing?"

"Well, comms viability's in the red, but still well within our version of 'normal.' You know how the Divide likes to eat comm signals. Otherwise, all systems nominal."

"That's good, right?"

His jaw flexed as he tilted his head. "Yes."

"Yet you seem disappointed."

"Honestly, boss . . ." Jackin leaned in, lowering his voice. "I was hoping it'd show something off with the thrusters—or at least a few faulty sensors. Something to account for that drift we had yesterday." He glowered at his screen for another few moments, then added, "I think we should run it again."

"Why?"

"I can write up a debugger quick and put it through at the same time. Maybe the diagnostic suite's finally giving out on this rust bucket."

Adequin blew out a heavy breath and glanced at the time on her nexus. "All right, if you think we need to. Go ahead." Not like she had anything better to do.

Jackin tapped the screen to reset the scan.

She paced up the steps and sunk back into the captain's chair, scratching her nose to mask a yawn. She returned to staring at the empty black viewscreen and tried to convince herself not to nod off. A few dull minutes later, her nexus chimed with a comm notification, snapping alertness back into her. She tapped her nexus to open the link. "Go for Rake."

"Sir, Bach here," Griffith's rumbling voice crackled through, staticky and startlingly loud in the quiet of the bridge. She thumbed the volume down. "Sir, I'm running preflight checks on the *Tempus*'s torus chamber, but I'm getting a spike in the SGL readings."

Blinking down at her wrist, it took her a second to process his words. SGL . . . she hadn't heard that call in years. At least since the Resurgence War ended.

Jackin glanced over his shoulder, quirking an eyebrow at her.

The rest of the bridge crew did a phenomenal job of pretending they weren't listening in.

Adequin cleared her throat. "Say again?"

"The SGL readings on the *Tempus*, sir," Griffith repeated. "I'll need to run diagnostics to troubleshoot, but I need your biometric clearance."

Jackin looked back, amusement tugging at the corner of his lips. "I got this, boss, go ahead."

"Protocol—"

He held up a hand. "Void, not with the protocolling, please."

"I'll come right back."

"I'd expect nothing less," Jackin mumbled as he refocused on his screen, then his look shot up again. "Hey—on your way there, we've still got a half dozen in the brig from that hydro debacle."

"Shit," she sighed. Last night, she'd thrown the entire third-shift hydroponics staff in there to cool off.

After Cavalon's little scuffle in the mess yesterday, the unrest had circulated, as it always did. This time, it'd ended up sparking a particularly destructive fight in the hydroponics lab. Half the nutrient tanks had been ruptured before Bray and the rest of the security team broke it up. She understood getting a little stir-crazy, but didn't know why that had to make them stupid and violent too.

"Thanks, Jack. I'll swing by and clear them for release."

She started for the exit, where Cavalon still intently mopped the same innocent square-meter area he'd been targeting a half hour ago.

"Oculus, you're going to swab a hole in the damn floor," she said. "With me."

She marched into the hall.

Jackin grumbled, "That means *follow*," then after a moment, hurried bootsteps trailed after her.

Cavalon exhaled a few curses as the squeaking wheels caught between panels of decking and the water sloshed over the sides. After a few seconds, he had enough sense to pick up the stupid bucket and carry it.

Adequin received courteous acknowledgment from the few passersby, but at mid-shift the halls were mostly unoccupied. She couldn't count how many times she'd cut this path over the last five years. The Legion's retrofit should have included moving the brig closer to the bridge; this was a post for criminals, after all. Though she appreciated any excuse to be up out of that damn chair.

She stepped onto the lift as it slid open, and Cavalon took a few quick steps to catch up before the door slid shut. "So, there was another fight, huh?"

She clenched her teeth, preparing her judgmental glare again.

"You come up with some of those creative punishments for them?" he asked. "Maybe one of those completely unnecessary cavity searches?"

Her readied glare faulted on deployment, overtaken by a scowl of disbelief. Though she really shouldn't have been surprised, he clearly wasn't the type to keep his mouth shut for very long. That he'd been quiet for almost five full hours actually impressed her, a fact which in turn nauseated her, but the bar for this one had been set painfully low. Pretty much on the ground.

He stretched out his right arm, the static gold and bronze Imprint squares glinting in the overhead lights as the lift descended. "Too bad I wasn't there to straighten them out, I guess."

"That fight was your fault, you know," she pointed out.

He scoffed. "I've never even been to hydroponics."

"Out here, unrest spreads."

"We talking viral or bacterial?"

Her gaze hardened, but he didn't seem to notice. "There was another fight shortly after in the research annex," she explained. "Two oculi ended up in medical. And those are only the ones that were reported—there were probably a half dozen more. The first round we've had in weeks."

He scratched his chin. "Interesting conjecture . . . Is this based on the verifiable science of being super bored at the edge of the universe, or do you think it's more magical in nature?"

"Maybe I should throw you in the brig with Barrow and let you collect some firsthand data."

His amusement melted away, then he mumbled, "Surprised you don't just drug everyone into submission."

"That's not sounding like a half-bad idea," she growled. The lift door slid open, and she marched out into the corridor toward Tres Sector.

This fucking guy. She'd never had an oculus act like this toward her before—in fact she didn't think she'd heard one voluntarily offer up more than a "yes, sir" or "no, sir" in the last five years.

He'd been so docile all morning, she'd thought they must have actually made some progress in her office yesterday, that at least some of what she'd all but beaten into him had stuck. Yet he still spoke to her like she was one of his vapid drinking buddies. He didn't think of her the same way that everyone else on the *Argus* did—they all saw their commander, someone to obey and respect. But he hadn't come up through the Legion; he didn't see any levels between them. That had to change.

As they approached the entrance to the brig, she rounded on him. His scuttling boot squeaks echoed down the empty hall as he stopped short and a splash of water sloshed over the edge of his bucket. She drew her shoulders back and faced him squarely. His chin dropped, posture slouching as he took a half step back and bumped into the wall, gaze flitting like a trapped animal.

"Uh, sorry, sir," he began. Some mix of regret and frustration tightened his grimace. "Just trying to lighten the mood . . . Everything's so doom-and-gloom around here. Hell, maybe I've caught a case of that viral unrest too."

She flexed her jaw, resisting the urge to raise her voice. "Shape up, or you can kiss that animus offer goodbye. We'll see how much your pile of diplomas helps when you're buffing floors for the next decade."

"I hear PhDs make them extra shiny."

She let out a low, crackling sigh that sounded more like the snarl of a combustion engine.

Cavalon's white cheeks paled another shade. "Sorry, sir. Again, sir. This probably isn't the shit-cutting you're looking for, huh?"

"Just stop talking."

"Yes, sir."

"You'll take a double shift tonight. After the brig's as spotless as the bridge, head to the mess. Then report to Circitor Lace in the hangar—there's a ruptured latrine tank that needs repair. After that, help with whatever else she needs. Report back to the bridge in the morning."

Cavalon's brow softened, and he didn't blink for a few long moments. She waited for it, that smart-ass comment that would get him into even more trouble—likely something about already giving up on her babysitting duty.

But instead, he drew up his posture and gave a curt nod. "Yes, sir."

Adequin deposited Cavalon into the capable hands of Rivas, the no-nonsense brig attendant, then released the hydroponics staff along with a firm reminder that repeat offenses wouldn't be met with such leniency.

When she arrived at the hangar, she found Lace hunched over a workbench, blue-white sparks from her welding torch flashing against her protective goggles.

The dismantled segments of a cargo-lift drone sat all around— some piled on the worktop, others on the floor, spare hardware and circuitry littered among them. Lace very well might have been the most skilled mechanic across all forty-some Sentinel vessels, but the messes she made were absurd. Adequin had no idea how she could possibly keep it all straight.

Lace flicked off the torch and looked up. "Sir."

"You wore them," Adequin said.

Lace gave a short nod, dropping her goggles around her neck. "I did indeed," she replied, looking quite pleased with herself. "You're welcome. What can I do you for?"

"Sending trouble your way this evening."

"Electrical or mechanical?"

"Biological."

Lace quirked an eyebrow.

"New soldier shipped in yesterday," Adequin explained. "He's in rough shape, but he'll respond if you're firm with him."

"I see, sir. And what should I inflict him with?"

Adequin pushed out a breath, shaking her head. "He's like a four-year-old in an engineer's body. Give him some toys to fix, and hopefully he'll wear himself out."

Lace's soft brown eyes shone with amusement. "Happy to field it, sir. I'm sure you could use a night or twenty off." She rubbed at a smear of grease on her chin with a gloved knuckle. "You walk all the way down from the bridge to tell me that? Coulda just pinged my nexus."

Adequin swayed her head toward the docking bay. "Here to help Bach with something."

Lace nodded as she eyed the *Tempus*, the fine lines around her lips deepening as she pressed them flat. "What's that he calls you, sir? If you don't mind me asking?"

"Dextera? Our rank during the war."

"No, the other thing, what's it—mo'acair? Sounds Northern Cautian. Your Titan call sign or something?"

"Oh that—no. Just a nickname he started using years ago."

"What's it mean?"

"You know, I never asked. You're from Cautis Prime, don't you know?"

Lace diverted her look as she knelt to pick up one of the magnetic claws of the dismantled drone. "I haven't been back in forty years . . . Maybe it's some kinda new slang."

"Maybe. I'll ask and let you know."

"Good idea."

Adequin eyed the alarming number of parts surrounding the workbench. "I'll leave you to whatever this disaster is . . ."

Lace smiled and reset her goggles, giving a curt nod. "Sir."

Adequin cut across the operations deck and entered the chilly docking bay, stepping up the steep ramp to duck into the air lock of the *Tempus*. Only modestly above average in height, she knew she had plenty of headroom, but still instinctively hunched as she crossed through the air lock into the main corridor. The passageways weren't any more cramped than any other vessel its size, but five years of living among the roomy corridors and high ceilings of the *Argus* made the barely over two-meter overhead seem that much more confining.

A flight of stairs took her down into the main cargo hold, split by four long aisles of metal shelving, two on either side of a wide thoroughfare. She found Griffith working in the main aisle, his silver and copper Imprints buzzing along his arms as he moved a storage crate from one side to the other. His nexus projected an inventory database screen, the orange glow of the holographic display casting his brown skin in an even warmer tone.

Adequin halted her approach, fists on hips. "SGL?"

Griffith flashed a grin. "Welcome aboard. Wasn't sure you'd remember that one."

"What *shit* could possibly have *gone lateral* in the practically empty cargo hold of your docked ship?"

"I need to report an infraction," he said, a furrow pinching his eyebrows. "The EX lied to me."

She glared.

"She swore we'd see each other before I left and . . ." He glanced at his open nexus. "We're T-minus fourteen hours and counting."

"Well, that's a shame. She's your CO, best you can do in this situation is file a motion of no confidence."

He gasped. "That's *mutiny*."

"Bloody void," she grumbled.

He laughed, shoving another crate across the aisle. "Figured you'd be stuck up there doing something stupid. You're welcome for saving you."

"Saving me by making me do inventory with you? You know you have subordinates to do this?"

"Look who's talking."

She rolled her eyes and stifled a yawn.

He grunted, pulling another crate from the bottom shelf and sliding it into the aisle. "Betcha haven't heard SGL since, what . . . ?"

"Well before Paxus," she said, wringing her chilled hands.

His lips pressed into a grim frown. "Yeah, well before, indeed. You know where it came from?"

"Assumed it was an old Titan tradition."

"Nah, I brought it with me from the Vanguard."

She quirked a brow. "You did?"

"Except we used it as a signal to switch to a new channel so we could rail on the brass behind their backs . . . rather than for arranging alcoholic rendezvous."

"Leave it to the Titans to make it about booze."

He chuffed a laugh and activated the control screen on the crate. Adequin smiled, surprised he'd offered up that bit of history. He rarely talked about his days in the Vanguard, even in generalities.

But even the brief mention seemed to affect him. His contentment faded and a frown flattened his lips as he refocused on his nexus to take stock of the crate's contents. He absentmindedly tugged at the left side of his collar, stretching it up over the tattoo at the base of his neck. Though over the years, the black ink had faded into his russet skin, the details of the emblem were still clear—*Volucris* scripted between two laurels of angular feathers, like dozens of keen-edged blades fanned into a crescent ring.

He'd had that tattoo when she first met him ten years ago; every Vanguard from that era had one—it'd been a rite of passage at the start of the Resurgence War. Humanity had enjoyed over two hundred years of peacetime after the Viator War, until the SCS *Volucris* arrived at the edge of the Outer Core for a routine mineral survey, but instead found a Viator fleet.

As the primary operations division of the First—the foremost command component of the Legion—the Vanguard had been the first to muster. For them, the tattoo served as a reminder of how unprepared they'd been for a real enemy to return—one they'd thought dead for two centuries. A reminder of what came from complacency.

The interface beeped as Griffith resealed the crate. He looked up at her, any trace of melancholy vanished, his features alit with his usual congenial amusement. "All I ask in payment for freeing you," he said, "is a few minutes of manual labor. Then you can run along back to the bridge, if you insist."

"Void, you're needy."

Griffith's Imprints buzzed softly, rearranging as he pushed the inventoried crate aside. "What, you losing your edge, Dextera? Life on the fringe of reality making you soft?"

She summoned a *little* extra strength from her Imprints and punched him square in the shoulder.

He let out a hard breath, equal parts laugh and pained grimace. "To be honest, I actually need the help. Lace is fixing the only working cargo lift, and we're the only two people on the ship with these guys at our disposal." He held up his arm and the Imprints flashed as they slid around the top of his wrist.

She shook her head. "Actually, not anymore."

"No?"

"New soldier came in yesterday with a set."

"Black market?"

"Nope."

He quirked an eyebrow. "*Another* Titan?"

She scoffed a laugh. "Definitely not."

"Then how the hell—" His confusion flattened and he let out a low whistle. "A royal? How'd that happen?"

"Shit if I know."

"Sounds fun."

Adequin sighed. "If by fun, you mean an exhausting trial of will-power, then yes." She unstrapped her jacket and tossed it aside. The short sleeves underneath left her bare arms exposed to the cool air. Her skin warmed, tingling as her Imprint squares energized, breaking from their default formation to spread across her back, neck, and shoulders.

"All right, what goes where?"

"Empties go to the cargo lift," he answered. "The others, move across the aisle and I'll take stock."

They spent the better part of an hour moving crates in circles, sorting out which still needed to be cataloged, which could have their contents combined, and which should be off-loaded.

Adequin put the last of the empty crates onto the cargo lift and wandered back to find Griffith at the end of an aisle, stretched over the top of few shorter, quarter- and half-sized crates.

"Ah, got it," he grunted. He shoved another smaller crate aside, revealing a sealed footlocker behind it. He tapped the access pad as the lid hissed open. A glint of light flashed across the necks of a dozen or so metal and glass bottles.

"Uh," Adequin began, leaning to look past him into the shadowed container. "Tell me we didn't move all these crates just to unearth your booze stash . . ."

Griffith slid her a please-be-merciful grin. "Not just any booze stash." He pulled a bottle free, angling it toward her. Adequin squinted at the brushed-metal bottle as she stepped forward, though she didn't need to be able to read the etched label to recognize it.

"Void," she breathed. "I haven't seen mellilla in fifteen years . . . Where the hell'd you get that?"

"Lugen gave it to me after I joined the Titans."

"Recruitment incentive?"

"Something like that."

"Damn. All he got me was five more years of war . . ."

Griffith laughed. "Well, I'm kind of a big deal, as you know."

She flexed her jaw, trying to look exasperated through the grin tugging at her lips.

He slid out from the maze of small crates, looking over the label carefully. "I almost forgot I had it—stashed it away forever ago for a rainy day."

"And today's that day?"

He glanced up at the beams of aerasteel truss lining the small cargo hold's ceiling. "Looks cloudy to me."

She crossed her arms. "It's the middle of the day, Griff."

"And?"

"And I'm the senior officer. I can't drink in the middle of the day."

He shrugged. "More for me, then."

"Void."

"You gonna write me up?" He palmed the bottle's seal, giving a feigned whine and frowning deeply. "I can't get it open—help."

She marched over and snatched the bottle from him, ignoring how pleased he looked with himself. Her glare drifted down and she turned the cool metal over to read the etched label: REDWIND DISTRICT SPIRITS, DISTILLED 182 AV with the official Seneca-IV export seal stamped below.

She patiently undid the four tiny safety nodules. Some feat of engineering allowed the aging process to continue until the seal was broken, so the task had been made purposefully difficult to serve as a reminder. With the latches free, she twisted the top off. It hissed and let out a belch of warm air, sending a sharp scent drifting up.

She angled the bottle at Griffith. "You mind?"

The corners of his eyes wrinkled with amusement. "Please."

She took a slow sip, letting the warm liquid roll around in her mouth. Though dryer than she'd expected, it came with a rich finish, and the slightest touch of honey smoothed the edge. She swallowed it and a spicy tinge lingered on the roof of her mouth.

Passing the bottle back to him, she breathed a sharp hiss from the back of her throat as the pleasant burn settled in the pit of her stomach. "You shoulda left it on the *Argus* instead of the *Tempus*. Would've aged longer."

Griffith let out a hearty laugh. "Shit, you're right." Hovering the bottle below his nose, he inhaled a breath before taking a purposeful drink. A smile creased his eyes and he licked his lips. "Damn. That really is as good as they say, isn't it?"

"Not bad," she agreed.

He passed it back to her. "Surprised you'll even drink Redwind, considering."

A knot tightened at the base of her rib cage, and she tried to loosen it with another drink. The Seneca-IV distillery district might be the only good thing to ever come from her shitty Outer Core home planet, as widely known for its unforgiving sulfuric rain as its dense samarskite mines—home to a much less widely known practice of systemic indentured servitude. Though the star system had been claimed as a colony of the System Collective over sixty years ago, and was technically under their jurisdiction, greased palms went a long, long way in the Outer Core.

She handed the bottle back to Griffith and shrugged. "Sometimes great things have shitty origins."

He nodded, his eyes drifting over her. "Indeed . . ."

She rolled her eyes. "That's not what I meant."

"Well, it's what *I* meant."

She leaned back to rest on the edge of the crate behind her. "If you're going to force me to engage in rampant misconduct—"

He rumbled a laugh mid-drink.

"—can we at least talk crew evals while we're at it?"

"Void." He sat on the crate beside him, sliding back to recline against the shelving. "All business with you, huh?"

"This really should not surprise you. Besides, the report's due in two weeks. It has to be done before you ship out anyway."

"Fine, fine." He scratched at his beard. "Honestly, I could use a few more people."

"You have fifteen now, should be plenty for a ship this size."

"It's not number, just talent—thinking I need to swap some."

She scooted back to sit fully onto the crate. The few sips of whiskey in her stomach had already spread a dense warmth into her chest and cheeks. "Someone coming up short?"

"No one's fault, merely shifting needs. Sullivan's been sitting copilot, and he's doing fine running the standard presets, but he's not a math guy. Can't adapt on the fly. No pun intended."

"What needs adapting?"

"There's constant fluctuations in the Divide's density that affect our trajectory."

"Since when?"

"Since always. The computer makes corrections, but it's reactive—and not efficient. There's got to be some way to chart it, anticipate it."

"You're one of the best pilots I've ever met, if you can't figure it out . . ."

"It's not about the flying, it's the . . . *nature* part. The Divide's just one big tract of dense gravity—I get that much. But the bodies of gravity I'm familiar with are generally round-ish, not flat-ish, and the computer's simply not made for it. If we got someone on board that could really study it, crunch the numbers . . . maybe we could get in sync with it, find that gravitational sweet spot and move along it faster. Possibly *a lot* faster."

"Back in three months instead of six?"

He smiled. "One week instead of two."

"Yeah," she agreed, "you probably need a physicist. But those types don't tend to end up Sentinels."

"Tell me about it. Can you recruit someone from the *Typhos*? *Accora*? There's forty other Sentinel ships, someone's gotta have an extra delinquent egghead lying around."

"Last I checked, they don't have shit for animus either. The *Typhos* has the biggest crew, I'll ping them with a request. Though honestly, it might be faster for you to just dock there on your way upward this time, ask them directly. Kharon Gate's been slow to deliver messages lately."

"How shocking," he mumbled, then took a long drink.

"In the meantime, I'll talk to Mesa, see if she's got anyone earmarked." Adequin cringed as an obvious but painful option came to mind. "That new guy might be a good fit eventually."

"Oh, Mister Imprints? Is that the one who came in on a private transport yesterday?"

"That's the one. But he's nowhere near ready."

"He in need of a little reforming?"

"Really just *forming*, to start with. I'll work on him—see if I can get him in shape by the time you're back next."

Griffith inclined his head. "Much appreciated, sir."

"What else?"

He scratched his beard. "Well, as the alert buoys get older, I really need some people who know their way around repairs. Or at least a chief to manage them."

"You already have six mechanics."

"Sure, but they're all riggers that came up through groundside ops. They could probably smart us out of a cave collapse with a piece of rope and a lighter, but they wouldn't know how to run a safe EVA if their lives depended on it. And their lives *literally* depend on it. I can keep escorting them for now, but you know . . ." He smiled. "A cap's not supposed to leave their ship."

"Who're you thinking?" she asked.

He paused as he slowly licked his lips, then all but mumbled, "Lace . . ."

She barked a laugh. "Somehow you look at me with a straight face when you say that."

He crossed his arms, jaw tight.

"No way, Griff," she said, shaking her head. "I need my hangar chief."

He scoffed. "For all the ship traffic you got comin' in and out of here?"

"She's also my peripherals mechanic." Adequin jutted a thumb down the aisle behind her. "She's the one fixing your damn drone right now, remember. You know how useful she is; you served with her for what—eight, nine years before the war?"

"Ten," he corrected, but didn't fall for the shift in topic. "You have two hundred people and Lace is really your only mechanic?"

"For life systems, at least. She's the only one that can convince the food processor to spit out anything other than basic protein strands, and definitely the only one that knows how to fix those ancient water recyclers."

"The *Argus*'s original complement was over a thousand. You can't need more than a few of those water recyclers working at once."

"We only *have* a couple working," she explained. "I requested a parts bin from the Legion months ago, but until it comes so we can fix a backup, we're maxed out. I already had to ration water usage for a week last month while one was down."

He blew out a long breath. "Well, if I can't have Lace, then it's gonna have to be you." She did her best to appear horribly offended and his features went flat with worry. "What?" he scoffed.

"I can't believe I'm your *second* pick."

He laughed.

She took the bottle back from him and sipped another drink. "If you need a thermal-control unit shoddily jury-rigged, I'm all over it. But I don't know shit about those alert buoys."

"That's only half the job," he pointed out. "And I've never seen someone shoot around so calm and confident like they were born with an MMU on their backs." He accepted the bottle back from her and took another drink. "That's what makes Lace the best of both worlds—you *personally* gave her that EVA crash course a few weeks back when the inward comms array shorted out."

"A few weeks? That was *two years* ago."

"And it's a great justification to give her a bump in rank—you've wanted an excuse to do that for years." His eyelashes fluttered. "Pretty please?"

She shook her head. "I can't budge on Lace, but I'll get an EVA course going. I'll keep an eye out for leadership potential, but we'll at least get a couple of people who know their way around a spanner trained up and ready for you to take next time you're back."

He smirked. "One benefit of time dilation—super-fast training."

"Super fast for you, maybe."

His amusement faded and his gaze drifted down. "About that—"

Down the aisle, someone coughed quietly, then pointedly cleared their throat. "Sirs."

Adequin's pulse spiked and a wave of warmth rose to her cheeks as she glanced over her shoulder. Lace stood at the end of the aisle, and she put her fist to her chest in salute while Griffith fought a smile and tucked the whiskey behind his back.

Adequin stood and faced the mechanic. "Circitor?"

If Lace had noticed the bottle, she didn't show any indication as she gave a casual, straight-faced nod. "Drone is repaired, whenever you're ready for it."

Griffith nodded. "Bring it to the lift, if you don't mind."

"Aye-aye." Lace turned to go, then hesitated. "Plan still on, sir?"

Griffith ran a hand down the side of his face. "Yeah, yeah, I'll get to it."

Lace nodded, then disappeared around the corner.

Adequin quirked a brow at him. "Get to what?"

"Nothin'," he said, letting out a sigh. "Just pestering me about stuff I've been putting off, as usual."

"Well, I guess if your mechanical brawn's back in working order, I'll leave you to it."

He scratched the back of his neck. "There's more we should discuss before I head out tonight—can we nightcap?"

"Yeah. Swing by after second shift."

He held up the whiskey. "Only if he's invited too."

"Twist my arm," she agreed as she backed away down the aisle. "But you'll have to leave a few hours after—so only one."

"One bottle?"

"One *drink*."

"When was the last time we had just *one* drink?"

He winked, and she rolled her eyes as she retreated up the aisle and back to the bridge.

CHAPTER SIX

What must have been moments after second shift ended, Griffith arrived at Adequin's door with the bottle of mellilla whiskey in hand. They proceeded to put away half of it during the evening's events: discussing the last batch of much-delayed headlines that came in from the Core, watching a bootleg film she'd confiscated from an oculus's bunk, and playing over an hour's worth of poker, at which she'd handily destroyed him.

Now she sat on the stiff couch in her quarters, wallowing in the warmth of an oversized gray Titan sweatshirt while Griffith lay on the floor beside the couch. Adequin tucked her legs up underneath her and nursed the remainder of the whiskey in her glass.

"More?" Griffith waved the bottle at her.

"No way, Centurion. Are you trying to kill me?"

He grinned, his cheeks flushed with slight intoxication.

"We should probably stop," she said. "You have to captain a ship in a few hours."

"Yeah, yeah. The thing basically flies itself."

"Speaking of—you wanted to finish talking about crew evals?" She spun the last few sips around in her glass, then took another drink.

"No . . . I wanted to talk about stepping down."

The swig of whiskey stalled at the back of Adequin's throat, and she almost choked. It blazed a fiery path into her stomach before she managed to croak out a wheezing, "Excuse me?"

"Relax," he said, amusement creasing the corners of his eyes. "Not from service. Just from my post."

"From the *Argus*?"

"The *Tempus*."

"What?" she asked, shaking her head. This was not a topic they'd discussed before, and the suggestion more than surprised her.

He kept his gaze locked on her. "Remember what you said yesterday? That it'd only be ten months before we're the same age?"

"Ten *years*, yeah." She upended her glass and finished the remainder of her whiskey. "Only a joke, Griff. Forty-two's not old."

"No, I mean . . . every month I'm gone, you get a year older? That's terrifying."

She scoffed and smiled. "What? You don't think I'll age well?" She set down her empty glass to pat her face and primp her hair.

He smiled up at her, but the amusement soon faded into a somber frown.

She took a minute to assess his seriousness, then slid off the couch to sit on the dark gray carpet beside him. "Step down?" she asked. "You love traveling the Divide."

He turned onto his side and propped his head up with one arm. "Love's a stretch, let's be honest," he said, tone weary. "It was exhilarating for a while, sure. And after they scrubbed the charting missions, certainly the next best option. But now, I think I'd be better off here, training soldiers. I'm not getting any younger."

"You mean you're not getting any older?"

It came out far more defeatist than she'd meant it. He smiled anyway, but it fell away as quickly as it'd appeared.

Pushing out a long breath, she lay on her side to face him, head propped up on her arm. She searched his tired eyes for some indication of what he was getting at. "What's this really about?"

"Life moves too fast while I'm gone. I feel like I'm missing a lot. Things change too quickly."

She scoffed. "Nothing's ever different on the *Argus*, trust me."

"*You* seem different. Did something happen?"

She shook her head. "Six months happened, Griff."

"Right." He let out a small sigh. "I've never been on the other end of it. It's hard for me to conceptualize the time difference. I'm sorry."

"Why are you sorry? It's your assignment, your duty."

"Because it's hard on you, I can tell. Every time I'm back, you're a little more tired, a little more weary—"

"I'm fine."

"—a little more jaded. You're not the same fierce Quin you were when I first left."

"I know," she admitted. "Life on the *Argus* isn't great, and having you gone hasn't made it easier. But I don't know what you want me to say. Like you said, we can't conceptualize life the same way. We live in two different time zones, literally."

He lifted his hand to the side of her face. Her cheeks warmed as he ran his thumb along her cheekbone, more familiar than she expected from her old friend.

"That's what I'm saying, Mo'acair," he said, his voice a low rumble. "I don't want it to be that way anymore." Her pulse beat up into her throat as he leaned closer, pressing his forehead to hers, his breath smelling of the honeyed whiskey. "I don't want you to grow old without me."

It took her brain a few seconds to process his round-about double negative. "Griff—"

Her breath left her as he pressed his lips to hers. On instinct her muscles tensed, but loosened just as quickly along with a wash of warmth down her back. She edged closer, and he wrapped his arm around her, drawing her into him.

Tilting her head, she paused to catch her breath. Her skin tingled as she inhaled his warm, leathery scent. Though she hadn't expected the night to take a turn quite like this, she couldn't say the thought had never crossed her mind. But he'd been gone for so many years now, she'd grown used to a life only occasionally punctuated by Griffith. She'd never considered he might someday return to stay. The thought alone stirred a sharp ache deep in her stomach.

"I don't want that either," she said. His chest deflated, worry creasing his forehead. She shook her head and tightened her arms around his waist. "To grow old without you, I mean."

Relief smoothed his brow, and he leaned closer again. "I don't want to leave again," he said quietly. "I should file my formal withdrawal now."

She shook her head. "I don't want you to quit the *Tempus* because of me. We can make the time difference work."

"No, we can't. Look how long it took us to get this far."

"You forget what life is like here, Griff. It's hard, and boring, and very uneventful."

"So's the *Tempus*. We just happen to be flying while everything is hard, boring, and uneventful."

Adequin let out a long sigh. "You really need to think this through. I want you to do this for the right reasons."

"You are the right reasons, Mo'acair. The only reason worth doing anything." He patiently awaited her response, his warm eyes steady. Earnest. He wasn't going to change his mind.

"All right," she said finally. "But you'll need to train your replacement."

"We can delay a day, and I can do that while we're docked."

"That's definitely not protocol."

His arm tightened around her back and he pulled her closer. "To the void with protocol. Even two weeks is far too long to be away from you."

"Since when?"

He chuckled. "Since right-the-fuck now. Eura's ready, has been for weeks."

"That's great, but you can't just throw command of a ship at her with no warning. You still have to do a check-ride."

"Fine. One more trip." He pressed his forehead to hers, and their eyelashes grazed each other's as she blinked at him.

She cleared her throat. "You mean, 'Yes, sir'?"

He pinned her hip to the floor with one hand, then tucked the other into her armpit and tickled her. Briefly overcome with giggling, she then got distracted trying to remember the last time she'd *giggled*.

He relented and kissed her forehead. Soothing, tingling waves flowed along her frayed nerves.

"This is fraternization," she said. "I'm going to have to report you to my CO."

His deep laugh rumbled in her chest. He gripped her waist and laid her back onto the ground, then braced on one arm to hover over her, his warmth enveloping her like a heavy blanket. His dog tags clinked together as they fell out from under his shirt, the cold metal and glass grazing the side of her neck.

"You're the EX," he said, his voice low and serious despite his grin. "You don't have a CO."

"Not aboard this vessel, maybe—"

He cut her off with another kiss, fiercer this time, sending her heart racing. His tongue found hers and their lips closed in on each other as three years/three months of pent-up desire let loose.

Adequin drifted slowly out of a deep, restful sleep. It took her a few long, wandering moments to realize what'd woken her—her wrist vibrating as her nexus hummed with a silent notification.

Griffith's slow exhales warmed the back of her neck, his arm draped heavy over her waist. It took a concerted effort of will to slide out from under its warmth. She shifted to the edge of the bed and sat up, swiping the notification open: the crew-evaluations report reminder she'd snoozed earlier. She dismissed it with a sigh, then rubbed the heels of her palms deep into her dry eyes.

The bed shifted, and Griffith let out a soft yawn. "Everything okay?" His hand trailed down her back.

Nodding, she slid her nexus band off and tossed it on the bed-side table. She turned and lay back down under the sheets to face him. "Fine, it was nothing."

He laid his arm over her shoulder, shifting toward her. "Tell me you don't normally get up at this time of night and work?"

"Not usually, no."

"You work yourself too hard, Quin."

"I don't mind having things to do. I need it that way."

"I know," he whispered, then kissed her forehead lightly.

"So . . ." she began, sliding closer, "how long have you been lying to me?"

His brow furrowed. "What?"

"Pretending not to have feelings for me?"

He smiled. "Oh, uh, I'm not sure I've done a very good job of pretending for quite some time. The way Lace acts, you'd think we'd been dancing around it for years."

"Is that what she's been giving you grief about? She knows?"

"Yeah. Hard to keep something like that from someone who's known you half your life. She probably knew before I even did."

"And when was that?"

"Since well before we came to the *Argus*. Hell, practically since we met."

She bit down on the inside of her lip. "Really, that long?"

"Yeah, that long." He let out a weighted sigh. "Back when I joined the Titans, well . . . you weren't with us at first, but you know how it was. After Redcliff, they were throwing commendations at me, then I finally gave in and came over from the Vanguard—"

"Back when Titans and Vanguards could still be in the same room without killing one another?"

"Right. Before we 'stole their war.'" His lips tilted in a smirk. "Your fault, by the way."

"I'm aware. But this isn't about me . . ."

He nodded. "I don't know if you remember, but for those first few years, they couldn't stop talking about everything that happened at Redcliff. They all acted like I was some divine gift to the Legion."

"Yeah, I remember," she said quietly. As a Vanguard, Griffith had been part of one of the first offenses against the new Viator threat—named after the cavernous gulch the worst of it had taken place in: Redcliff. It'd gone the true definition of SGL when shitty intel led them straight into a trap. As second-in-command, when

Griffith's CO died, the responsibility had fallen on him to get the company out. He'd managed to save dozens of Vanguards in a situation in which, by all rights, every one of them should have died.

Only a few weeks later, Lugen recruited him into the Titans, where his new comrades had been privy to every detail of the op and had just enough time to deify him before his arrival. From the moment Adequin arrived, the strange power dynamic had been obvious. They were all the same rank, all dexteras, but the others treated Griffith differently. They made him their liaison to upper brass, asked his permission for things he had no authority to grant or deny, and readily deferred to his opinions on the ground. They'd put themselves a class below, which had left him alone.

Adequin had seemed the only one unaffected by it. Coming straight from a delta-grade infantry unit into spec-ops training, she hadn't had the same access to reliable gossip, so it'd taken her time to piece together what Griffith had done, and why they were acting that way. Even after she found out, she'd been the only one that treated him like any other colleague. An experienced teammate— someone to learn from, certainly—but still a peer.

"It was still in full swing when I got there," she said. "They were trying really hard to give you a hero complex."

"Right. But you knew the truth of it," he said. "That'd I'd merely been the next person in line to take up the mantle. I'd followed protocol, used my training, and did what I thought would save the most lives. You were the first person I'd met who didn't either despise me or revere me for it."

"A single act can't define someone—good or bad."

"See, it's *that*."

She raised a brow. "What is . . . what?"

"That even-keeled wisdom. Way beyond your years." He pushed a strand of hair off her forehead. "But I know most of those years were heavy."

A lump built at the back of her throat, but she mustered an appreciative smile.

"Even if I didn't internalize it back then," he continued, "I think that's when I knew we could be more. Or I guess, that I might want to be more to you, someday."

"That was almost ten years ago. Why didn't you say anything sooner?"

"I don't know. I'm a lot older than you, for one." He rolled his eyes. "Whatever, that's a shit excuse."

She laughed. "Yeah, it's a shit excuse. Especially since you've already closed the gap by three years."

"There was just always a damn war on," he said, voice low and steady. "Then after Paxus . . . I didn't know if you'd be ready to hear it."

"Maybe not," she conceded. "But that was still *five years* ago."

"Only two for me."

"Right . . ."

"Honestly," he began, sidling closer again, "it's always been fear. Afraid if I told you, you wouldn't want me back, and I'd scare you off. That I'd lose you."

She leaned in and lightly kissed his bottom lip. He held his breath.

"You're a centurion," she said, "the most lauded Vanguard of our era, and as a Titan, part of one of the most successful spec-ops task forces of the last two centuries . . . but not brave enough to tell a woman how you feel about her?"

"Not just any woman."

"Oh, geez," she said with a hiss and a grin. "Feelin' pretty smooth tonight, huh, Griff?"

He smiled, then kissed her forehead lightly. "We can still get a couple of hours of sleep before I have to go."

"Just sleep?" she asked, biting her lip and smiling.

A wolfish grin spread across his face. "Who's fraternizing now?"

He locked both of his thick arms around her and pulled her into a deep kiss.

* * *

Adequin was sure there was no worse sight in the universe than Griffith standing by her door with a packed bag slung over his shoulder. How she'd put up with it for three years, she didn't know.

He swept some loose strands of hair behind her ear. "You gonna be here when I get back?"

"Where else would I be?"

"Honestly, every time I step off that ship, I'm surprised you're still here."

She scoffed. "This is my post, Griff."

He didn't immediately respond, taking a minute to regard her seriously. "Your punishment ended a long time ago. Or the Legion-issued one, at least."

"What's that supposed to mean?"

"You don't have to martyr yourself. What happened, happened. It's over—"

Her eyes sharpened, cutting him off mid-sentence. His jaw flexed, but he didn't continue. Griffith was the only person on the *Argus*, and one of the only people in existence, who knew why she was there. And he knew far better than to bring it up.

"Am I a bad EX, Griff? Do I not have anything to offer the Sentinels?"

He shook his head, grim solace in his eyes. "I think your talent's being wasted sitting on the edge of the universe, waiting for nothing to happen. You think they wouldn't jump at the chance to have you on the front lines again?"

"Front lines of what? War's over."

"They'd give you whatever job you want. I'm sure they'd love to plaster you on their recruitment posters."

"I'm sure they would."

"Just think about it, okay? We can talk to Lugen, get stationed anywhere."

"You don't have to stay on the *Argus*, Griff."

"As long as you're here, I'm here." He lowered his voice. "I didn't leave you on Paxus, I'm sure as hell not gonna leave you now."

"You're about to leave, literally right now."

"Hey, I'm just following your orders." He smiled, then wrapped his arms around her. He pressed his lips to her forehead and his beard scratched her skin as he spoke. "Last time. Six months. It'll make me that much less of a cradle robber when I get back."

She laughed, though it didn't lessen the sharp tightness in her chest.

"We've been through way worse shit than the Divide, Mo'acair," he said. "We got this."

She pressed her face into his chest and quietly murmured, "Aevitas fortis."

"Aevitas fortis," he echoed.

He kissed her one last time, then inhaled sharply and turned away. The door slid open and he stepped into the barren corridor. She leaned in the doorway as he strode down the hall. He turned back and smiled, the corners of his eyes wrinkling in that endearing way that made her stomach flutter.

"I'm sorry I wasn't brave enough to tell you before," he called back. "We'll make up for it in six months."

"Two weeks," she said. He laughed, then turned away and disappeared around the corner.

CHAPTER SEVEN

Adequin's whiskey buzz had almost worn off, and she felt jittery and anxious for reasons she couldn't put her finger on. So she showered, dressed, and headed for the bridge.

Though she wouldn't say she relished her time there during working hours, she found it a peaceful kind of calm in the dead of night. She'd spent a fair share of evenings reading her way through the old weapons systems manuals. She enjoyed visualizing how the dreadnought used to function two hundred years ago, when it'd still been the SCS *Rivolus*.

The bridge was in low-light mode when she arrived, three small, harsh lamps spotlighting down from the high ceilings. To her surprise, Jackin stood under one of the pools of light. He faced away from her, leaning on his terminal with clenched fists, head hung low.

"Jack, what are you doing here so late?" She stopped and rested her hands on the back of the captain's chair.

He remained silent for a few moments, then raised his gaze to the large viewscreen. "Did Bach get on his way?" he asked, tone flat, almost autonomous.

Adequin narrowed her eyes, not used to this kind of mood from her second-in-command.

"Yeah, they're off," she said carefully. Maybe Jackin had caught on that something was going on between her and Griffith. But the two men had always gotten along well—they were friends, as far as she knew. She didn't know what reason Jackin would have for this kind of despondency toward him.

"The *Tempus* hasn't responded to my hails."

Adequin withheld a scoff. "You know how well comms work near the Divide. Why're you hailing them?"

His eyes didn't stray from the viewscreen, didn't blink. "I'd wanted them to do some measurements on their way out, but . . . now I think I might want them to turn back."

She laughed. "Turn back? What are you on about, Optio?"

He finally broke his gaze to look down at his terminal. "I checked it. I double-checked, I triple-checked. I checked it . . ." His fingers flew through his holographic display, flipping dozens of numbers onto a main dock at the top of the interface. "Forty-nine times." He turned to look at her, his light brown skin gone sallow with shadowed bags encircling red, bloodshot eyes. "Think the fiftieth time's a charm?"

Any humor she'd reserved in defense of Jackin's strange mood fell away. She marched down the steps to stand beside him, locking her eyes onto his. "For what? What's going on, Jack?"

"We haven't drifted outward." He shook his head. "We haven't moved. Not fifty meters, not a meter, not a single *millimeter.*"

"It has to be the sensors."

"It's not the sensors."

"That's not possible. You're saying there's *less space* between us and the Divide, so we can't have *not moved.*"

"We can," he said.

"How?"

"If it's gotten closer to us."

"Right, but you *just* said we haven't moved."

He didn't respond and his dark brown eyes didn't flicker. Her heart raced and she swallowed hard, struggling to ignore what her subconscious tried to tell her.

"Get there yet?" he asked.

She gave a short, stilted laugh. "Be serious, Jack."

"I'm being dead serious, boss."

"Have there been any notifications from the other Sentinel ships?"

"Even if signals were getting through, no one sits nearly as close as we do."

"Okay, well . . ." She looked down at his terminal, the display showing a collection of coordinates and numbers she couldn't interpret. She looked up at the viewscreen, the same display of absolute black it'd always shown.

She took a deep breath. This was just a task, like anything else. A job to be done. What did they need to accomplish the mission?

Step one, before all else, would be to figure out what they were actually dealing with. The implication of this could not be taken lightly. They would need to test Jackin's findings and confirm the data before they could start throwing around unsubstantiated theories.

"What do you need to get the proper measurements?" she asked. "Something better than a buoy? I'll put in a request for—"

"When are you going to stop asking for stuff that'll never come?" His dark brows sunk as his eyes narrowed at her. "When was the last time the Legion granted you a special request? You think they give a shit if we're swallowed up by the Divide?"

"Whoa, slow down—"

"The signs were all there," he said, shaking his head in disbelief. "We've been riding the thrusters for weeks. The *Tempus* arrived three minutes early, then entered comms blackout a full twelve minutes earlier than it should have."

"There are many factors that could play into all of those things."

His eyes grew wide, equal parts fascinated and terrified. "Do you know what this could mean, Rake?" His mouth opened as he dragged his fingers down his cheeks and through his beard.

"*Could* is the operative word, Jack. We need to confirm—"

"You know how it used to be, right? The universe was expanding?"

"Of course," she breathed. "Like a *million* years ago."

"Then it stopped." He slid down the steps to the foot of the viewscreen, looking up at it in reverence, as if the screen itself were some fearsome, impervious foe. "Do you think this is how they felt when they found out?"

A chill ran up Adequin's spine.

"Probably not," Jackin answered himself, then began to chuckle. "Stopping in its tracks is one thing. About-facing's a whole different kind of formidable." His chuckle morphed into a full laugh.

"Optio, get a hold of yourself," she demanded. Her tone carried an impatient firmness she generally reserved for only the most unruly of soldiers. He ignored her and continued to laugh up at the screen. She descended the steps toward him two at a time, then took him by the shoulders to force him to look at her. "*Jackin.*"

His smile faded and the deranged fervor fell away from his eyes. He looked at his feet. "Sorry, boss."

"It's fine." She dropped her hands from his shoulders. "How far do your readings say it's moved?"

"It's hard to tell exactly. I'd say fifteen or twenty kilometers, give or take."

"Can you think of anything else that might be causing the readings you're seeing?"

He shook his head slowly, running a hand down the side of his face.

"We've eliminated sensor error, right?" she asked.

"Right. A few dozen times over."

"Griffith mentioned density fluctuations while riding it—could it be a bad flare-up making it seem like it's closer?"

"No. Those fluctuations might have an impact on the ships traveling on it, but they're nominal compared to the overall structure. We'd never see those kinds of readings from here."

"Okay," she said, crossing her arms. "What are we missing? What other phenomenon could it be?"

"No—this isn't theoretical, boss," he said, tone suddenly firm, all traces of his former shock replaced with sound assuredness. "I've checked it all, again and again. I just didn't realize what all the individual pieces meant until I looked at them as a whole." His gaze drifted down, and he let out a long sigh. "Until I took the laws of the universe out of my assumption. It's moving toward us—that's a fact."

Adequin's heart kicked against her ribs, and she took a second to steady herself before responding. "Well, here's another fact—it's still well over a million klicks away, and we've—*it's*—moved only a few kilometers. We have time to figure things out. I don't want to start telling people until we have to—but we can bring Mesa and some other brains in on it tomorrow if we need to. For now, I want you to get some rest. That's an order."

He nodded, then slowly ascended the steps toward the door.

"Jack?" she said. He stopped to look back at her. "Don't tell anyone about this. Understood?"

"Understood." Jackin disappeared into the dark hallway.

Adequin looked at the viewscreen to find the same field of solid black. If they'd already lost visual of the *Tempus*'s engines, they would soon be out of theoretical radio range. Not that the damn things ever worked anyway.

She climbed the steps to the communications terminal, sat down, and swept the interface open. She cleared her throat and opened the channel.

"SCS *Tempus*, this is the SCS *Argus*, hailing on high priority Legion X band, please respond."

She waited in silence, then expanded the frequency selection screen.

"*Tempus*, this is the *Argus*, I'm opening to wideband, broadcasting across all channels, unencrypted. Please respond."

She chewed her lip.

"*Tempus*, this is the *Argus*. Please be advised: Optio is recommending *Tempus* return to dock immediately."

She waited.

"*Tempus*, please respond."

Only static came back. She took a shallow, sharp breath.

"Griff . . ."

The light in her periphery bloomed as her unblinking eyes focused on the pitch-darkness of the void before her. She cleared her throat, forcing strength back into her voice.

"SCS *Tempus*, this is the *Argus*, hailing on all frequencies . . ."

CHAPTER EIGHT

Five years ago and ninety-three million light-years inward, Dextera Adequin Rake sits across a polished mahogany desk from the commander of the First, Praetor Reneth Lugen.

A single sheet of paper crinkles in the praetor's hand. He looks up from it, narrow face drawn tight across sharp cheekbones. He waits for her response.

"*Without us, you will perish,*" she says.

"That's all they said?"

"Yes, sir."

He folds the paper in half and leans back. He looks out the slatted floor-to-ceiling window and the honeyed glow of the setting sun warms his pallid complexion.

"Who else knows about this?"

For the first time in her career, she lies. "No one, sir."

"You expect me to believe you killed your way through ten kilometers of Viator and Drudger forces, *up a mountain*"—he points upward with an incredulous finger—"without any backup?"

"I'm a Titan, sir."

"That's true. And it's not that I don't believe you're capable of it. But I happen to know you flew a Levate cruiser off that planet."

She doesn't waver. She says nothing.

"Which takes two to fly."

She wavers. She's a terrible liar. "I'm sorry, sir."

"Your comrades are safe, I assure you. But I need to know who was there so I can mitigate the damage."

She considers lying. Naming someone else. Not implicating Griffith. But she can't. And he wouldn't want her to. "Bach, sir."

"Is that all?"

"Yes, sir."

"Thank you."

A drawer creaks open. He lights a match and burns the paper. They watch in silence as it's reduced to a pile of smoldering embers and ash atop his opulent desk.

He looks up at her.

"You've been granted the rank of excubitor, and all the rights and responsibilities the title carries."

Her heart stops. She expected to be court-martialed, hanged, drowned, thrown from a dropship in atmo, ejected out an air lock, publicly shamed, publicly executed. Not promoted.

"Excubitor? That's . . ." Her fingers twitch as she tallies the ranks mentally. "Four ranks."

"Yes, it is."

"I don't understand, sir."

"The events which occurred on Soldate 219–41 AV have been classified Caecus Level Alpha. You will never speak of the events to fellow members of the Titans, Legion officers or enlisted of any rank, civilians, or any sentient life-form or artificial intelligence, at risk of high treason. Understood?"

She opens her mouth to respond, but nothing comes out. Why isn't she being punished?

Her eyes drift to the glittering badges of rank pinned to his chest, and it hits her. It's obvious.

She's thinking like a guilty soldier. They're thinking strategically, politically, public-facing. Formally punishing her would be a matter of public record. The citizens would want to know why. They'd want to know about the mission, what'd really happened.

"Understood, sir."

"You are being assigned to the SCS *Argus*, effective immediately."

She refocuses her eyes. "Yes, sir." She doesn't know what that means, doesn't know what the *Argus* is. She doesn't care.

The praetor seems to glow for a moment, and his edges ripple away from him as he continues to speak. He begins to outline what will be expected of her on the *Argus*. She half listens as his form wavers, then flickers in and out of existence.

Her heart races.

She stands in the hallway outside his office. At the end of the long, wide corridor two armed guards await. They are there to escort her to her new assignment.

As she crosses the navy-carpeted expanse toward them, her attention is drawn to a vid screen recessed in the wall. It's playing a live newscast, but it can't be right. The screen shows the symbol of the Titans and a caption that reads: "Titan Forces Eliminate Final Viator Threat."

Behind the text, video loops of citizens celebrating in the streets of Elyseia, Viridis, Cautis Prime.

Text scrolls below it: "The Resurgence War comes to a close with confirmation from Legion officials that the last of the hidden Viator cohorts, along with the remaining breeders, have been executed on Paxus, under the command of the First and the Titans, helmed by Praetor Reneth Lugen."

Her chest constricts, her jaw tightens.

Lugen had gone a step further than she'd thought. He hadn't swept it under the rug. He'd called the mission a success.

He'd lied.

Then she sits atop the SCS *Argus*, legs folded beneath her. The Divide stretches out before her, infinite in its blackness.

It can't speak. That'd be ridiculous.

It says, "Aevitas fortis," and the words resonate in her chest like a bell being tolled. Warmth blooms and she feels a camaraderie with the edge of the universe.

Hull lights that don't exist flash. Blue and red, blue and red. Sound that can't exist in the vacuum of space blasts against her eardrums.

It's the *Argus*'s proximity alarm. Enemy ships are incoming. She stands to find the interlopers, to meet them head-on. She turns her back on the Divide and faces inward, toward the light of the universe.

Billions upon billions of stars blind her.

Adequin's eyes slid open.

Silence filled her cabin, save the quiet beeping notification on the holographic display on her bedside table. She rubbed the sleep from her eyes and turned to expand it. It was a request from Jackin to report to the bridge immediately.

The door opened and Cavalon Mercer rushed inside. He wore a standard white space suit with the sleeves pushed up, a helmet tucked under one arm. Adequin bolted upright in bed as he turned panicked eyes onto her.

"What are you doing?" he demanded. "You *cannot* be sleeping? Really?"

Her mouth gaped open, and she snatched the sheet to cover herself, instinctively gathering it around her. When she looked down, she realized she'd slept in her clothes from the previous day. She threw the sheet aside and stood.

"Oculus, are you fucking kidding me?"

He stepped toward her, extending his open palm. His gold and bronze royal Imprint tattoos slid frantically around his forearm. "This isn't really the time for a noble act of selflessness. You need to get on that ship. Now. Whether you want to or not."

Adequin pressed her fingers deep into her temples. She thought she'd woken up, but she must still be—

Cavalon grabbed her by the arm—not painful, but still fierce. Her skin pinched under his touch. It didn't feel like a dream.

Her tattoos rushed down her arm, and she shoved Cavalon away with a surge of Imprint-assisted force. He stumbled back.

"Dammit, Rake, we have to go!" he yelled.

Shocked by his temerity, she didn't know how to respond. His blue eyes narrowed. He reached for her again, but his form shifted and cracked, then peeled away as he disappeared out of existence.

Silence filled the cabin.

The door opened, and Cavalon rushed in again.

"What are you doing?" he yelled. He reached his open palm toward her, then his edges splintered and he disappeared.

She gaped at the door, but it didn't slide open again.

"What. The fuck."

Adequin inhaled slowly and tried to calm her nerves. That had easily been the most intense ripple she'd ever experienced. Her mind raced as she tried to determine how that situation could *ever* come to pass.

She took a deep breath and thought about what Griffith had told her about time anomalies. The crew of the *Tempus* were experts at dealing with them, after all, for in the interim time spent getting from the Divide to the *Argus* and back, they were inundated with the same phenomenon.

The general notion was: They meant nothing. They were a fabrication, aberrations of the potential of the future, and they certainly did not always come true.

The more recent the ripple, the more likely it would to come to pass, the fewer factors that could change the outcome. That bratty royal barging into her quarters implied a familiarity she couldn't fathom in the near, or even distant, future. So she pushed the incident from her mind, because it meant nothing.

She quickly changed, then left her quarters and headed for the bridge. Soldiers milled about in the corridors, some dealing with nearby doppelgängers, others clumped in groups sharing stories of strange interactions with the future. Apparently it'd been going on all night.

They snapped to attention as she passed, or dispersed to return to their tasks. She didn't bother to reprimand them, focusing solely on getting to the bridge as quickly as possible without actually running.

The bridge door opened before her, and Jackin looked up from his terminal, panic lining his eyes. The rest of the crew sat at their stations quietly working, giving furtive glances to nearby duplicates. Adequin strode past the captain's chair and down the short flight of stairs.

"Good to see you, boss," Jackin whispered, eyes darting to the crew members closest to them. "I've been riding the thrusters all morning to get us back in line, but they're *so fucking slow.*"

"Can't you set it to adjust automatically? Maintain the proper position?"

"I could write new code for that, yeah, but I don't have time. I have to make constant adjustments." He glanced back nervously at the crew. "And I can't exactly ask someone else to do it since I was ordered to keep it quiet."

She leaned closer and spoke as quietly as she could. "Forget keeping our position. Just crank up the thrusters. If we end up farther from it than we were, then oh well. Just get us away from it."

"Copy, boss." He leaned back over the terminal and got to work.

"Excubitor." An ethereal voice wafted down from the top of the bridge. Adequin turned to find Mesa standing behind the captain's chair, thin fingers drumming lightly across the back.

Adequin gripped Jackin's shoulder, then climbed the steps toward the Savant.

"I had to eat breakfast with myself this morning." Mesa's eyes sparkled with amusement. "What is going on?"

"Just drifted a bit outward."

Mesa looked over her shoulder. Cavalon stood with his mop in one hand, grinning at his future self, who also beamed with amusement. They lifted their mops in unison, attempting to mime one another. Mesa swung her gaze back to Adequin, who turned to exchange a worried glance with Jackin. They were going to have to tell people, sooner or later. They were only going to believe they'd accidentally drifted so many times.

"I'll admit," Adequin said, "the ripples have been a bit more frequent of late."

"It is really more of a reflection." Mesa's tone shifted into one

Adequin recognized well, one that more or less added the prefix "for your information" to everything she said. Mesa pressed her hands together and continued. "'Ripple' implies a degree of fluidity to time that suggests layered, concurrent dimensions acting in parallel to lead us toward a preconceived future. None of which has ever been substantiated. Even ancient Viator texts had very little information on tempology. You know, Excubitor, we are in an optimal location for data gathering as the closest vessel to the Divide . . ."

Adequin nodded along as the Savant continued. Mesa had no idea how accurate that statement was at the moment.

". . . *aberration*, maybe. Regardless, 'ripple' is wholly inaccurate."

"Yeah, I know, Mes. It's just what we call it."

"I know, Excubitor."

"Did you need something?"

Mesa's brows lifted. "Of course. The roster lists an oculus who has studied astrophysics, specializing in propulsion theory, but their name has been redacted. I would like to request him or her to assist on a project."

"You want them to join the research team?"

"For a time. If they are a good fit, I would consider a long-term arrangement. Can you point me to them?"

"Uh . . ." Adequin nodded over Mesa's shoulder.

Mesa looked back at Cavalon, now engaged in a mop-stick duel with his doppelgänger. She watched him fight himself for a few silent moments, then blew out a long breath as she turned back to Adequin. "I can see you are quite busy. I will leave you to your work."

Adequin laughed. "If you need him, Mes, he's all yours. But be wary, he's a handful."

Mesa sauntered away and murmured, "I believe you."

Adequin looked over at the new recruit and narrowed her eyes. "Cavalon," she barked.

To her surprise, both versions of him snapped to attention immediately. "Sir."

She didn't know which was real until the one on the right flickered. After a few moments, the duplicate disappeared, and a wave of relief washed over the bridge as more and more ripples subsided.

"How's that cleaning going, recruit?" she asked.

"Sorry, sir." Cavalon's downcast eyes suggested guilt, though his drawn brow made her think he was a little . . . mad. At himself, she hoped. At least he seemed to be trying to straighten out, even if he was bad at it.

"Just get to work, please."

"Yes, sir. Sorry, sir." He refocused his glower on the floor and began to furiously mop.

Jackin climbed the steps toward her two at a time. "All good, boss."

"Good. Let's go, uh . . . have a chat."

Jackin followed her down the corridor to her office. They didn't bother to sit, merely stepping inside far enough for the door to close behind them.

Adequin crossed her arms. "Long-term plan?"

He mirrored her, crossing his arms and facing her squarely. "I'm ready. Hit me."

She shook her head. "No, you hit me, Jack."

"I got nothin', boss."

"I need you to have something."

"I don't know what you want me to have."

She exhaled sharply. "Well, we've clearly got to get farther out of range than the thrusters can move us. How can we retreat at a quicker rate?"

"No idea."

"What about the jump drive? I know it's been decommissioned, but we have some people that might know their way around one— that new recruit's studied astromech and propulsion."

Jackin shook his head. "Even if there was a star out here to charge it, they pulled the primary components clean out and put them in some other ship."

"Seriously? No engine at all anymore?"

"Nope, it used to be where Novem Sector is now."

"Void. They really didn't want us going anywhere, did they?" She sighed. "How'd I go five years without knowing that?"

He shrugged. "Like you said, you're not really a ship captain."

"Maybe we just need to tell the Legion what's going on. Get a team out here to study it, help us figure out the best way to handle it."

He scoffed. "Even if they believe us, and even if we get them to send support to help figure this all out, fastest it'll get here is a month."

"Admittedly not ideal, but so what?"

"We don't have a month before . . ."

She stared at his dark brown eyes until the full reality of his seriousness sunk in. "Before what?"

"Before we all get to find out if there really is anything on the other side of the Divide."

"Is it speeding up?"

"Sure seems that way. I lined up all the data, and I've been trying all morning to figure out a timeline, but besides the constant interference plaguing our instruments, it's the same problem as always—nothing to orient us. I can't tell where we are versus where we were, other than how far our sensors seem to think we've moved, but they're just as in the dark as I am. No pun intended. Honestly, I don't even know if the thrusters are staying ahead of it at this point."

"Okay, forget the measurements." She rounded her desk and opened her terminal. "Let's get everyone safe, then worry about what's really going on. I'm going to send a priority message to HQ."

She slid open the comms interface and a red warning symbol floated to the top of her display. She glanced at Jackin. "It says link with Kharon Gate can't be established."

"Void." He pressed his fingers to his temples. "We've moved far enough at this point, we might've drifted out of range of the comm relay."

"Can we realign? Widen or boost our signal somehow?"

He ran an anxious hand through his hair. "I could try some things, I guess. Recalibrate the sensor array, maybe."

"Do you think it'd work?"

"Honestly, no."

She pinched the bridge of her nose. "Okay. What about a Hermes?"

"Not sure now's the time to go off on a charting mission, boss."

"Void, Jack," she said with a glare. "I *mean*, could we use a Hermes to travel to Kharon Gate, send a message directly from there?"

"Well sure, except it'd take like fourteen weeks to get there."

"Not at warp speed."

"The Legion doesn't give us warp cores with the Hermes. You know that."

"I've got a warp core."

Jackin laughed. "The fuck you do."

She maintained her level stare.

Jackin's eyebrows shot up. "Damn. Really, boss? Why didn't you tell me?"

"It's classified. It was the first thing I requested when I got here."

"Really?"

"Well yeah, it's not safe to leave two hundred people stranded in space with no FTL capabilities and shitty comms."

"Ya think?" Jackin said dryly, then shifted his weight and crossed his arms. "Okay. Show me this warp core."

They left her office to the amidship vestibule, then took a lift to the hangar, turning down a barren corridor lined with doors leading to unused storage facilities. Adequin pressed her thumb into the control panel beside one of the doorways. It confirmed her identity and the door opened. A single aerasteel case sat in the corner of the room.

"That's it," she said. "It's the only thing I asked for they ever actually granted. Took them eighteen months, but they sent it eventually."

Jackin knelt beside the case and opened it. He reached in and pulled the core out, a sleek metal canister the length of his forearm. Three long, narrow glass panes revealed the core's contents—a white-blue glow emanating from within.

Jackin turned it over in his hands, squinting and leaning closer. "One problem, boss."

"What?"

"This guy's almost entirely depleted."

She knelt beside him. "What? Shit. How? It's only a couple of years old."

"It probably came that way," Jackin grumbled. "They probably grabbed the shittiest one in the warehouse and shipped it off without even looking at it."

She frowned as she rubbed the back of her neck. "Can we refill it?"

Jackin leveled an incredulous look at her. "How would we go about that?"

"It needs acium, right? What do we have that uses acium?"

"Fuck, well," Jackin stammered, "I don't know, but even if we had some, without a fueling station, how do we get it into this thing?"

"I don't know, Optio, that's your area of expertise."

"I'm a pilot, and I know the ship's systems, but I'm no astromechanic. Put power in this and I can make it go, but how the power gets in it to begin with is beyond me."

She bit the inside of her lip, dreading her coming statement. "I think I know someone who might be able to help."

CHAPTER NINE

Forty-eight hours. Not half bad. He'd lasted longer than he'd expected, to be honest.

Cavalon had been following Bray down long corridor after long corridor, and with every turn, it became increasingly clearer where they were headed: the hangar. Those creative punishments Rake mentioned? He wasn't an idiot. Hangars were home to one of the few things he dreaded more than Rake's wrath: air locks.

He'd heard enough horror stories of marauders wandering the Inward Expanse to have earned a proper fear of the ways in which one could turn an air lock into a torture device. Sensory deprivation. Slow, drawn-out depressurizations. Or, what had to be far, far worse: the opposite. Hacking the controls and over-cranking the pressure. At least hypoxia would offer some fun hallucinations, or make you sleepy and oblivious after a time. But being slowly drowned in an excess of atmospheric gases until your cell membranes disintegrated, collapsing your lungs, detaching your retinas, while being overcome with vertigo and convulsions, all while puking your guts out? No thanks.

Rake didn't seem the needless-torture type, at least. A little tightly wound, maybe, but nothing a couple of weeks on a beach in the Outer Core drowning herself in cocktails wouldn't fix. So he had to assume if she bothered killing him, she'd probably do it quickly.

He blew out a long breath and sidelined the morbid train of thought, staring at the back of Bray's boots as he tried to put a finger on what had pushed Rake over the edge. Though he wouldn't be surprised if he'd screwed up and didn't realize it. He thought he'd been doing better, for the most part. Sure, he'd found that weird copy of himself amusing, and she'd rightfully reprimanded him, but he'd returned to his endless mopping and hadn't said a single snarky thing all day. And he'd fixed the literal shit out of that latrine tank the other night. Rake had to have noticed he was trying, even if he sucked at it.

He slicked his hair away from his forehead, plastered with cold sweat. Maybe it would just be a threat. *"Look what fate will befall you if you don't stop being such an arrant tool."*

Cavalon followed Bray around another corner and their pace slowed. He looked up to find Rake standing inside a small storage room with a man he'd seen on the bridge the last couple of days, usually hovering anxiously over his terminal. The conversation hushed as they approached.

Rake gave Bray a curt nod. "Thanks, Bray. You can go." Bray saluted and left. "Oculus, have you met Optio Jackin North?"

"Not properly, sir." Cavalon walked into the small room and shook Jackin's hand. "Cavalon Mer—er, uh, Cavalon. Sir. Good to meet you."

Jackin raised a thick eyebrow and gave Rake a sidelong glance. "Good to meet you too . . ."

Rake ignored Jackin's apparent skepticism as she held up a cylindrical container. She looked at Cavalon expectantly.

He cleared his throat. "You've, uh . . . got a warp core, there."

"We do," Rake replied.

"What's that all about?"

"That's classified."

His eyes narrowed, his instincts cultivating a handful of particularly snarky responses, but he hesitated. Rake wasn't giving him that look of exasperated tolerance he'd already grown accustomed to. Instead, she looked at him with a kind of calculated hope that made him worry he'd somehow already failed her.

"I understand." His eyes widened, surprised by his own response. "Sir."

"We need this recharged," she said. "Is that possible?"

"Theoretically or practically?"

"Immediately."

Her serious look didn't waver.

He nodded slowly. "Fair enough." He took the canister and turned it over in his hands. A small amount of glowing blue acium flowed along the glass encasement within. "Depends on the ship in question, but this is maybe a quarter of what you'd need just to do a baseline warp."

"Baseline?" Rake asked. "How far's that?"

"Not far enough," Jackin answered.

Cavalon raised an eyebrow. "How far is 'far enough'?"

"Kharon Gate."

Rake glared at Jackin.

"What?" Jackin shrugged. "He was your idea. He can't help us if we keep him in the dark."

Cavalon's face scrunched. Her *idea*? It sounded so disparaging, like he existed merely as a means to an end—some begrudgingly conjured solution. However, the more he thought about it, the more he realized it meant they actually needed him for something. Even if only to answer weird questions.

With an effort, Cavalon wiped the scorn off his face and refocused his confused displeasure on their decidedly odd line of questioning. "Kharon Gate? Why not Eris?"

Jackin shook his head. "Kharon's closer. By *a lot*—probably four or five hundred times."

"Really?" Cavalon asked. "That's not the one I came in on."

"No?" Rake's brow creased, and Jackin scratched his short beard with both hands.

"No . . ." Cavalon said. "We came in at Eris Gate, then limped our way here at warp speed, ate through quite a pile of cores. Took three weeks. Seemed like the long-ass way around to me." Rake sighed, and Cavalon's face warmed. "Sir," he added. But that didn't appear to be why she'd sighed.

She squeezed her temples with one hand. "Maybe Kharon's just overbooked."

"Yeah," Jackin said with a scoff. "Except there's about two things you can get to from that gate, and we're one of them."

"Off topic, Optio."

"Yeah, boss. Sorry."

Cavalon chewed the inside of his lip. Why in the universe did they need to get to an Apollo Gate? He took a breath and pushed the thought aside. He should just give them the information they wanted, then quietly return to his endless task of single-handedly spit-shining the entire dreadnought.

"So, is it possible to refuel it?" Rake asked.

Cavalon nodded slowly as he considered the options. Though he didn't have a truly eidetic memory, he'd gone through enough schooling that recalling facts on a whim had become second nature. "You have missiles?"

"Missiles?" Rake asked.

"Yeah, bombs? Warheads? In case the ghosts of the Viators show up? So you can blow them out of the sky? Sir."

She rolled her eyes. "Yes. Why?"

"Missiles use acium to fuel their thrusters."

Jackin scoffed. "That'd never be enough to fill this thing."

"Not from one, but this is an alpha-class dreadnought. You should have at least a few dozen fusion missiles. Right?"

"We do," Rake said.

"If you combined the acium from all of them, you'd have enough to warp to Kharon."

Jackin nodded. "Yeah, it's possible."

"A single warp?" Rake asked.

"You only need to get to the gate," Cavalon said. "You can refuel there for the trip back."

"Okay. Let's do it," she said. "Cavalon, take whoever you need to Octo Sector and pull those warheads."

"Me?" Cavalon scoffed. "Fuck, what? I'm just the idea man—"

Jackin's voice hardened. "You're whoever she says you are."

Rake gripped the optio's shoulder and his scowl faded. She

leveled a flat look at Cavalon. "You've got a degree that says otherwise."

"Yeah, a *degree*," Cavalon said. "Not practical experience."

"I'm not sure anyone has practical experience draining combustible elements from live warheads."

Cavalon's mouth gaped open. She couldn't be serious. Sure, he'd been well-schooled. He'd read texts and wrote papers and listened to professors drone on for practically his entire life. But it was a whole different affair to apply that knowledge empirically.

Rake lowered her voice. "If you wanted a chance, Oculus," she said, eyes earnest, "this would be it."

He shifted his weight, brow creasing. He knew what she meant: if he wanted to prove he could not be a fuck-up for once. She'd just said it more politely.

He blew out a long breath. "I'll need some supplies," he said. "Some kind of glass-lined steel pressure canisters—the kind your hydro lab would use for nutrient concentrates should work. Plus two of whoever's got the steadiest hands."

Rake opened her nexus. "Bray, this is Rake."

"Go for Bray, sir."

"Find Emery and Warner and escort them to Octo Sector, ASAP."

"Yes, sir."

Rake closed her nexus and looked to Cavalon. "Meet them there, Oculus. Take whatever you need from the research lab. And make short work of it."

Cavalon had thought with absolute certainty he was the most annoying person on this ship. Yet there she stood, proving him all wrong, chewing on her gum as if it were the most arduous task in the universe.

"*Flos*, actually, but that's just the last name every orphan on Viridis gets." Emery took a deep breath before continuing. "But whatever, those overrated gene pools gave me nothin', why would I want their fuckin' name?"

Cavalon sighed. This was still her response to, "I'm Cavalon. Nice to meet you."

Emery leaned against the armored wall of the dimly lit armament-repair suite and continued her rant, crossing one bare ankle over the other. She had her pants rolled up to below her knees, revealing shins covered in a mess of black-inked tattoos including a banner with the text "vita in via." "Street life," if memory served. Cavalon rolled his eyes.

She wore the hood on her vest up, and had ditched the undershirt in favor of displaying thin, bare arms covered in more black-inked tattoos, which were in turn covered in part by the Sentinel-issue, sparkling obsidian Imprints. She'd replaced the shoelaces on her boots with silver-glittered, neon-orange strings. It could *not* be proper dress protocol.

They'd been in the same room for about forty-five seconds, and Cavalon already knew her life story. Granted, recapping nineteen years didn't take long when most of it could be summarized with the phrase "pickpocket." She didn't seem particularly embarrassed by her unsavory history, but she did seem to think the Legion had been obligated to straighten her out, and that they'd failed her in that regard.

"Obviously," Emery concluded, slouching against the wall and crossing her arms. "Here I am, after all."

She continued gnashing her gum as she grinned over at Cavalon's second assistant. Warner stood hunched at the in-wall terminal—a stocky, thick-muscled man whose skin was almost the exact same shade of sandy brown as his buzzed hair. He had *literally* not spoken a word yet—not that one could be expected to get anything in edgewise with Emery in the room.

"I mean, they go to great lengths to say it's not a prison, but let's be real, guys. Right?" Emery shrugged. "But what-the-hell ever. This is the first time they've called me out to do somethin' useful. Plus, what better time to retrain my eye-hand coordination?"

Cavalon sighed. "I think a lot of times are better than when you're pulling unstable elements out of functioning warheads."

Her amusement dissolved and she squeaked, "Unstable?"

Cavalon bit back a smile. To be honest, it'd be relatively safe, assuming no random sparks. But it'd shut the girl up for half a second, so he considered it a win.

He let out a long breath, savoring the momentary silence. Despite his current irritation, he already had Emery earmarked as a useful contact. His three-month flight aboard the Mercer Royal Guard Luxury Cruise Liner had served as a lovely forced detox, but if he ever felt like having a bit of a relapse, Emery'd be the first person he'd go to. She might not be stashing vials of apex in her boots, but he could tell the type well enough. She certainly had the necessary connections, or at the very least a bottle or three of booze at her disposal. He wasn't overly picky about his vices.

With how delightful life had been on this ship so far, that day would come sooner rather than later. He'd never been able to kick it for long before, why would now be any different?

Warner growled a string of what might have been curses under his breath as he continued to tap at the holographic terminal screens.

Cavalon pinched the bridge of his nose to stave off the headache sprouting between his eyes, leaning back to rest on the workbench behind him. Extending over the small counter sat the articulated arm of a repair cradle, which would—in theory—retrieve a selected missile from storage for repair, if they could figure out how to use the damn computer system.

He really, really hoped the acium they could gather from the missiles in storage would be enough. If they had to go around to the ones already in the launch queues all over the ship, they'd be doing this for a week. Though he wasn't sure yet if that'd be better or worse than more endless mopping.

Warner grunted and turned away from the terminal. "It's no good," he rumbled, his gruff voice the tonal opposite of Emery's crisp, pitched timbre. "Giving some fuckin' error. Unless you happen to know what return code 485C means?"

Cavalon scratched the back of his neck. "Eh, afraid I'm a little rusty on my, uh . . . armament-maintenance software error codes. Who's your missile specialist?"

Emery snorted a laugh that turned into a brief coughing fit, and Warner just stared impassively.

Cavalon let out an exasperated breath. "There's gotta be some way to manually access the missile storage, right?"

Warner turned back to the terminal, tapping through screens. A few seconds later he gave a reluctant nod. "There's this weird list of drone protocols . . ." He jutted his square chin toward a narrow grate along the bottom of the wall, opposite the workbench. "That's apparently an access hatch for deploying automated repair drones. Could probably get in through that."

Cavalon's eyebrows shot up. "Automated?" That was one of his very favorite words. "Don't suppose you still got a few of those drones lying around?"

Emery chuckled, her constant mirth beginning to redden her pale cheeks. "Even if we did, would you know how to program it to do whatever weird-ass thing you got us doin'?"

Cavalon pinched his lips together. She had a point. "All right, looks like we'll be taking the hands-on approach."

He crossed the room, kneeling beside the access hatch to pull it open, but it didn't budge. Sucking in a breath, he grunted as he gave it another firm yank, making sure to keep his royal Imprints deactivated. After Rake's comment about the morgue, he wanted nothing to do with "volatile interfacing."

"This damn junk heap . . ." Emery slid away from the wall and slunk toward him. "Bet it's rusted shut."

He glanced back toward the workbench. "You guys got plasma knives around here?"

Warner breathed out a heavy grumble. He marched over, grabbed the handle with one hand, and yanked it open with seemingly zero effort. A haze of dust plumed out with it. Cavalon coughed as he accidentally inhaled a lungful, then slid Warner a frown.

The man crossed his arms over his broad chest, then rumbled, "You musta loosened it for me."

Cavalon breathed a laugh and shook the dust from his hair. "Right. Thanks, bud." He stepped back, sweeping his hands toward the open hatch. "Any takers? Don't all jump at once."

He looked between Emery and Warner, but they only stared back at him expectantly.

"Right," Cavalon sighed. Apparently this would be on him. "Shit-cutting. Shit-cutting . . ." He muttered the phrase to himself like a mantra as he knelt in front of the narrow hatch and peered into the pitch-dark beyond.

"What the hell're you sayin'?" Emery asked through her aggressive gum chomping.

Cavalon waved her off as he lay in front of the open hatch, then pulled himself into the dark. Stifling heat greeted him, the air gritty and thick, like sliding into a boiling river of sand. Sweat instantly beaded along his hairline.

"Bloody hell," he cursed, shimmying on his back until he slid fully inside.

The minimal light spilling in from the repair suite disappeared into total blackness a few meters in.

"It's dark as the void in here," he called back toward the square of light at his feet. "Can't see shit."

Footsteps squeaked and a few moments later, Emery's thin voice echoed into the inferno. "Incoming!"

A palm-sized disc skidded across the metal floor, landing centimeters from Cavalon's hand. He grabbed it, fumbling his fingers over the smooth surface.

"Switch's on the . . . side . . ." Emery's suspicion-filled voice called from the hatch.

He finally clicked the disc on, sending out a burst of blue-tinged light. Squinting as his eyes readjusted, he swept the beam to both sides.

The low overhead sat only a half meter above his face, comprised

104 J. S. DEWES

of rows upon rows of meter-long missiles, waiting in cradles to be grabbed by the automated system and whisked off to launch tubes all over the ship. Despite the sweat trickling down his back, a chill rushed up his spine, and he couldn't resist a shudder. It terrified as much as impressed him that one could fit so much destruction into such a small shell.

Unbidden, memories began to surface, and he clamped his eyes shut and tried to fight them away. But it was beyond useless. He'd known it was coming from the second the word "missile" had dropped out of his mouth. He'd held out hope he could put it off—at least get the task done, get through the rest of first shift, second shift, third, if that's what Rake wanted, then let his exhausted, feverish dreams work it out instead. But his brain didn't seem to care.

In an instant, his nostrils filled with the stale, dusty scent of the long-forgotten relief bunker under the eastern wing of his former home. He'd spent so much time in that old work space, it was too easy to visualize it filling into the darkness around him, frozen in time. The beam of the light disc became the glow of the work light shining across the worn counters and onto the hastily copied schematics tacked to the wall. The whir of the bobbin filled his ears, echoing off the reinforced concrete as it wound the strands of silver into wire. The air filled with the scent of burnt flesh as he charred the tips of his fingers over and over again with that damn handheld spot welder.

But any amount of pain he may have endured had been worth it. After a great deal of trial and error—and probably a little radiation poisoning—he'd made two of his very own, very customized replies to his grandfather's latest egomaniacal undertaking.

Cavalon had told exactly one other person his plan, he'd had no choice; he'd never had much of a mind for computers, and couldn't possibly figure out how to build the command circuitry on his own. Though they'd agreed to help, they urged him to reconsider, to try *communication* first—but only a Mercer could know how truly, utterly self-defeating that proposition was. His words had fallen on deaf ears too many times. If nothing else, this response had been too loud to ignore.

It'd taken him months longer than it should have, because he'd insisted both on smuggling everything directly into the manor—it wouldn't have been any fun if he hadn't built them right under Augustus's nose—and sourcing every component he couldn't literally make by hand from so far from the Core, no one within ten thousand light-years could be implicated.

Though as altruistic as that reasoning sounded, guilt that someone innocent might catch the blame had nothing to do with it. It had to be so *obviously* Cavalon's doing, that even by Augustus's absurd, roundabout logic, it couldn't be twisted into some ridiculous lie that would further his cause.

More importantly, whether or not Augustus concocted a cover story for the public, at least *he* would have to know the truth—who'd really been responsible. So he couldn't throw blame or sweep it under the rug, then ignore the problem entirely and stick Cavalon into another round of "reconditioning." So he'd have to actually fucking *do* something about it for once. He'd certainly called Cavalon's bluff on that.

He steadied his breath and tried to end it there, but the unwanted thought train rolled right on to the next suppressed memory: his last day at the manor. Cavalon had gone days without sleep, but somehow his fatigued limbs had propelled him forward as he stepped into Augustus's upholstered office, gilded depictions of his ancestors glaring down at him from the high-ceilinged walls. Despite the circumstances, his chest had been light, limbs energized, filled to the brim with a confidence completely fueled by blind relief. Because he'd done it—really done it, finally, after all those months spent working toward it. It was over, and now whatever happened, happened, and would be beyond his control.

Panic hadn't set in until the first unnerving sight of the Mercer Guard turning on him—the same people who'd shadowed him every damn place he went for the last twenty-seven years. Men and women he'd simultaneously hated, trusted, and relied on all too often to pull him by the scruff out of his own messes. Without so much as a second thought, they'd gone after him, treating him like any other miscreant as they shackled him and locked him in the cellar. Not that he could have expected anything different. They were Augustus's lapdogs, through and through.

Cavalon's chest tightened, the pressure weighing on his already strained heartbeat. The air thickened, and for a moment, he feared the oxygen had somehow been sucked out of the infernal missile compartment.

He closed his eyes and blew out a series of long, slow breaths, pushing every semi-adjacent, rage-filled memory from his mind. Some days, he truly hated the fact that he could remember every damn thing he'd ever seen or done. And shit-cutting, in all likelihood, did not include having a panic attack before he could even *begin* the task.

Summoning up a much newer memory of Rake's judgmental glower, he opened his eyes and refocused on his assignment. He slid back toward the closest line of missiles, the raised conduit tracks for the repair drones digging into his back as he shimmied.

Settling under one of the central racks, his eyes drifted over the series of articulated cradles clutching each missile. He had no idea if they were meant to be unloaded this way, but he didn't see what choice he had.

Turning onto his side, he folded his legs up and hunched into a massively uncomfortable crouch in the low overhead. He stuck the light disc against the underside of a nearby cradle and it adhered with a soft *shink*. Shimmying one arm up around the missile, he again resisted the urge to summon his royal Imprints to aid in the heavy lifting. He fumbled around with his other hand, hunting for some kind of release latch.

When he found it, the cradle snapped fully open. His royal Imprints triggered on instinct, flooding his arms and abdomen to help him catch the sudden weight.

He locked both arms around the casing as his heart leapt up his throat, heat flooding his cheeks—either from the shock of almost *dropping* a thermonuclear bomb, or from his Imprints activating, or probably both. Closing his eyes, he steadied his breath again.

Positive he'd die at any moment, Cavalon kept his Imprints activated long enough to guide the missile safely back to the small access hatch. It clanged to the metal deck *a little* hard as he pushed it out into the blissfully cool repair suite. Emery stood gaping, and concerned shock creased Warner's brow as he eyed Cavalon fumbling with the heavy missile.

Perspiration trickled down the back of Cavalon's neck to help drench his already damp collar. He flashed them a stiff grin. "I got it, guys," he huffed. "No worries."

He began to heft the missile up, and they both rushed over, taking some of the weight to help him lift it off the ground, then together they hauled it across the room to the maintenance cradle.

Pushing his sweaty hair off his forehead, Cavalon caught his breath for a few seconds while looking over the missile in the improved lighting. A series of identification and batch codes were etched into the casing, and, no surprise, every piece of it had been stamped with the Larios Munitions logo—a thick-bordered hexagon framing a splintered triangle. As one of the five royal houses of the Allied Monarchies, the Larios family had secured their role as primary weapons contractor for the Legion centuries ago. But they went by Larios Defense Technologies now—they hadn't been called Larios Munitions in ages.

Cavalon cleared his throat. "Uh, how old are these missiles?"

"The *Argus* is from the end of the Viator War," Emery answered. "So, a couple of centuries?"

"Void." He dusted off the nose of the missile to hunt for the command-controls compartment. "I figured you'd have updated firepower."

Warner scoffed and crossed his arms.

"Yeah, bud," Cavalon sighed, "I'm starting to get that vibe."

Emery giggled. "Yeah, they don't give us much to work with out here." She skirted the workbench and sidled up beside him. "All right, so what're we doin'?"

Warner moved forward and hovered over the tiny woman's shoulder, looking down expectantly. Cavalon's face warmed. He knew what he was doing, but something about the way they looked at him like he singularly possessed all the answers in the universe stressed him out. This whole being-useful thing would take some getting used to.

"Uh, well . . . I'll do this first part," Cavalon said, eyeing them warily. With only one cradle, there wasn't really a way to make this more efficient than one at a time. "But, grab me an impact driver? Should have a little star-shaped bit."

Emery knelt under the workbench, clanging around as she dug through the shelves, finally popping back up with an impact driver in hand. She passed the tool over to him, smacking her gum.

"Wire cutters next," he said.

She nodded and disappeared again, while he ducked under the nose of the missile to the other side of the workbench. He zipped off the six screws holding a section of the chassis in place, then pried the ancient panel free. He pulled out a clump of bundled wires.

Emery appeared over his shoulder, assaulting him with the fruity smell of her bubblegum. "Whatcha doin'?"

"Uh . . ." He lifted a brow at her, and she dropped the wire cutters into his open palm. "Disabling the arming unit."

Her curious expression stiffened. "Uh . . . manually?"

Warner grunted. "There's gotta be a way to do that through the computer."

"Probably," Cavalon agreed. "But I think we already established no one knows how to use the software."

With the edge of the wire cutters, he split the seal bundling the cabling, then singled out the wire in question and snipped it in half.

"Bloody void," Emery squeaked. "Yet you know how to do it *that* way?"

Warner shook his head. "And you were askin' *us* who the missile specialist was?"

Cavalon scoffed. "Trust me, I'm no specialist." He moved to the tail of the missile. "Anyone can figure out how to take something apart."

Emery's eyes narrowed.

"Pass me one of those canisters . . ." Cavalon began, then with a frown added, "and some safety gloves, if you have them." In any other circumstance, he wouldn't bother, but Rake would probably yell at him if he melted all the skin off his hands.

Emery shrugged off her skeptical look, digging under the counter again while Warner walked over with one of the mismatched canisters they'd appropriated from the research lab. Cavalon moved to the tail of the missile and unscrewed three different access panels before he found the right one. He lowered the cradle closer to the top of the workbench, then positioned the canister under it. Warner dropped a glass funnel into the top.

Emery surfaced and tossed a pair of gloves at Cavalon. He pulled them on, stretching the rubbery fabric up to his elbows. Inside the missile, he picked through the mess of wiring, fishing past the primary launch components toward the guidance module.

He expected to have to pry the smaller unit open to find the thruster lines, but to his delight, the black tubing instead lay affixed to the sides of it. With the wire cutters, he snapped the brackets holding it in place, pulled the rubber tubing free, then snipped it open. Twisting the missile a few degrees in its cradle, he angled the sliced tube until the thick acium began to flow out and into the funnel.

Concern tightened his chest as the element gathering in the canister emerged much as he'd feared: a very faint, soft blue glow. At full power, the element would be almost blinding in its luminance, even in such small quantities. Which meant the vacuum-sealed propulsion systems he'd researched must have been an advancement standardized sometime in the last two centuries.

"Well . . ." he said, yanking off the gloves. "Shit."

Emery leaned closer. "What's the problem, boss?"

Boss? With an effort he ignored it and shuffled closer to the missile, squatting to put his shoulder under the tail and lift it a few centimeters so the element would drip out slightly faster.

"It's good you guys never had to use these things," he said. "They'd probably have never made it to their target."

"Isn't this stuff supposed to last forever?" Emery asked.

"When it's sealed in an airtight core or lines, then yes. But it weakens when it's been exposed to oxygen for this long."

"Damn. We gonna need more of it?"

"Probably." Cavalon wiped a trickle of sweat off the back of his neck. "Can you call the optio up here?"

"Sure thing, boss," Emery piped.

"I'm not the boss," he grumbled, but she didn't react.

Emery crossed to the entrance and slid open the comms interface on the control panel beside the doorway. "Bridge, this is, uh . . ." She grinned and lowered her voice to speak in a conspiratorial hush. ". . . *special operations team alpha* calling from an undisclosed location in Octo Sector."

Cavalon leveled a look at her, and her grin broadened.

"Uh, go for bridge," Kamara's wary voice answered.

"Optio's presence is required for a critical inquiry."

"Emery, is that you?" Kamara admonished. "What are you doing?"

Emery rolled her eyes and returned to her normal timbre. "It's EX sanctioned, Kam, I swear. Just send the optio down."

"Yeah, copy that. I'll tell him," Kamara replied, then clicked off.

"Why we doin' this anyway?" Emery asked, returning to lean against the workbench beside Cavalon. "Don't we need these missiles to, ya know, be functional?"

"Er, it's . . ." Cavalon gave her a sidelong glance. "Classified."

Warner scoffed.

Emery laughed. "That's a pretty boss-like thing for a not-boss to say."

Cavalon forced a grin and chose to ignore them. "Might as well drain a few while we wait," he said. Every little bit would help.

Cavalon left them to monitor the acium collection while he returned to the sauna/storage room to bring out more missiles, more than happy to let them continue in their ignorance of his royal Imprints.

Emery rambled on while they worked, detailing stories she'd heard that sounded half made up about how Rake's predecessor used to decide on promotions and duty assignments, involving elaborate bribing schemes, indentured servitude, and climbing the ranks of cage-fighting tournaments. Rake's far less dystopian version of the *Argus* seemed reasonable in comparison.

"Sirs," Warner barked suddenly as Cavalon pushed a fourth missile out into the repair suite. Emery's back went straight so fast, Cavalon thought she'd give herself whiplash.

"Oculi," Jackin said. "What is it?"

"Cavalon has a question, sir," Emery barked.

Cavalon squirmed his way out of the hatch, narrowing his eyes at her in disbelief. Just that quickly, she morphed into a whole different person.

"Okay, as you were," Jackin instructed. They returned to the workbench and Jackin looked to Cavalon. "What's the problem?"

A few drops of sweat slid off Cavalon's forehead onto the missile as he rested it carefully on the floor. "These warheads are pretty ancient, Optio." He stood and found Rake had arrived as well. She leaned in the doorway behind Jackin, arms crossed.

"Yeah, they're Viator War leftovers," Jackin said.

Cavalon nodded to the dimly glowing canister. "You know, oxidation, and all that. Sir."

"Shit," Jackin grumbled. "I didn't even think about that."

"I know they pulled the jump drive out of this thing," Cavalon said, "but what about the accelerator lines?"

Jackin licked his lips, then his eyes went wide. "Man, you're fuckin' brilliant. There's no way they'd have bothered to drain the lines."

"And they should be airtight."

Jackin nodded, slowly at first, then with growing fervor. "Right. So if we vent the sector, get a space suit . . . we can drain what's left without any oxidation."

"Maximum potency," Cavalon agreed.

"That's great." Rake stepped up beside Jackin. "Where are the accelerator lines?"

Jackin's smile faded. "Where the jump drive was."

She let out a sigh. "So we have to evacuate all of Novem Sector?"

"Bulkhead doors, back, yeah."

Rake pushed her hair out of her face. "Okay. Jack, make the order. Send them to the mess. Try to keep it quiet, though, yeah?"

Jackin nodded. "You got it, boss."

Rake moved aside to let Jackin pass, and the optio scurried out the door. She eyed Emery and Warner at the repair cradle, then the line of missiles by the hatch, before looking to Cavalon. "This is some halfway decent shit-cutting, Oculus."

He flashed a grin. "Well, you gave me homework, and I'm clearly an A-plus student."

Her eyes glinted ever so slightly. She didn't grin, but she didn't *not* grin.

"So," Cavalon said, "I suppose you'll be expecting me to, uh . . . 'see it through,' as they say?"

She afforded him the tiniest of smiles. "Get on it, soldier."

Oddly, that same fire kindled in his stomach. He could see why everyone regarded her so highly. That look of approval was addicting.

CHAPTER TEN

The thick bulkhead door slid open, and Cavalon stepped out of Novem Sector and into the amidship vestibule, brow soaked in nervous sweat. Rake waited on the other side, leaning against the wall.

"How'd it go?"

"Good, sir," Cavalon said, voice muffled through his visor.

He set the acium-filled jar on the floor at his feet, then released the lock on his helmet. He lifted it off, and his ears popped as the pressure fully equalized. Glad to be free of the artificial air, he took a deep breath, but found it tasted just as stale as the suit's oxygen had.

"There was a lot of drip left in the line," he continued. "More than I expected. All sealed up tight."

He took off his gloves and pocketed them, then pushed up the sleeves of the white, pearlescent suit. He tucked the helmet under his arm, then picked up the jar.

Rake's hopeful visage faltered as she eyed his exposed arms and helmet warily. He found himself, yet again, afraid that he'd managed to screw up without knowing how.

"Everything okay?" he asked.

She gave a small nod. "Yeah. Just déjà vu."

Cavalon held the brightly glowing jar toward her like a peace offering. Rake stared at the acium and her unsettled look faded. The blue glow appeared a brilliant shade of emerald reflected in her amber eyes.

"You could probably warp to Kharon Gate three or four times with this," he said, with as much optimism as he could muster.

She nodded slowly. "Great. Let's go." She spun and headed for the other side of the circular vestibule.

"Go?" he squeaked. Though the other part of her statement concerned him more—just exactly how specific was her usage of "let's"? He slicked his sweaty hair off his forehead and took a few quick steps to catch up.

Though every part of him wanted to insist she elaborate, he kept his mouth shut and followed in nervous silence as she headed toward the lift.

At first, he'd been sure his involvement in all this would conclude at the odd-line-of-questioning phase. Then, he'd thought it'd be over after the warheads. This time, he'd been certain his final task would be venturing into a vacuum for the first time ever to drain the fluid from two-hundred-year-old accelerator lines. All while quelling his acute panic at being only one faulty warning sensor or clogged filter away from suffocation.

But she'd said "let's," and his feet were moving underneath him, and—even more oddly—he didn't feel all that compelled to argue with them.

A few minutes later, they entered the main hangar. In the docking bay across from where he'd seen the *Tempus* parked the day before, now sat a small, spherical transport vessel.

Jackin and Emery stood underneath the ship, lifting a crate above their heads toward the open hatch. Warner's thick arms reached down and grabbed it, then disappeared into the hull.

As Rake and Cavalon approached, Jackin looked over, cheeks flushed and sweat glistening on his forehead. Cavalon imagined the work of an optio rarely required such heavy lifting, but the real question was why the hell they were lifting anything at all. Loading a ship with supplies? This grew more and more suspicious by the minute.

Maybe Rake had finally had enough. Or maybe she and Jackin were secret lovers, intent on stealing away into the night, never to be heard from again. Cavalon had to grin at the thought. Not only did abandoning ship seem so not Rake-like, it was ludicrous, but the idea of her and Jackin together was just . . . silly.

The optio stepped away as Emery continued to hand supplies to Warner.

"Get what we need?" Jackin asked.

"Plenty." Cavalon held up the jar.

"Plenty indeed. But how do we get it into the core?"

"Well . . ." Cavalon heaved a sigh. "It's pretty complicated."

"How complicated?" Jackin asked, worry creasing his sweaty brow.

"Well, you'll want to use the vacuum-pressure glove box."

Jackin quirked an eyebrow. "Obviously. Then?"

Cavalon grimaced. "You're going to have to open the fuel port door on the core."

"And?"

"And then . . ." Cavalon lifted his shoulders in a weary shrug. ". . . pour it in."

Jackin's eyes shadowed as he leveled a flat look at Cavalon. Cavalon flashed him a grin, but Jackin didn't seem amused.

Rake glanced between them. "That doesn't sound hard."

Jackin didn't respond, but snatched the jar from Cavalon and headed toward a nearby workbench with a huff.

"Try not to get any on you," Cavalon called after him. "Burns a little."

"Ahh." Rake gave a quick nod. "A joke. Of course." She gave Cavalon an exasperated frown.

His cheeks instantly warmed, and the smile melted off his face. "Sorry, sir. Couldn't resist."

"Why don't you help Emery and Warner finish packing the supplies?"

"Yes, sir."

Cavalon gave Jackin a sheepish look as he passed by the workbench on his way toward the ship. He set the helmet aside and pulled off the space suit, then went over to help Emery lift a large aerasteel crate.

"What is this stuff?" he asked, eyeing the label on the crate.

"MREs," Emery said.

"Uh, yeah. What's that?"

Emery scoffed. "You really aren't a soldier, are you?"

"Who said I'm not a soldier?"

Warner peered down from the hatch above them and chuffed. Cavalon scowled, but chose to ignore it. It didn't matter if they knew he *wasn't* a soldier, so long as they didn't know what he *was*.

They lifted the crate, and Warner easily plucked it from their wobbling arms.

"Meals, ready to eat," Emery explained.

"Ahh."

"Note, that doesn't mean they'll stay down. Only that you can, technically, consume them with your mouth."

"Not the tastiest, then?"

"Understatement of the millennium. They've got a shelf life of, like, fifteen years if that tells you anything."

Warner reappeared in the hatch frame. "What else?"

"Just a bunch of pistol charges," Emery said. Warner raised an eyebrow. She shrugged, and they shared a wary look, equal parts clueless and nervous.

"Toss 'em up," Warner said.

Emery dragged over a pallet of narrow metal boxes. Cavalon recognized the worn cases as crates used to store firearm energy cells.

"Uh . . . why so much ammo?" Cavalon asked. "Where you guys goin'?"

"Shit if I know," Emery said. "Optio just gave us a list and told us to pack it."

She tossed one of the boxes up to Warner, then glanced over her shoulder. Jackin placed the last of the jars from the missiles into the vacuum chamber built into the workbench.

Emery lowered her voice, decidedly unamused. "No one ever goes anywhere. Like, *anywhere*. You probably know more than we do, boss."

It was partly true. He at least knew they wanted to get to Kharon

Gate. But that sliver of knowledge didn't do much to calm the knot in his stomach, which constricted with every passing minute.

He glanced over to where Rake leaned against the workbench, quietly speaking with Jackin as he worked. Cavalon wanted to stop packing and refuse to lift another finger until they explained what the hell was going on. Instead, he absentmindedly passed cases up to Warner and focused on trying to overhear Rake and Jackin's hushed conversation.

". . . supplies really necessary?" Rake asked. "Shouldn't take longer than a few hours to get there and back."

"Just being cautious, boss," Jackin answered. "Who're you gonna send?"

"I'll do it."

Jackin scoffed. "Well, that's just about the worst idea ever."

"We need rank to make that kind of request. And the higher it is, the more likely they'll listen. Technically, we need delta clearance to even relay this report."

"My rank and clearance will do. Send me."

Silence hung in the air for a long moment before Rake responded. "Fine. You're not going alone, though. Who do you want?"

"Just send these guys, they already know too much. No need to involve anyone else."

There it was again, that ambiguous plural that suggested Cavalon might be expected to continue down yet another stretch of this strange road.

Rake mumbled something, and Jackin huffed, then said, "That, I'm leaving up to you."

Warner dropped down from the hatch, then called out, "All packed, sirs."

With the filled warp core in hand, Jackin crossed over from the workbench, followed by Rake.

"Here's the situation . . ." Rake stopped in front of them, hands held behind her back. "You will be warping to Kharon Gate to send a request to HQ."

"Yes, sir," Warner said.

"Uh," Cavalon said. "Me too?"

"Yes, you too," Rake said patiently.

"Uh . . ." he began again. He'd been waiting for this shoe to drop, and he'd intended to fight her tooth and nail. But he quickly realized he didn't know which scared him more—fleeing to ask the Legion for help with . . . whatever, or staying behind on the ship they were fleeing from.

"Jackin's your CO for this mission," Rake said. "Heed his orders, and I expect you to treat him with the utmost respect. If I hear otherwise on your return, there'll be hell to pay. Understood?"

"Understood," both Emery and Warner barked in unison.

Cavalon had to clear his throat before his feeble response fell out. "Understood . . ."

"Your job's simple—head to the gate, put in the call, and come straight back." She turned to Jackin. "And Jack—ships. Right away, if you can."

Ships? Cavalon swallowed the lump in his throat. What did that mean? Like, backup? Like, "Enemies incoming, mobilize the fleet"? Cavalon looked to Emery and Warner for any indication of a reaction, but they still had their exemplary-soldier hats on, and their demeanors didn't waver in the slightest.

"Will do," Jackin said. "This'll be this Hermes's inaugural voyage, boss. What do you wanna call it?"

"Shit, I don't care."

"Just need something to put in the transponder when I boot it up."

Rake shook her head. "*SGL?*"

Jackin smirked. "Really, boss? The *SGL?*"

"I dunno, Jack. Does it matter?"

"Not in the least. Copy *SGL*. You'll need an admin terminal to clear us for departure. Where's Lace?"

"I dismissed her." Rake rubbed her hands together nervously. "I don't really want this to reach the bridge either."

"That's fine. Head to your office and call my nexus, I'll step you through how to unlock the bay controls."

"Thanks, Optio. Be safe."

"You got it, boss."

Rake faced Emery and Warner and saluted. "Good luck, soldiers." They returned the gesture, then climbed the flimsy ladder into the ship.

Oddly, Cavalon's feet wouldn't move. He looked down at them in annoyance.

Rake began to leave, but paused as she passed, gripping his shoulder.

"Good work today, Oculus," she said. "Thank you."

His cheeks warmed, and he hoped the surprise of being *thanked by Rake* would shock him out of his paralyzed reverie, but he still couldn't move. He glanced up at her, and he knew she could read his frozen, wide-eyed look for what it was: fear.

"You'll be fine," she said, so matter-of-factly he felt inclined to believe her. "Just listen to Optio North."

He nodded, and his body finally listened when he told it to turn around and climb into the ship. Jackin followed, and Warner secured the hatch closed behind him.

Cavalon spun to take in the layout of the Hermes—or rather the *SGL*—noting how well the inside matched the design of the outside: circular *everything*. The circular hatch sat dead center in a circular common room, complete with a circular table flanked by two half-circle benches. A small wedge protruding partway into the room outlined the cockpit, and in arcs on the outer wall sat doors to three separate areas. The one opposite the cockpit Cavalon knew would lead to the engines at the back of the ship, the others likely to cargo and crew quarters.

He finished his revolution and landed face-to-face with Jackin. The optio flashed a quick smile and shoved the brightly glowing warp core into Cavalon's chest.

"You can install that, right?"

Cavalon glanced at it. "Uh, yes, sir. Absolutely."

Jackin spun on his heel and disappeared into the cockpit.

"Need help, sir?" Warner called after him.

"No," Jackin called back. "Just need to get the transponder going, then put in some coordinates. It'll do most of it itself."

Emery began to help Warner sequester the supplies into the starboard room. Cavalon stood and watched, the cold steel of the warp core sending goose bumps up his arms.

"That is . . ." Jackin called out, "if someone installs the core so we can turn the warp drive on."

"Right," Cavalon said under his breath. That'd be him.

The lights faded up in the engine room as he entered. He walked up to the long, central console along the back wall and unlocked the fuel port, then tugged open the hatch in the floor. He lay on his stomach at the edge of the small cavity, dropping the core into the mechanism and locking it in place.

Twisting to reach behind him, he stretched up to the console and input the command for the warp drive to accept its new fuel cell.

"Acium core accepted," the computer said, then gave a negative chirp. "Error. Drive access lock not engaged." Cavalon grumbled, swiping the warning away, but the computer wasn't having it. "Please engage lock or give verbal confirmation to disengage safety protocols."

"Uh, okay. Verbal confirmation . . . granted?"

"Error."

"Disengage safety protocols, *please*."

"Error. Please confirm by stating the following: 'I understand the risks associated with exposure to hazardous elements. I wish to disengage safety protocols and understand that any repercussions are not the responsibility of the System Collective Legion.'"

Cavalon took a deep breath, clinging desperately to the last vestiges of his patience as he repeated it back.

The computer chirped, "Confirmed."

A series of small clicks preceded a soft roar of electricity sparking, and the floor shuddered as the ion engines roared to life. A familiar, unsettling sensation tugged down on him as the *Argus*'s simulated gravity swapped with the *SGL*'s notably less-realistic simulated gravity. His stomach flopped, and the ship lurched forward. All signs indicated they'd left the hangar bay.

Jackin's voice rang over the ship's speakers. "Cruising up to speed. We good, Oculus?"

Cavalon reached for the comms button. "Good to go, sir."

"Copy."

Cavalon lay facedown over the edge of the cavity and stared at the glowing acium. As sure as he'd been of the *theory* behind their jury-rigged warp core, he wasn't nearly as confident that it'd actually work. If it didn't look like it would catch properly, he at least wanted to have a chance at pulling it out in time.

"At speed," Jackin said. "Engaging warp."

Cavalon hovered his hands above the warp core, fingers twitching nervously. A soft click cut through the silence, but nothing happened. The acium sat placidly in the glass cylinder. His breath slowed to a stop.

Then the hairs on his neck and arms rose. The floor lurched and the acium floated upward. A high-pitched squeal began to build, then the element spun into a thin line and twisted through the core in a regimented corkscrew pattern. He knew it'd caught when the squeal cut off in favor of a low, constant rumble that vibrated deep in his chest. He breathed a sigh of relief.

When he returned to the common room, Warner and Emery stood near the circular table. He crossed the room toward them. "So, uh," he began, "what the hell's *SGL* mean anyway?"

Emery shrugged. "No idea."

"*Shit's gone lateral*," Warner rumbled, folding his arms over his broad chest.

"Really?" Emery snickered for a few seconds before the humor wiped from her face, white cheeks flushing. "But, wait . . ." she mumbled. "Does that mean shit's gone lateral?"

"It's an old Vanguard thing, s'far as I know," Warner went on, seeming not to have heard Emery's digression. "EX prolly got it from the *Tempus's* captain."

Emery's grin reappeared, eyebrows waggling. "That hunky centurion? How do you know he was a Vanguard?"

"Musta been—he was at Redcliff just before he joined the Titans."

"No shit?"

Cavalon quirked a brow. "Wait, there's *another* Titan on the *Argus*?"

"Sorta," Emery said. "He captains the *Tempus*, so he's gone most of the time." She leaned toward him, lowering her voice even further. "Both showed up here five years ago, just after the war ended. Weird, right?"

Cavalon shrugged. "I don't know, is it?"

"I mean, two Titans at the Divide? Can't be by choice."

"They musta pissed someone off," Warner agreed.

Emery flashed a diabolical grin. "Whaddya think they did?"

Jackin appeared in the cockpit doorway, a grim scowl lining his face. Emery flushed and Warner looked down.

"Is this a proper way to act, Oculi?" Jackin barked. "Talking about our EX behind her back?"

Cavalon's first thought quietly surfaced: *better than to her face*, but that newly developed self-preservation kicked in, and he kept his mouth shut.

"No, sir," Warner said.

"Sit down and shut up," Jackin said. "We'll be there in less than an hour."

"Yes, sir," Emery said. "Sorry, sir."

She and Warner sat on the bench, backs straight against the gleaming aerasteel wall.

Jackin turned his glare to Cavalon. He crossed his arms and stared down the optio. *They'd* been the ones gossiping—he hadn't done anything.

But instead of continuing his angry glare, Jackin's dark brown eyes relented in favor of . . . there it was. Disappointment. Far more effectual than anger, and Jackin knew it. He'd learned that from Rake, Cavalon was sure.

Warmth crept into Cavalon's cheeks. "Sorry, sir." He sat next to Emery and stared at his boots, the toes polished and unmarred. They looked downright naive next to Emery and Warner's—both scuffed and worn. He still had a long way to go.

CHAPTER ELEVEN

About twenty seconds after comms broke off, Adequin began to seriously question the sanity of her decision to send Cavalon. She leaned back in her desk chair and ran both hands through her hair.

Though he'd demonstrated both intelligence and competence, he still served as an unknown quantity—one who'd proven to be an unpredictable, aggravating nuisance. However, the last few hours couldn't be ignored. He'd stepped up more than she'd ever expected him to. She'd given him the tiniest sliver of trust and focus, and he'd all but entirely shed his volatile attitude.

But she knew that kind of compliance could be superficial. And temporary. A way to appease a subjugator, misdirect their focus while you scheme. It was how humans had won the Viator War, if on a far more complex and grand scale.

Adequin took a breath and refocused her thoughts. Cavalon wasn't a militaristic force assembling some complex strategy against her. He wasn't an enemy to outmaneuver. He was just a man—someone who had clearly lacked guidance, and who appeared to have the potential to thrive if given the chance. And she trusted Jackin without question. He would handle Cavalon well. She didn't need to worry about either of them.

"Excubitor, sir?" Kamara's voice rang over her nexus.

"Go for Rake."

"Sorry to disturb you, sir, but we've got a situation on the bridge, and I can't get a hold of Optio North."

"Jack's indisposed, sorry, Kam. What's the issue?"

"It's his terminal, sir. Positioning alerts are going off left and right. Seems we're drifting again."

Adequin grimaced. They were behind again already. She'd hoped flooring the thrusters earlier would give them a longer reprieve.

Pinching the bridge of her nose, she tried to compute how the hell to go about all this without Jackin. Though she'd learned some about the ship's systems in the last five years, she'd never had reason to actually *use* any of them before. She'd always relied on Jackin to liaise between her and the ship. That was an optio's job, after all.

If this thing were a starfighter, a cruiser, a recon ship—sure. She'd have it well in hand within a few heartbeats. But the *Argus* was no light spacecraft, quite the opposite, in fact—the very definition of a battleship. It required an entirely different kind of command, and a very different path through the Legion than the one she'd taken. It might as well have been a jump drive for all she knew about how to operate it.

A swell of annoyance, or maybe regret, climbed up the back of her throat. She needed help. As much as she preferred to stay discreet, she'd have to risk it to keep the bridge in working order with Jackin gone.

"Kam, call Circitor Puck to the bridge for me," she said. "I'll be there in a minute."

She pushed away from her desk and marched into the corridor. She rounded the corner and found Puck heading down the hall.

"Puck," she called after him.

He turned and stopped, putting his fist to his chest in salute. "Sir."

"Good timing, I just asked Kamara to call you."

"She did, less than five minutes ago. Sorry, came as fast as I could."

Adequin creased her brow. "Five minutes?"

"Yes, sir."

She rubbed her temples.

Puck ran his hand over the top of his shaved head. "Uh, what's wrong?"

"I don't think you're the Puck I'm looking for."

He raised a skeptical eyebrow. "Sorry, sir?"

"Just wait here a minute, Circitor." She continued toward the bridge, leaving a confused Puck behind.

"Uh, okay," he called after her, but his edges were already wavering. Seconds later, he flashed out of existence.

At least it acted as pretty solid confirmation Puck was on his way . . . which relieved her, because as she entered the bridge and approached Jackin's terminal, she didn't have the first clue what she was looking at.

A series of warnings and notifications had stacked up. She assumed from her encounter with future Puck that they indicated the *Argus* had again drifted too close to the Divide. Or vice versa, as the case may be.

She chewed her lip and tried not to let the reality of "vice versa" weigh too heavily on her.

She slid the holographic display into the air above the terminal, then flipped through the menu options, looking for a way to defer the warnings. She really wished she'd made Jackin stay, and gone to Kharon Gate herself. He would know what to do, how to handle it. She didn't know enough about their positioning with the Divide to make informed decisions, and though she had confidence in Puck's experience as it read on paper, she'd had very little chance to work side by side with him in the past.

"Can I help you out there, sir?"

Adequin turned to find Puck standing over her shoulder. Hopefully the real Puck.

"Yes. Thanks for coming."

"Oh, uh, sorry about the new kid the other day, sir." Puck looked down at his hands. "You hadn't assigned a work detail, so I figured he could help out in the mess. I didn't know it'd . . . well, that it'd explode."

"That's okay. You're not the only one that's had . . . *difficulties* with him."

"So, is he really royalty?"

"That's not your concern, Circitor."

Puck's shoulders drew back. "Of course. Sorry, sir."

She looked up to find his expression flat, but knowing. She lowered her voice. "Just, don't say anything. We've got plenty of other issues around here at the moment."

"Understood, sir."

Jackin's terminal beeped another alert.

"What's going on?" Puck asked, his voice low. "Where's Jackin?"

"He's indisposed. I know you have experience with all . . ." She swept her hand over the terminal screen. ". . . this."

Puck cracked his knuckles. "North better un-dispose soon, or it'll be 'Optio Puck' before he knows it."

"Yeah, yeah, Circitor. Just get on it, please."

"Yes, sir." He leaned over the display. With one swipe, he dismissed every notification, then flicked open the positioning and sensor menus. "We seem to be drifting outward at a pretty rapid pace, sir."

Adequin's heart raced. "Rapid? How exactly would you quantify rapid?"

"Honestly, I have no idea. How close do we normally sit?"

Adequin was pleased she actually knew the answer. She didn't know the specifics, but she'd memorized that stat years ago. "1.284 million kilometers."

Puck's face fell.

"What?"

"Ah, nothing. This estimation is just reading wrong, clearly."

She opened her mouth to let him know it probably wasn't wrong at all, but stopped herself. That would inspire a long line of questioning she wasn't ready to indulge.

Puck shrugged. "Not sure what'd be pulling or pushing us out so fast, but I'll engage thrusters to get us back inward."

"No—" Adequin began, but he'd already swept open the thruster control screen.

"Oh." Puck pressed his lips together and turned to look at her with acute alarm. He lowered his voice. "What the hell, sir? The thrusters are already pushing us inward at max speed . . ."

Her eye twitched as she mediated her anxious expression. "Any ideas on how to push us in a bit quicker?"

"Maybe, but . . . the Divide's gravitational influence isn't that strong this far out." Puck shook his head. "What the hell's moving us?"

"We don't know," she said, and a sharp pang of guilt fired in the pit of her stomach. Though, it wasn't precisely a lie. They truly didn't know what had caused it, Puck had simply assumed incorrectly about which had moved toward which.

She shoved the guilt aside and took a deep breath. Explaining it all to Puck was uncalled for. Knowing wouldn't change anything, other than that it would most assuredly cause him to panic. Which wouldn't help anyone.

"We need a temporary solution," she said. "Something to kick us back inward until Jackin can finish up with his permanent solution."

"Okay . . ." Puck crossed his arms. "Well, I might be able to, uh . . . trick it."

"Trick it?"

"Well . . ." He diverted his gaze and cleared his throat. "*Hack* it."

Adequin raised an eyebrow. "How so?"

"It's not really a Legion-sanctioned procedure, but I could reroute some of the life-systems power to the thrusters, push them beyond their specified limits and get a bit more kick out of them."

"How far can they be pushed?"

"From a strictly theoretical standpoint—"

"Puck. I'm the EX. I've read your file. I know exactly why you're here."

"Right." He gave her a sheepish grin. "Well, when I did a similar hack on the SCS *Somnium*, I got about two hundred percent more out of the engines before it—er, well. Before it stopped."

Adequin sighed. "Did they explode?"

"Little bit. Implode, really."

"I'd rather our thrusters not implode."

"It's totally different," he said hurriedly. "Trust me, this'll be fine."

These old dreadnoughts have incredibly thorough output sensors, assuming everything's still in working order." With a few hurried taps, he opened another screen on Jackin's terminal and scanned the display, nodding. "Yep, we're good—everything's nominal on the last diagnostic—run just yesterday. I'll be able to tell when they're at their max."

Adequin gauged his assured demeanor with narrowed eyes. "Best estimate?"

"Two to three hundred percent. But we'll have to cut power to a couple of sectors."

"That's fine. Novem's already evacuated, we can take Octo Sector off-line as well. Duo if you need it."

"Comms?"

"Yeah, they're basically defunct at the moment anyway."

Puck took that bit of news with surprising acceptance. "Okay, sir."

Adequin sent four members of the bridge crew to confirm that Novem remained evacuated and seal the bulkhead door manually, then do the same for Octo and Duo.

When they got the all clear, Puck began his work, fingers flashing expertly over holographic keys. He seemed to fall into a trance— eyes focused and unblinking as he flew through lines of code with consummate proficiency.

He only paused three times, each to allow Adequin to give biometric scans, granting him deeper access into the computer's architecture. She could have been giving him clearance to turn the whole ship rogue, and she wouldn't have had the first clue. Nevertheless, she had to trust him. She didn't really have a choice.

Less than an hour later, Puck sat back in the stool, wiping his forehead with the back of his hand. "Okay, that's all I can do, sir."

Adequin stopped pacing and leaned over the terminal.

"We're at about two-and-a-half times the speed we were," Puck explained.

She gripped his shoulder. "Thanks, Circitor. Let's hope it's enough."

"EX, sir?" Kamara said, tone tense. "Sir, we have a sensor alert. Reading outward, four degrees."

"What?" Adequin's chest tightened, and she looked up at the large viewscreen. "A ship?"

"No . . . or, I don't know. Nothing on radar, just a notification from the optical sensors."

"How far out?"

"Estimate is 35,990 kilometers."

"Mass?"

"Just says 'error.'"

Adequin stared at the enormous viewscreen, though it remained as black and placid as always. Kamara's console gave a short, negative beep.

"There's another," Kamara said. "At 35,720. Eighteen degrees."

Adequin swung her look to the right side of the screen, but saw nothing.

"Or—shit," Kamara continued. "Negative thirty-two degrees."

Every gaze on the bridge swung left.

Kamara let out a sharp huff as her console beeped again. "Never mind, I don't know. It keeps changing."

Adequin focused on the dark screen, her breath slowing as each uneventful second passed. Then, she saw it. Or, she thought she did. It disappeared before the signal could pass from her eyes to her brain.

A reflection? She glanced over her shoulder, but saw that everyone on the bridge had frozen in place, gaping up at the large monitor. No one stirred.

Adequin looked back at the screen. Moments later, it came again. Sharp and dry, like a static charge dancing across a wool blanket. She had no perspective, no way to judge the distance. But she'd definitely seen it this time. Whatever it was.

Kamara cleared her throat, but her voice still came out weak. "35,103."

Adequin kept her eyes trained on the spot, rounding Jackin's terminal to stand on the stairs, centered on the screen. The spark came again, sketching a thin, serrated line from port to starboard before evaporating. No one made a sound.

Heat crept up Adequin's neck. She turned her face to Puck, though her eyes stayed on the screen. "Lock down the bridge, please."

Puck clamped his gaping mouth shut and began furiously swiping through menus.

"Sir . . . ?" Kamara turned stunned green eyes onto Adequin. Eyes that were terrified, eyes that begged for an explanation. Adequin could only shake her head once.

She turned back to the viewscreen, catching another glint as it danced across the abyss. "Puck, let's go full dark."

"Uh . . ." Puck's voice wavered, then he cleared the hesitation from his throat. "Copy, sir." He raised his voice to address the rest of the crew. "Time to batten down the hatches, ladies and gentlemen. Get to your posts."

The crew snapped from their reveries, almost crashing into one another as they hastened to their consoles.

"Flynn, let's get those shields raised," Puck said.

Flynn, a stout man with a ruddy complexion, gaped at Puck for a few long moments. He let out a sharp breath, then sat at his terminal, and with trembling fingers began to type in commands. Commands he'd never had to type before, and that no defense engineer aboard the *Argus* had ever typed.

"Vega," Puck continued, "we need all hatches shut—the outward facing observation windows and hangar bay doors first, please."

"Yes, sir," Vega called out, already sitting at her console, navigating through menus.

"It's Roth, right?" Puck asked a gruff, older man.

Roth gave a curt nod. "Yessir."

"How's that cloaking system looking these days?"

The older man gave a relenting shrug. "Functional, s'far as I know."

"Check it out, let's see if we can get it online."

Roth nodded and leaned over his screen.

Puck raised his voice to speak to the whole crew again. "We've got power diverted *away* from Duo, Octo, and Novem Sectors, so do *not draw* from those systems—that's two, eight, nine. If you need additional resources, ask me first. The rest of you, start taking all nonessential systems off-line. Start outward-facing and work inward. Low-light mode, reduced O2 and grav in uninhabited sectors, the whole works."

Adequin watched Puck work in reverent silence. In the quiet, the tiny voice in the back of her head grew louder, judging her, calling her out on the futility of it all. She'd put the crew to work simply to keep them busy. Distract them to give herself time to process what this meant.

That wasn't an enemy rolling up to shoot them out of the sky. It wasn't a complement of Viator forces crossing over to wipe them out. She couldn't arm her soldiers and create a battle plan and give a fervent, rousing speech to inspire them to greatness. They could shut the blinds and lock the doors and pretend they weren't home, but it would achieve nothing.

But what else could she do? She'd already sent for help. They'd pushed the thrusters beyond their limits, and they had no engines. They were dead in the water. Thirty-five thousand kilometers from the Divide and counting.

Her brain did the math without her consent, estimating how much time had passed between Kamara's updates on the distance of the visual anomaly. Something in the realm of fifty thousand kilometers per hour.

"Forty minutes," she said, not realizing she'd spoken aloud until Puck turned a confused look onto her. Realization flickered across his eyes.

Before he could respond, Flynn interrupted, "Sir, the shield's sensors are going haywire. We're getting hit with . . ." He trailed off, his pink cheeks blanching.

"With what?" Puck asked.

"I don't know. It's like . . . a gravitational pulse, almost. Like a wave hitting in intervals."

The hiss of a door sliding open pulled Adequin's attention to the top tier of the bridge. Mesa drifted in, blue silk folds billowing out behind her as she swept toward them.

Adequin glared at Puck. "I thought I told you to lock us down."

"I did." Puck's brow creased in confusion. He looked at his screen for confirmation.

Adequin took a few steps up toward the top level. "Mesa, now's not a great—"

"Excubitor, there is a—" But before Mesa could complete her sentence, her form flickered, then disappeared out of existence.

Adequin groaned. Mesa walked in again, then followed herself in twice more until three copies of the Savant marched in rapid succession toward her.

"Bloody hell." Adequin pressed her fingers deep into her temples as the triplicate Mesas sauntered past the captain's chair.

Between the three of them, they managed to get out more of the announcement, though it was difficult to understand as they spoke over one another. "Excubitor, there is—there is a— Excubitor, there is—situation—outside—a situation—"

The first two evaporated one by one, leaving the third trailing behind with the lingering words "outside Octo Sector" before it disappeared as well.

The bridge crew exchanged nervous glances, but otherwise didn't react. Only the light beeps of console notifications punctuated the soft sounds of fingers sliding against screens. A raucous pounding shattered the nervous calm, and Adequin's breath caught as the hammering echoed through the silent bridge.

"Excubitor?" Mesa's muffled voice called through the thick door.

Adequin looked to Puck, who gave a small shrug. "I guess if it's not opening, maybe it's really her this time?"

"Open it for me." She ascended the stairs two at a time. As she approached, the door slid open. Mesa stood outside, cheeks flushed crimson, hands on her hips. She swept an appalled gaze around at the crew inside before landing on Adequin.

"Why is this locked?" Mesa asked, her breath labored. Savants weren't known for their stamina, and by the sweat glistening on Mesa's forehead, she must have expended quite a bit of effort in getting here. "I have been trying to call you on comms."

"Sorry, Mes, they must be down again. We hit a bit of a snag in here. There's a situation outside of Octo Sector?"

"Yes, how did you . . ." Mesa's face fell flat with realization. "A ripple. I see."

"Yeah, one or two," Adequin said with a sigh. "So, what is it? Fight break out, or . . . ?"

"Not exactly, I am afraid." Mesa lowered her voice. "Some of the men swore they saw something out the outward-facing observation windows. They began to argue like absolute *cretins*, but when they saw the hatches close, well . . ." Her look grew distant and harrowed, like she'd been made to recall a grisly dream. "Everyone started . . . freaking out."

Adequin's eyebrows raised. She didn't think she'd ever heard Mesa use such colloquial speech. "Can you be more specific?"

"Well," Mesa huffed, drawing back her shoulders. "Presently, they are trying to break down the bulkhead door to Octo to get to the armory."

"No, no, no." Adequin shook her head. "We cut power to Octo—grav and oxygen are off-line."

"You may want to get down there and explain that to them. They are under the fervent impression that they need to arm themselves."

"Shit." Adequin gripped the back of her head. "Okay." She turned to call down to Puck. "Puck, I have to deal with this. You have the bridge."

Puck's eyes just about bulged out of his head, and his mouth opened and closed a few times before he managed a response. "Oh, uh, okay. Sir . . ."

Mesa fell in beside her as Adequin left a shocked, silent bridge behind.

CHAPTER TWELVE

Cavalon's first thought as the *SGL* began to decelerate from warp speed was to wonder if his name carried enough clout to buy his way onto a transport.

After all, he should still have access to his private accounts, not to mention his trust fund. His father had been the progenitor, so Augustus, in theory, wouldn't have been able to touch it. However, that keyword, "theory," he couldn't ignore. His grandfather's reach was unmatched, and as the unofficial autocrat of the Allied Monarchies, he may have found a way to get his hands on it.

So Cavalon might have been destitute. He really didn't know. The more important consideration was if anyone at Kharon Gate would even question it. Cash on delivery to the Core—from the mouth of a Mercer. It could be a viable escape route.

But any contemplations of going AWOL quickly evaporated when they slowed to cruising speed and approached the gate.

"Uh . . ." Emery ceased her obnoxious gum-chomping as she gaped at the viewscreen. "Is that normal, sir?"

Jackin shifted uncomfortably in the pilot's seat. "No," he said simply. He opened the comm link again. "I repeat: Kharon Gate, this is the *SGL* via the SCS *Argus*, requesting permission to dock."

No response. Cavalon stood over Jackin's shoulder, trying not to gawk too openly.

The Apollo Gates were another technology owed entirely to their former subjugators, the exorbitantly advanced Viators. The relays were the only reason mankind had been able to traverse and populate as much of the galaxy as they had. Cavalon's understanding of how they worked started and ended at the involvement of teracene, a metamaterial devised by Viators that humans had yet to success-fully reverse engineer. As far as Cavalon knew, no one had been able to figure out exactly *how* it worked, only that it did, and that if they kept the stations powered and operational, the teracene con-tinued to function. His handful of degrees had focused on human-originated sciences, so he'd have to leave it to the likes of Mesa to understand anything beyond that.

The station's construction reflected the typical Viator design motif of everything in threes. Its hull gradually increased in size from aft to bow—a long, narrow, triangular prism of matte-black compressed aerasteel. Along the front face, three enormous, vicious prongs protruded from each peak of the triangle, like some horrible three-beaked swordfish. Nestled between the spikes, usually, sat the churning ball of teracene.

But not today. Instead of the raging yellow-green swirls of con-centrated light, ready to fire your molecules a million light-years across the universe, the entire structure sat dark. Not a single ship docked at the bank of air locks along the port or starboard side, and no one hovered nearby, waiting for their turn in the queue.

The *SGL's* spotlight cut through the abyss and swept across the outside of the enormous station, easily five times the size of the *Argus*. Though it appeared intact, it showed no signs of life.

They were still much too far from anything for any natural light to fall on the structure, but it shouldn't have been needed. Not only should the teracene have been operative, casting its sickly green hue out like a beacon into the void, but the structure itself should have been dotted with illumination from hull lights, or the glow of observation windows within. Even for a gate this far on the edge of nowhere, there should have been *some* activity. Even if only from the crew who ran the thing.

Cavalon scratched his chin. "I guess that's why I didn't come in this way."

Jackin broke his despondent stare out the front of the ship to look at him. "Yeah . . . I guess so."

Warner rested his thick arms on the headrest of the copilot's chair. "Sir, has it been decommissioned?"

"Not that I'm aware of." Whether Jackin's gruff tone came from annoyance at not being informed by the Legion, or the colossal-sized wrench this situation threw in their current plans, Cavalon couldn't say. "It doesn't matter," Jackin continued. "We're not here for the relay. We only need to use their comms."

"Yeah," Warner said warily. "But it doesn't look like anyone's home."

Jackin chuffed. "No, it really doesn't."

"Will we be able to dock?" Emery asked.

"Probably," Jackin said. "Assuming their basic systems are still online. But we won't be able to get through the air lock without access from the other side."

Cavalon licked his lips and squinted at the screen. To involve himself or not involve himself . . .

"What is it, Oculus?"

He looked down to find Jackin staring up at him expectantly. "Uh, just thinking . . ." Cavalon said. "We can still latch on, right? Equalize? Open the hatch?"

"Yes, but we won't be able to open the air-lock door beyond that."

"I can open it. Let's dock."

Jackin regarded him seriously for a few seconds, then turned back to the console. "All right. Let's grab that core and fill it up while we're here."

Jackin steered them toward the starboard air locks of Kharon Gate, and Cavalon returned to the engine room. He'd just pulled the partially depleted warp core from the fuel compartment when Jackin's voice rang out over comms.

"Strap in. Grav's going ninety in ten, nine . . ."

Cavalon hurried back to the common room. Emery and Warner had strapped into the half-circle bench, and Cavalon slid in beside them and harnessed in.

". . . two, one."

His stomach flopped, and his head grew heavy as he went from sitting on his butt to lying on his back. With a hollow clang, the ship drifted to a stop. A series of short handles hummed as they extended out from the floor—now the wall—leading up to the now-vertical hatch in the center of the room.

Jackin's voice crackled over comms. "Docked."

"Damn shitty, tiny transport vessels," Warner grumbled. The large man released his harness and slid awkwardly off the side of the bench.

Cavalon released himself, shimmying his feet to land on the wall—now the floor—beside him.

Jackin's head appeared through the doorway of the cockpit on the ceiling. "Latched on fine. Looks like their systems are still online." He reached out and pressed the release switch for the hatch, and with a hiss of air and a clunk, the circular door opened. He gripped the doorjamb and swung through, feet clanging against the metal floor as he landed inside.

Cavalon cradled the warp core in one arm and ascended the rungs, then dropped to the floor on the other side. A few narrow banks of crimson-hued lights dimly lit the primary air lock, the result of some kind of power-saving mode.

Warner dropped in next, followed by Emery. She had a weapons belt around her waist with three more clutched under her arm. She passed one to Warner, then Jackin, who strapped theirs on as effortlessly as one might tie a shoelace. She held the last one out to Cavalon, and he took it warily in his free hand, still clutching the warp core in the other.

Emery approached the door that led into the gate and surveyed the dimmed access screen beside it. "Systems are online. O2's reduced, but safe. Pressure's good."

Jackin joined Emery and pressed his thumb into the corner of the screen. "Kharon, this is the crew of the SGL via the Argus. We're docked starboard, requesting air-lock access at S6."

Cavalon tucked the core under one arm to try and fasten on his weapons belt, but the soft black leather slipped through his fingers. Emery caught it before it hit the ground. He gave her an appreciative nod, and she plucked the core from his grasp before offering the belt back to him.

"Kharon, please respond," Jackin said, his tone decorous, yet resigned. He clearly just wanted to be able to say he'd followed protocol. He knew no one would answer.

Cavalon fumbled for a few moments until he got the belt secured around his hips. On one side hung a narrow sheath which held a long, serrated combat knife. A heavy black laser pistol sat against the other thigh.

He flashed Emery a grin, trying to appear casual. No one here knew that he hadn't been taught to shoot a gun, and that he more than likely shouldn't be allowed anywhere near one. He suddenly wished he'd been made to endure the basic training required of all new Legion recruits.

Jackin crossed his arms and gave the air-lock door a skeptical once-over. "What's your plan here, Oculus?"

"This is a redundant air lock, right?" Cavalon asked.

"Yeah, this is the primary. Secondary we can unlock from inside, if we can get in there."

Cavalon walked up to the sealed doorway. "And we're definitely equalized?"

Emery, still clutching the warp core, stood on her tiptoes and squinted through a small observation window. "All green in there. Good to go, boss."

Cavalon pushed up his sleeves, and his skin buzzed as his Imprints energized. They wove a path up his arm, trickling into his back and shoulders. Mouth full of the taste of copper, he spared a short-lived thought of concern for "volatile interfacing," then ripped the door from its track.

With a small hiss, the air between the two spaces equalized, and to Cavalon's intense relief, they didn't lose pressure. The heavy door groaned as he set it aside. Jackin stared at Cavalon's arm with impressed interest as the gold and bronze squares settled back into their standard formation.

Jackin nodded slowly. "Huh."

"Holy shit," Emery said, mouth agape, her purple gum stuck between her tongue and teeth. "That was *awesome.*"

Warner leaned forward, eyes narrowing as he stared at the Imprints. "You're the one the guys have been talking about, aren't you? The royal?"

"Nope." Cavalon shook his head. "Definitely not."

"Royal?" Emery piped. "No shit?"

"That's ridiculous." Cavalon gave a stilted laugh. "What would a royal be doing in the Legion?"

Jackin crossed his arms. Emery and Warner just stood and stared at him.

Cavalon cleared his throat. "Should we go inside, or do you all just want to stand here and ogle me?"

Jackin and Warner shook their heads as they crossed through the open threshold and into the secondary air lock.

Emery remained, a smug grin on her face. "I think I'd rather ogle."

Cavalon rolled his eyes and brushed past, Emery following close behind.

Inside, Warner tapped the screen beside the secondary air-lock door, and it slid open. A dark corridor lay beyond, splitting off left, right, and straight, all lit with the same dim red lights as the air lock.

"Hold up," Jackin said.

Cavalon looked down to find the optio crouched beside the primary door. He squinted at a small, crooked device fastened low beside the door frame.

"What's that?" Emery asked.

"I don't know," Jackin mumbled.

"Doesn't look Legion," Warner said.

Jackin stood back up and took a deep breath, brow furrowed. "No, it doesn't."

Cavalon shifted his weight, doing his best to mask his discomfort. The more outwardly rattled Jackin became, the harder it grew to pretend like some seriously weird shit wasn't going on.

"Emery, Warner, take the core to the refueling station," Jackin said.

"Yes, sir," Warner replied.

"And it might appear abandoned, but be careful. Sweep the corridors, follow protocol. No shortcuts. Quick but safe."

"You got it, sir," Emery said.

"Meet us in the control room when you're finished."

"Yes, sir," she said. Warner followed as she turned on her heel and headed aft with the warp core.

"Cavalon, you're with me." Jackin turned the opposite way, toward the front of the station, and Cavalon fell in line behind him.

The eerily lit corridors matched the oppressive Viator design of the exterior, with walls of slanted aerasteel slabs layered atop one another like thick, dark scales. The angled walls narrowed as they moved deeper into the station, like traversing the dark bowels of some ancient, formidable beast, the innards constricting as they drew closer to the core. Cavalon tried to shake off his growing sense of unease.

He followed as Jackin made a sharp turn down another dimly lit corridor. How the optio knew where to go, Cavalon had no idea. Though he'd traveled via Apollo Gates a few times, he'd never had cause to actually dock at one. The way Jackin strode forward without question suggested a familiarity that went beyond a general knowledge of station layouts.

"You seem comfortable here, Optio," Cavalon remarked. "Were you stationed at a gate before?"

Jackin didn't respond at first, but after a few moments he spoke up. "No, but I know every asset in the Legion fleet."

"Oh? Were you an engineer, or . . . ?"

"I was chief navigations officer for the First."

Cavalon's mouth dropped open, partly from his bluntness, but mostly from the admission. "No shit?"

"No shit," Jackin said, tone completely devoid of sentiment.

"That's like . . ." Cavalon collected himself with an effort. "Really?"

"Really."

The next logical question went something like, "*Well, why the fuck are you here?*" but that seemed impolite to ask among Sentinels. And it would likely lead to retaliatory questions like, "*Well, why the fuck are* you *here?*" accompanied by accusatory, distrustful glares. Cavalon chose not to press his luck.

Yet he couldn't help his surprise. He didn't know the specifics of the Legion's hierarchy, but CNO was as household of a term as Praetor or Titan. Jackin would have been in charge of coordinating movements for an entire fleet. For the First, no less, which comprised the majority of the Legion's forces, including the Titans and Vanguard.

What was it with the *Argus*? It was like some isle of misfit war heroes. Cavalon was just waiting to discover Emery'd been a decorated centurion. Warner was probably a praetor.

Cavalon chewed his lip as a slew of questions conjured in his mind. Had Jackin been active at the same time as Rake? He had to be into his early forties, which meant he could have come to the *Argus* before the Resurgence War, though that would have made him a very young CNO. Even if they did serve at the same time, did the First even interact directly with the Titans? Or was that one of those things, like saying "*Oh, you're from Elyseia? Do you know Mr. Smith?*" as if you've met every single person on your planet?

Cavalon discarded his careening train of thought before it derailed entirely. He refocused his mental efforts on being unduly paranoid about the dark, ominous corners they walked past as the sinister walls closed in around him.

They finally came to the end of the corridor, which fanned out into a wide doorway. Jackin typed a code into a screen beside it, and the door slid open, revealing some kind of control room. Six stations sat in pairs around each face of a triangular platform. When active, the central platform likely showcased some kind of data center or map, but presently sat vacant.

Jackin slid into one of the seats and pressed both hands into the black monitors recessed into the top of the terminal. Moments later, the screens radiated a soft, yellow-green glow, and the terminal flickered to life. Jackin pushed the green holographic screens into the air, then sat back and swept through menus.

"The reactor is still fully functional," he mumbled. "Mainframe is online." He slid across a few controls with his thumb and the overhead lights raised to a dim glow.

"So, they just turned off the lights and left?" Cavalon asked.

Jackin shook his head as he stared at the display.

"When's the last log?"

"Three months ago," he said quietly.

Cavalon scoffed. "Three *months?*"

"Fuck." Jackin's brow furrowed, and he leaned back in his seat.

"What? Does it say why they left?"

Jackin remained quiet for a few moments, then took a sharp breath in. "It says *redacted*."

Cavalon slid into the chair next to Jackin. "Okay, let's be serious for a minute, Optio. Last I checked, relay gates are some seriously important strategic resources. When was the last time the Legion abandoned an Apollo Gate?"

Jackin continued staring at the interface. "Maybe during the Viator War."

"Yeah, the Viator War. Two hundred years ago. Something's going on."

Jackin finally broke his glower and turned to him, dark brown eyes equal parts worried and resigned. "Like what?"

"Well, I suppose the Viators might have spontaneously reanimated and murdered everyone . . ."

Jackin rolled his eyes.

"In which case, there's a distinct lack of blood and guts and destruction."

"Or?"

"Or . . . maybe the Legion's no longer supporting the Sentinels."

"They couldn't really lend us less support than they already do."

"Well . . ." Cavalon gestured at the lifeless station around them. "This certainly seems to demonstrate that."

"It doesn't matter," Jackin said, jaw firm. "We'll deal with that later. We're on a schedule. Let's get the comms on and get them on the horn."

Cavalon nodded. "You're the boss."

Jackin turned back to the terminal, sweeping through menus. After a few minutes, a negative tone beeped and the screen cast a red glow on his furrowed brow. He leaned forward, trying the input again, but got the same results.

"Damn," Jackin said. "We're getting interference."

"From what?"

"I don't know." He tapped the controls and tried again. "I might be able to boost the signal . . ."

"Physically or . . ." Cavalon wiggled his fingers at the computer. ". . . via the code?"

"Either." Jackin sighed. "Both."

"Okay, tell me what you need."

Jackin stared back at him skeptically.

Cavalon held his hands up. "Only trying to help, Optio. I can go adjust stuff in the comms room if you wanna do your thing with the code here. Divide and conquer, and all that."

Jackin's look faltered, then he cleared his throat. "We might need parts."

"Things they'd have here?"

"Not likely."

"Well," Cavalon said, "the *Argus* has a whole sector full of comms that don't work, right? We could pilfer that."

"There's no time to go back. We need to get them on the line, stat."

"You know, you keep talking about this deadline," Cavalon said. "Makes a guy a bit nervous—"

The piercing clang of an alarm drowned out Cavalon's voice. The dim room instantly filled with sharp flashes of blue and red light.

"Shit." Jackin slid out of the comms menu, then swept a video feed up onto the main viewscreen above the triangular platform.

He activated the station's hull lights, and a series of beaming spotlights fired out into the void.

Cavalon's mouth dropped open as a vessel careened out of the darkness, the station's lights illuminating the hull of a mangled, grisly cargo ship.

"That's . . ." Cavalon began, but couldn't continue, because all he could think was *fuck, fuck, fuck, fuck, fuck* . . .

Jackin swallowed. "Drudgers."

CHAPTER THIRTEEN

✦

The fighting had already begun in earnest when the lift door slid open and Adequin stepped out. The tension binding her shoulders loosened somewhat. If they were focusing on beating one another up, then they weren't focused on beating the door down.

Across the circular vestibule, more than sixty soldiers had gathered near the sealed bulkhead door of Octo Sector. Some merely argued, while others engaged in scuffles or tried to stop fights.

Adequin headed around the arcing corridor toward the commotion. Mesa followed just off her shoulder. They arrived on the outskirts of the pack, where a tall, brutish oculus clutched another in a headlock.

A young circitor, Walsh, stood nearby, furious. "Barrow, stand down!" she yelled. The man responded by wrenching his grip tighter. Walsh held up her wrist to indicate her nexus. "Don't make me."

"Oh," Barrow mocked, glaring. *"Don't make me."*

But Walsh already had her nexus screen open, then Barrow's face contorted and his knees buckled. He landed on all fours and his hostage tumbled to the ground as well.

Adequin picked up the discarded man by his shoulders. "To the mess," she growled, pointing a harsh finger toward the lift.

"Yes, sir." The oculus scrambled away.

Two other circitors stood among the commotion, fingers dancing across their nexus screens as they activated their oculi's Imprints to discipline them into submission. However, not everyone's CO was there, and they only had control over their direct subordinates.

Adequin turned to find Barrow up on his feet again. He grabbed another oculus by the front of his vest.

Walsh seethed. "Barrow, I thought I—" The circitor's mouth opened helplessly as she glanced between the standing Barrow and the Barrow still writhing on the floor in pain from his activated Imprints.

It was then Adequin realized there were more like thirty soldiers, accompanied by a whole host of doppelgängers. They flashed in and out of existence, an unwelcome addition to the chaos. Even on a normal day, time ripples put them on edge. Exacerbated by seeing something unknown outward—seeing *anything* outward? No wonder they were getting worked up.

"Soldiers!" Adequin shouted, but her voice barely cut through the din. No one reacted.

Her Imprints buzzed across her shoulders as she walked into the ruckus, heading for a fight that'd just broken out between two scrawny men. On the way, an oculus crashed into her, then sprawled to the ground at her feet. She picked him up by the front of his vest and tossed him toward the wall, but he disappeared before he hit it. A half second later, the same man crashed into her and she repeated the throw, but this time he slammed into the wall. He turned and glared at her, then recognition dampened his ire.

"Mess," she growled.

He immediately hurried away toward the lift.

Adequin took in the commotion around her: men and woman shouting, threatening, throwing punches, and arguing with their duplicates about which one was real. Cavalon's words from a few days ago gnawed at the back of her mind: *"Are you the warden?"* It'd been a serious question at the time, but she could just imagine the snarky way in which he'd redeliver it now. She was glad he wasn't there.

Although, she'd rather he was—that he'd already returned with Jackin, Legion transports in tow. She didn't know how much longer she could force calm.

She opened her nexus interface, finger hovering over the master control. She hated causing them pain, but she needed them to stop acting like Neanderthals for five minutes so she could concentrate on how to save their lives.

With a single swipe, their angry jibes receded into cries of pain. Most fell to their knees, cradling their arms. All except the doppelgängers, who continued to pop in and out of existence at a slow but steady pace.

After a few moments, the soldiers' pained wheezing ceased in favor of labored breaths. But the silence didn't last. They began to shout over one another, unleashing a tirade of concerns.

"We saw the lights!"

"Something's incoming!"

"What's going on, EX?"

"Barrow broke my fucking nose!"

"It's a Viator fleet!"

"Shut up," she barked, and their voices fell away. She swept her hardened glare across them. "What was the plan, here, soldiers?"

"We need the armory!" someone insisted.

"You do *not* need weapons," she said, letting out an exasperated sigh. She could only imagine how this would have gone if they'd managed to arm themselves first.

"We saw something outward," one explained.

"It's a ship or something!" another called.

"That was a visual anomaly, nothing more," she said. "We're seeing time ripples from crafts traveling the Divide elsewhere." She wet her lips, shocked by how easily the lie formed and fell out of her mouth. The soldiers gaped, as surprised by the assertion as she was.

"Since when does that happen?" someone in the back called out.

"What about the sealed sectors?" another accused.

"The rerouted power is part of routine systems maintenance," Adequin said.

Among the shuffling feet, a few brave souls scoffed. She clenched a fist but chose to let it go.

"Since you're all panicking like hysterical children," she continued, "I'm ordering a full lockdown. Unless you're assigned to an essential life-systems post, you're to remain in the mess until further notice."

After a heavy pause, Walsh's voice cut through the silence. "You heard her, Oculi! To the mess!"

The soldiers obeyed and rose to their feet, heading toward the lift. Adequin darted a glare to Walsh and the other two circitors. They shuffled over to stand in front of her.

"What the fuck, Circitors?" she said.

Walsh smoothed the front of her vest anxiously. "Sorry, sir, they just got so whipped up so fast—"

"Cut the excuses. You need to keep things calm while I deal with other shit."

"It'd help if they could go back to Novem, sir."

"Well, they can't. So, do your damn jobs and keep them in line."

Their faces fell into dejected frowns, but they nodded their understanding.

"Keep the instigators separated. I don't want any more fighting." Adequin opened her nexus and input a quick command. "I'm releasing full Imprint control to all circitors. Don't use it unless you have to, but do *not* let them break down any bulkhead doors, got it?"

"Yes, sir."

"Sorry, sir."

The circitors left toward the lift, and Mesa's lithe form drifted into Adequin's periphery. She'd half forgotten the Savant had come with her.

"I'm headed back to the bridge," Adequin said. "You okay, Mes?"

Mesa regarded her steadily for a few drawn-out moments before she spoke. "Yes, Excubitor. Fine."

"Thanks for letting me know. Sorry about the comms, I'll get . . ." Jackin. She wanted Jackin. ". . . someone on it."

"You are welcome."

Adequin inclined her head to the Savant and left, heading toward the bridge. She had every intention of actually going there, but as she passed the corridor to her office, her feet veered, and she found herself standing in front of her desk.

She needed a minute. Just a minute.

What was she doing? Lying to everyone and ignoring what was so clearly happening . . . It had to be some kind of denial. She had to snap herself out of it.

It didn't take long to determine why. She'd been crushing it under everything else, forcing it out of her mind because left unchecked, it threatened to overwhelm her.

Admitting the Divide had started moving toward them meant admitting Griffith was in trouble. Serious, mortal danger. And she couldn't do a damn thing to stop it.

She *could* have. She could have taken that warp core and that Hermes and headed outward instead of inward. She could have hopped on the Divide and tried to track down the *Tempus*. Warned them before it was too late.

But could a Hermes even withstand the turbulence of riding the Divide? It'd been built to handle warp speeds, but hadn't been cleared to travel via Apollo Gates. She didn't even know if that mattered. Relays were more like a shortcut through space-time than increased speed.

But she could have tried. Or at least asked Jackin if it were possible. But she'd lost her chance to go after him. She'd resigned Griffith to death.

Her heart seized, and she tried to force it to maintain a steady beat, but her breath came in short, hot rasps, and she couldn't impose calm. She braced both fists on her desk and leaned forward, looking down at her scuffed boots, head spinning.

Silken draped feet shuffled in behind her. "Excubitor?"

"Mesa. I'm . . ." Fine? Just having a think? Panicking?

"Overwhelmed," Mesa answered. "That is reasonable, Excubitor."

It wasn't. Not really.

Adequin sucked in a deep breath, then let it out slowly. She turned to face Mesa.

The Savant's brilliant eyes were patient and deadly serious. "Why are we drifting outward?"

Adequin opened her mouth, expecting another lie to fall out, but her breath caught in her throat.

"We're not." Puck's voice drifted in as the door whizzed open across the room. He marched up to stand over Mesa's shoulder, scorn in his eyes. "Are we, EX?"

Mesa turned her bewildered look away from Puck, back onto Adequin. "What?"

"Where's North?" Puck asked, tone full of impatient accusation.

Warmth flooded Adequin's face. Though every instinct told her to keep up the farce, she knew the time to come clean had long passed. "He took a Hermes to Kharon Gate to request assistance from the Legion. He's bringing ships back with him."

"Ships?" Mesa asked. "For what?"

"For the crew."

"Of the *Argus*? Why?"

Puck nodded, his suspicions apparently confirmed. "Because we need to get off this one."

Mesa's soft features paled.

Puck gripped the back of his head and the muscles in his face and neck wrung taut. "Why didn't you tell me this earlier? Is that what we were seeing on the bridge? That light?"

"I don't know what that was."

"So, they really did see something out the observation windows?" Mesa asked.

"Yeah," Puck said. "*The Divide*."

Mesa's overlarge eyes grew even larger. "They *saw* the Divide? There is nothing to see. And we are millions of kilometers—"

Adequin shook her head. "Not anymore."

"You should have told me when you first called me," Puck bristled. "I could have told you it wasn't going to be enough."

"Isn't it?" she asked. "Three times the thruster speed isn't good enough?"

"Fuck, no!" Puck said. "Not by half, not by anything! Its speed is increasing at a rate I can't calculate. We should be abandoning ship, not trying to salvage it."

"I'm not trying to salvage anything. *There's just nowhere for us to go.*"

"Yes, there is," he said. "We spin up however many away ships we have left in storage, and get everyone on board. Sublight will be fast enough to keep us out of it for a while. Then we figure something else out."

"How's that work, Puck?" she said derisively. "We could maybe cram *twenty* people onto one ship."

"So what? We'd only need ten ships to make that work. How many are in storage?"

"One."

"One, what?"

"One is in storage."

Puck's hardened grimace dissolved. "One Hermes?"

"Two, including the one Jackin's got."

"Fuck." Puck pressed his fingers against his mouth and let out a sharp breath through them. He lowered his hands and his tone softened. "It's gonna be here. Soon. We have to abandon ship. Now. If that's twenty people, then it's twenty people."

"No fucking way—"

"Yes," Puck said. "Who gets on the Hermes?"

Adequin's cheeks burned. "I can't make that call."

"You have to."

"I can't." Her heart raced, and that same loss of control threatened to seize her again. "I can't," she repeated.

Mesa nodded and laid her hands together lightly, her look sensible. The Savant's serene composure simultaneously soothed and infuriated Adequin. "Then we follow standard evacuation procedure," Mesa said. "There are no civilians, so protocol is rank, correct?"

Adequin nodded once.

"How many can we realistically put aboard a Hermes and not overweigh it?"

"Standard complement is eight," Puck answered. "Without warp, we're gonna need to save room for supplies—but they're built to accommodate a full crew for six months . . . Yeah, I'd say twenty's right."

"Very well," Mesa continued. "Are comms still inoperative?"

Puck looked at his nexus. "Working at the moment."

"Instruct the hangar to ready the ship, then summon the fifteen senior-most circitors to the bay at once. We will meet them there."

Puck opened a comms menu on his nexus. "Joss?"

Lace's static-filled voice came through seconds later. "Amaeus? What the hell's going on?"

"I'll explain later," he said, "just scramble that last Hermes, and get it ready to fly."

"Underst—" A din of crackling static overtook Lace's voice before the connection cut out completely.

Puck's brow furrowed. "Comms are down . . . Shit, whole network's gone. I can't warn anyone else."

Mesa gave a curt nod. "Very well. We will collect who we can along the way."

She and Puck turned together and headed for the door. Adequin didn't move. They stopped in the doorway and looked back at her.

"Sir?" Puck said. "Let's go."

"I'm not going."

"EX, you're at the top of the list. Like a dozen ranks above any of us."

"I'm *not* going."

"Like hell."

"I can't do that. You have my permission to take the last Hermes."

Puck marched back toward her. "Don't pull this going-down-with-the-ship crap. We need you with us."

Déjà vu swept over her at Puck's insistent tone. His eyes, both pleading and panicked, reminded her of something she couldn't quite put her finger on.

"That's not going to happen," Adequin said. "Jack will return from Kharon soon. They'll bring ships, and I need to be here when they do—help get everyone on board."

"Rake, that's *over*," Puck insisted. "It's too late. We have to take who we can and leave—right now."

"Twenty souls? That's your solution?"

"Better than zero," he growled.

Adequin's Imprints vibrated along with a spike of annoyance. "Watch yourself, Circitor."

"I'm sorry, sir, but we can't waste any more time. Remember when those visual pings said thirty-five thousand kilometers? Well, by now, they say ten thousand. If that's really the Divide rushing toward us, then we have *minutes*." He reached toward her, ready to usher her forward. "So let's go."

She looked at his open palm and realization washed over her as she recalled what this reminded her of. That time ripple where Cavalon stormed into her quarters and insisted she go with him to "the ship." She couldn't quite draw the lines between the two, but she supposed if she hadn't sent him with Jackin, it could have been him trying to force her to leave instead of Puck.

She cleared her throat. "Get whoever you can aboard that Hermes. Kharon Gate will be the rendezvous."

Puck dropped his hand. Mesa stepped up next to him, crossing her thin arms.

"Take as much food and water as you can," Adequin continued. "It's fourteen weeks at ion speed to Kharon."

Mesa's exasperated look remained patient. Puck's anger thawed, but the pity left in its place wasn't any better. They didn't say anything, but they didn't have to. She knew they meant to overrule her.

Adequin shook her head. "You don't make the orders here. Neither of you do. This is my choice."

Puck's scowl deepened. "There's no way in hell I'm—"

A din of blaring alarms buried the remainder of his words. Adequin grimaced at the piercing clang, then a sudden movement caught her eye. On her desk, the rings of the golden astrolabe spun wildly. It tilted slowly before spilling off the side of the desk as if knocked by some unfelt gust of wind.

"What the hell was that?" Puck called over the din of alarms.

Adequin shuddered and a sharp tingle rushed up her spine. She stumbled to catch her footing as the decking swelled and shifted, like a retreating wave pulling the sand from beneath her feet.

A surge of vertigo spun her vision, and the floor dropped. Her Imprints sped across her skin, rushing to protect her. Her shielded elbows and knees hit hard, the pain deadened as if the floor had been covered with thick carpet. The room bucked and swayed once more before settling still again.

Adequin's pulse hammered in her throat as she righted herself. Instead of returning to their default location, her Imprints fanned out, buzzing and clicking to take up a long-unused combat formation along the backs of her limbs, up her spine, wrapping around her abdomen.

A few meters away, Puck winced and shook out a wrist as he stood. Mesa picked herself up in an alarmingly dignified manner, waving off Puck's offer of assistance.

Adequin met Mesa's worry-lined eyes for a heartbeat before the floor vibrated again, sliding beneath her feet like a receding tide. The nape of Adequin's neck tingled sharply and her skin hummed, every hair on her body standing on end.

A rushing hiss drew her attention to the door, which unsealed of its own accord, locking into the open position. The blaring alarms shifted to a new, staccato rhythm, shrieking in sync with the pulsing crimson and blue beacon above the doorway—the alert to take up battle stations.

A burst of hard-edged white light flooded the outside corridor. Adequin and Puck rushed out, Mesa following in their wake.

Adequin jogged down the hall and around the corner toward a mid-sector bulkhead. At the farthest end of the long corridor,

156 ← J. S. DEWES

a blinding glint of sharp white light reflected off the decking and walls and ceilings, forking like bolts of lightning igniting across the metal. She gaped at the strange display until a sliver of movement caught her eye.

A ways down the long corridor, Bray rounded a corner and raced toward them, another man trailing a few meters behind. It took her a moment to recognize the other soldier, a stocky man with a mess of unkempt red hair whose duty vest hung open, unstrapped. Aller Erandus—a "problem circitor" who'd been dumped on her a year ago by the aging commander of the *Typhos*. She'd put him in Damage Control to try and give him some focus. Though incidents were rare, keeping a two-hundred-year-old dreadnought up to safety codes proved a literally endless task.

Bray and Erandus sprinted through the bulkhead door frame as if it were some kind of finish line. Erandus had already opened his nexus and touched it to the control screen to establish a local connection. Adequin dashed forward to intercept, but arrived too late. The massive bulkhead door blared a single warning, then roared shut.

"What are you doing?" she snapped. The door hissed and the control screen sounded an affirmative tone as the seal pressurized. "This is the only throughway to the bridge." And the fastest way to the mess—where she'd just sent over thirty soldiers to cool off. Thirty soldiers who were now trapped in the port bow of the ship.

Erandus turned his pallid, sweat-glistened grimace onto her. "Sorry, sir," he growled. "But there's no *bridge* anymore."

Bray pushed out a sharp breath and paced from the sealed door. Adequin gripped his shoulder, stopping him in his tracks. "Oculus . . ."

Bray's look snapped to her, his invariably neat, slicked-back black hair a disheveled mess, the usual steadfastness in his gray eyes overtaken by a haunted, glassy expression.

"What happened?" she demanded.

"No idea," Erandus answered, marching away from the control

screen. "Before the network crashed, the damage-control system said half the port bow's breached, but it happened damn fast. Whoever's shootin' at us must have some kinda new tech."

Bray shook his head and mumbled, "That's not what's going on . . ."

"Sir, what do we do?" Erandus asked, clueless to Bray's shocked stupor. "The auxiliary bridge was refabbed into the psych ward, right? We need some kinda helm control to try and reboot shields—it's cuttin' through us like butter. It's gotta be an energy weapon or somethin', but not like anything I've seen."

Adequin stared at him mutely for a few long moments, finding a strange comfort in the naivety of his earnest words. She truly, honestly wished it really were an enemy vessel—marauder, Drudger, Viator—hell, even first contact with a new, angry species going on some intergalactic murder spree. At least it'd be something they could fight, something they had a chance in the void at defeating.

Then she realized—the other soldiers would all be thinking the same thing as Erandus, that they were being fired on, that battle had commenced. That they should be running *toward* action stations . . .

But of course they didn't realize what was really happening. Why would they? The laws that defined the universe had changed, and she'd kept it a secret. She'd done nothing. Told no one, except Jackin, who she'd sent light-years away with their only warp core. Which meant she hadn't merely resigned Griffith to death, she'd killed them all.

A dense weight crushed against her chest, stealing the air from her lungs. She thought it was some kind of quick-onset panic attack until she glanced to the others—Puck, Mesa, Bray, Erandus—all wide-eyed, cradling their stomachs or clutching at their necks, seeming in various states of being choked to death.

Her eyes darted, searching for a cause while her lungs heaved, constricting and aching for breath.

Then in an instant, it vanished. The pressure ceased and air rushed back in like a valve had been opened. Adequin stretched her jaw as her eardrums popped, sending a spike of pain deep into her already aching skull.

"What's going on?" Puck choked out. He put a steadying hand on Mesa's shoulder as the Savant wheezed a series of short, sharp breaths.

"Bloody void," Erandus cursed, and Adequin followed his wide-eyed stare over to the bulkhead door.

A duplicate Erandus hunched over the controls, tapping furiously at the screens. His outline flickered and wavered, then morphed, the pallid, stocky form stretching upward and inward into a coltish, bronze-skinned man—Puck.

Duplicate Puck worked the controls, throwing furtive glances over his shoulder, sweat dripping down his temples. "I can't hack damage-control permissions without network access—acc—acc—" The ripple stuttered, blurred trails dragging out behind before it evaporated.

Adequin stood staring at the now-empty space, momentarily frozen in the still-blaring din of the condition alarms.

Erandus cleared his throat. "Good thing I'm here, I guess . . ."

Puck slid Erandus a suspicious glare, as if suddenly questioning the man's true existence.

The klaxons ceased, casting the corridor in a blanket of oppressive silence. A deadened thump still echoed in Adequin's ears, like an afterimage of sound.

She sucked in a deep breath and an order fell out of her mouth, the word cutting sharply in the unnerving quiet. "Hangar."

Puck nodded and spun to run down the hall. Mesa gathered up her silk folds and followed, with Bray close behind.

"Sir," Erandus said, pausing beside her, "the automated DC system is down. We should manually seal any bulkheads we pass, or the whole ship could depressurize before we even get to the hangar."

"Understood. There isn't another one until the amidship vestibule."

He nodded and took off, and Adequin followed. When they arrived at the circular vestibule, Erandus paused to quickly seal the bulkhead behind them. Across the way, a pack of soldiers stood gathered around the lift.

"Sir!" one called out across the open atrium. "The lifts aren't working, and we can't find a clear way to the bridge."

"With us," she shouted, then caught Puck's eye as they jogged around the wide arc. "We need to cut through crew quarters to the aft ladders. Can you repressurize Novem from here?"

Puck bared his teeth and gave a reluctant hiss. "*Technically*, no." But he approached the sealed door anyway, activating the control panel.

She used the reprieve to catch her breath and did a cursory head count as the newcomers joined them—fifteen total, sixteen including Lace. They could still save another four, if they could find anyone. She grimaced as a grating groan of metal roared and shook the ship. A shrill, onerous shriek reverberated through the walls, as if the entire deck might split at the seams. The noise vanished, the heavy silence left in its wake even more unnerving.

"Got it!" Puck called.

A much-needed swell of relief filled Adequin's chest as the door to Novem slid open. The group of soldiers fell in behind Puck and Mesa, filing into Novem Sector. Adequin started toward the open bulkhead when a deep-seated sense of dread descended, crushing into her chest until her breaths came short and shallow. Her boots gripped the floor less and less, her joints loosening, spine rounding as the pressure slackened until she'd lost touch with the ground entirely. Ahead, concerned shouts rebounded through the group as they were all relieved of weight.

"Sir!" someone shouted, panic lacing their tone.

Adequin craned her neck to look over her shoulder at Bray a few meters behind, reaching forward as he slid backward across the decking away from her.

She pivoted around her center of gravity to face him, but her prior momentum still carried her toward the Novem threshold. She growled, throwing her arms and legs out, frustration tightening her chest as she desperately tried to grab or kick something to propel herself back out. But in the weightlessness, any seam or bar or foothold lining the corridor had become hopelessly out of reach.

Bray's feet lifted from the deck and he tilted forward as he floated—no, *fell*—his body horizontal, as if only his gravity had flipped ninety degrees. He shouted as his feet clipped the railing, and he spun into the open air above the atrium, plunging straight across toward the port bow.

Adequin watched in stunned horror as pieces of the vestibule tore free—floor panels, terminal screens, fire-suppression rails, cabling conduits, light banks. Some dropped quickly, others slow, but none slower than Bray who fell away as if sinking through thickened water. The Unum bulkhead door lit with a blaze of colorless light, then—

Adequin blinked. She forced her eyes to refocus, trying to make sense of what'd happened. The wall wasn't there anymore, but it hadn't vanished. And there was *nothing* left in its place. She squinted, trying to force herself to *see* it, but it was futile.

For a fraction of a second, her mind tried to reject the idea, struggling for an accurate way to conceptualize it. The bulkhead hadn't been dismantled or disintegrated or vaporized—it just *wasn't*. The distinction settled in her bones unsettlingly quick. She inherently understood it, like any other force of nature—if she leapt off a cliff, she would fall; if whatever *that* was reached her, she would cease to exist.

A billowing suction of air yanked her sideways, then her weight slammed back into her and the deck rushed up. She tucked her chin and jolts shot down her shoulder and spine as she crashed all but headfirst into the grated metal floor, white spots flaring in her vision. She ignored the surge of pain and pushed up to her feet. But before she could take a single step to go after Bray, two sets of hands grabbed her from behind and yanked her through the doorway.

Still falling into the nothing beyond, Bray screamed, reaching toward her. Another flare of white light erupted, overtaking him.

The bulkhead siren blared, and the door slid shut in front of her, cutting off the rush of air. The hissing seal echoed in the dampened silence. Flares of white light burned in the backs of her eyes as she stared, unblinking, at the dull gray metal barrier.

Heat ignited in her chest and her Imprints tore across her skin. She blindly shoved away the people who'd grabbed her and leapt up. Her silver and copper Imprint squares coated the outsides of her fists as she banged on the sealed bulkhead.

Her pulse pounded in her ears, and she threw a fire-eyed glare to Erandus, who stood wide-eyed at the door controls.

"Circitor!" she shouted. "Open this door!"

Erandus hesitated, his pale skin flushed a deep red.

Puck yanked him back. "Go!"

Erandus took off down the hall.

Adequin balled her fists and clenched her jaw.

A thin, clammy grip tightened around her arm. Her Imprints buzzed on instinct, but as she turned to throw the offender off, she froze. Mesa stared up at her, a deluge of sweat dampening thin strands of black hair against her warm beige skin.

"There is nothing to be done," Mesa said, large eyes glistening, each breath labored and wheezing.

Though an influx of adrenaline still twitched in Adequin's fingers and quickened her pulse, the Savant's palpable worry extinguished her rage.

"Sir!" Puck shouted. "We have to keep moving!"

Adequin's eyes jolted up to the tail of the advancing group, where Puck waved an arm to urge her on, right behind . . . Mesa, who ran a few meters in front of him. The lithe grip on her arm firmed. Her eyes slid back to her side, but no one was there.

A burgeoning lump threatened to close her throat, but she swallowed it back, shaking the looping image of Bray screaming from her mind. She forced one foot in front of the other.

She rushed to follow, catching up as the group gathered at the entrance to the access ladders. She swept her clearance to unlock the door, and ushered each person down, watching the steady silence of the corridor behind her as if it might erupt into flashes of static light at any moment.

When the last soldier in line entered, Adequin made a cursory check for any stragglers, then followed them in. A wall of heat hit her as she climbed into the narrow shaft. Sweat dampened her jacket and stuck the heavy fabric to the skin of her back by the time she descended all four deep levels.

At the hangar entrance, they were greeted with a wash of warning beacons and blaring klaxons. A group of at least ten more soldiers had already gathered around the door. The handful of doppelgängers popping in and out of existence made it impossible to get an accurate head count.

Puck pushed into the gathered crowd toward the hangar door. Adequin followed, and boots squeaked on metal as they shuffled to give her room to pass.

"Sir, it's locked down," someone said.

Puck looked up from the control screen as she approached, then whispered, "I'd hack it but . . ." He indicated the crimson atmosphere gauge.

"Shit . . ." A vise tightened under her ribs. It'd already been breached. Lace would have been in there, working to pull the last Hermes out of storage. Her heart sped, pushing another wave of panic through her chest.

The strain in her chest loosened with a thought, and she locked eyes with Puck. "The other hangar."

"What *other* hangar?" a hoarse voice shouted from the crowd.

Puck's brow creased. "The starboard deck hasn't been used in years . . ."

"If Lace couldn't deploy here," Adequin said, "she'd try the other side."

He nodded, and she let him take point again, leading the pack toward the starboard access corridor. The decking rumbled as Adequin waited for them all to filter out.

Twenty-six—they'd be slightly overcapacity, but close to Puck's estimated limit. She took up the rear again and as they jogged, tried to steady her fraying nerves by reminding herself over and over again that they were saving as many people as possible.

When they arrived, the starboard entrance stood wide open. Inside, fewer than half the overhead lights illuminated the large, empty operations deck, like some sleepy, after-hours, mirror-image version of the port hangar.

The blaring condition klaxons echoed off the walls, the endless din driving a piercing spike between Adequin's temples.

She jogged to the front of the group, eyes locking straight across the deck onto the open launch bay, where a ship hoist sat clutching a gleaming white circular Hermes in its docking claw. The tension straining her every muscle slackened the smallest fraction.

Adequin took off across the large operations deck just as the decking shifted. She kept her footing but slid forward a few meters, bucked by another strange wave as if the metal had become rolling sand beneath her feet. She kept running, arriving right as the mooring claw released the ship.

Lace leapt from the raised seat of the ship hoist. "Rake—thank the void."

"We need to take off ASAP," Adequin said, her voice a dry croak. "We've got twenty-six; can we make it work?"

Lace's brow lined deep. "Sure, probably—but they better get here fast."

Adequin shook her head. "What?"

"If they're not here soon, we can't risk . . ." Lace went on, but the rest of her words faded away as Adequin spun to face the gathered pack of soldiers behind her.

But it wasn't a pack, not anymore, not nearly. Puck, Mesa, and Erandus stood flanked by *five* others. Five.

"Puck . . ." she croaked. "Where'd they . . ."

His gaze swept over the others, his mouth opening and closing wordlessly. They could not have *all* been duplicates . . .

"No way," Adequin said, stepping back toward the entrance.

Puck clasped her shoulder to stop her. "Rake—"

"It's not good enough," she growled.

"It has to be. Fuck—we tried."

The *Argus* rocked again, the few remaining lights flickering on and off while the decking drifted beneath their feet, and they all tumbled to the deck. Adequin pushed herself up, then turned and helped Puck to his feet.

Lace groaned, cursing under her breath, leaning heavily on her knees as she stood. "Just about sick'a that," she growled.

A soft wheezing drew Adequin's eyes toward Mesa. The Savant drew herself to her feet, but stood hunched, sweat pouring down her temples, sucking in air in short rasps.

"Help her aboard," Adequin instructed. "Get preflights done and get ready to take off."

Puck, Erandus, and the five other remaining soldiers escorted Mesa toward the flimsy ladder that led up to the underside hatch. Puck lifted Mesa up to two waiting pairs of arms, which pulled her into the belly of the ship. Lace's deckhands, maybe—that meant two more, at least. But that small solace did nothing to ease the acidic, bitter weight growing in the pit of her stomach.

Puck jogged back toward them. "Rake, we gotta go," he said, voice terse. He breezed past her for the launch controls console.

"I'll stay and man the controls," Adequin said, following him over. "Jack'll need someone on deck to give landing clearance."

Lace's brow furrowed. "What? North?"

"They went to Kharon," Adequin answered.

"I know, but . . ." Lace's confused disbelief swung to Puck.

Puck's scowl tightened. "Joss—it's giving an error. I can't set a delayed launch."

With a few quick strides, Lace joined him, then punched in a few short commands. "Shit. Problem's with the exterior hatch." She glowered at the screen, then mumbled, "Port-side control module needs to be repaired constantly—not surprising this one's fucked too."

Her annoyance softened, and she shared an anxious, almost contrite, look with Puck.

"I'll do—" Puck began, but Lace cut him short.

"No, I'll go. You take her," she said, jutting her chin toward Adequin. "She won't go willingly."

Lace knelt and yanked a space suit from under the launch-control counter. Adequin blinked in confusion as Lace tugged the glimmering white suit on. Puck grabbed Adequin's arm and pulled her back toward the Hermes.

"Lace . . ." Adequin croaked as she stumbled back. "Why are you putting on a suit? What are you doing?"

Continuing to tow her back, Puck mumbled, "There's manual control access on the hull. It's the only guarantee it'll open."

"On the hull? No—" Adequin shoved Puck off with Imprint-assisted force, and he tumbled out of sight. She rushed back to Lace. "I'll do it," she demanded. "I've logged a thousand more hours out there than you."

"I know, sir," Lace said, her tone unnervingly even. "But you don't know where the controls are, or how to work them."

"I'll figure it out!"

Lace ignored her, grabbing a helmet from underneath the launch-control counter.

The faintest tug low in Adequin's gut drew her glower back toward the open door to the operations deck. Her knees gave slightly as her balance tilted, and she felt like she was about to slide off the edge of a cliff. The few loose objects scattered throughout the derelict hangar slid toward the outward wall.

"Circitor," Adequin growled, throwing her glare back onto Lace, voice taut. "I'm ordering you to stand down. Get on that Hermes."

Lace continued sealing up her suit. Her narrow jaw flexed. "Sir, I lied before."

"What?" Adequin snapped.

"I knew what *mo'acair* meant. I just didn't think you did."

Adequin blinked, unable to turn her confused stupor into a response.

"My anchor."

A sharp heat sprung up Adequin's neck, clawing its way up her cheeks.

"That man loves you. Always has." Lace let out a soft sigh, brow creased. "Try to save him, if you can. Please."

A lump clogged the back of Adequin's throat. Her lips parted, but nothing came out.

Lace's eyes flickered, darting for the briefest moment over Adequin's shoulder.

Her Imprints were already running up her arm as she spun and Puck drew back his fist, but they were too late. Everything went dark.

CHAPTER FOURTEEN

Cavalon leaned forward so far, he almost slid off the edge of his seat. He squinted at the screen, his mind warring with the reality of the approaching ship.

Drudger vessels tended to be warped, surreal versions of Viator crafts, and this one proved no exception. It looked as if they'd taken a sleek, triangular Viator cargo ship in one of their brutish grips and bashed it into a rock—then proceeded to repair it with random salvaged debris, in the most haphazard way possible. Like a child pulling apart his toys and gluing them back together to create something new, yet unmistakably grotesque. Cavalon would take the mindless clone version of Drudgers his nefarious grandfather had conjured up any day to the barbaric version that barreled toward them now.

Jackin shook his head. "That device we saw in the air lock—they must have seen the station was abandoned and bugged the doors."

Cavalon ground his teeth. It was typical, and not surprising. At the end of the Resurgence War, the remaining Viator-allied Drudger forces had fled to the Outer Core and beyond. Though some had settled in remote systems and kept to themselves, others traveled in warring bands, looting and pillaging their way around the galaxy.

Not that those were new activities for Drudgers. They'd acted as the resident pirates of the SC since their inception at the hands of Viator geneticists a millennium ago. But it'd been different during the wars, when their sadistic inclinations had been focused on aiding the Viators. At least it clumped them all together, so the Legion could wipe them out easier.

"Well." Cavalon stood and dusted his hands off. "That's our cue to take our leave, I believe."

"We gotta send this message . . ." Jackin's voice withered and died in his throat. He stared at the screen, brow furrowed and desperate.

"How far out is the ship?" Cavalon asked.

Jackin's eyes refocused. "Maybe ten minutes until they dock."

"That's definitely not enough time to fix anything, Optio."

"No," Jackin agreed, then his tone waned again. "But we can't just . . . leave."

"It may not be ideal, but we can't fix the comms *ever*, if we're dead."

"We're four trained Legion soldiers," Jackin began, then sighed as Cavalon raised an eyebrow. "Okay, *three* trained Legion soldiers. We can fight."

"There could be fifty Drudgers on that ship!"

Jackin looked back to the terminal. "I'll do a scan, see if I can get a head count."

Cavalon paced for a few tense moments as Jackin worked.

"Uh, okay." Jackin cleared his throat. "Never mind."

Cavalon stopped in his tracks. "How many?" he asked, though he wasn't positive he wanted to know the answer.

Jackin flung open another screen, then slid across a command labeled "Station-Wide Emergency." A different ear-piercing tone rang out, and the blue and red lights from the proximity alarms were replaced with yellow and red.

"Hopefully Warner and Emery will get the hint." Jackin stood from his terminal. "Ready to run, Oculus?"

"*How many?*" Cavalon asked again, but Jackin had already hurried through the door. The optio accelerated into a jog, and Cavalon rushed to catch up.

Sweat glistened on their foreheads by the time they arrived back at the S6 air lock. Emery and Warner were nowhere to be seen.

"They're not back," Cavalon managed through stilted breaths. "What do we do?"

Jackin opened his mouth to respond, but hesitated as another, entirely different clanging alarm joined the chaotic din. Down the long corridor, an oscillating beacon lit up the S4 air lock door. The Drudgers had docked.

Cavalon turned his panicked look to Jackin.

"We stay," Jackin said, staring at the royal Imprint tattoos on Cavalon's right arm. "We hold the air lock until they're back."

Hold the air lock? Cavalon's mouth fell open, but the choice words he'd selected for expressing his total incredulity stuck in his throat. Jackin shoved him through the secondary air-lock door.

They rushed toward the *SGL*, and Cavalon hid behind the left side of the open air lock. Jackin took cover on the opposite side, knife out of its sheath, raised and ready. The half-serrated, dark steel blade glinted in the flashing emergency lights.

Cavalon's eyes darted to the *SGL*'s hatch. "Uh, Optio? Is sticking around really the best plan? Emery and Warner could be trapped on the other side of the station for all we know."

Jackin shot him a fierce glower. "Even if I were willing to abandon two of my crew—which I'm fucking not—we're not going very far without that warp core."

Cavalon swallowed hard. Dammit. He was right.

He fumbled his gun out of its holster and his mouth went dry.

Was there a safety? Did it need to be primed before it'd fire? Was there even an energy cell in it? How many times could he shoot before it'd need to be reloaded?

This was absurd. He hadn't been trained. Sure, he'd ripped a reinforced air-lock door from its track, but that didn't make him a fighter. He didn't know protocol, how situations like this were meant to be handled.

"Put that away," Jackin hissed.

Cavalon looked up, eyes wide. "I think it might be a good idea for me to stay at a distance . . ."

"Laser's no good against Drudgers." Jackin glared. "Bloody void, you really aren't a soldier, are you?"

Cavalon wiped the sweat from the nape of his neck. He really,

really wasn't. But he still should have known better. Thanks to the degree in genetic engineering his grandfather forced upon him, Cavalon had studied both the Drudger and Savant genomes, and the theories behind how they'd been designed.

So he already knew the Viators had passed along their segmented, carapace-like exoskeleton to their Drudger progenies. With the added bonus of an endoskeleton as well, both species proved incredibly tough—if slow—targets.

And in designing them specifically as war fodder, the Viators had gone a step further with the Drudgers, reinforcing the skin-covered carapace with metallic compounds, giving their gray exoskeletons a slight glint, and a whole lot of strength. Though plasma and most ballistics would do the trick, the armor-like plating could completely deflect laser fire.

Now if one were to shoot it in the same spot twenty or thirty times in a row, it might break through. But mostly it would just singe, distract, or annoy them, while not doing much in the way of actually killing them. Which was probably why his grandfather had zeroed in on them when masterminding his utopian clone-army scheme.

The soft connective tissue between the plates was vulnerable, however, if you could find a way into the narrow gaps. Which, Cavalon supposed, was why the basic loadout on his hip included a sharp, pointy knife. Though he'd bet anything the Sentinels were the only division of the Legion to be issued guns essentially useless against the only enemy they were likely to encounter.

Cavalon dropped his gun back in the holster. At least he wouldn't have to figure out how to use the thing. Yet. He pulled the knife out instead—heavier than he'd expected, and sizable. The blade alone ran longer than his outstretched hand. It felt just as foreign in his grip as the pistol had.

His breath caught as the air-lock siren ceased and a guttural grumbling echoed down the air-lock corridor from the main hull. He peeked around the corner far enough to catch a sliver, shuddering as a Drudger form came into view in the dimly lit hall beyond the secondary air lock.

It stepped cautiously through the threshold, rifle clutched in its taloned hands. Its wide head swiveled and its dark, thin lips twitched as it surveyed the empty room.

Cavalon had always tried to find a way to see their human side, but they looked so much like Viators, he had difficulty imagining they were anything but. They seemed more like bastard children than a different species, and that lack of distinction made them even more unnerving than they already were.

There were a handful of differences—they weren't extinct, for one. Their head and body shape had been altered, like they'd had their edges sanded off, or were slightly melted. Their wide-set eyes were the biggest disparity—Viators had four in total, two pairs, each comprised of one large, primary eye flanked by a smaller one which, for some reason unknown to Cavalon, never blinked. Drudgers only sported the larger of the two, and instead of the endless voids of all-black manifest on Viators, Drudger eyes were like overlarge human versions plucked out and stuck into a Viator shell. This served as the *only* aspect that even remotely likened them to their Savant counterparts.

Cavalon gulped as a second Drudger walked in behind the first—its gray complexion seeming almost pink in the flashing red light. It had deep red swaths of what looked like war paint across its flat cheeks and broad forehead.

Drudger skin came in a limited range of grays, often tinted with a unique design of teal and coral markings, all of which darkened as they aged, much like Viators. These two were clearly adults, but fairly young, with a light ash-gray skin the color of unfinished aerasteel.

The two Drudgers raised their rifles as they moved deeper into the secondary air lock. Cavalon retreated, pressing his back against the wall beside the door.

One growled out a string of unintelligible words, its voice muddled as if gargling water, *underwater*. Not that Cavalon would have been able to understand what it said anyway. Most Drudgers spoke only a heavy dialect of the Viator language, though some had a rudimentary understanding of the human tongue as well. Even then, their vocal cords were Viator, so what came out was generally a mere approximation of intelligible words.

The other Drudger responded with a similar string of nonsense, followed by a crunching metallic clang, vibrating through the metal wall. The other let out an angry snarl.

Cavalon knew one thing Drudgers got from humans: their vile tempers. For all their faults, the Viators could never be accused of having been short-fused. They'd been diabolical beings devoid of empathy or compassion—but they hadn't almost succeeded in wiping out sentience across the entire galaxy by being petulant.

The Drudgers shared another gruff exchange Cavalon couldn't make out, followed by a shuffle of footsteps that slowly grew quieter.

He tilted his head until he could catch a narrow glimpse of the room again. Instead of the empty air lock he expected, he found *three more* Drudgers had joined the first two. All five stood outside the secondary air lock. Three wore dark-gray Viator-issue jumpsuits, ratty and stained as if they hadn't bothered to change their clothing since the Resurgence War. Two of the newcomers wore strange, mismatched pieces of armor—molded sheets of rust-colored metal lining their limbs and chests. Yet it didn't seem strapped on, hovering over the body as a suit of armor might, but instead, it lay flush with their hardened skin. Bolts protruded from the top of each piece, as if the armor had been riveted directly to their exoskeletons. Unlike their jumpsuited counterparts, neither carried a pistol or rifle, but instead had sets of sharp, curved metal blades built into the tops of their hands, extending their talon-like fingers into rusted claws.

One of the jumpsuit Drudgers knelt to inspect the door frame where the device Jackin had found was installed. Another's gaze shot up toward the SGL, taloned fingers dancing across the side of its rifle.

Cavalon slid back behind the wall, then clamped his eyes shut and held his breath. It had *definitely not* seen him.

Searing bolts of plasma fire flew through the open doorway and struck the wall below the hatch. Before Cavalon could even begin to consider what to do, one of the armored Drudgers rushed forward, unaffected by its comrades' fire pinging off its shielded back. The creature spotted Cavalon first, roaring and swiping at him with a rusted claw. He stumbled back as the blades ripped three short tears in the front of his vest and his royal Imprints darted across his skin.

Jackin leapt out, kicking the Drudger in the back of the knee. As it collapsed in a clatter of metal, the optio grabbed its armored collar and with surprising strength, hauled it out of the open door frame into cover with him. He plunged the knife between two panels of armor at the base of its neck. Wrenching the blade free released a fountain of grisly black-red blood.

The Drudger thrashed and clawed at the wound, blood pooling up and spilling onto the floor.

Jackin slid back up against the door frame while the creature spasmed, then fell still. A barrage of plasma bolts continued to pelt the meter-wide swath of open floor between the two doors.

Cavalon gaped, his fingers grazing the torn fabric at his stomach. His heart thrashed in his chest as he realized how close he'd just come to being gutted. He pressed his back against the wall, breaths coming in ragged gasps. His gaze darted to the knife gripped in his hand, and it suddenly seemed distant, disembodied, as if he were merely a spectator in someone else's field of vision.

"We can throttle them here," Jackin called out, voice raised over the unending din of fire. "They'll get impatient and come to us."

As if on cue, the Drudgers' firing ceased. Jackin raised his bloodied knife and angled toward the door frame. Cavalon swallowed hard and slid back, bumping into the cold metal of the air-lock door he'd detached earlier, still leaning against the wall behind him. He tightened his sweaty grip on the hilt of his knife.

A clank sounded and something bounced off the wall behind them, landing at Jackin's feet. Cavalon froze, staring down at the small metal object, its escalating, high-pitched squeal cutting through the temporary silence.

Jackin tried to kick the grenade back out at the Drudgers, but it'd already clawed its little needled feet into the floor, and stopped Jackin's boot in its track.

The taste of copper filled Cavalon's mouth before he even registered that he had an idea. He grabbed the detached air-lock door, angling it to soak up the relentless plasma bolts as he crossed the open threshold.

"Move!" he shouted, and Jackin dove to the side as Cavalon felled the door atop the squealing grenade. He dropped onto it, pressing into the metal as hard as he could, his Imprints humming as they fueled his strength. With a hollow, chalky crack, the door popped up a half meter. As it landed back on the ground, his elbows gave way, and he collapsed face-first into the cold metal. Dark smoke billowed from the edges and a bitter metallic smell lingered in the air.

Plasma bolts peppered the hatch wall in front of Cavalon's face. Jackin grabbed him by the back of the vest and pulled him up against the wall, farther from the unending deluge.

"Void, Oculus," Jackin cursed, gritting his teeth. Cavalon gulped, certain he was about to get yelled at, but Jackin remained silent as he stood, black brows high, panting breaths suddenly loud in the silence.

Cavalon's heart kicked. Why was it silent?

"Shit—use the door to block it!" Jackin shouted. He passed his own knife into his other hand, then yanked Cavalon's from his trembling grip.

Cavalon opened his mouth to ask "Block *what?*" but the simultaneous pounding of four sets of Drudger boots clanging down the hall answered it for him.

Cavalon's eyes darted to the felled door, kinked at the center from the explosion. His mind said *no fucking way*, but his head nodded yes and his hands grabbed the bent metal up off the ground. He shoved it in front of the empty threshold and the metal clanged as bolts pinged it. He pressed his back against it and Jackin jammed his shoulder up to help brace it.

The door slammed against the back of Cavalon's head as the Drudgers crashed into it. He pressed against the onslaught with as much strength as he could muster, feet planted, legs bent. His Imprints spread themselves thin to accommodate the grueling request.

The Drudgers growled and spat, their taloned fingers clawing their way through the gaps around the edge. Cavalon held his breath as a waft of putrid, earthy BO assaulted his nostrils. With a knife still gripped in each hand, Jackin braced his arms on either side of Cavalon. Despite the optio's aid, the hard metal rammed his back again and again. He gritted his teeth and endured it.

Rake's words *"You'll be fine"* rang through his head and he half snickered, half growled. Jackin shot him a disdainful look, his light brown skin flushed crimson as he pressed into the door, though the man's efforts were feeble compared to Cavalon's Imprint-assisted fervor.

Jackin's scowl vanished as a decidedly human roar thundered from the other side of the door. The pounding stopped and the pressure ceased. Cavalon glanced over his shoulder and through the small window in the door-shield behind him.

In the other room, Warner punted a Drudger square in the chest and sent it crashing into the wall. Warp core in one hand, knife in the other, Emery kicked it in the jaw as it hit the ground, then thrust her blade into its exposed throat. Warner stabbed his knife between the segmented plating on its chest, and it fell still.

"Two left!" Warner called as another Drudger rushed up behind him. Emery swept its legs out from underneath it, but its talons tore a bloody gash in Warner's thigh on the way down. He growled, but the pain seemed to fuel his strength as he spun to pin the Drudger while Emery dealt the killing blow—another swift knife deep into its throat.

Cavalon had just wondered where the last remaining Drudger went when a metal-clawed hand burst through the small observation port in the braced door. The glass shattered, raining down his shoulders. He ducked as the bloody arm clawed blindly. Jackin spun away too slowly and the metal claw caught him across the top of the shoulder, tearing three long slices through his uniform.

The optio growled and blood seeped from his shoulder, but he didn't hesitate. He lunged and crossed both knife blades through the inside of the rogue arm, slicing it to the bone, right at the fleshy inside of the elbow. The Drudger bellowed a roar and ripped its arm back, bloody flesh catching on the jagged glass shards.

Cavalon grimaced and fully pressed his back against the door again. He clenched his teeth, glaring at the floor as sweat dripped off his forehead and onto his boots.

"Another squad's incoming!" Warner bellowed, hissing as he gripped the bloody gash on his thigh.

Cavalon twisted to look down the hall. Emery pulled her knife free from her target's chest—the mangled-arm Drudger, who twitched violently before slumping the rest of the way to the ground. Behind her, five more stood just inside the secondary air-lock door frame. They looked at their fallen comrades, then their overlarge eyes trained on Warner and Emery.

Cavalon took a deep breath, and his skin ignited as his Imprints flew into action. They sped his movements, boring down into the muscles of his back as he turned, flipping around to cradle the door in his open arms.

"Watch out!" he called.

Emery and Warner dashed to either side of the air lock as Cavalon stepped forward, spun the door horizontal, and threw it down the hall into the clump of Drudgers.

All five toppled to the ground as the door flew through their ranks. The gnarled metal landed with a resounding clang against the doorjamb of the secondary air lock, then fell back onto the pile of prone Drudgers.

Warner scoffed a laugh. "Shit."

Cavalon stumbled into the wall below the hatch, panting as the full strength of his Imprints subsided. His skin and muscles burned as the squares slid back into their standard formation.

"Install that core!" Jackin ordered.

Emery rushed past Cavalon, warp core clutched under one arm, filled to the brim with glowing acium. She scaled the rungs and disappeared into the ship.

Warner stumbled up, gripping his thigh in one thick hand. Blood poured between his fingers, though he seemed mostly unfazed. He gave Cavalon a weary grin. "Nice one."

Cavalon panted and nodded, but there was no time for warm fuzzy bonding, because half a second later, the discarded, beaten door clanged as it flew aside and the Drudgers scrambled to stand back up. Jackin grabbed Cavalon's shoulder and threw him toward the hatch as a bolt pinged off the metal beside him.

"Inside!" Jackin barked.

Cavalon scrambled up, then fell through the hatch into the *SGL*. His Imprints rushed to protect him, coating his knees and palms before he landed hard on the metal floor—though it was actually the wall.

"Core's up!" Emery called. Her neon-laced boots appeared, and she gripped Cavalon's arm to help him stand. Warner slid through the opening and down the wall, with a great deal more grace than Cavalon had managed.

Jackin immediately swung from the hatch into the cockpit as bolts flew through the opening, burning streaks into the ceiling. Warner pounded the control switch with his open palm, wiping blood down the screen. The hatch slid shut and the din of plasma fire dampened.

"Clear!" Warner called. The ship rumbled and jerked, pulling away from the air lock.

"Shit. Grav's gonna flip, guys!" Jackin called from the cockpit.

Cavalon tried to determine what surface he should hold onto in order to negate the effects of the switch, but his senses were still too muddled from adrenaline and panic. So he just let it happen, falling awkwardly into the wall as it became the floor again.

Emery and Warner handled it with slightly more finesse, pressing their backs into the wall and sliding down onto their butts as the gravity shifted back to normal.

"I have to snap-warp so they can't lock on!" Jackin shouted. "You guys okay back there?"

"We're good," Emery called.

A high-pitched squeal rang out from the engine room as the warp drive spun up. The floor shook and the drive let out a troubling crack—the result of engaging before any kind of acceleration. Cavalon could hardly believe the hyper-restrictive Legion ship computer had allowed Jackin to do that.

Sweat dripped into Cavalon's eyes, and he wiped it away with the back of his hand. He unbuckled the front of his torn vest and let it hang open, welcoming the cool rush of air. He slid across the floor to lean on the wall beside Warner.

Warner groaned, slouching heavily against the wall. His arm and leg were torn and glistening red, though the bleeding appeared to have slowed. Emery sat on his other side, bruised and sweating, but seeming mostly unscathed. They sat for a few long moments with only the sound of their labored breathing and the rattling of the still-tremoring ship.

No surprise, Emery perked up first. "Okay, that was a little fun." She flashed them a grin.

Cavalon's pounding, frenzied heart disagreed. As did his aching muscles, which burned and cramped from overuse of his Imprints.

Despite being decidedly not amused by the events themselves, he did feel an odd sense of satisfaction at the outcome. He couldn't be sure, but he thought he'd handled it relatively well. It could have gone better, but it also could have gone far, far worse.

For the first time since they'd met earlier that morning, Warner's mouth turned up into an actual smile. Emery joined as well, and they both began to chuckle.

A lump grew in Cavalon's throat, and he couldn't bring himself to join in their display of relief, or exaltation, or whatever was going on. It was too absurd. Absurd, maybe, but their reality. It said something grim about the state of life on the *Argus* that the Sentinels were happier to be in mortal peril than at the relative safety of their post.

But at the pit of his stomach, a deepening well of acid churned—because he knew that wasn't the real reason he couldn't bring himself to revel in the victory along with them. Because if it'd been up to him, those two would be dead right now. He'd have left them behind in less than a heartbeat.

He'd seen the very archetype of it in action on an almost daily basis growing up, far too many times not to recognize it now for what it'd really been. A ruthless selfishness that went beyond fight or flight, that dug deep into the very moral center of what it meant to be human: seeing numbers where people should be, assigning value to lives like they were just any other commodity to be bartered, manipulated, or expended to achieve an outcome.

Emery and Warner's value had only exceeded the risk of waiting for them because of that damn warp core.

Warner elbowed him, and Cavalon refocused on the glint in the man's sandy brown eyes. A glint that looked suspiciously like approval. "You did pretty good, princeps."

A thickness built at the back of Cavalon's throat. He tried to clear it with a hard swallow, but his voice still came out stiff. "Princeps? Can we not do that?"

Warner gave a half shrug. "We'll see."

The ship's rumbling finally ceased and the high-pitched squeal cut off into a long, low thrum as the warp drive finished its acceleration. They were on their way back to the *Argus*.

CHAPTER FIFTEEN

Five years ago and ninety-three million light-years inward, Dextera Adequin Rake stands holding a rifle to the head of the last Viator breeder.

In the bright wash of lights from the purring generator, everything is more detailed, more nuanced. This close, this exposed, she sees more than usual, more than she's comfortable with.

Stark flecks of maroon stipple the breeder's segmented, slate-gray carapace—they're middle-aged for a Viator, fifty or sixty years. Tiny reflections of her rifle's barrel shine in each of their four glossy eyes, black as oil slicks, black as the void. A black she won't know a true comparison for until well after she's ended this.

The lines of pleated skin on the breeder's forehead pull taut, loosen, then quiver before stiffening as their thin lips turn down—a look Adequin is incapable of interpreting. On a human, it could be called a gathering of will, a precursor to defiance, a judgment, a fleck of pity. But one expression cannot be all these things, unless you know what to look for. It's a level of detail only another of their kind can fully grasp, one that requires the inherent understanding of one's own species. So her interpretation is meaningless, and she knows better.

Under her hardsuit, sweat-slicked fingers twitch. She reaffirms her grip, stock tight to her shoulder.

The largest two of the breeder's dark eyes blink slowly. They're patient. They wait.

Many thoughts run through her head at once.

Where the fuck is Griffith? is predominant. He'd been clearing the mountain pass behind her, but he hadn't arrived yet. He should be here. She needs him.

But if Griffith is captured or dead, does it change anything? She'd killed dozens of Viators on the way up this mountain. She'd run her bloody gauntlet without hesitation and without questioning a single pull of the trigger.

There is a bitter pleasure in being here, alone, sole witness to the end of something so hard fought, something earned with so much blood and pain over so many endless, tiring years. This moment has been built on the lives of billions over millennia. How can something so far-reaching culminate in something so intimate—a single breeder on a single planet with a single soldier, a finger's twitch away from—

Xenocide. That's what this is.

Even then, she doesn't realize she's hesitating for any reason other than to savor the moment.

This is it. The culmination of a brutal nine-year war. The result of everything the Legion gave her. Every deadly mission, every comrade lost, everything she'd prepared for since she was sixteen. They've sculpted her, trained her, trusted her. She's a Titan among men.

She stands before the last of them as an example. She's supposed to be the best mankind has to offer. When she pulls that trigger, she'll have made a decision for her entire species. And she won't be able to hide behind an order or a mission objective or a greater purpose. There's a limit to what you can justify in the name of precaution.

But they'd killed *so many.*

Mankind had been decimated in the wake of the Viator War. Billions had died. Not to mention the half a dozen other sentient species that had been wiped out completely. Then only humanity remained, persistent, unwilling to lay down and die.

So the Viators had taken matters into their own hands and tried to take humanity's future, their virility, and they'd almost succeeded.

Four hundred years gone, and they still hadn't recovered, and they didn't know if they ever would.

But when the war was over, it was over. And they'd thought that was the end of it.

Yet here they are on the fringes of the Outer Core, breeding and plotting and amassing. Conspiring with Drudgers and enslaving Savants, gathering a force to take back what the humans had unjustly ripped from them. And she knows from experience, they will do so in the most bloody way possible. Not because they're spiteful, but because it's easier.

So now a new war, a new objective: not to "win," because winning is no longer enough. Now they must give it in turn, take the Viators' future just like they'd tried to take their own, and this, now, is the final play, the last breeder, the crowning glory of a war forged across a galaxy for a thousand years.

But if she kills the last of them, then *she kills the last of them.* Not Lugen or the First or the Allied Monarchies or the Quorum or whoever else one wanted to say gave the order. Just her. They can't make that call for her. She has to make it for herself.

She doesn't lower her weapon.

The breeder opens their mouth and speaks in the Viator tongue. The words are a threat, but the tone is grave petition. "Without us, you will perish."

She doesn't know what it means. But she's already made her decision.

Adequin's immediate sensation upon regaining consciousness was that she didn't weigh enough.

". . . the fuck . . ." she grumbled. She reached up to touch the bruise swelling on her upper cheekbone. Her eyes fluttered open.

A dim gray ceiling—but she knew immediately what that ceiling belonged to: the crew quarters of a Hermes.

The fuckers had hauled her aboard, like a goddamn piece of cargo.

She scowled and a hazy form appeared above her. Her eyes adjusted and focused on his bronze skin and shaved head.

"Now, sir—"

Her feet hit the ground, her grip tightening around Puck's throat before she knew what she was doing. She thrust him against the wall of the cramped quarters, then shoved him aside. He slid down the wall, coughing. Mesa crouched beside him, light fingers grazing his neck.

Adequin swallowed some copper-tinged saliva and crossed the room in two strides. She pressed herself against the long, narrow observation window.

Static bolts danced across the void beyond the black silhouette of the *Argus*. Or rather, what remained of the *Argus*.

She clamped her eyes shut. Against the back of her eyelids, Bray reached out before disappearing into a wave of white light. She tried to reason it out, his existence unspooling, just as the pieces of the ship had been, just as they were now. But her swollen eye ached and her head pounded, mind straining with the effort of it.

"What did you do?" she growled. Her ragged breath fogged the ice-cold glass.

She turned her ire back to Puck. He was on his feet again, rubbing his throat. Mesa stood beside him. Erandus appeared in the doorway from the common room, looking alarmed.

Adequin's glare remained on Puck. "What did you do?" she repeated.

"Excubitor," Mesa began carefully, "we needed you among the survivors, and—"

"You had no right!" she yelled.

"You're the only one with that right, Rake!" Puck yelled back, taking a step forward. Mesa's hands lifted as if to stop him, but retreated. "And you were being too stubborn!"

"I told you to leave without me," she said, stepping face-to-face with the taller man. "You defied a direct order."

Puck stood his ground, but his eyes were hesitant. Maybe even apologetic.

"No one is trying to challenge your authority," Mesa assured.

"It's not about authority, dammit!" Adequin took a step away from Puck and swung her arm to point out the observation window. "There are two hundred people on that ship!"

Puck wrung his hands. "Not anymore . . ."

"Shut the fuck up, Circitor," she said, her voice low and steady. "Or you'll wish you were among them."

Puck swallowed.

"Adequin," Mesa said quietly. "I know this is difficult, but there is nothing more we could have done."

Adequin stared at the Savant, furious at her composed demeanor. But also envious. That should've been her. Calm and cool under pressure. An unwavering beacon of logic amidst the fucking *impossibility* of this situation.

She took a few deep, slow breaths and tried to shut off the part of her mind that seethed. The part screaming about Griffith and Jackin and Lace and Bray and the two hundred soldiers who relied on her for their safety, whom she'd just completely and utterly failed.

A commotion erupted in the other room. Light sparked across the ground.

Adequin looked down as it flashed again, masked on the floor in the long, narrow shape of the observation window. Erandus laid his fingers over his lips and approached the glass. Adequin stepped back to the window and Puck followed. She had to squint as the flashes grew more intense.

When the flare ebbed, she could finally see the *Argus* clearly, but it was not right. Not whole. Like a clean slice had split the ship in half, chopped off with a sharp blade. Yet no debris flew free, no chunks of aerasteel sparked and shot off in every direction. There was no implement with which the destruction had been caused. One half of the *Argus* was simply not there anymore.

It was surprisingly slow.

In some dark recess of her mind—a part that allowed her to conceive such atrocities with unhindered wonder—she'd imagined it'd be fast. It moved at thousands of kilometers per hour, gaining speed every minute. Why did it take so long?

But she knew it wasn't that simple. The Divide was a singular beast, governed by a set of laws even the Viators had never been able to fully understand. She imagined it had to do with some kind of dense mass or dark energy—or lack of mass or dark energy. Forces playing against one another that hadn't come into effect since the universe stopped its expansion millennia upon millennia ago.

She knew one thing for certain: whatever the cause, there was nothing beyond the edge, and could be nothing beyond the edge, and thus as the edge encroached on the *Argus*, the *Argus* became nothing as well.

As for the speed, she couldn't reason it out. Maybe they were seeing it in segments—partly in the future and partly in the present—a series of ripples laid atop one another to create the illusion of a slow-motion slice from existence.

She squinted at a new burst of light—the familiar trails of a thousand blue-white bolts converging into a colorless orb. A ship had dropped from warp speed and landed between them and the *Argus*.

"There's another Hermes!" someone called from the other room.

"Shit." Puck pressed closer to the glass. "Is that North?"

Adequin could only nod in response. The *SGL* slowed as it sped forward, silhouetted by the sparking static lights of the Divide as it continued to consume the *Argus*.

She waited. Waited for more familiar flashes that would indicate more ships decelerating from warp speed—Legion ships come to their aid. But there was nothing.

And Jackin was too close. He'd landed *too close*. He still sped toward the Divide.

"I need them on comms *yesterday*," Adequin barked, peeling away from the window and storming into the other room. She didn't look at the faces of the too-few crew members in the common room as they split before her on her march to the cockpit.

"Got them!" someone said.

Whoever'd taken the helm slid away and disappeared as she sat into the pilot's seat. She pressed the comm link.

"Jack."

"Boss." Jackin's voice cut through, full of static and distortion, but audible. "What the—"

"Jack, shut up. Turn the ship around. You need to head inward as fast as you can."

"Shit, shit, shit—"

His ion engines roared to life in a glow of blue, and the ship slowly turned inward. But they didn't accelerate; they sat hovering, as if held still by some invisible grip.

Jackin's voice returned. "The Divide's gravity's pulling us outward. We're too close to it. Warp won't engage. Rake—I don't think I can get out of it."

"Oh, come now," she said with a dry, pained laugh, "you always said you were the better pilot. Time to prove it, Optio."

Jackin didn't respond at first, then his voice reappeared, light and airy. "Damn right I am."

Adequin shifted in her seat and let out a breath. "Flip those landing thrusters and kill grav. You'll be lighter on your feet."

"Rake, I—"

The comms cut out completely. Adequin's stomach roiled. Her fingers hovered above the holographic controls and she stared at the viewscreen. She pressed the link again.

"Jack, you there?"

Nothing. The fact that the comms had worked at all was a miracle.

The *Argus* continued to shrink in a colossal shower of static light behind the *SGL*. Jackin's thrusters rotated and lit up, discharging outward. The ion engines continued to fire. They inched forward almost imperceptibly, slow but steady. Adequin gnawed on her lip, waiting.

After a few minutes, instead of breaking away, Jackin's ship came to a slow stop.

His garbled voice reappeared. "It's—use—free."

The ship continued to struggle, and the light storm carried on behind it. The *Argus* was almost two-thirds gone.

Adequin slipped to the edge of her seat, leaning over the controls. "Jack, listen. In a minute, I need you to break right on my mark, then floor it. I'll flash our search light at you once. Understand?"

The comms crackled with a short, unintelligible response.

"I need confirmation. Do you copy?"

By some miracle, his voice came back loud and clear. "Copy, boss. Break right on your mark."

"Hold on," she announced to no one in particular. Feet shuffled around her as she slid back and slipped the seat belt harness over her shoulders and across her chest. She swept the steering controls into the air above the console, then turned the ship to speed directly toward Jackin.

She took a deep breath. She hadn't flown a ship in five years.

She became vaguely aware of protests around her—shocked gasps and murmured dissent. Mesa appeared beside her and said something in her ear, but she didn't listen.

She could have shut them up by explaining that regardless of the fact that she'd never leave Jackin behind to die when there was something she could do to stop it, they also needed something very important from the *SGL* in order to make it out of this alive.

Instead, she ignored them and focused on quelling her nerves about the maneuver she intended to attempt.

"I need a read on that gravitational field," she said to anyone who'd listen. In the corner of her eye she saw Puck slide into the copilot's seat, swiping open menus.

"It's at 541 klicks," Puck said. "Current approach speed is 16,058." He fumbled his harness over his shoulders and strapped in.

Adequin's mind raced, trying to confirm the math as quickly as possible. "Okay, I need a hard mark at 22.6 klicks. Lead me up to it."

"Yes, sir, but uh," he stuttered. "What're we doing?"

"Helping Jack achieve escape velocity."

"Uh, okay—and you've done this before?"

"Yes," she said, firming her jaw. "Sort of."

"Sir . . ." The edge of his voice creaked.

She blew out a heavy breath. "I used it once to pull a crippled fighter from planetary orbit. This is . . . similar." Similar enough. She hoped.

"But it worked?" Puck asked.

"Yeah, mostly."

"Mostly?"

She sighed. "I mean, the other ship flung a little . . . fast, and ended up in a spin, and it didn't have working engines to right itself, so there were some g-force-related issues—void, it doesn't fucking matter, okay? The point is, it worked and it will again." It had to.

Puck hesitated only a heartbeat, then his reply came steady. "Understood, sir."

"I'm taking the wheel. Ride that speed for me. I need it right at five percent."

Any slower and they'd leave Jackin behind. Any faster and they'd crash face-first into them. It'd be one way to go. At least she'd have tried, and not left him to fly toward the collapsing edge of the universe without even knowing what he was headed into.

"Yes, sir," Puck said.

With both hands, Adequin passed her holographic menus to Puck. They slid across the console and he caught them. He rearranged the screens in an arc in front of him.

"Two hundred," he said.

Adequin pressed a button on the cold metal console, and two control sticks raised up.

Someone behind her whispered in awe, "Old school . . ."

"Clear the pit," Adequin said.

With a shuffle of feet and a door whizzing shut, the tension in the air settled. It was just her and Puck. Just them and the controls. Just their Hermes and Jackin's.

"Can we push our weight to starboard bow?" she asked. She wasn't sure what these basic exploratory vessels were capable of.

Puck swept to a menu and dragged a slider up to max. Adequin's weight pressed down into the cushioned seat.

"Density's at max," Puck confirmed. "One hundred."

"Give them that flash at the two mark."

"Copy, sir."

Adequin took hold of the control sticks and their cool, soft gel molded to her grip.

After a beep, the computer's voice spoke up. "Confirm settings."

"Confirmed," she said, and the gel solidified. Her Imprints ran into her arms and hands, ready to aid her reflexes.

"Here we go," Puck said. "Ten . . ."

Adequin's eyes flickered to the flashing scene behind Jackin. Less than a quarter of the *Argus* remained. She refocused on the SGL.

"Seven . . ."

Proximity alarms blared, blasting against her eardrums and bathing the console in flashes of red light.

"Caution," the computer warned. "Approaching mass detected."

She ground her teeth. She should have disabled that.

"Five . . ."

This was just a modified slingshot. Or even more apt: like taking a very brief and quickly aborted "ride" on the Divide. Though she'd never done it, she'd learned the concept when she came to the *Argus*, and Griffith had bored her with theoretical discussions about it plenty of times over the last three years.

"Three . . ."

Just a perfect balance of speed, mass, angle, and gravity, with a fraction of a percent margin of error. No big deal.

"Two . . ."

Puck flashed their spotlight at Jackin.

"One."

Adequin swept the controls forward, and the ship lurched, banking left just as Jackin's ship launched to its right.

"Caution: Impact imminent."

The *SGL* staggered forward, and their hulls swept within centimeters of each other as their paths came together. The straps of her harness dug painfully into her shoulders.

Jackin's ship swung to her viewscreen's far right as the two ships turned to face the same direction. It stayed in sight for a few microseconds, then fell off the edge of the screen. Adequin's neck muscles tensed, and her head snapped back against the headrest as their momentum surged.

"—fuck—shit—" Puck bleated out a string of expletives, but she couldn't spare a look to check on him.

She'd gotten a *little* closer than she'd intended . . .

The computer beeped another dark warning. "Caution: Velocity increase approaching dangerous levels. Please decrease rate of acceleration."

"What's our position?" Her voice wavered in her chest as the ship shook.

"We're—right on—it," Puck managed through clenched teeth.

The rate of vibration increased, and Adequin's jaw ached as her teeth threatened to be shaken free from her skull. "Tell—me—escape—velocity."

"Coming—up," Puck warned. Moments later, he called out, "Now!"

She wrenched the controls and the ship banked left, careening away in a subtle, but definite arc. She spared a look to the right of the screen, and relief washed over her—the *SGL* still dragged alongside them.

"Comms," she said.

"Up!" Puck called.

"Jackin, you keep those engines floored inward. Twenty degrees, then we'll arc out. You got it?"

A static-filled, incomprehensible response came back. "—what—bloody—fuck—doing?"

The computer spoke up again. "Velocity stabilizing."

The vibrations slowed and fell away, and the flashing red emergency lights ceased.

Puck let out a wavering breath. "We're clear."

Adequin released her sweaty hands from the control sticks, her fingers stiff from the fierce grip.

Puck passed the comms menu back to her, and she pressed the link. "Jack, you read me?"

Only garbled static came in reply.

"Jack. You guys okay?"

More static, then a sharp click. "All right, all right," Jackin's voice spluttered through. "We get it. You're the better pilot."

CHAPTER SIXTEEN

Adequin took a few long, steady breaths. She wiped her sweaty hands on the front of her jacket, then unhooked her harness.

Puck let out a resounding sigh. "And *that's* why I punched you in the face."

Adequin turned a fierce glare onto him.

His demeanor sagged. "... sir."

She slid to the edge of her chair and swept open a menu to check their speed.

"We're good, sir," Puck assured. "We're outrunning it for now. But it's picking up speed. We'll need a long-term solution ..."

He continued to speak, but his voice faded away as her mind reeled. She swallowed hard.

It didn't even matter if Legion ships came at this point. They wouldn't be able to get to the *Argus* to save the crew, then back out of the gravitational pull. If they tried, they'd just be sucked into the Divide as well.

"Adequin ..." came Mesa's calm voice again. She'd entered the cockpit, and Puck now stood over her shoulder.

"That was impressive, sir," Puck said.

"You saved them," Mesa agreed.

Adequin didn't respond.

If Jackin almost got pulled in that easily, what chance did the *Tempus* have? That was another sixteen souls she was responsible for. It was a larger ship, sure. With more powerful engines, designed to withstand the bizarre gravitational influences of the Divide. But they'd been barreling toward it at full speed without realizing it also barreled toward them. Even if they'd accelerated safely, how long would that balance last if it was moving—a calculation they wouldn't know to account for?

Puck cleared his throat. "What now, sir?"

She blinked the dryness from her eyes and tried to remember what the plan had been. "They have a warp core," she said. Even if they hadn't refilled it at Kharon Gate, they should still have enough to make another trip.

"Okay," Puck said. "We'll all have to get on one ship."

Puck and Mesa stared at Adequin expectantly, but she barely noticed.

How could she return to Legion HQ with fewer than fifteen of the two hundred people she'd been responsible for? How could she face their families, or Lugen—or anyone? And how could she leave the Divide without knowing if Griffith was safe?

Mesa stepped to the console and pressed the comm link with one dainty finger, as if warily squishing a bug. "Optio North, this is Animus Mesa Darox."

"Uh, go for North?"

"We are going to get a safe distance away, then transfer your warp core and your crew onto our vessel."

"Is Rake okay?"

"She is fine."

"Okay," he said, then cut away for a few seconds. "Hey, we have a lot of supplies on board, maybe you should come here instead? Might be easier to pass people than crates."

Adequin narrowed her eyes at the comms screen. Why did supplies matter? They'd hop to Kharon Gate, inform the Legion, then get on the first bus back to the Core for reassignment.

Mesa looked to Puck. "Do we have enough suits?"

"No, but the sectors can be vented separately," Puck answered. "We can get everyone into crew quarters and take a few shifts."

Mesa's eyes drifted to Adequin. Adequin gave a stilted nod.

Mesa pressed the comm link again. "Very well, Optio. We will call back when we are ready to board."

Adequin stared at the control screen, watching as their speed approached maximum.

"EX," Puck said. "You wanna head over first so you can talk to Optio North?"

"I'll go last. I'll stay and man the pressure."

Puck didn't respond at first, but eventually gave a short nod. "Yes, sir."

He headed into the common room, and Mesa stood in the doorway and looked back at her. "Puck and I will get the first round prepared for transfer. I will call when we are ready, and we can align the ships."

"Thanks, Mes."

She nodded, then disappeared into the common room. Adequin waited for the door to close again, then turned back to the console. "Jack."

After a short bit of static, his voice rang through. "Hey, boss."

"Where's the Legion?"

The connection clicked on, and only empty static crackled on the air for a few long moments before he spoke. "Not coming, boss."

"Not coming? At all?"

"Let's talk about it once you're here."

She leaned back in her chair. "Okay . . ."

How could they refuse aid? How could they send no one, do nothing? And why had Jackin returned so quickly? Though anxious to find out, she knew better than to discuss it over the radio. If anyone overheard, it'd only incite more panic. And she'd had just about enough stress for one day.

Puck's voice rang on her nexus. "EX, sir?"

"Here, Puck."

"We're far enough if you want to link up with them. We've got six suited up."

Adequin called Jackin back. They reconciled velocities, then spun the ships and aligned the hatches, thousands upon thousands of kilometers away from the careening Divide.

Once the crew transferred and she confirmed everyone had dis-embarked, she pulled on her space suit and helmet, then launched her weightless self out the cockpit door. She grabbed onto the hatch and swept the access screen with clumsy, gloved fingers, and the door opened.

The *SGL* stood above her, though it didn't really feel like above when nothing pulled down. A tether had been strung between the two ships. She grabbed it and, hand-over-hand, drew herself across the six-meter expanse between the two ships.

Partway, a glint in her periphery caught her eye. She turned to look outward, back from where they came. A tiny flashing electri-cal charge lit in the starless pitch-dark of the void, thousands of kilometers away. It fizzled and died and didn't return. Though too dark and much too far to tell, she knew it was the last of the *Argus* blinking out of existence.

She looked back at the *SGL*. Two helmets stared down at her from the open hatch. She let out a slow breath, then continued to pull herself along the tether.

Puck and Cavalon were the two waiting to greet her. They reached through and guided her in, then Puck shut the hatch door.

His voice buzzed through the comms in her suit. "EX secured. We're clear."

With a hiss, gravity pressed down on her again, and her feet hit the floor.

Jackin's voice crackled in her ear. "O2's back online."

She released her helmet and pulled it off. Pressure assaulted her eardrums, and she stretched her jaw to try and pop them. Puck and Cavalon removed their helmets as well.

"Good to see you, sir," Cavalon said, his face flushed and dirty, sweaty blond hair plastered to his forehead. He smiled at her wearily.

She gave him a nod, then looked over as the doors across the circular room slid open. Nine soldiers walked in from the crew quar-ters, Emery, Warner, and Erandus among them. Some wandered in shocked reverie, others clumped into small groups, murmuring among themselves.

They stepped aside to make room as Adequin headed for the open cockpit door. Mesa stood inside, talking quietly to Jackin. She'd shed the flowing top layer of her navy dress, and now wore the fitted vermillion undersuit, ornately embroidered with contrasting reflective thread.

Their conversation ceased, and Mesa inclined her head. "I will let you two speak."

She left into the common room, swiping her hand over the door control as she did. It slid shut behind her.

Adequin leveled a flat look at Jackin. "You guys talking about me?"

Jackin marched up to her, and to her surprise, wrapped his arms around her, lifting her off her feet.

"That was the fucking coolest thing—"

"Jackin . . ."

"—I have ever seen in—"

". . . Jack."

"—my goddamn life." He set her down, but kept his arms wrapped around her. His grip loosened into a soft hug, and his tone became serious. "That was unbelievably dangerous. Thank you. Never do it again."

"You're welcome."

He stepped back to look at her, eyes widening. Her face flushed in confusion, and a sting of pain along her cheekbone reminded her of being punched into unconsciousness by Puck.

Jackin's eyebrows lifted. "What happened to your face?"

She scowled. "Rampant insubordination."

"What?"

"It doesn't matter. What the fuck is going on? Where's the Legion?"

His brow furrowed into concern. "Boss, no one's at Kharon Gate."

"Well, they don't always station additional troops at some of the less frequented gates—"

"No," he said, shaking his head, his voice growing quiet. "*No one* is at Kharon Gate. It's deserted."

She stared at him, half expecting him to break into a grin and say "*gotcha!*" but he just stared back, unblinking.

"Were they attacked?"

He shook his head. "I don't think so. There's no signs of struggle, no bodies or blood—and nothing in the logs. Systems were in reserves, gate's off. It's been abandoned."

"It's off?"

He nodded.

"Did the comms work?"

"No."

She let out a hissing sigh. "Of course not." Why would they?

"And it gets better." He pulled on the torn collar of his shirt, revealing a shoulder covered in bloody scrapes. "It was bugged by Drudgers."

"Shit, Jack . . ."

"They pounced on us once we were already inside, and we had to retreat. We barely got out of there."

"Are the others okay?"

"Fine. Warner took a couple hits, but we patched him up."

"Well, shit." She cleared her throat. "So, to clarify . . ."

He put his hands on his hips and nodded. "Go ahead."

". . . the only place we can reach via our single warp core, in our overpacked exploratory vessel devoid of armaments, is a defunct Apollo Gate currently occupied by Drudgers?"

"Replace 'occupied' with 'overrun,' and that about sums it up."

"How overrun?"

"There were over fifty on the bio scan I did. We didn't stick around to confirm."

She chewed her lip for a few moments. "Fine. Let's go."

Jackin blinked in surprise. "Let's go?"

"What other option do we have?"

"Well, none, but . . ." He shook his head. "What's the plan, exactly?"

"We're going back, and we're going to fix those comms. And since we can't take a Hermes through the gate, we'll take the Drudgers' ship."

Jackin barked a laugh. "*Take* the Drudgers' ship?"

She picked up a discarded weapons belt off the copilot's seat. "Sentinels may only have laser pistols, but my clearance will grant us access to the arms lockers on the station so we can get our hands on some better firepower." She flashed a grin. "And we're fifteen Legion soldiers. That's almost half a platoon."

"See . . ." Jackin began, crossing his arms and sighing. "You say *almost* half a platoon, but I say *not even* half a platoon."

"Set the course, Jack," she said. "We're taking back Kharon Gate."

Adequin had never put much thought into the existence of a higher power. In a universe somewhere in the realm of twenty-thousand-billion light-years wide, with countless galaxies, solar systems, planets, and forms of life, it seemed too inconceivable for one being, supernatural or otherwise, to orchestrate.

But if one did exist, then Adequin knew for certain they'd decided to focus their spiteful gaze upon her. For what sin, she didn't know, but it had started to get annoying.

Not ten minutes into their trip, the *SGL* decelerated from warp speed in a glorious shower of flashing light and misdirected acium charge. She picked herself up off the cockpit floor and Jackin looked down at her from the pilot's chair.

"Boss, we got a problem."

"No shit."

Jackin's fingers flew over the controls. "I think something might have, uh, jarred loose during our little maneuver."

"Jarred loose?"

"Yeah, I'm getting a malfunction . . ." He leaned over the console and enlarged an overhead of the ship. "There." He pointed to a flashing red icon on the port quarter. The small distress symbol meant nothing to her.

"Can it be repaired?" she asked.

"Maybe. We'd have to go out and see what's actually going on."

"We can't reach it internally?"

"No. Sorry."

Adequin ran her hands through her hair, pulling it from its tie and letting it fall past her shoulders. "Okay, let's take a look."

"*Let's* being . . . ?" Jackin asked warily.

"You?"

"I'm no mechanic."

"Mechanic?"

"It's part of the warp drive."

"Okay. Who do you think can help?"

Jackin shrugged. "I don't even know who all we have left—" His shoulders dropped.

Adequin's gaze flitted to the ground, a knot twisting in her stomach.

Lace. They needed Lace.

She didn't even know if warp drives had been part of Lace's skill set, but the woman had a thousand stories of all the different shit she'd had to fix over her forty-some years as a legionnaire. She'd have found a way to fix it, she always did. Always *had*.

"Sorry," Jackin continued, his voice haggard. "I'm just not sure who knows what."

Adequin cleared her throat, then gathered her hair back up and retied it. "Let's find out."

She opened the door and walked into the common room.

"Soldiers," she called. The soft hubbub died and their frightened faces turned to look at her. "Everyone okay?"

Their response came in murmured agreements and tentative nods.

"Who has a background in astromech?"

Feet shuffled, and no one spoke up.

"Mechanics? Engineering? Anyone?"

A tentative hand raised in the back. Emery and Warner turned around to look at the volunteer standing behind them, revealing a pair of nervous, tired blue eyes.

Adequin sighed. Right. Degree number whatever: astromechanical engineering. Of course.

"Cavalon, with us." She turned and headed back into the cockpit. Cavalon appeared moments later, Puck gripping his shoulders as he led him inside. The door slid shut behind them.

"We meet again," Jackin said.

Cavalon flashed a nervous grin. "Hey, Optio. Long time no see."

"You okay working with him again, Jack?" Adequin asked. "Did he give you any grief?"

"No," Jackin said. "He did great, actually."

Adequin raised an eyebrow. She'd have believed "didn't get us all killed," "not awful," or even "decent." But "great"?

Jackin gave a small shrug to indicate his sincerity, however hard to believe.

Cavalon crossed his arms and huffed. "Try not to look too surprised."

"Not surprised," she assured. Not *just* surprised. "Pleased."

"We got tossed from warp, right?" Cavalon said. "What's going on?"

Jackin walked over to the flight console and Cavalon followed. "We've got a class G malfunction, it says. Not overly specific systems computers on these little transport vessels. Any ideas?"

Cavalon rubbed his chin as he stared at the readout. "Huh. Well, that's a catchall classification. Could mean just about anything. I guess you might have had a hull panel lift up when—" He scoffed a laugh and turned to Adequin. "When you did that ludicrous mass pull. That was fucking awesome, by the way."

She dampened the smile that tried to tug at her lips. His boyish incredulity was a little endearing, if very annoying and ill-timed.

Cavalon turned his smirk onto Jackin. "Or when you snap-warped earlier, I suppose."

Adequin leveled a flat look at her optio, who scratched the back of his head and did a fantastic job of ignoring her.

"You were saying . . ." she said, turning back to Cavalon. "About a panel?"

Cavalon's amusement faded, and he refocused on the display. "Right. Well, you might have caught some debris, or rattled something loose during that slingshot. If a hull panel around the engine's nacelle lifted or bent, it could have exposed part of the outer engine and be giving you a reading like this. Might just need tightening back up."

"Might?" Jackin asked.

Cavalon shrugged. "Yeah. Mighta ripped something clean off too. No way to know without getting eyes on it."

"All right, Oculus," Jackin said. "Get an MMU from cargo and get suited up."

Cavalon's eyebrows raised as he looked to Jackin. "Get a what, now?"

"An MMU," Jackin repeated, as if Cavalon simply hadn't heard him. Then dawning realization crossed Jackin's face and he ran a hand through his black hair. "Oh, void."

"Cavalon?" Adequin said.

He swung his high-browed look to her. "Yeah, sir?"

"You've never done an EVA?"

"Me? No. Well, I don't know. What is that?"

"Extravehicular activity?" she said. "You've never spacewalked?"

Cavalon's eyes widened. "Oh, right. No." He shook his head fervently. "I worked on engines with my feet on the ground, full of gravity." He grinned and let out a nervous laugh. "Might be the only certified astromech that can say they've never been in space."

Adequin forced out a steadying breath. She could imagine it now: their only hope at repairing the warp drive, slipping his tether and bumping off the hull or triggering his thrusters, then rocketing off into the depths of space, spinning endlessly until he ran out of air.

"I'll tandem with him," Puck said.

She quirked a brow, eyeing the circitor carefully, though the offer appeared genuine. He certainly seemed to be trying to make up for jacking her in the face earlier. "You sure, Circitor?"

"Sorry, 'with him'?" Cavalon tried to interject, but Puck ignored him.

"Positive, sir."

"How many times have you walked?" Adequin asked.

Cavalon cleared his throat. "As in *Puck and Cavalon . . .*"

"Just in basic," Puck answered.

". . . *go on a spacewalk?*" Cavalon continued.

She shook her head. "I'll go. We can't risk this."

"Shit, Rake—" Jackin started, but she held up a hand.

"I'm going. End of discussion." She grabbed a discarded helmet off the table and shoved it into Cavalon's chest. His face paled to a rather unhealthy shade of white. "Suit up, soldier."

CHAPTER SEVENTEEN

For the third time that day and the third time in his life, Cavalon stepped into a space suit. He'd started to wonder if he should just keep it on all the time.

The rest of the crew had been sequestered into the other sections, and he stood alone with Rake in the common room. She'd already suited up except for her helmet and gloves, and now strapped a multitude of tool holsters to her arms and legs.

Cavalon withheld a groan as he bent to lift his suit over his shoulders. Despite the short, fitful nap he'd taken on their ride back from Kharon Gate, his skin and muscles still throbbed from overworking his Imprints during their Drudger encounter.

Rake finished tightening down the last of the tool holsters, then crossed the empty room toward him. He began to carefully overlay the folds of the suit, but she pushed his hands away to do it herself. Her fingers flew up the seam with practiced proficiency, and the pearlescent, nanite-infused fabric stitched itself together seamlessly as the folds met. The swollen bruise on her cheek had started to darken.

"Where'd you get that shiner?" he asked.

"Your CO."

Cavalon scoffed. "Puck?"

"Yeah." Her eyes remained focused on sealing up his suit.

"Punched you?"

"Yeah."

He lowered his voice. "Did you deserve it?"

She gave him one of those glares that made his stomach flop, and his cheeks burned.

"Joke. Sorry, sir."

She finished with his suit then gave the seal a pointedly firm pat, and he had to take a step back to catch his balance. She picked up a mess of black strapping, untangled it, and held it up in the proper shape.

"The tandem harness," she explained.

He took it and shimmied it up around his hips.

Rake grabbed his shoulder and turned him around, then pulled the loose straps up his back. He felt like he was being dressed by a valet—a rather harsh valet—to attend some Allied Monarchies formal affair. He honestly wasn't sure if that would be more or less fun than what he was about to do.

He bent his elbows back to slide his arms through, and his shoulder muscles screamed in pain. "I don't know about all this," he said warily.

"The key is no sudden movements," she said.

He spun on one heel as she twisted him back around. No sudden movements? Was this spacewalking or escaping from a predator?

She tightened the harness straps with a series of curt tugs. "A tiny bump can send you careening out of control."

Careening. *Careening* . . .

"So, keep your movements slow and methodical. Or better yet, just let me drag you along. Don't even participate."

"Don't participate. Copy, sir." That, he could get behind.

But he couldn't stop thinking about how agitated he'd felt when he'd done his depressurized walk in Novem Sector earlier. Gravity had made it seem far less real that nothing but a pitiless vacuum existed on the other side of that glass. It'd still been awful, but it'd been tolerable. He didn't think this would be the same sensation.

Rake dropped his helmet onto his head, and it buzzed as it sealed itself shut.

The display flickered to life against the glass visor. His eyes darted across the information. His vitals sat on the left: heart rate, respiratory rate, blood pressure, temperature. The suit and external temperatures were listed on the bottom along with a series of questionable numbers.

Text flashed across the center of his vision: "MMU attachment detected." It vanished and a percentage counter appeared at the top, showing his emergency thruster fuel to be at a hundred percent.

Emergency? The heart-rate indicator blipped and switched from green to yellow.

Rake took his wrist and activated the nexus interface built into the arm of the suit. She pressed in a few commands and the display in the helmet disappeared.

"Comms are still on, but you don't need all that HUD junk distracting you." Rake pulled on her gloves, then secured her own helmet. "We're clear here, Jack."

"We are?" Cavalon croaked.

She picked up a tether from a winch on the front of her own harness and fastened it to the front of his. With a thunk, she patted his helmet, and he thought he saw a reassuring smile through the glass. "Yes, we are."

Jackin replied through comms. "Copy, boss."

A second later, the room depressurized and his feet lifted off the floor. The tether connecting them wound through the air, slithering like a weightless, slow-motion serpent. Rake moved into the open hatch and floated down until she disappeared from view. The slack left the tether, then tugged on his stomach.

"Cavalon?" Rake's voice crackled through the comm link.

"Yes?"

"Ready?"

"Oh. Yes."

He pressed against the wall beside him, then lightly pushed away and drifted feetfirst through the opening. He floated past Rake, who held onto a handle bar outside the hatch.

"Don't look down," Rake said. He half thought she was joking, but her tone came flat and deadly serious.

Of course, he immediately looked down. Or rather, past his feet, because down was no longer relevant.

And there it was. Nothing. Just infinite black nothing. But as he looked down even farther, he saw the beginnings of it—a faint gradient of stars that became denser and denser as they moved toward the center of the universe. Compared to the total abyss when facing outward, inward shone with an almost blinding luminance.

He couldn't stop staring, and moments later he realized he'd tilted quite far forward—nearly parallel with the bottom of the ship.

"Void," Rake cursed. A small tug on the tether pulled on his stomach and twisted him around to face her. She looked at him from beside the hatch over two meters above. "By not participate, I didn't mean let yourself drift off," she chided.

His cheeks warmed. "Sorry."

With the tether in hand, she carefully pulled him back toward her.

"Hold onto that." She pointed to a handle bar, and he gripped it with both hands. Rake took another handle, then pulled herself from bar to bar across the bottom of the ship like she was in a weightless jungle gym. She stopped, releasing the tension on the tether enough to turn around and face him.

"Cav."

Cav? She hadn't called him that before.

"Cavalon," she repeated.

"Yes? Sir?"

"You coming?"

"Oh, right." With a shaking hand, he reached forward and grabbed onto the next bar.

"Just one at a time," she encouraged.

So he did it, literally one at a time, getting a firm grip with both hands on each bar before reaching to grab the next. He caught up with her, and after a few endless minutes, they arrived at the edge of the ship. Rake let go and palmed her way up the side, then disappeared around the corner.

"Just let go," Rake said. "I'll pull you up."

The slack in the tether disappeared. With a focused effort of will, he unclenched his fingers. He hovered free for a moment, then the tether pulled him forward and up the side of the ship.

Rake rested a meter up, arm hooked through a long handle on the side of the hull. She guided him up, and he grabbed onto the same bar.

He gestured to the MMU on her back. "Why don't we use that thing to get around?"

"Safer if we don't. Less chance of an accident."

"Accident?" He barely choked out the word.

"It's only for emergencies."

He nodded numbly as a wave of warmth rolled through him.

"You okay?"

"It just . . . it feels so claustrophobic, you know?"

"I know," she said, her tone patient. "It does. It's normal."

He let out a shallow breath. "Sorry, is it hot in here? Out here? Here?"

"No," she said. Blood rushed to his head, and her voice grew muffled. "It's actually very, very cold. Well, not technically, but you know how it works."

"Right."

Cavalon reached to wipe sweat from his forehead, but just thwacked his hand into the glass of his helmet. He squinted as a bead of sweat rolled off his brow and floated past his eye. He imagined the heart-rate indicator in his HUD would have been a particularly vibrant shade of red by now.

"I just feel like I shouldn't be this hot," he croaked, the words thick in his suddenly bone-dry mouth. He looked up at the endless black above him. Except it wasn't up—there was no fucking *up*. He tried to take a deep breath, but the air had solidified. It caught in his throat and his windpipe constricted.

He needed out of this suit. It was suffocating him.

He reached up to paw at his neck.

"No! Bloody void, Mercer!" Rake gripped his arm and pinned it to his side, pressing him against the hull.

"Jack?" Rake barked.

"Go for North."

"Cavalon's vitals reading okay?"

"Heart and respiratory rate are elevated, but his temp and blood pressure are good."

"He's acting like he's freezing to death."

Cavalon shook his head. "Not cold. Hot. I'm too *hot*," he insisted.

Somewhere in the back of his mind, he knew that when humans got too cold, they started feeling too hot, but he couldn't focus on trying to justify his illogical behavior.

"Temp reads good on my end," Jackin said, "but his pulse spiked again. I'd try to calm him down, boss."

Cavalon clenched his eyes shut, but his head still spun—like that level of drunk right before blacking out. He'd much, much rather be drunk or blacked out.

He tilted his head back farther, trying to counteract the vertigo.

"Whoa, hey now . . ." Rake's voice came through his earpiece again, calm and patient, but firm. "You're spiraling, Cavalon. Rein it in."

"Okay. Okay." His hand cramped as he clenched the handle bar even tighter. He opened his eyes and tried to focus on her instead of the absolute nothing reaching out in every direction around him.

"Listen," Rake said. "You're fine. But do you wanna talk about what to do if you lose pressure?"

Cavalon's wavering vision steadied. He liked knowing things . . . And of course, she'd know what to do. She was a Titan. She'd probably done a thousand spacewalks. Who knew what valiant feats she'd accomplished while traipsing about in the vacuum of space?

"Okay." His heartbeat slowed enough he could hear clearly again.

"If you lose pressure, exhale. First and foremost. Just exhale. Don't hold your breath."

"Right. Exhale." He exhaled. "Got it."

"Use your Imprints to coat the skin around your neck and chest."

"Okay. Imprints. Check."

"You'll only be conscious for a few seconds after that."

"A few seconds?" he croaked.

"Fifteen, maybe. But it'll take another ninety seconds or so for you to actually die. That's plenty of time for me to toss you back into the ship."

"Ninety seconds? That long?"

"Maybe even two minutes."

"You swear?"

She tentatively released his shoulder, then held her palm toward him. "On my life, soldier."

"But what about the temperature? You said yourself it's freezing."

"It's well beyond freezing."

"Oh, void—"

"No, no, listen," she said hurriedly. "It all takes time. Your body doesn't instantly lose all its heat. There's no convection, conduction, any of that shit. You're a fucking scientist three times over; you should know all this."

"I know, it's just—" He took a sharp breath in but gained nothing from it. He couldn't let it out, and he couldn't try for more. He couldn't breathe and couldn't find his voice back.

"Cavalon, don't freak out on me." Rake released her grip from the handle bar.

His heart hammered against his chest. She'd just *let go*.

Yet she didn't drift away, or go firing off into the void. She merely hovered, floating gently toward him. No sudden movements.

She held onto either side of his head with both gloved hands, then pressed the front of her helmet into his with a soft, hollow thunk.

Her hands blocked his peripheral view, and the endless nothing around him disappeared. He could see nothing except her face, lit by the blue and white flashes of her suit's display.

"You're fine," she said quietly. Wisps of hair hung across her eyes. Her black eye. Why had Puck *punched* her? "You're safe. I promise."

He swallowed hard. The knot of tension in his chest loosened, and he found his breath back. His throat and chest ached from the stress, but he believed her.

"Can you do this, Cavalon?" she asked seriously. It wasn't a challenge, but an offer. This was his way out, if he wanted to take it. She would let him.

He cleared his throat. "I can do it."

"Good." She released his helmet and drifted back. "Now, let's get this over with."

Slowly, meter by meter, Rake pulled them along the arc of the hull to the port quarter of the ship. He knew she continued to take it easy for his sake—that she'd have rocketed right over there and latched on in two seconds if she didn't have to tote his incompetent ass behind her.

Finally, with a high degree of relief, he saw it—a crumpled panel on the shell of the warp drive's exterior housing. "That's it," he said.

"Good. Heading up. Hold here."

She released the winch and palmed her way up the side of the ship, toward the bar closest to their destination, though it sat over a meter too far away. They'd have to perform the repair without holding onto the hull.

Rake pulled him up to her, then switched his tether from the front to a hook on his lower back. She then fastened a short tether from the back of her own harness to the bar. Rake let go again—*completely*—and floated away from the hull, taking him by the shoulders and guiding him toward the broken panel. She placed him right in front of it, and let go.

"Remember, slow and steady." She remained hovering just off his right shoulder.

"Got it." He gave a short nod, then carefully gripped the loosened panel.

It didn't budge, a fact which relieved him greatly. Something probably hadn't ripped off entirely if there wasn't an open, gaping hole in the side of the ship.

"I need the—" Rake's hand appeared, holding the zero-g impact driver. "Thanks." He slowly took it from her grip. How was everything so *fucking hard* without gravity? It made no sense.

Cavalon moved the drill toward one of the bolts on the bent panel, and as he pressed down, his body floated away from the hull. His hand shook, and his grip loosened. The drill began to float away, but Rake grabbed it and pressed it back into his hand. His breath started coming in shorter gasps again.

Jackin's voice crackled through. "Rake, kid's vitals are spiking again."

"Cav, just relax. Pretend you're back at university."

He took a wavering breath. "Which one?"

"Whichever you did astromech at."

Cavalon secured the drill onto the bolt, then began unscrewing. "Altum Institute."

"Okay, then. You're back on Elyseia."

"Shit, I don't want to be back on Elyseia," he grumbled. He finished removing the first bolt, and it floated away. Rake grabbed it, and he moved on to the next.

Even if he *could* go back, even if the full force of the Mercer Guard wouldn't come down on him the second he hit atmosphere, he'd die a happy man if he never had to breathe a single lungful of that scrubbed, over-oxygenated air again. The news vids, propaganda poorly disguised as SC tourism initiatives, and even the historic records would have everyone believe Elyseia was the closest example of a utopia humanity had yet to have the good fortune of witnessing. Though each of the royal families' home planets had their own unique offering of sins, Elyseia alone embodied everything Cavalon hated about the Allied Monarchies and then some: a rampant and worsening caste system; systemic oppression; an unbalanced, wildly corrupt legal system; the list was endless.

Cavalon cleared his throat as he removed another bolt. "I mean, not that I want to be *here*," he clarified, "but I definitely don't want to be *there*."

"Okay . . ." Rake said, letting out a soft breath. "Then, what's your favorite planet?"

"Artora. Easy." More bolts floated off and Rake caught them.

"You're on Artora, then."

He could almost feel the warm, humid spring air on his cheeks. The panel floated loose, and Rake's hand appeared in his periphery and grabbed it. He inspected the open hull and found the secondary nacelle paneling bent as well. He began to unscrew the bolts fastening it down.

"What am I up to on Artora?" he asked.

"Well, no good, certainly," she grumbled. "But for now, you're just at the spaceport fixing a ship."

"Which port?"

"Hera."

"Wait, who the hell's flying a Hermes around the Core?"

"I don't know," she said. "Just some old explorer guy."

"Old explorer guy? You can do better than that."

"What?" she scoffed. "You expect some elaborate backstory?"

"I mean, if you want . . ."

Cavalon finished removing the secondary panel and passed it off to Rake. He peered down into the opening, where a resonance dampener coil floated loose.

"Ah, see?" Cavalon grabbed the coil. "*This* should be attached."

He turned it over in his hands, checking for damage, but found none. It'd merely shaken itself loose.

"Solder knife, please."

Rake secured the loose bolts in the front pouch of her suit, then replaced the impact driver in his hand with a soldering tool. He lowered the copper coil back into place and began to reattach it.

"Probably caught a speck of debris," he explained. "Worked its way through the two sets of panels and bumped into this guy."

"A speck could cause this?" Rake asked.

"At the speed you were going?" He laughed. "Definitely. You should be glad the whole hull didn't rip off."

She sighed.

"The debris probably just tweaked it. The vibrations caused by that velocity ramp are likely what shook it loose," he explained. "Now, you were saying about our explorer?"

"Right." She cleared her throat. "Well, he's a haggard sort. From, uh . . . the Inward Expanse."

"No shit?"

"No shit. He thought he'd bring his Hermes into the Core and get it traded for a decent Evorsor."

"Oh, a *starfighter*." He grinned to himself. "Whatever for?"

"Well, see . . ." She took a beat, either for dramatic effect or to try to think up something to say. Either way, he appreciated the distraction. "After a lifetime of charting the IE," Rake continued, "he'd finally found what he'd been hunting for all along."

"And what's that?"

"The Drudger horde who'd killed his family."

Cavalon let out a low whistle. Damn. That got dramatic fast. He finished the last of the soldering, then doubled back around to confirm solid connections.

Rake continued. "So now, he has some reckoning to do."

Jackin laughed through the comms.

Cavalon grinned. "What's his plan?"

"He's going to buy a ton of ammo and plasma charges, then take his Evorsor and follow the trail. But first, you gotta fix his stupid Hermes so he can make the trade."

"Well, if it's for revenge, I'm all-in." He confirmed the stability of the last connection, and the coil held securely in place. "Optio?" he called tentatively.

"Go for North."

"What're your sensors telling you in there?"

"Hull breach warnings are up, but our original malfunction is clear."

"Fixed?" Rake asked.

"Fixed," Cavalon confirmed.

"Nice work. Let's wrap it up."

Bolt by bolt, he secured both crumpled panels tightly into place while Rake detailed the old explorer's plan for avenging his family.

"We're all green in here," Jackin said finally. "See you guys back inside."

Cavalon let out a deep breath. "Thank you, sir." He craned his neck to look at Rake. "I mean, for distracting me. My brain works better when it doesn't realize it's in mortal danger."

"I've noticed."

Cavalon turned to hand her the impact driver, but the bit scraped against the side of the hull and it fell from his grip. On instinct, he dropped his hand down to catch it, but the stupid thing stayed floating.

The damage had been done, however. His elbow hit hard against the hull with an innocent thunk, and he bounced away at a speed slightly faster than he felt comfortable with.

He cursed at himself. He'd gone so long without any sudden movements.

"Shit," Rake said, quickly releasing the tension on the winch, presumably so he wouldn't boomerang and come crashing back into the ship too fast. "What was *that*?"

"I dropped the drill!" he called out, as if he needed to accommodate for the distance stretching between them.

"You can't *drop* anything!" she yelled back. "There's *no gravity*!"

Dammit. She was right.

Rake took a deep breath, crackling through the comms with forced patience. "I'm going to rein you back in."

Heart hammering against his ribs, Cavalon twisted and grunted, struggling to reach behind him to grab at the tether hooked to his back.

Any hint of calm in Rake's tone dropped away. "Don't *even* fucking touch that!"

But it was too late. His reckless, grasping fingers had managed to trigger one of the manual thruster switches on his MMU, and he learned the practical definition of careening as he rocketed away from the ship.

The air drained from his lungs and vertigo overtook his vision. It appeared only one side had been triggered, as he spun in one direction, faster and faster. The SGL flashed by once every few seconds, then once a second, then faster until it almost seemed like it stood still again. The tether twisted around his torso, tightening as the length expended from Rake's winch.

"Turn it off!" Rake yelled.

He grasped at the switch again and the thruster ceased, but he continued to spin. Moments later a hollow poof sounded, then something clamped down hard on his shoulders. His body stopped, though his vision continued to reel. His stomach lurched, and he swallowed bile back down.

He must have been facing outward, because he could see nothing ahead of him, nothing in his periphery, just black, starless, galaxy-less, nebula-less nothing.

"Fucking void, Mercer," Rake cursed. "Are you *trying* to die?"

The grip on his shoulders released, then Rake's arm crossed his chest and pinned his back to her.

"I panicked," he said, then realized he was wheezing.

The ire fell away from her tone. "Try to breathe."

"I'm sorry. I panicked."

"I know."

"How did you do that?" Grabbing onto him like that should have sent her into the same rotation.

"I counteracted your spin with my thrusters." She let out a long breath. "Fuck. I knew I shouldn't have given you an MMU."

Cavalon had to agree. That one was on *her*.

"Sir?"

"Yeah?"

"I think I'm going to be sick."

Rake sighed.

CHAPTER EIGHTEEN

Adequin pinched the bridge of her nose with one hand and lightly patted Cavalon's back with the other as he buried his face in the latrine and expelled the contents of his stomach. Again.

The poor guy hadn't stopped throwing up since they'd repressurized. At least he'd made it that far. She'd thought for certain he would hurl in his suit on their way back to the ship.

"He'll be fine," Emery assured quietly. The oculus had offered her support upon hearing him vomit for the tenth time. "Probably a combo of nerves and zero-g. His body's just not used to it."

"Thanks, Emery," Adequin said. Cavalon heaved again. "Do we have anything we can give him that might help?"

Emery shook her head. "Nothing for nausea. Bone knits, apex, saline."

"Saline's better than nothing, I guess. It'll keep him from getting too dehydrated. Mind grabbing a few cartridges for me?"

"Sure thing, EX."

Emery left the sequestered washroom through the staggered doorways. The light from the brightly lit common room flashed across the darkened crew quarters as Emery exited, leaving Adequin alone in the latrine with the vomiting prince.

"Sorry." Cavalon's voice cracked, raw and haggard, echoing in the metal bowl of the toilet.

Adequin knelt beside him. "I bet this isn't the first time you've found yourself hunched over a toilet, huh?"

Cavalon laughed. Then hurled again. He spat into the latrine, then sat back on his heels with a resounding sigh. She passed him a towel. He wiped his mouth as he crumpled backward to lean awkwardly against the wall. Dark bags hung below his bloodshot eyes, his skin ghostly pale.

"I think that might be it," he said, then hiccupped. "All my insides are in there now."

She flushed the toilet and tried to smile reassuringly, but it came out a sympathetic grimace. "Sorry, Oculus. Believe it or not, I'm not trying to get you all injured or killed."

"It's not your fault. I think I just overdid it a bit. With all the zero-g, and the panicking, and wearing out my Imprints earlier."

"Imprints?"

"When we were leaving Kharon Gate." He coughed into the towel. "With the Drudgers."

"You participated in that?"

He shrugged. "I, uh . . . threw a door at them."

She nodded slowly. "Of course you did."

Emery appeared with a sealed pack of saline cartridges and a biotool, a Legion-issue medical multitool that provided a whole host of functions from disinfection to cauterization.

"Sir, do you want me to . . ." Emery began. Adequin stood and waved it off.

"I can do it." She took the pack from the oculus. "Thank you."

"No problem, sir. Anything else?"

"Not now."

Emery left, the din of chatter filtering through from the other room briefly before being hushed as the door sealed again. Adequin sat on the floor beside Cavalon. She tore open the package and took out one of the saline cartridges. All Titans had at least some combat medic training, and though she hadn't had cause to treat anyone in over five years, it'd be pretty hard to kill someone with saline. Though, at the moment, he looked like he might find death preferable.

Cavalon let out a soft groan and slid partway down the wall, resting with one shoulder jammed into the corner, neck craned upward.

"That doesn't look comfortable." She turned on the biotool's interface and set it to disinfect.

"You don't have to do this, sir," he said. "You've got subordinates out there. You should shunt this to one of them." He hacked into the towel a few more times. "Or just leave me to die. That'd be fine."

"I'd rather deal with this than sit in the cockpit, waiting. I feel better when I'm doing something."

His mouth turned up into a decidedly weak, pathetic grin. "Like me."

She gave a small smile back. "Yeah."

His eyes drifted closed. She took his arm, his skin clammy but warm.

"Sorry, my hands are cold," she said, pushing the sleeve of his uniform up above the elbow. He only grunted in response.

She swiped the biotool across the inside of his elbow until the interface glowed green, indicating the skin had been disinfected. She loaded the saline cartridge into the side of the tool.

Cavalon's gold and bronze Imprint squares glinted and sprung to life, quickly laying themselves across the inside of his elbow.

"Cav . . ."

"Sorry." He let out a wheezing sigh. "They're just trying to protect me. I don't like shots."

She tried not to laugh, but a sympathetic chuckle came out anyway. He slid the rest of the way down the wall to lie fully on the floor. He draped the towel over his face.

"Void, you're a mess," she said.

He groaned.

She waited, rubbing her hands together to warm them up. Finally his Imprints receded, falling back into their standard formation.

She repeated the disinfection process, then switched the biotool into injection mode and pressed it against the crease of his elbow. The tool hissed as it let out the solution. The muscles in his arm twitched, but otherwise he didn't react. Moments later, his skin flushed with color.

"Damn, that works fast." He tilted his head up and pulled the towel from his face, then flopped back down. "Still feel like I'm going to hurl, though."

"This'll only help hydrate you. We don't have anything for the nausea aboard."

"Cerenozine."

She nodded. "We'll get you some when we get to Kharon Gate."

His brow furrowed. "We're headed to Kharon Gate?"

"Yes."

"But—" He hiccuped. "But Drudgers."

She sighed. "Yeah, I know. We'll take care of it."

"You will," he mumbled. She quirked an eyebrow, surprised that his tone lacked all traces of sarcastic incredulity. He sounded like he had every confidence in her statement.

She pushed herself across the floor and sat against the wall beside him.

"Sir . . ." he croaked. "What's . . . going on?"

Swallowing hard, she slid another saline cartridge in the biotool, then set it aside. She'd wondered when he would start asking questions.

"What happened to the *Argus*?" he continued. "And what caused that gravity field you pulled us out of?"

"We don't know for certain . . ." Her instinct was to play it down, let him rest, not add to his stress. But she'd grown tired of lying about it—to others and to herself. Maybe saying it out loud would help. She took a deep breath. "The Divide appears to be contracting."

He let out a wheezy snort.

"Unfortunately, I'm not kidding."

He stayed silent for a few long moments before he spoke, his voice hoarse. "The Divide is the edge of the universe."

She nodded. "You are correct, Oculus."

"And you're telling me you think it's contracting?"

"Yes."

"As in, the universe is collapsing?"

"Right." Adequin chewed her lip while she waited for his response—for an onslaught of panicked questions or accusations about how she'd handled it all wrong. But after a few moments of heavy silence, he merely rubbed his palms down his pale face and let out a deep sigh.

"If it's okay with you," he said, "I'm going to file that away for later processing."

She bobbed her head slowly. "Me too."

Cavalon fell quiet, and his breath slowed until she was sure he'd fallen asleep.

She craned her neck to look out the staggered doorways into the pristine crew quarters, hunting for something to busy herself with. Unfortunately, she saw nothing that needed doing. She tucked her legs up to her chest and laid her forehead on her knees.

As disconcerting as it was, she wasn't actually worried about the Divide. Yet. As long as they had access to FTL, they'd be safe for the time being. But what about the thousands of other Sentinels at the Divide? There were dozens of ships just like the *Argus* stationed along it. Had they met their fates as well, been scrubbed from existence like the soldiers left in her charge? Or did they still have time to warn them?

She breathed into her knees and tried to focus. She needed to take it one step at a time. A task like any other. Step one: Gain access to Kharon Gate so they could fix the comms, contact the Legion, and get new orders. The rest could be determined later.

She took a slow breath and let her eyes drift closed, but had to force them back open a heartbeat later. Every time she shut her eyes, she couldn't stop seeing Bray screaming, falling away from her, unspooling from existence. And Lace's defiant glower as she sealed up that damn suit.

Lace had been like family to Griffith, and Adequin had let her die. Her stomach roiled at the thought of having to break that news to him. If she ever even got the chance. Void only knew where he and his crew were. It'd been almost a day since the *Tempus* left, but to them, it'd have only seemed a couple hours. If they'd even safely joined up with the Divide to start with.

What she didn't want to admit was how selfish that pain in the pit of her stomach was. She worried for the crew of the *Tempus*, of course she did. She wanted them all safe. But Griffith was her best friend, her oldest friend, and the only person she'd call family. They'd worked side by side for over ten years; she hardly remembered what her life was like before he was in it. He'd been there when she completed her spec ops training, when Lugen took her under his wing, and for every major campaign to minor skirmish since she joined the Titans. They'd followed each other into the fray countless times, but she didn't know how to follow him this time.

And she knew she'd be enjoying the same sense of gut-wrenching anxiety even if they hadn't recently become . . . intimate. Loving him, romantic or otherwise, had always been what made life at the Divide tolerable. Even with how much he'd been gone, she always knew he'd come back. But not this time—he couldn't. There was nothing for him to return to.

So ultimately, it wasn't Kharon Gate, or the Drudgers, or the other Sentinels, or the Legion's mysterious disappearing act that worried her. It was just Griffith Bach's fate. He rooted her to this life, and without him, she'd be lost.

She let out a sharp breath and dragged her hands through her hair, pressing her cold fingers against the warmth of her scalp.

Cavalon coughed, and his groggy voice startled her. "Have you been to Artora for the decennial fall equinox?"

She let go of her head and lifted her face from her knees. He remained lying faceup, eyes closed, the pink in his cheeks stark against his pallid skin.

"No," she said.

"It's ridiculous." A weary grin tugged at his lips. "It's when they swing so close to their binary, Myrdin, it takes up half the sky."

She glared down at him. "Are you trying to distract me?"

"Is it working?"

She didn't respond at first, but after a few moments, she quietly mumbled, "Not really," though her tone betrayed her. Mindless chatter felt better than mulling over everything she could have done differently in the last day.

"Okay." Cavalon grunted as he propped up on his elbows, then slouched against the wall beside her. "You told me a story," he croaked. "I'll tell you one. Are you ready?"

"I guess . . ."

"Once upon a time . . ." He cleared his throat. "There was a kingdom led by shitheads."

She scoffed.

"It gets interesting," he assured. "Trust me."

She nodded. "Go on."

"So, in this kingdom led by shitheads, there was a preeminent leader—a king of kings, if you will. The shittiest of them all."

"Ah." She fought back a smile. This was to be autobiographical, then.

"After decades of unhindered tyranny," he continued, "the shithead procreated. By some unequivocal miracle, and despite years of brainwashing disguised as a royal education, his spawn was *not* a shithead. The spawn wanted to change things, but he wasn't allowed to truly lead. He was throttled, puppeteered by the shithead himself."

"A figurehead," she offered.

"Exactly." He nodded. "Years later, the spawn spawned, and thus introduces the hero of our story."

Adequin quirked an eyebrow. "Hero?"

"Leading man?"

"No."

Cavalon frowned. "All right, our *protagonist*—we'll call him 'the boy'—led a fairly clueless childhood. Thankfully, the shithead was busy enough with his evil endeavors that most of the childrearing had been left to the spawn and the shithead's wife, who was also unquestionably *not* a shithead."

"The boy's grandmother?"

"Right."

"I met her once."

Cavalon's face fell slack. "You . . . did?"

"Corinne Mercer?"

He gave a wavering nod. "When?"

"Shortly before the war started. My first posting after basic was at Legion HQ. She attended a summit where I was a security escort for a senator. I think she was there bidding to get Legion-held Viator tech released for private sector research."

Cavalon nodded slowly, his pale skin gone gray in the dull light. "That would have been right before she went missing. I—uh, the boy was eleven. He doesn't remember it that well."

The solemn look in his eye told her that wasn't the entire truth. If anything, he'd *tried* not to remember it. But Adequin certainly did. It'd been one of the biggest news stories around the time she enlisted, and a point of bitter contention between the Allied Monarchies and the Legion for many years after.

"She was a geneticist, right?" Adequin asked.

Cavalon's lips twitched with a weak, fleeting smile. "Aren't we all?"

"Do you have any idea what happened to her?"

He shook his head, and his voice came out a dull croak. "No."

Adequin chewed the inside of her cheek, trying to decide whether she could believe that. People went missing all the time, all across the galaxy. But not high-ranking members of the royal families. In fact, she couldn't recall another instance in modern history. Surely he had some notion of what'd happened.

But her doubt melted away when she looked back over to Cavalon, shoulders stiff as he slouched against the wall beside her. He stared down with a doleful glower as he wrung his hands. Someone, somewhere, may have known what happened to Corinne Mercer. But her grandson clearly didn't.

"Sorry," Adequin said quietly. "I didn't mean to derail the story."

"It's okay." Cavalon rubbed his eyes, and some of the color seemed to return to his cheeks. "I always encourage audience participation."

"What's next?" she prompted.

"Right. Well, for the sake of brevity, we'll skip over the years from sixteen on, in which the boy attended university and stayed as

224 ◄ J. S. DEWES

far, far away from the shithead and his shitheadedness as he could. Because the real fun began when the boy became second in line and was expected to return home, for good. To fall in as the shithead's right hand."

"Wait, second in line? What happened to the father?"

Cavalon remained silent for a few long moments. When his voice returned, it came muted and gravelly. "I was kinda hoping we could skip that part."

A lump grew in her throat, and she swallowed. "Okay, what happened next?"

"He returned to find the shithead had made an even more epic shitshow out of the SC than the boy could have ever imagined."

"He really didn't notice it while he was away?"

Cavalon diverted his gaze, looking down as he picked at his fingernails. "His . . . uh, recreational habits . . . had hindered his ability to clearly see what'd been going on."

She gave a grim nod. "I see."

"Though honestly, it'd always been bad. Since before he even left. But he'd been inside it for so long, he hadn't been able to see it for what it really was."

"He couldn't see the forest for the trees," she offered.

His bloodshot eyes flit up to meet hers, almost startled. As if he didn't think she'd actually been paying attention. "Right. Exactly." He shimmied against the wall to sit up straighter. "He could see it all so much clearer—including how the shithead had managed to get away with everything he did. How flawed the whole damn system was."

"The System Collective?"

He nodded.

"How so?"

"Well, think about it," he began, and his voice picked up strength. "It was created seven hundred years ago by a society that'd been wracked by endless war for centuries. They'd been battle-hardened, guarded, and rightfully fearful—and the tenets of the government they built reflected that. It served a certain purpose, but that's not what we need now."

"And the boy wanted to change that?"

"He wanted to try, at least. See, he'd realized something through all this . . . that he was just one of many, in a line that stretched back hundreds of generations. That it wasn't his burden, but his responsibility. There was more at stake. And to change things, he'd have to root out the festering tumor at the heart of it. He needed to dethrone the shithead."

"And how'd he plan to do that?"

Cavalon shook his head wearily. "To be honest, there wasn't much of a plan. For a time, he tried to forge alliances, garner some respect so he might be able to replace the shithead on the Allied Monarchies' board."

"I'm assuming there's a 'but'?" she asked.

He nodded. "*But* he was railroaded at every turn. The shithead knew the boy's plans opposed his vision for the future of the SC. He wouldn't have him taking over, wouldn't let him tear down everything he'd built. So the boy responded the only way he thought could make the shithead listen . . ." His jaw tightened, and he rolled his neck side to side a few times as he let out a breath through his nose. "By blowing it up."

Adequin threw him a surprised look. "Wait . . . literally?"

"Quite. The boy picked a location where it'd hurt the most. He went for the jugular, as his father would have said. Then he built himself a couple hydrogen bombs."

"He built them himself?"

"He built them himself," he confirmed. "Because the shithead had eyes and ears everywhere. The shithead owned majority shares of every weapons manufacturer in the Core. The shithead's fingers were in every fucking proverbial pie. He was infallible."

"Until . . ."

He shrugged. "I guess, until his spawn spawned a halfway intelligent kid who also came with a backbone and absolutely zero sense of self-preservation."

She blinked at him for a few long moments, then had to forcibly close her gaping mouth. She'd imagined a whole slew of immature stunts he could have pulled that would have sent Augustus Mercer over the edge once and for all . . . but this? She'd have thought he was lying if he didn't look too exhausted to be deceptive.

"What was the jugular?" she asked. She hadn't caught this bit of news from the Core yet. Though maybe it'd been conveniently removed from the headlines.

"A state-of-the-art Drudger-cloning facility," he answered. "Set to be unveiled and opened the following week."

"Before it was occupied?"

Cavalon gave a small shrug. "The boy's not a murderer."

"This facility . . . It was meant to clone the Drudger army?"

"Right. The *Guardians*, as the shithead so modestly coined them."

"And how'd that work out?"

"It didn't. It slowed things down, hindered progress. And it pissed the shithead off, which was almost worth it in itself." Cavalon closed his eyes and his voice faltered as he continued. "But it changed nothing. The shithead is still on his throne, and now the boy is at the edge of the universe, where he should have already died, but . . . didn't. For now."

"Well . . ." Adequin sighed. "That story's kind of a downer."

"I said it got interesting, not that it had a happy ending."

"I gotta say, Mercer . . ." she began, blowing out a long breath. "I didn't expect you to be a revolutionary."

He coughed out a nervous, brisk laugh and threw a furtive look around the small washroom. "Void, don't say that too loud . . ."

She tried to curb the smirk that tugged at her lips, but from the amused glint in his eye, he'd already noticed.

He shook his head. "Don't worry, I'm no revolutionary. But I *was* raised a politician, remember. I just didn't come out the way Gramps wanted."

"Clearly." She scoffed and leaned her head against the wall. "So you took out an entire Mercer Biotech facility? That was . . ."

"I know. Stupid and impetuous and childish—"

"Brave."

Cavalon's eyes opened past a sliver for the first time since they came back inside. He turned his shocked look onto her.

"I mean, it was all those things too," she assured. "But sometimes you have to fight fire with fire. I get that."

He maintained his unreserved gawking. "Yeah . . ."

"And you were risking everything you knew," she continued. "Everything that made life easy. Because you believed in something. That's commendable."

"You mean, the boy did."

"Right."

"'Cause it's totally made up. A story."

"Right."

They stared at the toilet in silence for a few long moments.

"Hey, sir?" he said.

"Yeah?"

"I'm sorry for how I acted when we first met."

"It's okay."

"My Augustus-appointed therapist always said it's a defense mechanism. Obviously I was feeling extremely . . . defensive. Not that I'm trying to give an excuse," he added quickly. "I'm just . . . I'm aware. And I'm trying to be better."

"I know," she said quietly, then added, "I think getting rid of that therapist was a good start."

He laughed, but it soon faded away, and his tone fell serious. "And thanks for talking me off a cliff out there. Taking my own helmet off in space would have been a really, *really* ridiculous way to die."

"I agree." She let out a long breath. "And you're welcome."

CHAPTER NINETEEN

✦

Adequin gave Cavalon another injection of saline, then helped him into a bunk. She grabbed a clean shirt and vest from storage, and Cavalon started snoring before the door slid shut behind her. Puck patted her on the back, and Mesa gave her a weary smile, but otherwise she avoided the gazes of the crew as she crossed through the common room to the cockpit.

Jackin sat in the pilot's chair, feet up on the console, snoring softly.

"Jack."

He jerked awake. "Void."

She slid into the copilot's seat. "Good morning."

"Hey, boss." Jackin wiped his brow.

She held up the fresh uniform. "Thought you might want to change."

He looked at the torn shoulder of his vest, caked with dried blood. "Shit. Yeah."

She slid the clothes across the console toward him. He stood and pulled his vest off, then yanked his torn shirt over his head. As his undershirt tugged up, she caught a stray glimpse of his lower back, where countless streaks of deep scars marred his light brown skin.

She tried not to stare, keeping her eyes focused on the collection of holographic screens in front of the copilot's seat.

Yet her thoughts stayed fixated on those scars. They were old, at least ten years, and not the kind one got from battle, but from a much different style of warfare. She knew Jackin had been CNO for the First through most of the Resurgence, and she'd managed to glean a few other bits over the years. But he tended to be closed-lipped about what'd happened before the war, and even more so about what'd landed him at the Divide. Despite her taking advantage of a plethora of opportunities to encourage him to open up, he'd skillfully avoided it every time. And his were the only sealed service records she'd come across since joining the Sentinels.

He could have been captured during the Resurgence, she supposed. Though as CNO, that would've been very unlikely. Regardless, physical torture wasn't common for Viators. They were more the slow psychological breakdown types. Drudgers, maybe, but it wasn't likely he'd have survived it if that'd been the case.

Jackin finished tucking in his shirt, then sat as he strapped his new vest closed. "Thanks, boss."

"How long till we're there?"

He leaned over the console and blinked heavily. "Fifteen minutes. What's the plan?"

"I'm wondering if I should just go in myself."

"Void, Rake," Jackin cursed. "What's this all about?"

"What?"

"This martyrdom bullshit. Mesa told me what happened on the *Argus*. You tried to stay behind?"

"Because what, Jack?" she said defensively. "I deserve a spot over someone else?"

He scoffed. "Fuck, yes. Maybe you don't value your life over anyone else's, but we all do. And going into Kharon alone is suicide. This isn't the war. You aren't the last soldier. You don't have to do it alone."

She met his gaze head-on, his dark brown eyes serious. Mesa had been smart to go to him. Not that their opinions didn't matter, but Jackin's mattered more, and the Savant knew it.

Adequin grazed the sore bruise on her cheekbone—a reminder of what her stubbornness had forced Puck to do.

"The Sentinels are behind you," Jackin assured.

She leaned forward onto her knees and looked at her boots. "I know."

"But you need to talk to them," he said seriously. "They're scared and confused. Most of them just saw the *Argus* and two hundred of their comrades disappear before their eyes. What are they supposed to think is happening?"

She could only nod slowly in response as her heart thudded heavily against her chest. Jackin's features softened. He took a deep breath, stood, then crossed the small cockpit and knelt at her feet, eye level with her.

"I know we lost a lot of people, boss," he said quietly. "But wherever they are now . . . it's probably better than here."

She nodded. She wanted to believe that. But that was that higher power thing again. Could there really be a place every soul went when their time was up? And if so, did that still hold true for those who were *erased from existence* by leaving the confines of the physical universe?

With an effort, she steadied herself before meeting Jackin's gaze again. "Is there any chance the *Tempus* survived this?"

He shook his head. "I have no idea."

A breath caught in her throat, a swell of heat rising up her neck. Jackin's thick brows knit together, and he wrapped one of his hands around both of hers. "One thing I do know," he said quietly. "Bach's smart, and tough as hell. If anyone could get them away from it safely, it's him. He's the one person I know who could give you an honest run for your money when it comes to flying."

Nodding slowly, she slid him the best version of a grin she could manage. "No, he can't."

Jackin smiled, though his eyes remained creased with sympathy. "If we can get the sensor suite working on Kharon, we'll do whatever we can to find them," he assured.

"Yeah, okay. Thanks, Jack. And I do hear what you're saying about the crew."

He gave an appreciative nod.

"I promise I'll talk to them. But let's get aboard Kharon safely first."

"Okay." He gave her hand a squeeze, then returned to the pilot's seat. "What's the call?"

She took a moment to collect her thoughts, then looked up at him. "Let's drop out of warp early and cruise up. See what's going on."

"We have no cloaking." Jackin sighed heavily. "There's really not much of anything on this ship."

"Well, it's an exploratory vessel. So one thing it has is decent long-range scanners. We'll edge up till we can get a read and see what we're up against."

"Whatever you say, boss. But just so you know, when you get into Titan plan-of-action mode, without someone inside, the air locks aren't accessible."

"How'd you guys get in?"

Jackin gave a short laugh and tilted his head toward the cockpit door. "Kid ripped the primary air-lock door right off its track."

"Cavalon?" she asked. He'd said he'd thrown a door at the Drudgers, but she didn't think he'd meant the *air-lock* door.

"Yeah, *Cavalon*," Jackin said, his tone suddenly sharp. "Or should I say *Mercer*."

He stared her down. She blinked once.

"Yeah," he scoffed, "don't think I didn't overhear that little slip on the comms while you two were out parading around on the hull."

She crossed her arms and leaned back. "That was hardly a parade."

"That kid's goddamn royalty?" Jackin said, voice high with disbelief. "Why didn't you tell me?"

"Why's it matter?"

"If he gets hurt or dies on our watch, and we end up on some Allied Monarchies' shit list?"

"Sadly, I don't think we'd end up on any list. I'm pretty sure that was the goal."

Jackin's eyebrows raised. "What?"

She shrugged. "He's been disowned, cast out."

"Wait, who is he?"

"The heir."

Jackin froze, his face stiff, as if cut from stone. "Augustus's grandson?"

"Yeah . . ." She narrowed her eyes at his casual use of the monarch's first name. "*Augustus?*"

Jackin's jaw skimmed back and forth slowly, and he didn't respond, didn't even appear to have heard her.

"Jack?" she said. "Do you know the Mercers somehow?"

He remained silent for a long time, then finally, his voice came quiet and low, in a tone she hardly recognized as his. "I can't lie to you, Rake," he said, turning to look at the console. "So let's pretend you didn't ask me that."

Staring back at her optio, her brows knit together. She'd never seen him like this before. "Jack, what's wrong?"

With a few fluttering blinks, he seemed to snap back into himself. "Nothing." He licked his lips, head shaking. "Why's he here?"

"Long story, and not mine to tell," she said. "But basically, they wanted to get rid of him. They shipped him off to die—they probably figured he'd be dead already."

He huffed. "Well, he might be if it weren't for you."

"Give him a little credit."

Jackin pinched his fingers together and squinted through them to indicate a very, very tiny amount. "This much. I give him this much."

"What unit is that measured in?"

He let out a breathy laugh, but the humor fled his face in an instant.

"You said earlier he did *great*," she reminded him.

"Yeah, well," Jackin began, then shrugged. "He's not half bad. But green as shit, I mean—the EVA thing? *Come on.*"

"I know, I know. But he's learning. And fast."

"Yeah," Jackin agreed, leaning back in his seat. "Talk about a shitstorm. Ever think about blaming him? All this started when he showed up."

Her brow creased in amused disbelief. "You think he brought the Divide with him?"

"Maybe not, but a whole pile of bad karma."

"The point is," Adequin said, steering them back on track, "if ripping the door off worked, we'll rip the door off again. Or maybe Puck can hack it."

Jackin held up one finger. "Small problem."

"Go ahead."

"We may have forcibly ejected ourselves from that air lock before it had a chance to seal and depressurize."

"May have?"

"Did."

She sighed. "Well, that's not ideal. But the gate should have automatically sealed off that sector. We'll just have to dock at the other set of air locks. Which side did you break?"

"Starboard."

"Then we go in port."

Minutes later, they decelerated out of warp speed, and Jackin flew them inward until Kharon Gate appeared on their long-range scanners. On the viewscreen, Adequin could just barely distinguish the tiny black shape the deserted gate carved out against the backdrop of endless stars.

"Huh." Jackin slid open a few menus, then leaned closer to the interface. "Huh . . ."

"Jack."

"Yeah, sorry." He slid the scanner display to overlay on the viewscreen, then spread his hands to enlarge it to full width. The orange holographic map showed a wide, gridded expanse, with a single, long, narrow blip on the farthest edge.

"I'm not seeing anything other than the gate itself," Jackin said. "No other ships. I think they left."

Adequin nodded. "It'd be just like Drudgers to get bored and leave. Let's head in. Dock port."

"Okay, boss. But if the doors on starboard were bugged, port might be as well. They could be headed back shortly after we dock."

She shrugged. "We can be sitting ducks here, on a ship with no armaments, or sitting ducks in the station, where we can mount a defense."

"Fair point." Jackin swept open the interface and typed in a command. The ship rumbled as the ion engines roared to life, and they sped toward Kharon Gate.

A few minutes later, they were docked. Adequin disembarked first, welcomed to the P1 primary air lock by blaring sirens and flashing emergency lights. From the control screen, Puck both quelled the station-wide alarm and opened the air lock—without the need to liberate the door from its track.

Jackin thoroughly checked both the primary and secondary doors, but found no device like the one they'd found on the starboard side.

The rest of the crew unloaded into the main corridor. When they were all gathered, Adequin reluctantly made her way up the ramp leading deeper into the station, then turned to face them.

"Listen up," she said. They fell silent and turned to look at her. "We have reason to believe there could be a Drudger ship incoming to this location."

Their reactions were a bit more shocked and appalled than she'd anticipated, and they erupted into a furor of questions and concerns. She crossed her arms.

Jackin's harsh voice cut through the din. "Shut it!"

They shut up, and Jackin moved to stand beside her, glaring down at the soldiers.

Adequin cleared her throat. "We need to get unloaded and prepared for that possibility."

"Where is everyone?" someone called out.

"I know you have questions. We'll do a briefing as soon as we get this Drudger thing under control. But we need to keep this gate at all costs; it's our only foothold out here until we can get it operational again. So for now, we're in full defense mode. Got it?"

A mixture of tentative verbal affirmations rippled across the soldiers.

"I want a base camp set up at the end of this hall," she continued. "If they dock, it'll be this side, and we'll throttle them here. There are arms lockers down the main corridors; let's get those unlocked and gather as many plasma guns as we can. Set up ammo drops and distribute biotools. Let's do a temporary med station down this hallway as well. You guys know the drill."

A stronger wave of affirmation came with a series of sharp "yes, sir"s.

She pointed down the corridor toward the port bow. "Port-side control room will be our base of operations. Nexus comms should be working on the local network, but if you need anything, you can find Optio North and me there." She turned to Jackin. "What else?"

Jackin nodded. "Emery, Warner, grab two others and head to the port-side fuel depot. Fill and bring back every warp core you can find."

"Yes, sir," Emery said.

Jackin turned to Erandus. "Coordinate getting everything pulled off the *SGL*, but leave the essentials on board in case we need to—" He let out a slow sigh. "Er . . . retreat."

Erandus gave a sharp nod. "Yes, sir."

The others shuffled their feet and exchanged nervous glances.

"Get to it," Adequin ordered.

They saluted, then peeled away. Cavalon remained standing at the back, sweaty and flushed, holding one hand over his mouth, the other arm cradling his stomach.

Adequin caught the eye of a nearby oculus.

The short, dark-haired woman snapped to attention, facing her. "Sir?"

"Can you find the med station and get that oculus an injection of cerenozine?" She tilted her head toward Cavalon. "It'll probably knock him out for a while, so bring a few cots up as well. Then pull whatever other supplies they have and bring them over. And check with everyone else, make sure no one was injured when we fell out of warp."

"Right away, sir." The oculus marched off.

Adequin caught Puck's eye. "Puck, with us."

Puck and Jackin followed as she made her way toward the portside control room at the bow of the vessel. When they arrived, Puck immediately slid into one of the six work stations congregated around the central, triangular platform. Moments later, the overhead lights came on, and the displays of every terminal flickered to life, including a series of large maps and status outputs above the central hub.

Adequin gave a nod of approval. "Puck, get the bio scanners up first. Let's make sure we're the only ones on board."

"You got it, sir." Puck leaned forward to hunker down at the terminal.

Adequin turned to find Jackin staring at her, arms crossed. "That's not *exactly* what I had in mind when I said you should talk to them."

"I know." She sighed. "But let's focus on not getting ambushed by Drudgers first."

CHAPTER TWENTY

—✦—

Cavalon woke to find a weapons belt draped across his chest. The laser pistol he'd had before had been replaced with a sleeker, dark chrome gun of similar size. He had to assume it was a plasma pistol from the station's armory, or at least he hoped.

He lifted his head, then sat up slowly, expecting a surge of nausea to overwhelm him, but none came. His head spun, but once upright, he felt normal. Decent, even. His raw throat still ached, and he didn't think he'd ever find cause to consume food again. Otherwise, he didn't feel half bad. He rubbed his stomach, grateful it had given up on trying to murder him.

While he'd slept, the once-empty room had been transformed into a makeshift medbay. Six cots sat against the walls with stacks of aerasteel cases between them, lined with biotools, cartridges, and various other medical supplies. But not a Sentinel to be seen.

He hoped that didn't mean the Drudgers had arrived. Not that he'd lament missing out on all the fun, but he'd feel a little bad if he'd managed to snooze through the whole thing.

He fastened the weapons belt around his waist and walked out into the brightly lit hallway. At the end of the corridor toward the air lock, Warner and two others stood post.

Cavalon headed the other way, toward a light murmur of chatter. The next doorway stood ajar, and inside the remainder of the Sentinels had taken up shop. Emery and two other soldiers snoozed on cots in one corner. Another two chatted quietly between themselves while chewing on bricks of brown gravel that Cavalon assumed were MREs. The dark-haired woman who'd given him the shot sat cross-legged against the wall on the other side of the room, cleaning her gun methodically.

A half dozen filled warp cores lined one wall, casting the room in a soft blue glow that reminded Cavalon of the vast network of glass tunnels under the oceans of Viridis. Only without the school of immanis sharks hovering, looking hungrily down at the humans watching them. Though Cavalon thought he might prefer the vicious, six-meter-long sea creatures to the horde of Drudgers that might be lurking outside.

He didn't know how much time had passed, but considering how far along the Sentinel's base-camp efforts had come, he assumed it'd been at least an hour or two. The efficiency with which they'd put all this together impressed him. It was as if they'd run the "abandon ship to the nearest defunct Apollo Gate" drill dozens of times. And, being the oh-so-helpful tool that he was, Cavalon had slept right through it. Just like that, he'd become a totally useless outsider again.

He stepped into the room, finding a clear piece of wall away from the others to lean against. He let out a sigh, louder than he'd intended. The soldiers eating MREs looked over at him passively, but soon returned to their soft chatter.

He didn't know any of them, and he could only imagine what they thought of him. To them, he was just the guy who'd started a fight in the mess less than four hours after intake. The guy who was so obviously not a soldier, everyone seemed to immediately know. And the guy who'd somehow ended up here, alive and well, even though their friends were all dead.

His eyes drifted over the six soldiers, and despite his sincerest objection, his mind tallied up the reminder of those he'd seen in the SGL. Fourteen total. Only *fourteen* of the two hundred people on the *Argus* were here.

A mass twisted in his gut with a realization—because by all rights, he should have been on that dreadnought when it went down. Rake sending him on that mission had been a fluke—a temporary lapse in judgment by an otherwise rational mind. Or maybe she'd wanted to test his mettle, see if her shit-cutting exercises had sunken in. Either way, if she hadn't forced him onto that Hermes, he'd be dead right now.

He didn't know why being alive upset him. It's not like he'd asked Rake to pull him into all this. It wasn't his fault. The remaining Sentinels didn't really seem to care, or even notice.

Regardless, an annoying, bitter weight that felt suspiciously like guilt had lodged itself deep in his gut.

A short, thin woman walked through the doorway and landed beside him. Cavalon did his best to avoid eye contact until he realized with a start who it was.

Mesa—he hardly recognized her. She'd changed from the embroidered jumpsuit into a regulation uniform. The straight lines appeared even more boxy and utilitarian on her lithe form. Her black hair had been drawn into a single, long plait down her back.

She gave Cavalon a curt nod, then held up a clear plastic water canteen. "After expelling so much bodily fluid," she said, "it is important to hydrate."

He frowned. "Heard that, huh?"

"*Everyone* heard it," she said decisively.

His cheeks warmed. *Great.* So now he was also the guy that'd obnoxiously thrown up for an hour straight. He took the water bottle. "Thank you."

She nodded once.

He gave her uniform a pointed once-over. "So, you're a combat soldier now, huh?"

"I always have been," she said simply.

"What? I thought you said Savants didn't enlist."

"I did say Savants did not enlist. I did not say *I* did not enlist."

"Well, then . . ." He lifted the new chrome pistol from its holster. "You can help me with this thing then, right?"

She made a small clicking sound with her tongue, then sighed heavily. She took the weapon from him and slid open a compartment on the side, revealing some kind of power cell. She dumped the charge onto her hand and held it out.

"This is a standard IGW cartridge."

He blinked and flashed a grin. She pursed her lips.

"Ionized gas weapon," she explained. "In this instance, a standard-issue plasma pistol. It is very simple. Smaller end goes forward." She held up the narrower end, capped with light silver metal, then dropped it back into the compartment and slid it shut. "Point and shoot. No prime required." She dropped the pistol back in his holster, then pointed a thin finger to his knife. "That, I am fairly certain, is pointy end forward. To the face."

Cavalon let out a short laugh. "Face?"

Mesa draped her hands together. "Eyes, specifically."

He grinned. "Not chest—not heart. *Face*. Damn."

She licked her lips, unaffected by his amusement. "As I am sure you realize, the Viator, and thus Drudger, torso is completely covered by the carapace-like plating which comprises their protective exoskeleton. The muscle tissue within is so dense, and the endoskeleton structure so concentrated, and the spacing between plates so narrow that the Viator ventricle unit which sits perfectly centered within the chest cavity . . ."

Cavalon's eyebrows raised as Mesa took a deep breath.

". . . is incredibly difficult to reach, particularly for those inexperienced with combat."

The corner of his mouth pulled up. "Yeah, yeah. Okay. I will definitely go for the eyeballs first."

She nodded curtly, seeming pleased he intended to take her advice. "Then, when they are blinded," she continued, "you can take your time finding the correct attack point to reach their aortic vessel."

She lifted his arm and drew two fingers along his flank. "The best access point is here, where the fourth and fifth rib meet and wrap around to the spine—though, it is *their* sixth and seventh rib. The spacing is very, very narrow. Perhaps a millimeter, so it will be very difficult to insert, assuming the individual Drudger's plating even allows for it. You will have to apply a great deal of thrust."

Cavalon chuckled, but she didn't seem to notice.

"Depending on girth," she continued, and he had to bite his lip to keep from laughing, "the organ can be located as deep as twelve to twenty centimeters within the thoracic cavity. If you need additional time to locate it, you can also puncture one of three respiratory organs to subdue them further."

She used two fingers to point out one spot at each collarbone and one at the base of his neck.

Her brow furrowed and she huffed. "This is somewhat pointless without a proper anatomical model." She glanced over her shoulder, as if she expected to find a Drudger carcass lying around to use as a subject.

Cavalon grinned fully, no longer trying to temper his amused incredulity. Mesa was fucking scary.

"That's okay, really," he said. "I'll keep all that in mind. Thanks."

Mesa lifted her chin. "You are welcome."

"Though, it's been hours. Maybe they're not coming?"

"Adversaries rarely appear when it is convenient."

"True. Well . . ." He held up the water canteen toward her. "Here's to hoping they have better things to do than monitor a busted Apollo Gate at the ass-edge of the universe."

Mesa pinched her lips together, like she'd tasted something sour. "Yes. Here is to . . . hoping."

He took a deep swig from the canteen, and it tasted like ice-cold heaven—fierce and dark and beyond refreshing. The cold water surged down his throat and coated his stomach, and the welcome chill raced directly into his blood. He coughed lightly as he pulled the canteen away from his lips, shocked by the water's intensity.

Mesa's overlarge eyes regarded him steadily. He stared back.

She cleared her throat. "That water is laced with epithesium."

He laughed. "Oh, yeah?"

"For subcellular hydration, alveoli oxidation, et cetera. For energy."

"Yeah, I know what it is."

"It is natural and perfectly safe. You have experienced a trauma."

"Thank you," he said.

She gave a small nod.

He took another swig, this time less surprised by how intensely refreshing it tasted. "You seem to know a lot about all this fighting stuff. Did you serve in the Resurgence?"

"I no longer fight," she said plainly, as if that in any way answered the question. "But it is all knowledge, like anything else. I find that can be an equally powerful weapon, when correctly applied." She straightened her back and kept her eyes on him. "I think that may be something we agree on."

Cavalon smiled. "Yeah, I think so."

Mesa let out a small sigh, and for the first time, Cavalon noticed how bloodshot her eyes were. Her beige complexion had lost some of its warmth, thin blue veins visible through the skin.

"Have you had a chance to get any rest?" he asked.

She shook her head once. "Now is as good a time as any, I suppose."

"You can sleep easy," he assured, patting the pistol on his thigh. "'Cause now I know how to use this."

A thin smile spread across her face. "I have never felt safer."

He inclined his head. "I do what I can."

She took a few steps toward the doorway, then turned back. "If you are wondering what it is you should be doing, consider finding your commanding officer."

Right. He had one of those now.

He nodded. "Good idea. Thanks, Mesa. I mean . . . sir?"

"You are welcome." She strode away, shoulders straight, hands clasped firmly behind her back as she rounded the corner.

Cavalon finished the rest of his water, and, feeling particularly energetic, strode out into the hallway to look for Puck. Warner and the two circitors still kept watch at the end of the corridor. The older, male circitor with wild red hair elbowed the blond female circitor as Cavalon approached.

Warner nodded in greeting. "Hey there, princeps. You met Circitors Erandus and Murillo?"

"I have not," he said, giving the pair a courteous nod.

The stocky, red-haired Erandus quirked a brow at Warner. "This the guy? The royal?"

"Aw, come on." Cavalon glared at Warner. "I thought we were buddies."

Warner narrowed his eyes. "Buddies?"

"You know, like comrades in arms. We survive battle together, then we don't share secrets about each other?"

Warner stared placidly at him.

Cavalon frowned. "That meant nothing to you, did it?"

"Are those tats like Rake and Bach's?" Erandus asked.

"Uh, I'm not sure, actually," Cavalon said. "Wait, who's Bach?"

"He flies the *Tempus*."

Oh, right. The "hunky" centurion. The *other* Titan.

"Which family are you from?" Murillo asked. "My cousin once dated a Saxton—said they're all total narcissists."

"That's true." Cavalon gave a sharp nod.

"Oh, what about Watts?" Erandus asked. "A guy I dated at basic had an uncle who worked for Watts Automation. Said they were obsessed with 'keeping the bloodlines clean.' All kinds of incest."

"Uh, yeah. Also, true." Cavalon diverted his gaze. They were narrowing down the families pretty quick. It might be best to get out before the process of elimination prevailed.

To his surprise, Warner gave reprieve. "Come on, guys, we don't need to grill the guy. What'dya need, princeps?"

"I'm looking for Circitor Puck."

Warner pointed down the hallway behind him. "Control room's 'bout fifty meters down, on the left."

"Thanks, big guy." Cavalon gave Warner a pat on the back, then headed into the hall. Fifty meters down on the left, he peeked his head through the doorway.

Rake stood with her arms crossed beside Jackin, who leaned over a terminal, swiping away at the holographic display.

Puck sat at a terminal on the opposite side of the triangular platform, leaned back in his chair, resting both hands atop his head, eyes heavy and bloodshot. "We should have a plan B," he said.

"I had them stockpile warp cores," Jackin replied. "We'll need quite a collection if we end up having to warp to Eris Gate."

"Will there be enough?" Rake asked.

"Enough acium, yes. Enough cores? I don't know. There's a starboard fuel depot as well, we might find more empty cores there."

"Let's wait until we can coordinate a full team to head that far into the station," Rake said. "Everyone needs to get some rest first. For now, let's stay focused on getting a hold of the Legion."

"Rake . . ." Jackin began.

"What?"

Jackin continued carefully. "They abandoned this gate and didn't even tell us."

"So what? They'll send help if they find out what happened."

"I don't know if that's true."

"Really? You think if we get a hold of them, they're just going to say, 'Sorry, we're out. Best of luck'?"

Jackin scoffed. "Honestly, boss? Maybe."

Puck covered his face with both hands and breathed deeply. Cavalon went unnoticed as he stepped up to lean against the door frame.

"Then I'll talk to Lugen," Rake said, tone firm. "They're not just going to leave us here."

"We don't need anything from the Legion in order to *start the gate*," Jackin said. "We can say fuck comms and focus efforts on that. You can make the call—"

"This *is* the call," she said. "We can't put a Hermes through an Apollo Gate anyway. It's too risky."

Puck sighed and dropped his hands. "She's right about that, Optio."

Rake nodded her appreciation, then turned back to Jackin. "We need them to send a vessel. We're stuck until they do. Get the Legion on the horn."

"Okay, boss." He ran his hands down his face. "But we've had no luck so far, and it's been hours."

"What more can we do?" she asked.

"I've been avoiding it because it'll take internal comms down as well," Jackin said, "but we can do a full manual reboot of the mainframe and comm systems. Even if it doesn't help with comms, the sensor grid is on the fritz too—we didn't get more than a few minutes warning when the Drudger ship arrived. A reboot might help that as well."

"Okay, let's try it," Rake said.

"We have to do it manually. From the server room."

"I'll go."

"It's at the other end of the station, and the conveyance system's down. It's at least a forty-minute walk, one way."

"Sounds good."

"Remember that sleeping thing you promised to do?" he scolded.

"I'm *fine*," she insisted. "I need to be doing something. I can't take all this waiting around."

"All right," Jackin huffed. "But when you get back, you're sleeping, whether it's willfully or not."

"Fine," Rake agreed. "You wouldn't be the first subordinate to render me unconscious today."

They both looked to Puck. He raised his eyebrows, entwined his hands, then stretched them high above his head before leaning back over his console and busying himself.

Rake patted Jackin's back firmly. She picked up a weapons belt and strapped it around her waist, then turned and marched toward Cavalon. He stepped back, worried he'd be reprimanded for listening in, but she hardly registered his presence.

Jackin called after her. "Don't go alone. What if . . ."

Rake ignored the optio, giving Cavalon a nod as she passed on her way out the door.

Cavalon watched her go, and when he turned back, he found Jackin staring at him. Cavalon diverted his gaze to his feet. He rubbed a light scuff mark on the toe of one boot with the heel of the other.

"Oculus," Jackin said.

"Yes. Sorry, sir. Just looking for Puck. I wasn't sure what I should, uh . . . be doing."

Jackin crossed his arms. "You're feeling better?"

"Good as new, sir."

A groaning creak of metal rang out from the direction Rake had gone. Cavalon looked over his shoulder, but couldn't see her.

Jackin let out a slow sigh. "Go with the EX, please."

"Uh . . . yes, sir." Cavalon gave a quick, awkward salute. He hadn't tried that yet. It felt weird. By the grimace Jackin gave him, it must have looked equally strange.

Cavalon shrugged it off and turned to hurry after Rake.

CHAPTER TWENTY-ONE

Rake had already made it ten meters down the corridor. Cavalon quickened his pace to catch up.

A small weapons locker sat recessed in the wall, and the once-locked metal door rested mangled and warped on the ground below it. Cavalon stopped to look in. A single plasma rifle was missing from the half dozen lined up inside the locker.

His fingers drifted to the small pistol on his thigh. Though it should in theory do the trick if they encountered a stray Drudger on the way, the station weapons looked far more formidable. Besides, following Rake's instincts had to be the right call.

He grabbed one of the rifles, then took an extra power cartridge and hurried after her.

"Mercer," she growled, glaring at him but not decelerating her pace. "What are you doing?"

"Uh, Optio North—" He almost dropped the rifle and ammo, stumbling as the floor sloped upward. "He, uh, told me to go with you."

"He did, did he?" she muttered.

Cavalon couldn't quite infer how best to respond, so instead, he focused first on walking, and second on trying to figure out how to load the rifle.

He fumbled with it for a minute until Rake turned and snatched it away from him. Without missing a step, she pulled her already loaded rifle off her back, dropped it into his hands, loaded his in one fluid movement, then slung it across her back.

Cavalon pulled the strap of his new rifle over one shoulder. Despite her purposeful march, he kept up easily, and his heart thrummed and fingers twitched with unused energy. The cold epithesium still coursed through his veins, making his body and mind restless.

Rake took a sharp right to head down another corridor, and the walls narrowed as they wound their way deeper into the station. After a few more minutes of silence, Cavalon took a couple of quick steps to fall in next to Rake.

"So, why'd Puck punch you?" he asked. "Sir."

She grimaced. "To force me to abandon ship."

Cavalon nodded, not in any way surprised. He'd been wondering how they'd stopped her from going down with the *Argus*. Though he had to admit, his congenial CO punching her into submission hadn't been the *first* on his list of possible explanations.

It also explained her half-angry, half-annoyed, and fully despondent attitude. She'd been forced to leave most of her soldiers behind, and from the sound of it, the Legion hadn't done a damn thing to prevent it from happening. But that seemed like a grim topic he wasn't quite ready to broach.

"So, uh, AJ, huh?" he said. "What's the J stand for?"

She ignored him, staying focused on the corridor as they walked.

"It's only fair, right?" he continued. "I mean, you know mine. *Augustus*, ugh. Dick." He rolled his eyes. "I bet he wishes he hadn't given me his name now, huh? Thanks for keeping that from the others, by the way. Or trying to—I think they're going to figure it out. These Imprints are like a beacon, and I'm *so clearly* not a soldier, and they already know I'm not a Saxton or a Watts, and this fuckin' blond hair—"

"Bloody hell, recruit," she said in disbelief. "Did someone give you quill or something?"

He gaped, dropping his hand away from mussing up his hair. "Why would the Legion have psychotropics on board?"

Her face tightened into an incredulous scowl. "Void, they don't. I was joking."

"Ahh. Epithesium, sir."

"What?"

"Mesa put some epithesium in my water. Actually, she said she 'laced' it. That sounds kinda nefarious, doesn't it? Did you know she enlisted?"

"How much did she put in?"

"I have no idea. It's been a while since I've had any. I forgot how awesome it is." He drummed his fingers in the air and grinned. "Tingly, a bit."

"Well, calm down, Oculus. You had a rough go of it. If you get too worked up, you'll end up over that latrine again before we know it."

"Noooo, thank you. Okay, I'll calm down, sir. It's your turn anyway. So, go ahead."

"My *turn*?"

"Yeah. You told the one about the old explorer guy who wanted revenge. I told the one about the boy and how he ended up at the Divide."

"So?"

"So, it's a thing now—"

"No, it's not."

"—which means, it's your turn."

She scoffed. "I don't think so."

"You could tell the one about the girl," he prompted. "How *she* ended up at the Divide?"

She gave him a stoic glare that sent a shiver up his spine. "That's classified."

He laughed. "I knew you were gonna say that."

Rake refocused on the corridor in front of her and didn't respond.

Though certainly curious about how she'd ended up on the *Argus*, what he really wanted to know was how her faith in the Legion had remained so steadfast, despite how poorly they treated the Sentinels. He'd have grown bitter long ago, and though he didn't consider himself the most steadfast person in the universe, he was fairly certain extending her faith this long should be considered nothing short of delusional.

"Maybe that specific story is classified," he assented, "but you must know more stories. How about the girl who became the most lauded Titan of our generation? Origin stories are the best."

"What's this all about, Oculus? Why all the questions?"

"You said you like knowing someone before you ask them to risk their life for you."

"Yeah."

He cleared his throat. "Well, I like knowing the people who are asking me to risk my life."

It hadn't sounded so serious in his head. But it caused her scowl to fade, and she grew quiet for a few long moments. "That's fair."

"And that little hull jaunt makes . . ." Cavalon counted off to himself. "The *third* time since we met. Arguably four."

The muscles in her jaw flexed. "Four? Dumping those warheads does *not* count."

"Oh, no? Well, what if I'd dropped one and the command-trigger wiring had sparked the firing set and triggered the missile?"

"You're making that up."

"You don't know that," he huffed. "Sir."

Rake just shook her head. They reached a peak in the hallway, and the floors began to slope down instead of up. The slanted, scaled walls became subtly wider again, indicating they'd passed the center of the gate, and were on their way out to the starboard edge.

Cavalon rubbed the nape of his neck, unsure of how to prompt Rake without pissing her off. "Okay," he said finally. He gave her a grin, which she completely ignored. "I'll take a stab at it myself." He threw his shoulder back to reseat the awkwardly long plasma rifle, then rubbed his hands together. "Just let me know when I veer off track."

She let out a long breath through her nose, but to his surprise said, "Fine."

"Once upon a time there was a Legion brat. At least third generation." Her exhausted head shake indicated he'd already gotten it dead wrong, but he continued anyway. "Eldest child of a pair of Legion officers. She grew up in the Core, but always dreamed of following in her parents' footsteps, and at age eighteen she enlisted, ready to sail for the stars . . ." He swept his hand in an arc in front of him, showcasing the imaginary vista. He looked over at her and smiled.

"Damn," she said. "You're terrible at this."

"Feel free to correct me."

Rake pushed a strand of hair out of her face. "Well, she was a *single* child from the *Outer* Core. Came from a shit planet, with shitty parents, and even shittier relatives who begrudgingly took her in after the shitty parents died."

Cavalon frowned. Well, fuck. He really had been wrong.

"Outer Core, huh?" he said. "Whereabouts?"

"Unlikely you've heard of it."

"Probably have, honestly. It was a key feature of my princely training to learn about all the places outside SC jurisdiction we might be able to exploit."

"You'd have to fight the Saxtons for it. Seneca-IV."

"Void, that shithole?" A wave of heat flooded his face. "I mean . . . no offense . . ."

She gave a firm shake of her head. "None taken. I stopped claiming any association with it long ago."

"The Saxtons run a tidy little mining outfit outta there, right?"

"If you want to call forced labor a 'tidy little outfit,' then yeah."

Shit. Warmth crept into his neck and ears, and he scratched at the stubble on his jawline. There he went again, with his sociopathic tendencies. "Sorry, sir," he said quickly, "I, uh, I didn't mean to make light of it. I really do realize how bad things are in the Outer Core."

"It's fine."

He cleared his throat, considering what to make of her lack of outward emotion. "So, uh, if she was all the way out in Seneca, how'd she end up a legionnaire?"

"The Legion was the only way off-world, so when she was sixteen, she ran away and enlisted."

Cavalon gaped, then stumbled, almost tripping over his own

feet. She was *sixteen* when she enlisted? That meant she'd been with the Legion half her life.

"Uh, how'd she join so young?" he asked, taking a few quick steps to catch back up.

"She told them she was eighteen." She gave a small shrug. "The recruitment officer didn't really believe her, but . . . he probably felt bad for her."

"Bad for her? Why?"

"Kid shows up looking like that?" Her brow furrowed. "Asking just to push a mop or spit-shine your boots, so long as it's anywhere but there. Took some begging, but it wasn't hard to convince him."

Cavalon waggled his eyebrows. "Oh, she used her feminine wiles?"

There was that "if looks could kill" glare again. Cavalon gulped.

"Don't be disgusting," she chided.

"Sorry . . ." he said, rubbing the back of his neck. And he really was. For whatever reason, she'd decided to be candid with him. He hadn't meant to derail it with one of his asinine comments. His worry eased with a twinge of relief as she continued of her own accord.

"She didn't *want* to exploit his sympathy," she explained, eyes flickering to the floor. She almost sounded ashamed. Like the only improper thing she'd ever done in her life had been to schmooze this guy into lying on her intake paperwork.

Yet Cavalon had to smile at the mental image—a doe-eyed young Rake with grease-smeared cheeks, batting her eyelashes at some gruff, no-nonsense Legion recruiter.

"But she had to," Rake continued. "It'd been too hard for too long. Enough was enough."

Cavalon's amusement faded and he swallowed, not entirely sure what to say. Part of him wanted to know every grimy detail. But he also really, really didn't. The thought of Rake subdued to the point where the best option had been to join the Legion at a time when they were on the cusp of all-out war . . . He couldn't begin to imagine it, and he didn't want to.

He cleared his throat. "So, even after they got you—*her* . . . off-world, she stuck with it? All those years?"

"At first, it was a means to an end." She gave a small shrug. "But she stayed because it was structured and safe and . . . really, the only thing that ever made sense."

Cavalon's amped-up zest dwindled along with a realization. This blind faith of hers wasn't at all what he'd assumed. It didn't come from some regimented upbringing where everything began and ended with the Legion. She wasn't a mindless soldier-drone born and bred to serve. The Legion had taken her in and raised her. Rescued her. Maybe even saved her life. It was far worse than he'd thought.

He had to wonder if she'd ever be able to accept what had already become painfully clear to everyone but her—the Legion was wholly unconcerned with the likes of the Sentinels.

They walked in silence for a few minutes, eventually crossing into a familiar area—the corridor that ran along the outside of the starboard air locks. Cavalon barely recognized it under the wash of white overheads instead of the grim, red emergency lighting of his last visit.

He paused outside the sealed-off secondary air lock to S6 and peeked through the small observation window. Inside, a handful of Drudger corpses floated aimlessly, their ashen skin now an icy blue-gray.

Rake retreated a few steps and peered in as well. "Guess it got the air lock sealed in time. We could have docked this side after all."

Cavalon nodded as he watched the bodies float—five of which had been killed in the fight, and at least another three or four that'd been sucked out before the gate's emergency systems kicked in and sealed the air lock off.

"It's still a ways farther," Rake said, continuing down the corridor. "Better keep at it."

Cavalon followed her into a maze of shorter, dimly lit hallways. At least ten minutes passed as they walked, and Cavalon wished he had one of those Legion-issue nexus bands just so he'd have a vague notion of the relative time of day. Yet another aspect of life in space he'd have to get used to. If they survived long enough for it to matter.

Finally, they turned into a dead-end hallway with a closed door on either side. Rake swept her hand across one of the keypads, but it flashed red and gave a negative beep.

She opened the comms interface on her nexus. "Jackin, it's Rake."

"Go for Jack."

"It's locked. Can you let us in?"

He responded after a brief pause. "Puck's on it. Remember, boss, comms will be off-line during the reboot, and mainframe systems will be down temporarily as well. They'll spool back up on their own one at a time, but we'll be dark for a little while."

"Understood." Rake shouldered her rifle. Cavalon fumbled with his strap, then did the same. Without even sparing him a glance, Rake added evenly, "Finger off the trigger, please."

He frowned, then carefully laid his finger on the side of the trigger guard. "Sorry, sir." It'd be just perfect if he stumbled and shot the EX in the back. That'd get him spaced for sure.

Moments later, the screen flashed green and the door slid open. Rake stepped inside, swinging her aim to clear the corners of the hot, cramped server room.

She slung her rifle, then called Jackin back. He walked her through the steps to reboot the communications systems and the mainframe, which—once Puck had hacked the system to give them clearance without a biometric scan—equated to throwing a couple of large levers, waiting a few minutes, then flipping them back on. When the screen beside the mainframe barrack indicated the commencement of a successful reboot, they started their trek back to the other side of the massive vessel.

As they reentered the maze of hallways that'd led them to the starboard air lock, Cavalon found he still itched with unused potential, and he suddenly wished Mesa had cooled it a bit on the dose of epithesium. He was ready to crawl out of his skin.

"I have a follow-up question," Rake announced as they rounded a corner. "About the boy."

Cavalon's eyes widened. A *follow-up* question? That, he had not seen coming. He cleared his throat and tried to act casual. "Go ahead."

"Why did he care?" she asked, tone fervent yet perplexed. "About the shithead building the Guardians? They were meant to replace Legion soldiers, but what repercussions did that have for the boy?"

"It wasn't about him."

"What was it about, then?"

Cavalon let out a long breath. "Well, two points. One—replacing Legion soldiers with mindless clones might seem all nice and humanitarian on the outside. But it means one very bad thing."

"Which is?"

"Well, so . . . your troops are like robots, right? Fleshy and meaty, sure, but ones you can control. They may have protocols to act their rank autonomously, but that's all just for show. They're all the same, and you can control their every move, if you want. So the *real* power would lie in only one place. With whoever's sitting at the controls."

"The man who made them," Rake confirmed.

"Right."

"So Augustus Mercer has control over the clones, and thus control over the Legion."

Cavalon nodded. "And thus control over the SC."

Sweat beaded under his collar as they turned a corner into a warmer corridor.

Rake pushed her sleeves up to her elbows. "Okay, and the second point?"

"Let's just say . . . the elder Mercer's interest in genetic engineering doesn't stop with creating fodder for wars."

"How so?"

"Well," he said, scratching his chin. "How caught up are you on Mercer family history, Viator War-era edition?"

She blew out a long breath. "The basics, I guess. What we learned in school. Renowned geneticists and genetic engineers who helped stop the virility mutagen from spreading, then reverse engineered it to turn it against the Viators. Some think that was the real tide of the war, that we'd never have been able to win without it."

"Right. So, Augustus takes that legacy very, very seriously, and as a result has some, uh, interesting opinions about genetics."

"Like what?"

"He thinks the Viator War was an *opportunity*. A chance for mankind to start fresh, a way to sculpt the human population into something . . . unpolluted, clean. Weed out the weak and ineffectual."

"Eugenics."

He nodded, readjusting the strap of his rifle as it dug into the side of his neck. "A thousand-year war with billions of deaths gives us a much smaller crop to choose from. In theory, some of the stronger and smarter folks survived. He thinks we need to take the chance to be more selective. Breed a stronger, healthier species."

"But what about the mutagen?" she asked. "Some of the mutations have taken generations to surface. That's not much of a clean start."

"Exactly. That's the whole problem. He has a relentless, obsessive need to correct it all. To thin every single genetic defect from the population, whether residual from the Viator War, or just natural—even things that aren't technically defects, just things he doesn't like."

Rake rubbed the nape of her neck, shaking her head. "Admittedly not great. But what's that have to do with cloning Drudgers?"

"I'd say for now, it's about trust. The Mercer family supplies the SC with replacements for their Legion soldiers, and they get to send thousands and eventually millions of *human* daughters and sons and husbands and wives home alive and well. That puts him in a pretty good light in the eye of the general public."

She shook her head. "Sure, except the general public's not going to love the idea of using clones—Drudger or otherwise."

"Five, ten years ago, I'd have said the same thing. But Augustus has been hard at work on that too. The Legion continues to push even peaceful Drudger clans farther into the outer sectors, while any anthropologists or scholars applying for visas to go study their cultures are summarily rejected."

Rake pinched the bridge of her nose and gave a weary sigh. "They're dehumanizing them."

"Exactly. We clone animals all the time, no one gives a shit. If Drudgers are considered nothing more than simple creatures, Augustus will get far less backlash. Then the benefits will easily outweigh any residual distaste for cloning."

"All right, point taken. So he's got the people's trust, he builds his clones, then what?"

"Then he can gain clout for his platform of using that same tech to perfect mankind. Along with a series of intense breeding laws, of course. It probably involves some kind of mass murder he'll call *'a horrific accident'* or some shit. It's just one piece of a massive, probably homicidal puzzle. It's always a longer game with him."

She scoffed. "The Quorum would never go for any of that."

He chewed his lip and didn't respond at first. She apparently had about as much misplaced faith in mankind's elected officials as she did the Legion. Why did he have to be the one to break it to her?

"A lot's changed since the war," he began carefully. "The Quorum's more firmly under the thumb of the Allied Monarchies board than ever, and you already know who has control over the board."

"But genetic cleansing?" she said, tone incredulous. Unease stiffened her expression as she pulled her hair from its tie, the elastic snap loud against her wrist in the lingering quiet of the empty corridor. "It's one thing to keep the royals all interbreeding, but how could you possibly implement that across the Core? Never mind the outer colonies? It's too much."

"Not when you have a mind-controlled army at your disposal to ensure compliance."

Rake aggressively retied her hair while cutting a hard left into the brightly lit starboard air-lock corridor. Cavalon hurried to catch up.

"If the clones are meant to deputize soldiers," she said, her tone stiff and flat, as if reciting an official statement, "that means the Guardians are part of the Legion. To use them to administer planetside law enforcement, he'd need martial law."

"Then he'll find a way to get it," Cavalon said. "It wouldn't be the first time he masked one conflict with another."

"What?"

"You remember the labor strikes in the Bennius system? Or the riots on Chiran-III?"

Rake kept her brisk pace but threw a discerning look at him, edged with measured curiosity. "No . . ."

"Exactly. Augustus did his usual housekeeping. It wasn't systemic discrimination, it was *'safeguarding our future.'* Not a civil uprising, but *'an organized terrorist plot.'* Eventually those kind of cover-ups weren't cutting it, and they would have done anything to stop it—not excluding conveniently happening upon a Viator fleet."

Rake shot him an incredulous look. "Conveniently?"

"A distraction. One that worked, I might add."

Cavalon almost ran squarely into Rake's back as she stopped dead in her tracks.

"What—?" he began, but cut short when Rake clamped a hand over his mouth. She held a finger to her lips and stared down the air-lock-lined corridor. The floor rumbled along with a hiss of air.

Hand still over his mouth, Rake pulled him into a narrow alcove across the hall, jammed beside a vertical support beam. His stomach turned with a wave of nausea, the silence around them oppressive.

Then came the short blare of an air-lock siren, a hiss of air pressurizing, the sound of a door sliding open, and a shuffle of trundling footsteps, followed by the half-witted grunts of a half dozen Drudgers.

CHAPTER TWENTY-TWO

Cavalon clamped his eyes shut—as if eliminating his sense of sight would somehow make him quieter or still his pounding heart. Rake's hand fell away from his face, and he found the nerve to open his eyes, mostly to confirm she hadn't abandoned him.

Rake still stood mere centimeters away. Her fingers flashed across her nexus, and the comms interface showed a red warning symbol. The mainframe hadn't fully rebooted. They couldn't call Jackin and the others.

Rake looked at him, her warm eyes serious, breath slow and controlled and deadly quiet. She appeared the exact opposite of how he felt. How was she not in a total panic? It had to take a special kind of temerity to stand there, a meter from at least a half dozen armed Drudgers, shoved in an alcove with a man who'd never fired a gun in his life, and maintain that degree of composure. It was honestly unsettling.

Rake kept her eyes locked on his, then raised one finger to her lips and waited.

Shut up. He could do that. He gave a short nod.

She curled her fingers into a fist.

Stay put. He gave another short nod.

Rake shouldered her rifle, then slid out of the alcove. After a frenzied squeak of boots on metal, a barrage of gunfire erupted— the sharp, chalky twangs of a plasma rifle. He really hoped *Rake's* plasma rifle.

Mere seconds later, the bombardment ceased, punctuated by a meaty thunk, then the heavy galumph of a body falling lifelessly to the floor. Then silence.

An odd sense of calm washed over him. If Rake had lived, then he was safe. But if Rake had died, then he was dead too, and it'd all be over. And that sounded easy, and peaceful, and would sort of be okay.

A fist reached in and grabbed him by the front of his vest, pulling him out of the alcove. Rake stared him down, rifle slung over her shoulder and her knife—*bloody* knife—in the other hand. He glanced past her, gaze flitting from corpse to corpse as he tallied the body count. Four—no, five. Five Drudgers. One Rake.

"Probably a scouting party," she explained, voice hushed. "They'll send more once these don't report back. Do you think you can find your way back to Jackin?"

Cavalon's reluctant nod took a hard turn and circled into a fervent shake of his head. "No. No. I have no idea how we got here."

She didn't seem to register his admission. "The mainframe is still rebooting. Jackin may not even know it's docked."

"Yeah," Cavalon said, eyes wide, nodding emphatically. "That was some *great* timing on our part."

"Oculus," Rake said, voice sharp. "You need to go back and warn them."

"Yeah, let's do that," Cavalon agreed. "Let's get backup."

She shook her head. "They're over a half hour away round trip. I can't let the Drudgers get a foothold on this side of the gate just to wait for a few more guns. They have double our numbers and this place is a maze. They'd be able to overwhelm us easily."

Cavalon's mouth gaped open as he processed what she meant. She wanted *him* to get backup. She had no intention of joining him.

"But, wait," he sputtered. "What are *you* gonna do?"

"I'm going in."

"No way," he said, then, somehow, he found himself adding, "I'm not leaving you here alone."

Rake's eyes sharpened. "I'm sorry, did that sound like anything other than an order?"

She was right, it had sounded suspiciously like an order. But then his stupid mouth opened again. "I *am* following orders," he said, voice wavering. He cleared his throat. "Optio North told me to go with you. Not to follow you until a ship of Drudgers showed up, then turn tail and run."

"You're not running; you're getting backup."

"Backup I'll probably never find my way to, and backup that, by your own admission, will come *too late*," he insisted.

"Fine. Stay here." She turned away and bent down to pluck the power cartridges from the pockets of one of the fallen Drudgers.

"Rake, wait," he said, surprised at his own adamancy. "I'm going—" He stopped himself, knowing he needed to choose his next words carefully. He was in no position to demand anything of her.

As if to reiterate that point, Rake stood slowly, then turned to face him even slower, staring at him with expectant challenge in her eyes, just waiting for him to say something stupid enough to justify punching him in the face.

He steadied his breath, thinking back to the fight in the air lock hours earlier—how together, he and Jackin held the gate, and together, the four of them cleared the air lock long enough to make their escape. It was the same dogma all the recruitment initiatives spouted, the same motto on all the propaganda posters from the Resurgence War. Staying together was what made them strong—a tenet the Legion as a whole had been doing a really shitty job of adhering to lately, at least when it came to the Sentinels. And he didn't ever want to be able to count himself among those who'd abandoned Rake.

He squared his shoulders, locking eyes with her. "Let me go with you."

Rake crossed her arms in utter, incredulous exasperation. "Seriously?"

"Seriously," he assured. "Shit-cutting, remember? But you gotta give me a chance."

Her glower wavered slightly, then she let out a brisk sigh. "Fine. If this is how you want to die, I'm not going to stop you."

"Your faith is touching."

"But if you want to stay, you need to fight," she insisted. "You can't be dead weight. I can't have to protect you."

"You won't have to." Bloody void, where'd he get the balls to say something like that? He shook his head. "Uh, but, just so you know, I've never shot a gun in my life."

She glanced down at his right arm, then met his gaze again. "Then don't use a gun."

Cavalon turned his arm over and the gold and bronze Imprint squares glinted as they caught the light.

"From the way you kicked ass in the mess the other day," she continued, "it seemed like you might have had at least a little combat training."

Cavalon took a moment to relish that morsel—Rake thought he'd *kicked ass*?

He composed himself and cleared his throat. "If bar fights count as combat training, then yes. I'm well-versed."

She tilted her head in contemplation. "So, you're scrappy. Like when you threw a door at the Drudgers earlier."

Scrappy. He could work with that. He shrugged. "Yeah, I guess."

"How about this: Try not to engage at all, just watch my back. If you get caught up in it, stay inside their guard so they can't shoot you. Use your knife if you have to, but use your Imprints for defense, first and foremost."

"What about . . ." He lowered his voice and leaned toward her. "Volatile interfacing?"

"So long as your Sentinel Imprints aren't activated at the same time, you'll be fine."

He frowned and gave her what he knew to be a sheepish, pathetic look.

"I *promise* not to activate them," she assured. "And the mainframe is still rebooting, so the controls won't work anyway." She scoffed. "Plus, why the fuck *would* I?"

"I don't know," he said. "If I do something stupid . . ."

"Well, *that's* guaranteed. But I still don't see the logic in taking down my only ally when it's two against fifty." She turned and looked at the pile of bodies behind her. "Forty-five, I guess. Maybe forty after the ones you guys killed."

Forty. Forty Drudgers. That's what he'd just agreed to. No, not agreed to—*insisted* on. What the hell was wrong with him?

"Hey, calm down," she said, gripping both his shoulders. "You're not off to a good start."

"I'm fine," he squeaked, eyes darting around. "What makes you think I'm not calm?"

Rake blew out a heavy breath and dropped her hands from his shoulders. "Okay, we don't have time to keep talking about it. You wanna do this or not?"

He nodded and tried to focus on the cool, refreshing epithesium coursing through his blood. Maybe that had been what'd turned him suicidal. Did an abundance of unfocused energy equate to blind, illogical courage? Could this even be called courage?

He mustered every ounce of nerve he had in an effort to steady his voice. To sound confident. To sound like he wasn't panicking about willingly putting himself in mortal danger. "Yes, sir."

Rake gave him one last assessment, her narrowed eyes sharp and serious. He was sure she was about to change her mind, insist he leave her, find his way back to Jackin and the others, and get some real, proper help.

But instead, she took a step toward him, lowering her voice to a growl. "You stay on my six."

He managed a single nod, his stomach doing that unsettling flop that sent warm tingles up his spine. "Yes, sir."

Rake unslung her rifle and headed down the hall toward the air lock where the Drudgers' ship had docked. Gun raised, she quickly swept the secondary air-lock door before crossing through the threshold. Her feet moved silently beneath her with unsettling deftness, and Cavalon felt like a lumbering oaf in comparison, boots shuffling loudly against the metal floor. Rake's movements were clean and methodical, aim focusing into each corner and crevice as they made their way through the redundant air locks. Cavalon found himself glued to her heel.

She glared back at him over her shoulder, then whispered, "I'm happy to be your human shield, but you really don't need to stand so close."

He gulped and nodded, letting her take a few steps ahead before following again.

They walked through the open hatch of the Drudgers' ship and into a dingy vestibule, which forked into two corridors leading to either side of the vessel. The stale air reeked of earthy Drudger musk, but there were no Drudgers in sight.

The bare bulbs cast the area in dim but harsh light, throwing the corners into deep shadows that made Cavalon's skin crawl. Rake didn't seem disturbed, likely instantly dismissing their threat due to the fact that they weren't large enough for anything to hide in, or that Drudgers simply weren't patient—or smart—enough to hide in them. He supposed the one easy thing about fighting Drudgers was their brash impetuousness. They'd charge toward you headfirst without a second thought, or even a care for their own well-being. Strategy or deftness didn't play into it, so you always knew what to expect.

After Rake cleared the entrance, she breezed past Cavalon to head to the other side of the room. She didn't appear keen to partake in the Drudgers' head-on approach, because instead of moving down one of the two hallways, she motioned for him to follow as she crouched in front of a large grate in the wall.

She pulled the cover loose, then set it aside and crawled in. He shuffled forward and crouched, heading in after her. The vent allowed barely enough room for him to crawl on his hands and knees. After a few meters, they stopped in front of another grate. Rake leaned in, first peering through, then turning her ear to press against it. Cavalon could barely make out a few grunts and shuffling noises.

Rake looked back at him, her closed fist signaling him to hold. She spun around, then tucked her legs to her chest and in one quick motion, punted the metal with both feet. It flew off and into the room beyond. So much for subtlety.

Rake launched herself into the room, and Cavalon peered out far enough to watch in stunned silence as she, by every definition of the word, *perfectly* executed six Drudgers.

The one she'd kicked the vent cover into died first, via a plasma bolt to the head even as it flew back against the wall from the force of the grate. She simultaneously stabbed another Drudger in the flank. How her knife had ended up in her hand, he didn't even know.

She turned that motion into a sweeping kick, knocking a Drudger to the ground at her feet. The knife slid directly from the flank of the other Drudger into the chest of the prone one, just as Rake's rifle swung up in her other hand. She fired off two shots to the far right—past Cavalon's field of vision, though he could hear grunts and the sounds of bodies collapsing.

Rake yanked the knife out of one torso and turned into another as it charged from the left side of the room. She'd apparently received the same anatomical training as Mesa, because all the Drudgers that met her knife died instantly.

The alarmingly impressive affair lasted all of ten seconds. If this was her "rusty," after five years of idleness aboard the *Argus*, he couldn't imagine what she'd been capable of during the war.

Rake stood among the six dead Drudgers, hardly winded. Every bare patch of skin on her neck and arms glittered with silver and copper Imprint squares—so many more than he'd seen in their default layout on her right arm before. They receded into their standard formation, the hundreds that had flowed into her arms and neck disappearing beneath her shirt.

He had to wonder where she kept them all. She must have way, *way* more Imprints than he did.

Cavalon pulled himself out of the dusty ventilation shaft and into the room. A series of stiff-looking, hard-backed couches lined the walls. Food wrappers, piles of discharged energy cells and power cartridges, and other garbage littered the floor.

He wiped his dusty hands off on his chest. "Well," he began, but realized he had no words for what had just happened. Rake tossed her rifle to the ground, then picked up one of the Drudgers' beefy plasma pistols. She checked the cartridge, seemed satisfied, then stuck the gun in the strap of her weapons belt.

Cavalon's eyes lingered on the splayed body of a nearby Drudger. "All this subterfuge is fun, but why don't we just rig the engines to blow and call it a day?"

Rake sighed and shook her head as she pulled her knife from the chest of the last Drudger she'd killed.

"I can arrange that for you, you know," he said.

"I'm sure you can. But even if that wouldn't put a massive fucking hole in this side of the station, we need this ship. It's our only shot at getting through this gate in one piece."

"Oh . . . right." He scratched the back of his neck. Relay gates, much like jump drives, required a certain mass—a stability threshold of sorts—in order for the ship to arrive at its destination in one, unmangled piece. He'd completely forgotten. Or rather, thinking that far ahead never even crossed his mind.

But what worried him more was the look Rake now regarded him with as she cleaned off the blade of her knife: discerning and a bit . . . concerned.

He couldn't blame her. He wasn't sure how to feel about the two apparent faces of his battle instincts: turn and run the fuck away as he'd wanted to the first time the Drudgers boarded, or now, to just blanket it all with wanton destruction.

Throat tight, he plastered on a smile. "A long-term plan. That's good thinking. Guess that's why you're the boss."

"Leave your rifle," she instructed. "It'll be too narrow."

He wanted to ask *what's* too narrow, but instead, he fumbled his rifle off his back and set it aside, then confirmed his own plasma pistol and the heavy combat knife still rested in the weapons belt on his hip.

Rake marched over to one of the couches. Her Imprints flickered as she easily pushed it aside. She knelt, ripped a black panel off the floor, then swung her legs down into the opening and disappeared.

Cavalon scurried across the room, following Rake into the dark.

CHAPTER TWENTY-THREE

Cavalon shouldered through the narrow shaft after Rake. She apparently knew the layout of this ship very well. He supposed memorizing the design of enemy vessels would have been part of her training. Infiltration, covert ops, advanced weapons—all the crap that made a Titan a thousand times scarier than an average soldier.

Rake's boots—or what he could see of them in the practically nonexistent light—suddenly stopped, then disappeared *upward*. By the time Cavalon shimmied forward and craned his neck to look up, she'd already cleared the vertical shaft. She looked down over the edge at him from five meters up, loose strands of hair swinging in her face.

He gaped at her. How in the void did she expect him to get up there?

"Use your Imprints," she whispered. He just stared dumbly back at her, and she added, "For *grip*."

"I don't think mine work like that," he mumbled. He turned over, looking up into the dark vent toward Rake's annoyed grimace.

"Should I have brought the winch?" she asked. It took his brain a couple of seconds to register the dry snark in her tone. He scowled, but said nothing.

He summoned his Imprints and they rushed down his arms and into his hands, coating his palms and fingers with gold and bronze squares. He reached up and pawed at the vent, but his hands slid right over it, slick like metal on metal.

"See?" he hissed.

"You have to *think* about it," she insisted. "Imagine you just, I don't know, stuck your hands in a vat of glue. That's something you'd do."

He rolled his eyes, but couldn't precisely disagree. Seeing no other way out of this than to listen or get left behind, he decided to try her advice. He imagined his hands were sticky, willed them to adhere, *believed* them to be grippy enough to claw his way five meters up a metal tunnel.

When he ran his hand over the metal again, to his total shock, his fingers gave a dull squeak and caught immediately. He gaped at them, then stuck his fingers to the bare skin on his cheek. The Imprints had taken on a dense, tacky quality. They pulled painfully at the stubble on his jaw as he dragged his fingers over his skin.

"Ow," he grumbled.

Rake sighed.

He turned his arms over in wonder, staring at the Imprints he'd clearly been using wrong the last nine years. He could have gotten up to *so much more* shit if he'd known that trick. He wondered what else Rake knew about them that he didn't.

"Come on, Mercer," Rake prompted. "These Drudgers aren't going to kill themselves."

He shook off his awe and set aside the catalog of questions he planned to interrogate Rake with once they weren't skulking through the bowels of an enemy ship.

Cavalon reached up and pressed his hands to either side of the duct and secured a firm grip. With a grunt, he pulled, but couldn't squeeze through. He told himself to *think small*, then forced the air out of his lungs and tucked his shoulders forward to make himself as narrow as possible. He huffed as he pulled, then managed to barely wedge his torso into the duct.

"Void . . ." Rake grumbled.

"Come on," he breathed, "cut me a break. I have broader shoulders—*man* shoulders."

"Stop talking," she whispered. "Your oafish grunts are loud enough."

He let out a series of *quiet*, sharp breaths as he squirmed into a standing position, then began to palm his way up the passage. He gained tenuous footholds at the seams of the ductwork, and his knuckles went white as he pressed into the vent as hard as he could without actually punching a hole through the metal.

He awkwardly climbed for a few grueling minutes, then a glittering silver and copper hand appeared, dangling beside his face. He braced his feet, then let go with one hand and gripped Rake's forearm. With consummate ease, she hauled him up over the ledge into a much larger vent shaft. And much cooler. Cavalon sat back and exhaled with relief, while the muscles of his arms and legs burned from his Imprint-assisted climb.

He got the impression they were now on the second deck of the ship, possibly even higher. The wall at one end featured a meter-wide grate backed by a series of thin, wide slats—some kind of bladeless fan system. A mess of tangled wires wove into a metal trellis behind it, all coated in thick dust. Hazy, thin light peeked through the slats.

Rake silently crawled toward the large fan and Cavalon followed. While she inspected the contraption, he carefully peered through the slats to look into the room beyond. Or below, as the case happened to be. The vent exited about three meters above the height of the floor, looking down on a spacious room.

A mini command center consisting of three terminals lined one wall, with a mismatch of tables and chairs scattered in the center of the room. A putrid approximation of a kitchen took up another wall—filthy dishes and food waste strewn about on the counters and overflowing from the sink and garbage chute.

Two Drudgers sat across from each other at a table, gnawing on crumbling food bricks. A third snoozed on a couch below the grate.

Rake caught Cavalon's eye and jerked her head back, motioning for him to follow. They crawled back a ways, then she whispered, "Those bolts are reinforced, and there's a few dozen. I'll need your help kicking out this grate."

His back straightened. "Okay."

"But stay up here until I'm done," she warned. "I can't get a good visual, so I'm not sure how many are down there. Don't follow me into the room until it's over."

"Got it, sir."

She slid the commandeered plasma pistol from the back of her belt to the front, then crawled toward the grate. He followed, mirroring her position as she leaned back on her elbows, feet lifted. His Imprints moved into his legs, and her silver and copper squares appeared to do the same, disappearing under her shirt.

Cavalon reserved a handful of his Imprints for his forearms, and willed them to take on the same tacky quality to help keep himself in place. He nodded at Rake. She silently counted, and on three, they drove their heels hard into the grate.

Rake slid away before Cavalon even realized they'd succeeded. She disappeared off the edge into a storm of white dust. A clang of metal rang out as the grate hit the ground, accompanied by a chorus of shocked Drudger yelps.

Cavalon coughed as he scrambled forward to make sure she'd landed okay. But the thick coating of dust sent him gliding over the slick metal just a *little* too far—right off the edge after her.

His Imprints cushioned the fall, but a shock of pain still coursed through his right side as he hit the ground hard. Rake had already gotten to her feet—or maybe she'd landed that way—dust raining down on her as she sliced the throat of the napping Drudger. The stunned Drudgers at the table were still clamoring to their feet as she rushed toward them. She simultaneously stabbed one and shot the other. Two more Drudgers appeared in an open doorway at the back of the room and she moved to intercept.

As Cavalon picked himself up, another Drudger came from an alcove to his right, behind Rake's field of view. His heart slammed against his chest as it stared across the room, distracted by Rake executing all its friends and seemingly unaware of the idiot lingering helplessly just two meters away.

Now, Cavalon supposed, would be exactly the time to prove he wasn't dead weight.

He fumbled his pistol from its holster, aimed it straight at the Drudger's wrinkly forehead, and pulled the trigger.

And literally nothing happened.

"Shit," he hissed, but he had no time to troubleshoot as the Drudger started for Rake.

"*Scrappy,*" she'd said. He might as well own it.

So he chucked the gun as hard as he could at the Drudger's head. It had the decency of looking briefly stunned—though more likely by the inanity of the action than anything—stopping in its tracks as the gun bounced pointlessly off its forehead.

With as much Imprint-infused, epithesium-fueled rage as he could muster, Cavalon charged the Drudger and slammed it into the wall. "*Stay within their guard,*" Rake had said. Check.

He grappled with the disgusting thing, pinning its neck to the wall with his forearm. He coughed and tried not to choke on a lungful of putrid Drudger stench. Summoning his Imprints, he pressed harder to keep the Drudger against the wall with one hand as he fumbled his knife out of its sheath with the other.

Clamping a sweaty hand around the hilt, he recalled Mesa's advice: "*Sixth and seventh rib. Apply a great deal of thrust.*" He took aim, his mouth burning with the taste of copper, and stabbed it into the Drudger's side, praying he didn't miss.

But he missed, he definitely missed.

Pain shot up his arm as the blade hit directly into one of the hard, glinting metallic exoskeletal plates. The knife twisted, skimming a layer of thick, gray skin off the plating, before wrenching from his grip and clattering to the ground.

"Bloody void—" Cavalon hissed.

The Drudger took advantage of the distraction and threw Cavalon to the floor, then leapt after him. His Imprints flew into his torso, and he barely rolled away in time as the creature pounded its fists into the ground where he'd just been.

He scrambled to his knees and grabbed the legs of a nearby chair and swung. The light metal crumpled against the Drudger's chest, and it collapsed into the wall. Cavalon crawled forward and straddled it before it could regain its senses. His Imprints rushed to his thighs and a few sped to his arm as he pinned the Drudger's wrists with one hand. He grabbed the knife. *"Pointy end to the face."*

However, even as the gross creature snarled and snapped at him, its large blue eyes full of hate and willing to kill him the second it got the chance, Cavalon knew he couldn't do it. Those were Savant eyes—*human* eyes. Killing it was one thing. Stabbing it brutally in the face beforehand? That was something else.

So he mustered himself and took aim at the chest again—he hoped better aim—then stabbed with all his strength.

This time, the blade found purchase, slicing between the carapace plates, sliding between the ribs, and lodging deep into the Drudger's chest. It let out a guttural groan and its body shuddered, hacking up a splutter of crimson blood that sprayed across Cavalon's chest. Moments later, its eyes rolled back into its head, and its muscles slackened as the life left it completely.

Unmoving, Cavalon stared at the corpse under him. His sweat-slicked fingers shook as he released his grip from the hilt of the knife. He thought about removing it—he might need it again. But he couldn't, right at the moment, so he left it buried in the dead Drudger's chest.

He only then realized the fight might not be over. He turned quickly to look for more adversaries, but the room had gone still and silent.

Rake watched him steadily, standing among her pile of bodies. Seven, at least. Even she looked a little spent, a few wisps of hair stuck to the sweat beading on her forehead, olive-skinned cheeks flushed with exertion.

"You okay?" she asked.

Cavalon stood, knees wobbling beneath him. He wanted to spit out the overwhelming metallic taste, but his lips and mouth had gone dry. He ran his hands over his chest and willed his senses to function again—to tell him if he'd sustained any injuries. Other than exhaustion and his frantic, rapid breaths, he seemed to be functioning normally.

"Fine," he managed. "Yes . . . fine."

She looked down at the body at his feet, then back up at him. "You sure?"

His gaze floated to the ground, and he clenched his jaw. She didn't mean *physically* okay.

He stared at the spattering of crimson staining the backs of his hands. He never saw himself as a particularly sheltered person. But there was something uniquely disturbing about watching the life dissolve out of something while its hot blood spilled onto you until it became silent and unmoving and gone forever . . . Even if it was only a Drudger.

The boy wasn't supposed to be a killer.

He had to ask himself—why were they doing this again? In anticipation that the Drudgers would have done the same to them, in a heartbeat. And they would have. Under no provocation, they'd have killed the Sentinels, simply to take whatever meager supplies they had, or so they could declare themselves the victors, or whatever.

But the Drudgers would have lost. If the Sentinels' single most useful fighter and single most *useless* fighter could take so many of them out, then the entirety of the group would have been just fine. So he told himself they'd have died either way. Because they would have.

"It's only a Drudger," he said, trying to sound like he believed himself, but his voice came out weak.

"It doesn't matter. Taking a life is never easy." She gripped his shoulder, face creasing into a concerned grimace. "I shouldn't have let you come."

"I'm fine," he said, surprised by the hardness in his tone. "Really. Let's keep going."

She assessed him cautiously, then nodded. "Let's find out where the rest are."

She crossed to the bank of terminals against the opposite wall. Cavalon followed and stood over her shoulder as she brought up the scanners. Three blips showed on the holographic overhead of the ship—all located in what appeared to be the cockpit.

"Only three?" he asked.

She shook her head. "There should be fifteen or twenty more, at least."

"Maybe Jackin's scan was off?"

"By almost half?"

"They were gone for a few hours—maybe they dropped a few off somewhere else," he suggested.

"Dropped them off where?" she asked, but it was rhetorical. Obviously Cavalon had no idea, and she didn't either.

Rake dismissed the menu, then stepped over to the Drudger Cavalon had killed. His stomach fluttered as she yanked his knife from its chest.

She swept the flat of the blade across her pant leg, wiping the blood clean, then handed it back to him, hilt-first. "Ready?"

He hesitated, then sucked in a breath. He took the knife and re-sheathed it. "Yes, sir."

CHAPTER TWENTY-FOUR

To Cavalon's surprise, instead of slipping into another vent system, Rake simply strode into the hallway. They'd been so stealthy up to this point, it felt odd to just waltz out into the open, but he tentatively followed. He didn't have to worry for long, when a couple of meters down, Rake stopped at another vent, similar in size and structure to the first. She pulled off the grate and climbed through, and Cavalon trailed after.

A minute later, they came to a dead end capped by another grate, hard light streaming in from the other side. Rake paused, holding a finger to her lips. As if she had to remind him to be quiet just in case he'd forgotten he was in mortal danger.

She pointed to the grate and scooted to one side. He shimmied his way next to her, peering through the narrow slats into the cockpit. He squinted as his eyes adjusted to the relative brightness of the room beyond.

A single Drudger stood between the pilot and copilot's chairs, watching a video message play back over the ship's main console. The holographic screen cast a blue glint against its steel-gray skin—it was older than most of the others Rake had killed. That *they'd* killed.

Unlike the others had, it wore a relatively clean Viator-issue uniform, with badges of rank pinned carelessly to the shoulders. Though Drudgers didn't bother much with rank distinctions, he assumed this one must be the ship's captain.

The Drudger in the recording gargled something Cavalon couldn't understand, and the message ended. The captain dismissed the video interface and stepped aside, revealing a display of brilliantly bright, crisp white holographic screens. They looked nothing like the dim, muddy displays lined up over the cockpit terminal.

Cavalon craned his neck to catch a glimpse of the source of the screens—a polished gold pyramid about thirty centimeters wide, sitting on the terminal counter.

The displays were shaped like nothing Cavalon had ever seen—curved, equilateral triangles with the edges bulging out. Dozens layered atop one another, stacked and linked in a pattern not dissimilar to the scaled walls of the Apollo Gate corridors. The Drudger's body and the pilot's chair obscured much of the view, but from the various overlaid grids, he thought it might be some kind of structural blueprint, like a large, multileveled building or starship.

Cavalon quirked an eyebrow at Rake, and she returned it with a clueless shrug. The Drudger captain grumbled something to itself, reached down, and the strange displays disappeared. It shoved the pyramid aside, then swept open a menu from the cockpit terminal.

Out of sight on the far right of the room, another Drudger muttered a series of unintelligible words. The Drudger captain grunted a terse response, then the other started a long-winded reply.

Rake must have been able to understand the thick dialect, because she turned to look at Cavalon with raised eyebrows, as if to say "that's our cue," then thrust her palm into the grate. It shot halfway across the room and clattered into the pilot's chair. Rake pulled herself free and fired her plasma pistol twice to the right side of the cockpit.

Cavalon leaned out to find two additional Drudgers on that side of the room, now very dead. The captain managed to claw one of its taloned fingers down Rake's arm as she grabbed it by the front of its jumpsuit.

She threw the captain to the ground face-first, twisting one of its arms around and pressing a knee into the small of its back to pin it to the floor. She flipped her grip on the knife and held the serrated blade to the side of the Drudger's throat. It roared and spat, but she held firm, the silver and copper squares on her arms jittering. She didn't even spare a glance at the jagged slice it had carved down the side of her arm. Blood flowed to her wrist and across her knuckles, dripping onto the Drudger's back at a troubling rate.

"What are you doing out here?" Rake barked. She leaned into the Drudger's back and it groaned in pain, but didn't answer. Rake slid the blade closer to its neck.

A sparse formation of Imprint tattoos slid up from under the captain's collar, the glossy white squares stark against its dark gray skin. The Imprints spread thin to try and protect its neck.

"Where's the rest of your crew?" Rake demanded.

It gave a guttural half laugh before spitting out a response Cavalon couldn't understand.

Rake untwisted its arm and pinned its wrist to the ground in front of its face, then stabbed the back of its hand with the knife, skewering it to the floor. A few of its white Imprints slid onto the top of its hand, but they were far too late. The Drudger roared and thrashed beneath her.

Rake growled. "This can be easy or hard, Drudger."

"Easy, easy, legionnaire," it pleaded in a horrific approximation of the human tongue, the obviously unfamiliar language gnarled on its lips. "I coop'rate."

Rake let out a gruff breath and yanked the knife free from its hand. In the microsecond she was off balance, the Drudger's Imprints surged. It twisted out from under her knee, throwing an elbow as it spun. She blocked it with her free arm while slicing the knife cleanly into its chest with the other. The captain spluttered a mouthful of blood, and its eyes rolled back as it fell limp.

"Fucking Drudgers . . ." Rake muttered under her breath and stood, sheathing her knife. She headed straight for the main terminal and began sliding through menus, blood dripping down her arm.

"Void, Rake." Cavalon pulled himself out of the duct and glanced around. The primary flight console sat flanked by two smaller, catchall terminals sitting behind the pilot and copilot chairs, facing each of the side walls. He went from station to station, scouring the filthy cockpit for something not disgusting to staunch her bleeding with.

"Cav, it's fine," Rake assured.

He glanced back. Her Imprints glided around the cut, and the flow of blood ceased as they sealed up the wound. Moments later, it scabbed over, like it'd been healing for days. Rake absentmindedly swabbed the excess blood off with the back of her hand, then wiped it on her pant leg while staring at the terminal.

"Don't you get tired?" Cavalon nodded at her Imprints as they receded from her wounded arm and reset themselves.

"Yes," she said simply, scratching at the fresh skin.

"I could *never* use mine as much as you have in the last half hour. I'd have dropped dead by now."

"You have to treat them like a muscle," she said, continuing to swipe through the screens. "Exercise them."

"Really?"

"The more you use them, the more your body gets used to it. You won't get tired as quickly."

"What kind of regimen are we talking?"

She glared. "Must we talk about this *right now*?"

"Okay, okay." He held up his hands in submission. "Sorry, sir."

Cavalon added that to the list of points to question her on later. Her eyes darted back to the display, and he walked over to the terminal. He picked up the strange golden pyramid the Drudger had been using. It was heavy for its size, and oddly warm. A series of etchings ran along each of the four facets in an uninterrupted, geometric design. He turned it over in his hands, running his fingers along the asymmetrical grooves, but could find no way to activate the display. He set it back down, then went to hover over Rake's shoulder.

"What are you doing?" he asked.

"Checking their logs to see where they've been."

"And?"

"And . . . nothing," she said, shaking her head. "They've traveled a good distance the last few days—stopped at a couple of random coordinates. Nowhere I recognize as being anywhere. But I'm mostly concerned about where they just came from, and where those other twenty Drudgers are."

"Is there even anywhere they could get to in only a couple of hours?"

"Other than the *Argus*, no. Their last trip put them literally on the edge of nowhere. Halfway between the *Argus* and the next buoy, but a few hundred thousand klicks inward. There's nothing there."

"Maybe it's a loot drop. You know—secret places they stash contraband between runs."

"Yeah . . ." She stared vacantly at the screen.

"We could watch that message it was playing," he suggested. "Maybe it'll give us a clue where the rest of them went."

She raised her eyebrows. "Good idea." Again, she seemed a bit too surprised for his liking.

Rake closed the ship's logs and opened the comms menu. Only one video message sat in the queue, and she swept it onto the larger viewscreen. She pressed play, and the recorded Drudger's image appeared. Its shadowed face glared from the screen as it spoke, its words strikingly crisp compared to the garbage-disposal version he'd just heard from the others.

He took a step closer and squinted at the video, because something else wasn't right. The lines of the Drudger's neck and face and shoulders were too sharp, too rigid. Its skin was a deep, charcoal black with a dull, matte finish—no glinting metallic shine. The eyes he'd thought had been in shadow were in fact pools of inky, empty black. And there were not two eyes, but four.

His breath caught. "Rake—"

She shushed him with a silent hand wave, staring at the screen, brow creased in contemplation. But not surprise. She seemed stern, if anything. Maybe worried.

Cavalon's heart beat hard and a feverish chill washed through him. It had to be a trick. Or some kind of mistake. Because if that

"Drudger" had *four black* eyes, then it was not a Drudger. And the alternative was impossible.

Rake pressed play, and the message looped. She watched it carefully, then played it a third time, and it froze on the end frame when it finished. She crossed her arms and didn't replay it again.

Cavalon stared at her. "You understand their language, don't you?"

She nodded slowly, not taking her eyes from the screen.

"What'd it say?"

He wasn't sure she intended to respond at first, but after a few long moments she answered quietly. "It said, 'First you must' . . . something." She mumbled a few incoherent syllables. "Restart, I think. Yeah, restart. 'First you must restart the station marked on the atlas.'"

"Restart the station?" he asked, voice thin. "Like the gate?"

"No, they have another word they use for the gates. *Arc'antile.* It said something more akin to . . . station or sector. Node, even."

"What else did it say?"

"Then it said, 'You have the . . . supplies,' I think. Or 'components,' maybe. Then, 'I'll forward the remainder of the instructions shortly.'"

"Instructions? Like, orders?"

Her expression tightened, lines furrowing her brow. Her gaze remained focused on the screen, deep in contemplation. "No, it was instructions," she assured. "There are different words for orders or demands. It meant . . . like, directions. Steps to follow."

"Either way, that sounds fucking nefarious."

"Yeah . . ."

Cavalon crossed his arms and stared at her. "You do not seem appropriately shocked."

"This message could be decades old. We don't know when it was recorded," she said, voice steady.

"Yeah we do!" He pointed to the timestamp in the corner of the screen—mere days ago.

Her lips twitched as she glared at the evidence. "Timestamps can be altered."

He scoffed. "Why would they bother to do that?"

She didn't respond, continuing to stare at the frozen frame of the vid message.

"How are you not freaking out?"

"Relax, Mercer," she said, voice suddenly harsh. "Not everyone jumps to the absolute worst case scenario and starts panicking."

"They do." His head rocked fervently, chin bobbing to his chest in an exaggerated nod. "They do about *Viators*. And what about that weird"—he flicked his fingers at the gold pyramid—"thing he was looking at? That looked like schematics, or a map. Is that the 'atlas' it mentioned?"

She let out a sharp breath through her nose. "This is not our concern."

"*What?*" He gaped, wide-eyed. He *literally* could not believe those words had just come out of her mouth.

Rake's eyes sharpened into an impatient glare. "I'm not sure if you've noticed, but we're in a bit of a life-and-death situation out here at the moment. We need to confirm all the Drudgers aboard Kharon have been eliminated, get the gate operational, and get everyone safely back to Legion HQ. And *that's it*."

"Really?" he said, unable to temper the incredulity in his tone. "We've got Drudgers at the Divide, armed with weird maps and instructions from real, live, breathing *Viators*? And it's not our concern? Isn't this your—" He stopped and took a deep breath, letting the panic in his voice subside. "Isn't this our whole point? As Sentinels? What if another round of Viators has come? From wherever they came to start with?"

She shook her head. "After thousands of years?"

"Well, they were all dead as of five years ago! You should know— the Resurgence? Paxus? That was all you."

Her jaw clenched, then she reached out and grabbed the strange pyramid-shaped device. "We'll take this back to Mesa and see what she thinks." She shoved it into his chest, lifting a finger to point at him, then narrowed her eyes. "But don't breathe a word of this to anyone."

He nodded fervently and a cool tingle of relief washed through him. She'd found a sliver of her sanity back, at least. "Yes, sir."

CHAPTER TWENTY-FIVE

Adequin stayed a few steps ahead of Cavalon as they marched their way back to the other side of the gate in silence. She turned the oddly warm artifact over in her hands, studying each of the four facets for some indication of how to activate its displays, but found nothing.

When they arrived at the port-side control room, Jackin stood hunched over his terminal, frantically typing in commands. Mesa and Puck hovered on either side of him, staring down at the screens in anxious anticipation. Puck's fingers twitched against the grip of his holstered pistol.

Adequin walked up behind them and cleared her throat.

Jackin jumped, turning to face her. "Void, Rake, where've you been?" He let out a sharp breath. "The mainframe just popped back up a second ago. A ship's docked starboard—"

"We know," Adequin said. "We took care of it."

Jackin looked her up and down, eyeing the blood splattered across her uniform. His gaze slid to Cavalon. "We?"

Cavalon frowned grumpily, but said nothing.

"Yes, we," Adequin said. "Puck?"

"Sir?"

"Get a team together to do a quick sweep of the Drudgers' ship. Confirm they've all been eliminated. There's twenty more somewhere; let's make sure they're not here. Then get the ship docked on this side and do a full search, including inventory. I want to know what they're up to."

"Copy, sir." Puck activated his nexus and began summoning other soldiers.

Jackin stared at the red scab running down Adequin's left arm. "What happened?"

She held up a finger, then turned to Mesa and passed her the pyramid. The Savant took it with a raised eyebrow. Adequin opened her mouth to explain, but got cut short by pretty much the last noise she ever expected to hear: a voice crackling over the gate's comms.

"Khar—this—is—"

Jackin froze, hands floating over the display. He gaped down at it in disbelief, like if he bumped it, he might lose the connection forever.

A tingling warmth radiated through Adequin's limbs. Rebooting the mainframe and comms had actually *worked?* This was a long-overdue miracle.

The voice returned moments later, still crackling and almost incomprehensible. "—Gate this—Legion Command Soter—"

Adequin stepped forward as Jackin carefully typed in a few slow commands, narrowing in on the signal. He backed away, then she sat and pressed the link. "This is Excubitor Adequin Rake with the SCS *Argus*, hailing from Kharon Gate."

"Copy, sir," a male voice responded. "Loud and clear. Sorry, sir, did you say the *Argus?*"

"Yes. Who am I speaking with?"

"Oculus Rio Murphy, sir," he said, his youthful voice wavering.

"Where are you, Murphy?" Adequin asked.

"The Drift Belt, sir. Soteria cluster, Poine Gate."

Adequin scooted closer to the edge of her chair. "Soldier, we were forced to evacuate our post aboard the SCS *Argus*, stationed at the Divide. We've regrouped at Kharon Gate, but it's been abandoned. Do you know what happened to the troops that should be stationed here?"

"Uh, sir, sorry, sir," Murphy said quickly. "But, uh, the SCL has withdrawn from the Divide, including Kharon Gate. Eris and Zelus too, and some others . . ."

Jackin scoffed. "Did they plan to tell *us* that?"

Adequin pressed the link again. "Oculus, are forces being summoned elsewhere?"

"No, sir."

"Then why are we withdrawing?"

"Sir, that information is Caesus Level Delta, sir."

"I have Alpha clearance."

"But I don't," he said. "I don't have that information, sir."

"Is there someone there who does? Where's your CO?"

"Off-site, sir. We're on skeleton crews here."

"And you know nothing about why we're withdrawing?"

"Well . . ." He cleared his throat and hesitated.

"Speak freely, soldier," she encouraged.

"Nothing official, but there's been talk. The withdrawal order came down right after the LPWA passed."

She glared at the comm link in confusion. She had no idea what that meant.

"Fucking goddamn—" A gruff voice began a tirade of exasperated cursing, and Adequin turned around to find Cavalon gripping his hair with both hands.

"Oculus . . ." she warned.

"Sorry," he said, releasing his head. He lowered his voice. "That's Augustus's doing."

"Explain."

"LPWA—Legion Personnel Welfare Act." He gritted his teeth. "The *Guardians*."

Jackin crossed his arms. "Excuse me?"

Adequin sighed. "They intend to start replacing Legion soldiers with cloned Drudgers."

Vaguely aware of a clamor of hushed voices rising up behind her, Adequin tried to stay focused on Jackin as his brow furrowed. "You're saying these Guardians are supposed to come replace the Sentinels?" he asked.

Cavalon shrugged. "Maybe, or at least to start. Probably some kind of trial run."

"But why pull us away before sending replacements?" Adequin asked.

Jackin scowled. "More importantly, why'd we never get a withdrawal order?"

Adequin turned back to the comms screen and pressed the link. "Murphy, we never received an order to withdraw."

"Sorry, sir. I can't speak as to why that—"

"Then give me someone that can," she snapped back. The why of it didn't matter, but this kid was useless. She needed someone with enough authority to give them some guidance, tell them what they should be doing next. Or even just how to turn the gate on so they could get back to the Core.

"I can . . . try to call my CO, I guess . . ."

She shook her head. "I want to talk to Lugen."

Murphy's voice wavered. "*Praetor* Lugen? I can't make a summons like that, sir."

"I'm invoking the Titan prius statute. I order you to connect me directly to Praetor Reneth Lugen."

Murphy hesitated, more than likely having never heard that directive enacted before. He came back on moments later. "It's two in the morning here, sir."

"You think I give a fuck?" she barked. "You want to be on a Titan's shit list, Oculus?"

"No, sir," the kid sputtered.

"Then get me Lugen. Now."

"Okay, sorry, sir. I'll need to rouse our comms tech, then we'll have to call around to find the praetor, but I'll call you back."

"Do not break this connection," she warned.

"I won't, sir," he assured. "I'm locking it in. I'll be back."

He clicked off and left only a stream of steady static behind. Adequin fixated on the comm link and waited in the heavy silence of the room, unmoving, her heart pounding loudly against her ribs.

She didn't even know where to start. If the Legion had *purposefully* abandoned Kharon and fully withdrawn from the Divide, then their negligence in not telling her was unheard of. She had no idea how to react.

But that'd just be the icing on the proverbial cake of shit that'd been the Legion's behavior toward them since she'd arrived at the *Argus* five years ago. Getting anything beyond the essentials to survive was like pulling teeth. Now, they'd all but gone radio silent. Abandoned them to their fate at the edge of the universe.

Her initial instinct was righteous indignation. She wanted to march straight to Lugen and demand an answer. But she knew it wouldn't be that easy. She might always technically have the prerogative of having been a Titan, but in sending her to the Sentinels, they'd made it clear they didn't intend to extend those privileges.

But Lugen had trusted her implicitly, once. She'd been his strategist, his right hand. If anyone would send aid, be willing to help them, it was him. But she didn't know what, if any, sway she'd have with the praetor anymore. He'd sent her here, after all.

Jackin's calm voice broke through her thoughts. "I wouldn't hold your breath, boss."

She let out a sigh, pulling her eyes away from the silent comm link. Over Jackin's shoulder, Puck stood with Warner and the other soldiers he'd summoned. She didn't know when they'd arrived, but by the looks on their faces, they'd heard quite a bit. Puck and Warner's expressions were wary, but the others' were tight, angry, confused. Oddly, they mostly glared at Cavalon.

"How do you know about that act?" One of the circitors turned to face him, a man with thinning black hair named Snyder. "That LPWA?"

Cavalon's mouth dropped open, but nothing came out. He pulled at his collar. "I, uh, read about it in the news."

"And *Augustus*?" Snyder growled. "How is it you're on a first-name basis with Augustus Mercer?"

Warner walked up beside Snyder. "Cool it, guys. Why's it matter?"

"Wait a minute, I recognize you." Another oculus shuffled forward, ignoring Warner and pointing at Cavalon. "You were in the vids a few years back. They thought you were involved in that Ivory Hall stuff on Elyseia—those college kids using veterans as drug mules. But it all got buried, disappeared from the news."

Cavalon's face went bright red, and he glanced anxiously at Adequin. Snyder stepped forward, face-to-face with Cavalon, who met the challenge head-on, jaw tight.

"You're not just any Mercer, are you? You're the heir . . ." Snyder's shoulders swelled. "You know your granddad's little 'Heritage Edict' forced my entire family off Viridis? We'd been there for *five* generations."

Cavalon gulped.

"Then, when they tried to get the mutation corrected," Snyder continued, "they were refused treatment since they were no longer Core citizens 'in good standing.' That's quite a fucking loophole."

That sent them all into an uproar, and they began slinging a host of other accusations at Cavalon. Adequin expected him to jump on the defensive, but he stood his ground and remained silent. She didn't know how he could tolerate letting them rail on him like that. All they saw was a name. They had no idea how sympathetic he was.

Adequin watched the anger circulating through the small group of soldiers, thinking back to their conversation before the Drudgers' arrival. He'd called the timing of the Resurgence "convenient." He thought the SC had instigated the war in order to cover up this kind of unrest. It'd sounded so far-fetched at the time.

But the longer it sat with her, the more sense it made. Fielding the newly exposed Viator fleet had required a decisive and unified offensive. The Legion had long since been split into duty zones—by planets or systems or sectors. But after that day, for the first time in two hundred years, the First had been reunited in order to move against the new foe.

And a sweeping, galactic-wide sense of patriotism had come along with it. For the first time, Adequin had seen the real value of the System Collective, the reason so many on her home world had worked so hard and sacrificed so much to gain full citizenship.

That pride—that sense of unity—had fed her confidence in the early days of the war. And her resolve as the years dragged on. She couldn't stomach the thought of it all being orchestrated.

Snyder's fists clenched, and he took a threatening step toward Cavalon. Adequin moved to intercede.

"Soldiers!" she barked. They fell silent and looked at her. "Not that I should have to justify a goddamn thing to any of you, but this kid's more than pulled his weight in the last thirty-six hours. So why don't you cut him some slack—"

"Bullshit!" Snyder shouted. "What use is an entitled prince, never mind a *Mercer—*"

Adequin grabbed the circitor by the front of his vest and pushed him into the wall beside the door. Blood rushed through her veins, fueled by rage, and her head pounded in protest. She kept him pinned with one hand and pinched the bridge of her nose with the other, then took a deep, slow breath and fixed her glare on Snyder's wide eyes.

She unclenched her teeth, keeping her voice low and calm. "I'm just now remembering your file, Snyder. Conspiracy and solicitation, right? Blackmailing superior officers, aggravated assault, and a whole handful of counts of being drunk at your post."

Snyder's cheeks darkened.

"He may have fucked up too," Adequin continued, "but he's the reason we had enough fuel in the warp core to escape the Divide. He's helped fight off Drudgers twice, and he repaired the hull of the Hermes so we weren't all stranded in space *forever*. How many times have *you* saved our lives in the last twenty-four hours, Snyder?"

His Adam's apple bobbed a few times before he found his voice back. "Uh, zero, sir."

She gave him a few slow, deliberate nods. His head bounced as he followed her eyes.

"Zero." She shoved him against the wall again, then let go. "So *shut up.*"

He nodded quickly. "Yes, sir. Sorry, sir."

"Puck," she growled, gesturing to the doorway.

"With me, soldiers," Puck called out, spinning one finger in a circle and heading for the door. Snyder and the others fell in line behind him and disappeared into the hallway, leaving Adequin in the control room with Jackin, Mesa, and Cavalon.

Adequin looked at Cavalon. His cheeks were beet red, glower focused on his feet—either embarrassed, mad, or some of both, but she didn't care. Her reserve of patience was dwindling very, very quickly.

"Mesa?"

"Yes, Excubitor?"

Adequin nodded at the golden pyramid in the Savant's hands. "Please take whoever you need and look into that."

"It would help if I knew more about its origins."

"Probably Viator tech. That's pretty much all I know."

Mesa glanced down at the device. "It certainly appears that way, but where did you obtain it?"

Adequin hesitated only briefly—too tired for subtlety. "The Drudger ship. The captain was reviewing the data on it after receiving a recorded video message from a Viator."

Jackin leapt to his feet, but she held up her hand to shush him, continuing to stare at Mesa. The Savant's mouth dropped open.

"It produces a holographic interface," Adequin explained. "It looked like schematics. Please, just see if you can unlock it."

Mesa's large eyes blinked rapidly a few times, then her shoulders drew back. "Very well, Excubitor." She stepped to the doorway, then stopped to look back. "Cavalon?"

Cavalon snapped from his reverie and looked at her. "Uh, yeah?"

"With me, please." She sauntered through the doorway, disappearing into the hall.

Cavalon looked at Adequin, eyebrows high. She nodded her assent, and he followed Mesa, leaving Adequin alone with Jackin.

"Rake?" Jackin said, voice wavering.

She put her hands on her hips and looked at her boots, not turning to face him. "Jack?"

"Care to give me a quick sitrep on *what the fuck is going on?*"

She took a deep breath and turned to look at him. "There was a video message. Instructions sent to the Drudgers on how to do something. I don't know what."

"Sent from a Viator?"

"It appears so, yes."

"Appears so, or *is* so?"

"It was a recorded message. There's no way to know for certain."

Jackin's eyebrows sunk low over his dark brown eyes. "I'm getting really sick of hearing that shit come out of your mouth."

"Watch yourself," she warned.

"Wake up, Rake!" he yelled. "The time for delusions is over."

Her cheeks burned, and she clenched her fists, then looked away to keep from punching him.

"The Legion abandoned this gate—and at *least* two others—without telling us," he continued, voice harsh. "They withdrew from the Divide *without telling us.* And now we have a Viator giving orders to Drudgers. And, *oh yeah,*" he added wryly, "the universe is shrinking! You gonna come up with a reason how *that* might not be real too?"

"None of that follows, though, Jack," she yelled back. "None of it. I can't connect them. It makes no sense."

"Why do they need to be connected?" he growled. "It's shitty thing A, B, and C. Let's not pretend like any or all of them won't get us killed. Together, or separate."

"B and C might get us killed, yes. But there's got to be an explanation for A. The Legion wouldn't just leave—"

"Void, Rake," he spat, his anger flaring again. "What don't you get about this? I'm so sick of tiptoeing around this blind devotion." A swell of sudden determination hardened his expression, and he pointed a stiff finger at his flank. "These scars—and yeah, I saw you worrying on them earlier—"

Heat rose to her face, but she kept her glare locked on him.

"—where do you think they came from? Viators, Drudgers? I was safely tucked away on a capital ship the entire war, Rake."

"How am I supposed to know where the fuck they came from, Jack? You've never told me a damn thing about what you did before the war. Do you know how many times I've tried to get you to even tell me why you're *here*?"

His scowl deepened, voice lowering. "I can't tell you why I'm here; that's the whole damn point."

"What?"

"If I did, and they found out I told you—"

"*Who*?"

"—then they'd know I give a shit about you, and you'd be next."

"Next for what?" she said, but her question went unheard as Jackin's haunted gaze drifted toward the door.

"Especially now," he mumbled, "with that kid here . . . It's a good thing I never told you."

"Cavalon? What the hell does he have to do with this?"

"I hope nothing. I really fucking hope nothing."

"What? You think he's a spy for the Allied Monarchies?"

"I wouldn't put anything past Augustus Mercer, Rake," he said. "And you shouldn't either."

A hard lump rose to the back of her throat as she stared at the fury in her optio's eyes. But it wasn't the blind, lack-of-sleep anger it'd first appeared to be. Jackin was scared.

"The noble Legion you're so devoted to," Jackin continued, "they don't give a shit about us. The sooner you wrap your head around that, the better off we'll all be."

She stood silently for a few long minutes. "Jack, I . . ." She looked down. "I'm sorry for what happened to you. And I understand if you can't tell me."

He stared vacantly at the console, head bobbing slowly.

"Just know that, if you ever need it, you have my confidence. Always. You can trust me."

His bloodshot eyes darted over, urgent to meet hers. But he remained silent, the muscles in his jaw twitching with unsaid words. After a time, he cleared his throat. "I'm sorry for yelling, boss. I'm a bit sleep-deprived."

"I know. But don't be sorry. You're right. I've been on the extreme side of caution with all this. It's just a lot to take in."

"I know."

"We've got the Drudgers' ship now, at least. If we can get the gate turned on, we can get everyone back to the Core. Then we'll worry about this . . . *Viator* situation later. Do you know how to restart the gate?"

He dragged his fingers through his short beard and groaned. "No fucking clue. They don't exactly get shut off on a regular basis. Or, *ever.*"

"Just see what you can do."

"Copy." He sat at the terminal and opened new menus, punching out commands with sharp impatience. "You might as well take a breather, boss. I'm sure that kid'll have some hoops to jump through before he gets a hold of Lugen. This could take a while."

Adequin dropped into the chair beside Jackin, and he reached over to grip her shoulder before returning to work. She stared at the flashing holographic displays for a few silent minutes, and soon found herself slouching into the padded chair. Her eyes drooped, and though she tried to hold onto consciousness, she eventually gave in and let sleep take her.

Griffith smiles, warm eyes glinting in the moonlight. "Where'd you learn to shoot like that?"

Adequin stands and slings the sniper rifle over her back. "I had a decent teacher."

"Oh, yeah? Bet he's a great guy."

She shrugs. "Just some old man."

His amused grin persists, but he shakes his head and sighs. "Will this spot work?"

"If the intel's right."

"And if it's wrong?" he asks, scratching his beard with one hand. "And they really are on Haudin-IV, or way off somewhere in the Perimeter Veil? Not Paxus?"

"Then we're alone on this planet," she says, then lets out a listless breath. "And that's just fine."

A small ovoid drone with spindly arms flies up to hover in front of them. It drops the carcass of a fat, juicy carnis hawk at their feet, shot through the forehead with a single plasma bolt. Adequin swipes across her nexus screen to dismiss the drone back to camp, and it speeds away. She kneels and picks up the garnet-feathered bird, then looks to Griffith.

"I caught it, you cook it."

The corners of his eyes wrinkle. "Deal."

They turn back toward camp, walking along the edge of the embankment, which falls away steeply into a wooded valley.

"You know," Griffith says, "your teacher might be an old man, but with age comes wisdom."

She grins. "With age comes being tired a lot."

His voice falls to a low, serious rumble. "You tired, Quin?"

"Aren't you?"

He sighs a weary, heavy sigh that says more than any words could. "It'll be over soon."

She tries to look at him, but can't. His edges aren't clear, aren't sharp. He's there, but not. If she tries to reach out and touch him, she's sure her hand will pass right through.

They pause and look out across the valley toward the foot of the mountain, where a placid river snakes through uncut wilderness. Tomorrow it will burn, all of it.

"Sir?"

Adequin shot awake so quickly, she almost slid off the front of her chair.

"Whoa, boss," Jackin said, still hovered over his terminal. "It's just Puck on your nexus."

She looked down and saw her comm link flashing, then tapped to open it. "Go for Rake," she said, her voice gravelly from disuse. She checked the time in the corner of the screen, relieved to see she'd only been asleep for forty minutes.

"We've swept the Drudgers' ship and have it docked at P4," Puck began, his voice hesitant.

"But?" she prompted.

"Well, sir . . . you're going to want to see this."

"I'll be right there." Adequin stood and shook out her tired limbs, slightly sore from using her Imprints, but *very* sore from sleep deprivation. "Jack, keep an eye out for Lugen's call, or anyone's for that matter. Patch them through to my nexus."

"You got it."

Adequin made her way down the corridor to the port-side air locks and through the Drudger ship's hatch, where Puck stood waiting, wringing his hands nervously.

Her chest tightened. "What is it?"

His response came as a curt nod over his shoulder, indicating she should follow. They headed down the hall, then took a lift down into the belly of the ship. The door slid open, revealing a large cargo area packed haphazardly with crates. A few soldiers stood around taking inventory.

Adequin stepped out of the lift to follow Puck, who entered the maze of crates and pallets and led her to the far side of the expansive area.

"We've found all kinds of shit down here so far," Puck explained. "Weird shit. There's cases upon cases of chemicals, metamaterials, a half dozen slabs of raw aerasteel, some metals and alloys I don't even know the names of. It's like a chem lab down here."

"For what? Explosives?"

Puck shook his head. "No idea. There's no casings or detonators, at least that we've found so far. Just a lot of raw materials."

She chewed her lip. This was not what he'd brought her down to show her. "What else?"

Puck sighed. "Well, other than loads, and I mean *loads* of Viator tech, these guys also have loads of, well . . ."

He stopped at an open bay door that led into a secondary hold. The space sat packed wall-to-wall with Legion-issue equipment and supplies.

Adequin stared at it for a few seconds, then looked up at Puck with a furrowed brow. "Where'd they get all this?"

"I wondered the same thing." Puck walked over to a stack of crates that had been secured to the floor with a taut canvas tarp. He lifted the cover up. Brandished across the side of the crate was the Sentinel logo above the words "SCS *Tempus*."

Adequin's heart stopped briefly, then slammed hard against her chest to catch back up. She swallowed and stepped forward, running her fingers along the etched words. Its sharp edges were cold and solid. It was real. Not an illusion.

Heat crept up her neck, but she steadied her voice and focused all her efforts on remaining calm.

"Puck."

"Yes, sir."

"Get the coordinates from the ship's logs. I want their last location."

CHAPTER TWENTY-SIX

Adequin stood at the helm of the Drudgers' ship, stared at the blank viewscreen, and waited.

They'd been at warp speed for almost thirty minutes and would be decelerating shortly to land at the coordinates they'd found in the logs of the ship—named after a Viator term that roughly translated to *Synthesis*. They were headed straight back outward, which was such a bad idea, not to mention irrational and reckless. But she couldn't find a way to care.

It might have been a long shot, but it didn't matter. They'd lost too many aboard the *Argus*; she had to know she'd done all she could to find the *Tempus*. And if it wasn't enough to risk it for her own reasons, she found plenty of justification in doing it for Lace's sake. It'd been her final request, and Lace was the closest thing Griffith had to family. Adequin had to do whatever it took to honor that, or she'd never be able to forgive herself.

Jackin sat harnessed in the ratty copilot's chair, throwing anxious glances at her while the kilometers ticked by on the main display. He'd insisted on coming, and she'd been too panicked to argue. He'd set Puck to take over his task of figuring out how to restart the gate, then grabbed Erandus, Warner, and two other oculi while following Adequin to the air lock.

She hadn't wanted to endanger anyone but herself for this admittedly rogue mission, but Jackin hadn't given her a choice. Though they didn't need more than two to adequately fly the ship, she knew she'd be glad for the extra bodies if they ran into another enemy vessel on the way.

The deck rumbled lightly as they decelerated from warp with a flash of light. An outward sea of absolute black welcomed them on the viewscreen.

Jackin opened the scanners, and a single blip twenty kilometers away sent a sharp spike of adrenaline through Adequin's veins.

"Light," she ordered.

Jackin engaged the ion engines and flew the ship forward, slowing after a time to swing their spotlight across the void. It tugged back as it hit the edge of a hull, dragging along a plain expanse of gray aerasteel until it came to a rest at the numerical call sign along the port aft. *SCS-4146–02*.

Adequin fled the cockpit and took the steps down to the main deck two at a time.

"Rake, wait!" Jackin called after her. He scrambled to follow, fumbling his helmet on, calling out rushed orders for someone to lock down the helm and keep the engines warm.

Jackin, Warner, and Erandus barely made it inside the small auxiliary air lock before Adequin sealed the door. "Helmets on?"

"On," Warner called through the suit comms, strapping a plasma rifle to his back.

"On," Erandus confirmed.

"Go for it, boss," Jackin said.

Adequin pressed the air-lock controls and with a hiss, the room depressurized. Her feet lifted and the hatch door opened.

She reminded herself not to rush, to stay calm—no sudden movements—then swung out and released the retractable tether from outside the hull. She pressed away from the *Synthesis* and launched herself toward the hatch of the *Tempus*.

Inside, the *Tempus*'s halls sat silent and dark. Thin strips of red emergency lights lined the entrance corridor.

Jackin's fingers danced across his suit's nexus. "Life systems are online," he confirmed. "It's in standby."

With a hiss of air he released his helmet, and Adequin did the same. Warner and Erandus set their helmets aside and took up their rifles in both hands.

Adequin raised her pistol and started down the hall. Jackin hovered to her right, Warner and Erandus off her left shoulder. They cleared the entrance corridor quickly and silently, room by room, seeing no signs of life or struggle.

Down a deck, the cargo hold and life systems were similarly quiet. At the aft of the ship, Adequin led them up a ladder to the engine-access deck. She didn't know whether to be anxious or relieved by the piles of Drudger corpses they found littering the corridor.

She signaled the others to keep an eye on the hall, then knelt beside a cluster of bodies. They wore the same jumpsuits and carried similar weaponry to the Drudgers she'd killed aboard the *Synthesis*. This had to be the rest of the missing crew.

Adequin turned a few of the bodies over and examined the wounds. Though a handful of poorly aimed laser shots had singed their uniforms and left char marks on their gray skin, most had been cleanly executed by a mixture of perfectly accurate plasma bolts and precise knife slices.

"They put up a fight," Jackin noted, standing over her, gun raised as he kept a wary eye on the corridor ahead.

"Looks like it. But where are they?"

Jackin only shook his head.

Adequin left Erandus to keep watch on the corridor, then motioned for Jackin and Warner to take the left side of the hallway, while she went for the first door on the right.

Inside the small common room, some of the lockers along the far wall sat ajar. Their contents lay strewn across the floor: clothing, playing cards, tablets, and drink bottles, all collected along one wall. It didn't seem to be the result of uncleanliness, but rather some kind of turbulence.

Adequin chewed on the inside of her lip as several scenarios ran through her head. Had they pulled away from the Divide, then the Drudgers happened to find them? Or had the Drudgers also been riding the Divide, then shot them down somehow? The *Tempus* hadn't appeared to have any hull damage, but she hadn't really waited for the full report before running to the air lock.

She took a breath and shook it from her mind. She needed to focus on finding the crew. They would have all the answers she needed.

Adequin ducked back outside and continued down the corridor as Jackin appeared in a doorway across the hall.

"Clear," Jackin said.

Adequin didn't spare a look back as she slipped into the next room.

"Clear," Warner called from the hallway, just as Jackin said it again, though he couldn't have cleared another room that quickly.

Adequin swept every corner of the room and a small supply closet, but found nothing out of the ordinary.

Warner called another all clear as she went back into the corridor and turned toward the last door on her side—the engine-access room. The red screen beside the closed door indicated it'd been manually locked. She tried to swipe it open, but the screen flashed a warning: "Biometric clearance required." She pulled her glove off and stuck her thumb to the pad. The door slid open, accompanied by a waft of burnt metal and charred rubber.

And there he was, lying on the floor in front of one of the ion-engine access doors. Her feet crossed the metal floor in a few short strides, and she slid to her knees at Griffith's side.

"Griff?"

He didn't stir. Sweat beaded on his forehead, and the fine lines on his face appeared deeper than ever. The gray peppering his beard and hair somehow seemed even lighter. A bloody, Legion-issue combat knife lay on the floor beside him.

Her fingers fumbled to his neck—his skin blissfully warm—searching for the spot just below his jaw. She pushed out a few purposeful breaths to steady herself long enough to sense it. A sliver of relief cut through her when she finally felt it—his heartbeat strong, his thick chest raising and lowering slowly. He was breathing.

"Jack!" she called over her shoulder.

She carefully looked Griffith over, but saw no wounds.

"Griffith," she said, shaking him gently. "Wake up, Centurion."

Her heart fluttered as he groaned. His head lolled from one side to the other.

"Griff, look at me." She held his face in her hands and turned his head toward her. His eyelids flickered, then opened, revealing bloodshot, tired eyes. They were the same warm brown, but in the dim light they appeared dull, as if the color had faded.

"Fuck," he grumbled, his voice a deep rasp. His brow creased. "Quin?" He craned his neck and slid his elbows back, as if trying to sit up.

"Don't." She gripped his shoulder to stop him. The door behind her hissed open, followed by the shuffle of feet. "Find a biotool, guys?"

"Mo'acair . . ." A grin tugged at the corner of Griffith's mouth as he stared up at her. "I didn't even get off at the right stop, and I still found you. You really are my anchor."

Her throat closed as Lace's final words sounded in the back of her mind again, the sincerity in the circitor's soft brown eyes crushing the air from her lungs. She had to swallow down a swelling lump before she could breathe again.

Griffith pulled her to him, locking his dry lips around hers. A few tears escaped the corners of her eyes as she clamped them shut, letting the anxiety and tension she'd spent the last two days meticulously constructing seep away.

The door hissed again, and a rush of boots squeaked across the metal floor. Adequin pulled away to find Jackin standing over them, eyes wide. He made a production out of clearing his throat, then said, "Uh, when did *that* happen?"

The door slid open again, and moments later, Warner knelt beside her.

"Biotool, *please*," Adequin said, not sure why they were making her ask again.

"Yes, sir." Warner hopped back up and disappeared.

"How did you find me?" Griffith asked. He ran a trembling thumb along her bruised cheekbone, and his tone hardened. "What happened?"

"It's a long story," Adequin said. "How did you end up here, Griff? What happened after you left the *Argus*?"

"We got on the Divide, same as always. But after only a few minutes, we started drifting. The sensors kept going off, reading like we were steering into it."

"Or like it was steering into you," Jackin said grimly.

"Exactly. It *was*," Griffith said. "I think it's moving inward."

"It is," Adequin said.

Griffith coughed, then grumbled, "See, this is why I needed a physicist."

She sighed. "How'd you end up all the way out here?"

Griffith swallowed. "Once I realized it was moving, I tried to edge us away slowly, keep in that sweet spot, but it was moving too quickly—I couldn't accommodate. Eventually I had no choice: either keep going and crash into—or through—it in a matter of minutes, or, well . . . I could rip away."

"Wait, what?" Jackin said, eyes wide in disbelief. "Are you saying you disengaged without slowing down?"

Griffith gave a short nod, then groaned and sucked in a shallow breath.

"Why didn't you decelerate?" Adequin asked. "Slow down like normal and exit?"

"It was moving too quickly—the angle too sharp. If we slowed down, I wouldn't have met escape velocity before it'd have overtaken us. Our only chance was to pull away with enough speed to rip free entirely."

"Void, Bach," Jackin cursed. "How'd you pull that off?"

"I locked the crew up in the torus chamber and took manual control."

Adequin let out a sharp breath. With the crew locked in the torus chamber—where for safety, everyone should be during the autopiloted entrance and exit from the Divide—they should have been safe from the effects of deceleration, even one as sudden as this had been. However, in the cockpit, Griffith would have been exposed. To what, she didn't even know; she wasn't sure anyone did. As far as she knew, no one had ever tried a maneuver like that before.

"At that speed . . ." Jackin mumbled, running a hand through his hair. "How'd you get enough power?"

Griffith cleared his throat. "I overclocked the ions. That hacker kid told me how to circumvent the Legion shackles a while back—one of the circitors, Amaeus something."

Adequin raised her eyebrows. "Puck?"

"Right. More a thought experiment than anything—never thought I'd actually need to use it."

"But it worked?" Jackin asked.

"Yeah, but the force slung us away really fast. Too fast." He shook his head, his demeanor wilting. "There was this weird gravitational . . . billowing, almost. Thought every organ in my body was gonna explode. It worked, but tossed us around until I could get the engines under control, and we finally came to a stop . . . here. Wherever here is."

Warner crouched beside Adequin with a biotool and an armful of cartridges. She took the tool and switched it to scanning mode. A green beam shot out the front, then fanned into a grid. She ran the light over Griffith's chest.

Jackin glanced back at the corridor. "How'd those Drudgers even find you guys?"

"Shit if I know," Griffith growled. "I'd barely gotten the torus chamber opened to check on the crew before they pounced on us. We took a ton of them out, but they overwhelmed us pretty quick. So I routed them down here to give the crew time to lock themselves back in the chamber, then I shut myself in here to wait it out. I watched the door access on my nexus—looks like they just off-loaded our cargo, then left."

"Why'd they bother off-loading the supplies?" Jackin asked. "Why not take the whole ship?"

"Engines are shot," Griffith said. "And you know how Drudgers are."

"Can we fix the engines?" Adequin asked.

"Hard to say." His jaw flexed, eyebrows pinching together. "And my mechanic got stabbed by a Drudger."

"Ivana?" Adequin asked.

Griffith gave a grim nod. "Last I saw, Eura was dragging her into the torus chamber. Not sure if she made it or not—or if any of them did for that matter—nexus comms have been down. Have you guys been to the command deck?"

"Not yet," Adequin said.

"Then they must still be locked in there. I'm not sure they'll be able to figure out how to unlock the doors without officer codes."

Adequin looked to Jackin. "Go get them out. We'll meet you up there."

Jackin and Warner nodded their understanding, then took off into the hallway.

The biotool beeped, indicating its completion. Adequin pushed her hair out of her face with a heavy sigh, then took a look at the readout. Though there were a few lesser fractures and strained muscles, it showed no indication of serious injuries. She let out a sharp breath. The results should have reassured her, but the knot of worry bound even tighter in her chest.

Griffith gave a pained scoff. "Can't be *that* bad, Quin. My Imprints took the brunt of the trauma." He looked down at his bare forearms. The silver and copper squares shuffled wearily as he stretched his hand. "I might have broken them . . ."

He grimaced and closed his eyes, sweat beading on his wide forehead. His teeth clenched, brow furrowed in pain. She'd seen him hurt before, badly at times. Countless stray bolts that his Imprints weren't able to shield. Third-degree burns from not quite making it out of the blast radius of a grenade. And once, a knife slice across his neck that, if a medic hadn't been there to immediately cauterize it, likely would have bled out in seconds. Unfortunately, that didn't make it any easier to see him in pain now.

"I can give you something for the pain," she said quietly. "If you want it."

"Can't hurt," he agreed.

She unstrapped his vest, then unbuttoned the shirt underneath, revealing thick muscles marred with garish purple lesions. A few Imprint squares remained, marooned among the sea of bruises. One copper square skipped back and forth along the same short path over and over, trying to pass back to its default location, but unable to make the journey. Maybe he really had broken them.

She picked through the collection of cartridges, hoping he couldn't sense her deepening worry. She'd seen Griffith's Imprints take the impact of a point-blank electromagnetic bolt without so much as a minor glitch. If this crash had caused them this much damage, she could hardly believe he'd lived through it. She couldn't imagine how bad the deceleration could have been if he hadn't had Imprints to protect him.

She found a localized painkiller, then loaded the cartridge into the biotool. He gritted his teeth as she carefully injected a portion near his sternum, then moved to the left, then right side.

She got to her feet and called on her Imprints to assist as she helped him stand. He towered over her, leaning heavily on her shoulder before settling into a semi-stable position. She kept hold of his forearms as he steadied himself. He closed his eyes and took a long, deep breath.

"You sure you're up for this?" she asked. "I can just take you straight to the ship."

"Just tired, don't worry. Hey . . ." He opened his eyes and swept the hair out of her face. "Aevitas fortis."

She gave him a tired smile. "Aevitas fortis."

He wrapped his arms around her and pulled her close. She laid her head against his chest, inhaling his warm scent.

He let go, then put an arm around her shoulder for balance as they started for the door. After a few steps, he gained his stability back and leaned on her less and less as they approached the hall.

"Aevitas fortis," he said.

She raised an eyebrow and looked up, but his weary grin had disappeared. He shook his head.

Then she heard her own voice, elsewhere. "Aevitas fortis."

Griffith's face slackened. They turned around.

Back near the engine access doors, Griffith stood, his arms wrapped around her, warm eyes glistening as he smiled. Her hair was a mess, pulled up into a heap atop her head, and the bruise on her face had darkened to a sickly blue-green. She looked up at the much taller man, almost disappearing in his embrace as his thick arms pulled her closer.

Adequin stared at them, but it didn't compute. She couldn't process it. Her mind knew what it meant, but at the same time, it tried to protect her. So for a fraction of a second, she ignored her panic and enjoyed the sight.

They looked exhausted, but happy. Relieved that they'd found each other. And good, together. That Adequin looked at that Griffith like she couldn't live without him. And that Griffith looked at that Adequin like she was the only person in the universe.

Then reality began to seep back in. It was something she'd never seen before, never heard of before. She didn't think it was possible.

A time ripple *the wrong way?* A time ripple that told the past instead of the future? It wasn't a thing. It didn't happen.

The doppelgängers wavered and flickered, then disappeared. They stared at the empty space for a few heavy seconds.

"Quin . . ." She turned to meet Griffith's humorless gaze, and the pain that furrowed his brow had deepened into concerned shock.

She opened her nexus. "Jack." No response came. "Jackin? Warner, Erandus? You guys read me?" Only static in return.

She looked back through the open door into the corridor, where another Adequin supported the weight of another Griffith, helping him limp down the hall toward the stairs that led to the air lock. Moments later, she wavered and flashed away, but Griffith remained, leaning on nothing as if her doppelgänger still held up his weight. Then he flickered until he no longer leaned, but cradled his ribcage and walked of his own accord.

"Shit," the real Griffith grumbled. He scratched his beard and watched, mouth agape. "What's going on?"

"Time ripples . . ."

He looked back at her with raised eyebrows, as if to say "no shit," but instead he said, "Where are we?"

"We're inward. Far enough inward . . ." She tried to conjure up the will to do the math, based on how fast it'd been contracting when they left the *Argus* hours ago, but she couldn't get her mind to focus on it. "We're about halfway between the first buoy and the *Argus* . . . or where the *Argus* was. But quite a ways inward."

"Where it *was*?" he asked.

She shook her head. Now wasn't the time to catch Griffith up on the last twenty-four hours. Now was the time to get the hell off the *Tempus*.

＋

CHAPTER TWENTY-SEVEN

Cavalon flicked on the plasmic welding tool, and the end sparked to life in a white-hot blue flame.

This is what it had come to. After almost an hour of poking and prodding at the stupid gold pyramid, Cavalon had started to question if he'd ever really seen the holographic screens come out of it in the first place. Maybe it had just been a fancy paperweight, obscuring something else on the console that had projected the weird displays.

Gum-chomping pulled him from his thoughts, and he refocused through his protective glasses onto Emery as she stared at the impressively bright light.

"Don't look directly at the arc," he grumbled.

Emery pulled her eyes away and gave him a mellow grin.

Apparently, she had been a "trusted laboratory technician" of Mesa's a few times in the past. Though her suggestions of the various ways in which they could attempt to *destroy* the object had been creative, they had not been precisely productive. Not that Cavalon had managed to offer anything useful himself. This was his strategy, after all. Frying it with a plasma torch.

He zapped every facet of the pyramid with the tool, dragging it along every etching and groove, but nothing happened. Whatever material it was made from didn't react to the twenty-eight thousand degrees of hot plasma arcing into it. Didn't even leave a mark.

He set down the tool and sighed, pulling off his glasses and gloves. He leaned back in his chair and crossed his arms, meeting Mesa's gaze across the wide table they'd set up in the middle of the makeshift medbay.

"What about biometrics?" Cavalon asked.

Mesa pinched her lips together. "Viators disfavored that manner of security, though it is possible. It would most likely be regulated to a single user, if that were the case."

"Then we should cut off the hand of the Drudger captain," he said with feigned cheer. "Try that on for size."

Emery leaned forward. "Except the EX just took the Drudger ship to void-only-knows-where. Think she's abandoning us?"

"I assure you," Mesa said, "she is not abandoning us. Please focus, Miss Flos."

Emery shrugged and leaned back in her chair, chomping her gum.

"They did remove the corpses before they left," Mesa said. "Though I am not sure if they have ejected them out the air lock yet. So, that may yet be a possibility."

Cavalon took his knife from the sheath and held it up along with the palm of his other hand. "What about a blood sacrifice?"

Mesa frowned. "Even if it was biometrics, it certainly would not be *your* biometrics," she said, scorn evident in her tone. Then her scowl faded, and she licked her lips and slid to the edge of her chair. She pulled the pyramid toward her, then snatched the knife from Cavalon's grip and dragged the blade along the palm of her hand.

"Mesa!" His eyes went wide and he sat up straight. "I was kidding!"

She glared at the pyramid ruefully as her blood dripped down onto its peak. "No marked change," she murmured.

Cavalon's chair groaned against the metal floor as he stood. He grabbed a biotool and a pack of gauze from the crates of medical supplies along the walls.

Mesa continued to turn the pyramid over in one hand as Cavalon took her injured hand and held it flat. He disinfected it, then switched to cauterization mode and closed the small slice. Mesa winced, but her focus remained on the pyramid. Within seconds, the wound had fully sealed over with new, pink skin. The nanite-enhanced cauterization would leave no scar.

Emery grinned up at him, leaning her chair onto its back legs, arms crossed. "Know your way around a biotool too? You get more and more useful every time I turn around."

Cavalon eyed her, certain any second she would tip over in her chair and ensure he'd be tending to her foolish injuries next. He wiped the rest of Mesa's blood off her hand with the gauze. "I was pre-med for about ten seconds before August—" He shook his head. "Before I switched to genetic engineering."

"I think you may be correct," Mesa said with a light sigh.

"Correct about what?" He tossed the bloody gauze in an incinerator chute on the wall, then returned to stand across the table from her.

"I will test a few more theories," she began, "but please see if you can find the Drudger captain's corpse and return with its hand. You may take Miss Flos with you."

"For the love of the void, Mes," Emery growled, leaning forward until the front legs of her chair clanged back to the ground. "Just call me Emery."

Mesa ignored her. "The hand alone will do. Wrist, up." Without looking away from the pyramid, she slid Cavalon's knife across the table toward him.

He grimaced and picked it up, returning it to the sheath at his hip. "You got it."

Cavalon kept his eyes on the ground as he and Emery passed two soldiers standing guard at the air locks. He didn't know if they were among those that had been present during Rake's chat with the Legion, but he still imagined their heated gazes boring into him as he passed. Even if they hadn't known before, the news of his accidental admission had likely traveled fast.

He still didn't know how he felt about that whole incident. Relieved—and maybe a little flattered—that Rake had bothered to stick up for him. However, it'd come with a healthy dose of humiliation. Pretty much the only thing that could make this situation worse would be if he became known as a teacher's pet.

The already-rank mound of Drudger corpses was not difficult to track down. They sat a few meters past the P4 air lock, piled beside the wall. Unfortunately, it seemed the captain had been one of the first bodies to be removed, as he and Emery had to unstack most of the other corpses before they found the right one. Cavalon immediately recognized the one he'd killed from the wide gash along one of its flank plates where his knife had skinned off the fleshy covering. Then the second, gaping entry wound that'd made it through the ribs and reached its heart, deflating it and draining its life, beat by beat.

"Elyseia to Cavalon." Emery snapped her fingers at him. He looked up from the corpse and stared at her. "One of these our guy?" She motioned to the bodies at the bottom of the pile.

He nodded numbly, then knelt and turned one of them over. "This is the one."

He traced his fingers along his gold and bronze royal Imprints. They were tired—*he* was tired—but he might be able to muster enough energy . . .

"I could just carry the whole body back," he suggested.

She gave him a flat look. "They already reek. We don't want a whole dead Drudger back there stinking the place up. You heard the Savant. Wrist, down."

He gulped and took his knife from its sheath, staring down at the steel-gray, taloned hand of the Drudger. He may have been briefly pre-med, but he hadn't gotten to the dismemberment part of medical school. He had no idea how to remove an appendage.

Emery let out a disgusted sigh. "Bloody void, ya big wuss."

She snatched the knife from his hand and without even the briefest hesitation, sliced the serrated blade deeply into its wrist. Cavalon had to look away for the rest, though hearing the wet, meaty sawing wasn't really any less nauseating.

With a sickening crack of bone, he knew it was over. Emery held up the bloody hand and waved it at him, the taloned fingers flopping about lifelessly.

"Asset acquired." She grinned.

His stomach turned, and he tried to return her smile, but he was sure it came out more of a grimace.

A glint caught his eye, and he looked over at the dismembered Drudger. Around its coral- and teal-tinged neck lay a thin silver chain, half-hidden under the collar of its uniform. Drudgers weren't known for accessorizing.

Cavalon tried to ignore the bloody stump on the end of the captain's arm and reached to pull the necklace over its wide head. The blackened silver chain held a thin, tarnished gold medallion of three interwoven triangles.

He exchanged a curious look with Emery, who shrugged. He pocketed the necklace and turned to head back down the hall, but three unexpected guests stood in their way.

A pasty man with thinning black hair stood with his arms crossed in the middle of the hallway—Snyder, the rather angry circitor that'd overheard Rake's conversation on the comms earlier. Behind him stood the two air-lock guards they'd passed earlier, a thickset man with greasy brown hair, and a tall, broad-shouldered woman who had a mess of old scars covering the left side of her jaw and neck. They both looked equally displeased.

"Hey, Mercer," Snyder said, a light smile playing at the corner of his thin lips. "I was wondering where you'd run off to."

Cavalon's heart sank. He gave a quick look around the empty hallway—for help? He didn't know why he thought that would exist.

"Have you met my friends?" Snyder gestured to his two bodyguards. "Their families were also displaced by the Heritage Edict. Small universe, huh?"

"Guys," Emery groaned, holding up the severed Drudger hand. "We're on kind of an important mission here. Can your schoolyard-bully thing wait?"

Snyder shook his head, and the scarred woman strode toward Emery. The top of Emery's head came up roughly to the woman's armpits, but Emery didn't cede her ground.

"All right, all right, hold on *just* a sec . . ." Emery flashed the viscera-covered blade of Cavalon's knife, then pointedly wiped each side clean across the front of her pants. "I should get the Drudger guts off first. Wouldn't want you to catch their stupid." She jutted her chin out as she glared up at the tall woman looming over her. "Y'all don't need any more of that now do ya?"

In one swift motion, the tall woman caught the wrist of Emery's knife-wielding hand. Emery glowered as the woman wrenched the blade from her grip, then tossed it away. The clatter echoed down the silent corridor.

"Leave her out of this," Cavalon growled. His royal Imprints shuffled along his arm, though they stayed mostly in formation as he fought to keep them still. He knew what sliding Imprints implied, and that Snyder would see it as a threat. As much as he wanted to put the circitor and his beefy cronies in their place, he was fairly certain that wouldn't fall under the category of "shit-cutting."

Snyder turned his forearm out to showcase the glowing holographic screen of his nexus. "Guess what?"

Cavalon swallowed. "You're gonna take the high road?"

Snyder's mouth curved up into a sneer. "Your best friend the EX did something kinda stupid earlier."

"I doubt she's ever once done anything *stupid*," Cavalon said, in the most level tone he could manage.

Snyder nodded. "You're right. I'm sure it seemed like a good idea at the time. But her mistake was in not fixing it afterwards. She's been a little busy, so I get it. But it's unfortunate for you."

Cavalon raised an eyebrow. He didn't have the first clue what this guy was on about. Snyder grinned, then swept two fingers across his nexus.

Cavalon's knees hit the cold metal floor before he even registered the lance of hot pain firing through his left arm and down his spine. His vision faltered, and for a few endless moments, he knew nothing outside of the pain—each grueling second ten times worse than the agony he'd experienced when receiving either set of Imprints.

When it finally ceased, a stockpile of leftover pain lingered along every nerve on the left side of his body. But at least it was manageable. He could function again, use his other senses.

He glanced around, realizing he was on his knees, sitting back on his feet. The taste of blood filled his mouth as he panted through gritted teeth. Through a haze of wetness in his eyes, Snyder's boots approached. Then came a voice, muffled through a fog of pain.

"See, back on the *Argus*, they were all fighting like idiots and things were getting chaotic, so she unlocked Imprint control to all circitors." Snyder crouched down and took Cavalon's chin in his fingers, forcing him to meet his gaze. "And she's not here to protect you now, is she, princeps?" He stuck out his lower lip. "She left you all alone."

"Void, you guys," Emery hissed, "Leave him alone!"

She tried to push past, but the tall woman blocked her, gripping Emery's shoulder and shoving her back to pin her against the wall.

Cavalon somehow found the will to reach up and shove Snyder away weakly. The circitor's shoulder barely turned back with the pathetic attempt.

He snickered. "Is that all the fight you've got left?" He gave a small shrug. "That's probably my fault. I figured we'd see what the intensity slider was like at 'max.' The EX had it at a measly twenty percent. Kinda lenient, in my opinion."

"What do you expect me to say?" Cavalon growled, surprised at how haggard and dry his voice came out. "I wasn't even born when that damn edict passed. I had nothing to do with it."

"That's not the point," Snyder said. "My family suffered, so *his* family is going to suffer."

Cavalon glared. "It's *hilarious* that you think he gives two shits if I suffer. You'd be doing him a favor."

Snyder smiled. "Nice try. Your pathetic lies only make this all the more fun for me."

A wash of copper flooded Cavalon's mouth as he clenched his fists. As much pride as he took in his shit-cutting prowess over the last twenty-four hours, enough was enough. He'd tried. Shit-cutting wasn't going to cut it this time.

In a rush of glittering metallic, the gold and bronze squares on his right arm dispersed from their default formation, speeding his movements as he leapt to his feet. With Imprint-fueled force he lunged for Snyder.

But the man had already started to swipe at his nexus controls. Cavalon had been too slow.

A tidal wave of hot pain tore through him, igniting every nerve. His muscles seized, and his view of the hallway tilted and skewed until his cheek met the floor. Sparks of azure light cut across the backs of his clenched eyelids.

A shrill, grating tone rang through his ears, vibrating across his skin, clawing through every one of his muscles and burrowing deep into his bones. The pain pulsed, echoing, building on itself—an endless feedback loop of agony.

It was an unprecedented level of pain. One that raised the bar, that set a new standard for intolerable. But Snyder had already set it to max. Why was it so, so much worse this time?

Then somehow, between the seconds, came a brief, almost imperceptible moment of clarity. Cavalon detached from the pain just long enough to feel it: how his royal Imprints struggled to climb up his arms and down his legs and across his back. How they jittered along his skin in disjointed, drunken motions. And how the black Sentinel Imprints on his left arm grew hotter and hotter with each passing second—each square an electric diode firing a lightning bolt's worth of energy out across his body . . . and into his royal Imprints.

Then he realized . . . this was it. Volatile interfacing. This was what they'd been warning him about—something that could really, actually, get him killed.

With a rush of panic, he realized he had to not use them. He had to *stop* using them.

The millisecond the thought fully registered in his brain, his royal Imprints terminated. Yet instead of sliding back to their default formation as they always had—as they never, not even once, hadn't—they simply stopped dead in their tracks, like hundreds of tiny metallic bits marooned all across his pale skin.

The grueling, feedback-like waves of electric pain ceased immediately, leaving only the regular torture caused by the activated Sentinel Imprints. But that was cool and easy and almost tolerable in comparison.

His muscles still twitched with the residual pain, body curling instinctively into a fetal position. His nails dug into his palms as his hands tightened into fists, and the urge to summon his Imprints persisted. He had to use every ounce of will to fight his instincts, to assure his royal Imprints didn't reactivate while this bastard had control over the other set.

Though hell, maybe he had it coming. After all, he'd sat on his hands for twenty-seven years without doing a damn thing. He'd cowered behind brazen indifference, and it'd taken his own father's death to snap him out of it, for fuck's sake. Maybe he really was the bad guy.

A high-pitched voice shouted through the din, angry. Emery, maybe? He tried to peel his blistering eyes open but the pain grew all-consuming.

He poured all of his efforts into focusing on keeping his royal Imprints inactive. He became vaguely aware of boots impacting his stomach, over and over—deep, thudding blows in the meat of his guts. The strikes themselves didn't hurt, as his nerves were already overloaded with the pain of the activated obsidian Imprints. But he knew the beating would hurt later, assuming they didn't intend to kill him. So he tried to clutch at his stomach, protect it as much as he could with his forearms, until someone turned him over and held his wrists down. Then fists joined in.

He didn't fight back, he just waited for it to end, doing his best to deflect as many of the impacts as he could. He just had to hold out.

Although . . . what was he holding out for, exactly? Rake had left. Jackin and Warner had left. Puck sat glued to a screen in the control room, trying to save everyone's lives. Mesa would never be able to stop brutes like this. No one was coming to save him.

CHAPTER TWENTY-EIGHT

✦

Adequin pulled herself up the last few rungs of the access ladder into one of the secondary passages of the *Tempus*'s command deck. More corpses littered the corridor and her breath caught in her throat. Fewer than half were Drudgers.

A few meters away, Erandus crouched over one of the human bodies, his fingers pressed firmly under their jaw. He shook his head then let out a soft sigh, shifting to unhook the soldier's dog tags.

A sharp prickle ran down Adequin's spine as her eyes drifted over each of the twelve fallen Sentinels, small holes scoured into the fronts of their navy vests from clean, close plasma fire straight to the chest. All but three still had their knives sheathed and pistols holstered. They'd been caught off guard.

And why wouldn't they have been?

The *Tempus* was a scouting vessel in name only, and nothing more than a flying repair kit in reality. The crew's endless cycle of struggling to keep a two-hundred-year-old alert system in working order while micromanaging meager supplies meant readiness drills weren't even part of the regimen anymore. In all likelihood, no one on the crew had seen combat training in years. She'd failed them in that regard too.

Griffith grunted, and she tore her gaze back down to the ladder, offering him a hand up out of the hatch. She hauled him up and her Imprints brought a metallic surge to her tongue, morphing into a sulfurous, bitter taste as it mixed with the acid that'd risen from her stomach.

He exhaled as he straightened his back, then stood unmoving

for a few long moments, eyes drifting slowly over his fallen crew. He ran a stiff hand over his mouth, then blew out a long breath before moving forward to join Erandus. He knelt beside the oculus and began to quietly speak under his breath.

She could only catch a few syllables, but didn't have to hear any of it to know what he recited—a traditional Cautian elegy, used by nonsecular and atheists alike. Countless times during the Resurgence, she'd stood beside him as he spoke those words for their fallen comrades—far too many times. She'd hoped to never hear them again.

A dense pressure rose in her chest, and she found it difficult to catch her breath. Not from memories of the war, but because she hadn't once thought to offer any kind of parting words or last rites for the *Argus*'s crew. For Lace, for Bray, for the hundreds of others she'd left behind.

As heat rose to her face, she had to close her eyes and remind herself it was far from over. The time would come to mourn the dead, to pay homage to those they'd lost. For now, she had to focus on finding a way to make sure they didn't add themselves to the list of casualties.

She swallowed the surge of guilt back down, then caught Erandus's eye. She nodded a silent order to stay with Griffith, then left the men and rounded the corner toward the central corridor of the command deck.

Jackin stood outside the torus chamber door, hands on hips, boot twanging against the metal floor. Warner stood nearby, arms crossed. A gurgling, rushing hiss of liquid and gasses from within the walls indicated the effusion process taking place—which meant for some reason, the chamber's dampening effects had been activated, and were now resetting. The counter on the screen beside the door read 95 percent.

"Effusion?" Adequin asked as she approached.

Jackin shrugged. "To discourage the Drudgers from trying to beat the door down, I'd guess. Took us a minute to figure out a way to disengage the mode manually. Where's Bach?"

"With Erandus, collecting tags."

Jackin frowned.

"We've got a couple of things we should probably discuss . . ." she added reluctantly.

Jackin closed his eyes, then took a deep breath through his nose before letting it out slowly. He reopened his eyes. "Hit me."

"For starters, comms aren't working." She held up her nexus's flashing red comm link as proof. "And, time ripples."

He didn't react at first, then turned his ear toward her as if he'd misheard. "Sorry?"

"If we're seeing time ripples here, how long do you think until the Divide reaches Kharon?"

"Well, shit. That . . . depends. I mean, we used to see ripples when we were still over a million kilometers away." He sighed and rubbed the back of his neck. "We more or less flew straight outward from the gate . . . so assuming it's moving uniformly inward, which it very well might *not* be . . . maybe twenty-four hours? Thirty-six? That's a total bullshit guess though, boss. I have no way to know for sure."

"Before we left the *Argus*, Puck said it appeared to be accelerating. If it's *still* picking up speed . . . ?"

Jackin buried his face in both hands. "Yeah, uh . . . so maybe definitely less?"

"And, Jack?" Adequin began quietly, though she knew Warner could still hear, so she wasn't sure why she bothered. "We saw a ripple . . . of something that already happened."

Jackin dropped his hands and looked at her steadily for a few long moments. "I'm pretty sure that makes *you* the ripple."

She glared. "I'm not the fucking ripple, Jackin."

He shook his head. "That's not possible. You can't have seen the past—"

Jackin's voice disappeared under a din of klaxons as the ship violently jerked. A sudden pressure buffeted the air, and the oxygen sucked from Adequin's lungs as a wall of flame engulfed her vision. She spun away too slowly, and the left side of her face smoldered with heat before an Imprint-induced numbness overcame the pain. Her vision disappeared into inky black as she tumbled away from the burst of fire.

She landed on her back, writhing as she panted ragged breaths through clenched teeth. Her head spun, and her fingers drifted to the tingling, Imprint-coated skin at her left cheek. They'd protected her from the brunt of it, though a subdued twinge of pressure told her they'd been just a little too slow. Her saliva filled with a metallic bitterness as the Imprints buzzed, working to heal the burn.

Groaning, she rolled onto her side to sit up, her still-reeling gaze cutting across the smoke-laden corridor. The fire-suppression system wailed, spewing out a coating of thick white foam across the smoldering debris. To her left, a half-meter-wide hole sat charred in the polished aerasteel wall opposite the torus chamber, blackened chunks strewn across the corridor.

Jackin's boots caught her eye, and she twisted onto all fours and crawled toward him. He lay on his side, expressionless brow coated in black soot—breathing, she realized with a pang of relief.

"Shit. Jack?" She shook him lightly, but he didn't stir.

Like her own uniform, his fire-resistant vest had repelled most of the flames, but the fringe of his collar had melted and caked into the blistering skin of his exposed neck. Glistening red and white burns seared the right side of his neck and jaw, scorching a path up through his beard to his cheek bone. It had fortunately missed his eye, though only by centimeters.

"Dammit," she growled. "Jack, wake up." She rolled him onto his back, loosening the top strap of his vest to peel the fabric from the smoldering flesh before it had time to dry into the wound.

Her eyes shot up as Griffith and Erandus ran around the corner, just as the fire-suppression foam snuffed out the last of the licking flames.

Erandus paused to help Warner, who cradled his elbow, but appeared otherwise uninjured.

Griffith rushed over, kneeling on the other side of Jackin. "What happened?" he called over the screaming din of klaxons.

"No idea," she shouted back, then a tingling flutter of relief washed through her as Jackin hacked out a series of sharp coughs. Griffith put a steadying hand on the unburned side of Jackin's face. "Hey, Optio. This is really no time for a nap."

Jackin sucked in a breath, then his eyes flickered open, sharpening a glare at Griffith through a sneer of pain.

The knot in Adequin's stomach twisted. "You okay, Jack?"

He gave a short nod, then hissed under his breath as his fingers drifted to the raw burns on his cheek. "Yeah, I'll be fine, boss, but what—"

"Warning," a computerized voice rang over the monotonous rhythm of sirens. "Core systems compromised. Gaseous breaches detected on deck one, quadrants A, D. Deck two, quadrants A, C. Deck three . . ."

Adequin exchanged a concerned look with Griffith as the computer continued to list the affected areas of the ship. She glanced at her nexus, but she'd lost her connection with the mainframe.

Griffith tapped at his own nexus, shaking his head. "Network's glitching. I can't tell details but it looks like the effusion cylinders have been breached."

"Effusion cylinders?" she asked.

"The tanks that house the buoyancy cocktail for the torus chamber. Unsealing the door must have triggered it—it's leaching ammonia and hydrogen into the other systems."

Jackin groaned as he pushed up to rest on his elbows. "How the hell would that have happened?"

"Fucking Drudgers probably left a parting gift," Griffith growled. "They couldn't salvage the ship themselves, and they sure as shit didn't want us to be able to get it going and come hunt them down."

Adequin's brow creased. "So they rigged the whole thing to blow?"

"'Rigged' is probably a bit generous," Jackin explained with a pained grimace. "They very well could have blown themselves up in the process, but a dozen or so mags worth of plasma arcs would have done the trick. No brainpower required."

Adequin steadied herself as the floor hitched and vibrated for a few seconds, like an aftershock tremor from a far-off blast.

"Damage-control systems fatigued," the computer announced. "System-wide deflagration imminent. Immediate evacuation advised."

"Uh . . ." Erandus's alarmed look shot toward them. "Deflagration means what I think it does, right?"

"Shit," Adequin cursed.

"Shit indeed," Jackin said, pained grimace hardening into resolve. "We need to get the crew free and hightail it outta here, boss."

"The effusion stalled out," Warner said. "Doors are still locked."

Adequin stepped to the torus controls screen, gripping the edge of it as if she could somehow wring out the last percent. She tapped through a few menus to try and reset it, but the system didn't respond.

She threw a look back to Griffith and Jackin. "We gotta get this door open—fast. Ideas?"

"When the computer fails . . ." Jackin began. "I'd say our best bet is brute force."

Griffith looked to Warner and Erandus. "There should be a boarding kit in the arms locker."

The two rushed away, returning a minute later with a large gear case. Adequin threw open the case, tossing aside a pack of small charges. More explosions would have to be a last resort.

Underneath a smattering of small electronics and hacking tools lay two thick crowbars. She pulled one out and extended it, the nanite-laden metal weaving itself together to form a single, long handle.

She caught Griffith's eye. "You up for this?"

He gave her a flat look. She tossed him the crowbar, then took the other for herself.

"It's one of the few reinforced entries on the ship," Griffith explained. "There'll be a blast door on either side of an inner seal."

"Copy that," she sighed. This would be a one-for-the-price-of-three kind of deal.

She walked to the torus chamber entrance, fitting the flattened end of the tool into the seam where the door bisected. Griffith did the same, facing the other direction. Adequin counted down, and together they heaved. She summoned every one of her Imprints to aid her, which sent a jolt of prickling hot pain to the left side of her face as the ones that had been dedicated to numbing and healing her burns rushed to join the others. A handful of squares slid to wrap low around her core, the rest rushing to bolster her upper-body strength.

Griffith bared his teeth, the pain evident on his crumpled brow. She eyed the alarming number of Imprints on his arms that remained static—stranded, malfunctioning.

The seam finally gave way, opening a couple of centimeters. Griffith held his side steady as she worked her crowbar farther in to find stronger purchase. They heaved again, repeating the process until the outer blast door's safety mechanism triggered, and it slid itself into the open position.

Adequin swept the beading perspiration from her brow, wiping her damp hand off on her pant leg before resuming her white-knuckled grip on the heavy crow bar. Unsurprisingly, the inner seal proved the most stubborn, but with even more Imprint-infused effort, it gave way a minute later along with a short burst of cold, pungent, ammonia-tinged air.

"One more," Griffith said by way of encouragement, though the edge of his voice came strained under a tight grimace of poorly masked pain. He clearly still suffered from the effects of the forced deceleration, but she knew he'd be too stubborn to admit it—right up to the point of passing out. Yet even injured, with half his Imprints malfunctioning, he still outmatched the others in strength. So as much as she wanted to force him to stop and send him directly to the *Synthesis*'s medbay, she had to let him see it through if she wanted to get the crew out in time.

They positioned the crowbars again and sweat stung Adequin's eyes as they heaved, growling through the final few centimeters until the inner blast door clicked and skated open the rest of the way.

Inside the dimly lit, circular chamber, three Sentinels stood shoulder to shoulder, pistols aimed straight at Adequin and Griffith in the doorframe. Front and center stood Griffith's second-in-command, a young circitor with short, black hair named Eura.

Eura's blood-stained hands trembled as she lowered her pistol, brow creased in confusion. "Excubitor? How . . ."

Beside her, the other two soldiers—both oculi—exchanged relieved glances. Though their faces were a mixture of flushed, scared, and angry, they all stood upright and appeared uninjured.

Eura nodded to Griffith, her worry loosening a bit. "Sir. Good to see you made it."

"Likewise," Griffith rumbled. He wiped sweat from his brow, then rested a forearm on the door frame.

"Everyone okay?" Adequin asked.

The two oculi holstered their weapons, then stepped aside. On the ground behind them lay Ivana—the *Tempus*'s mechanic, unconscious, her alabaster skin a sickly shade of pale blue. Smears of glossy crimson coated the torn remnants of Eura's duty vest strewn all around, clearly used to try and staunch the bleeding.

"She's in a bad way, sir," one of the oculi said. "Needs blood ASAP."

A jolt rocked the ship, sending a groan of steel creaking through the metal walls. Adequin stumbled, but kept upright despite how slow her fatigued Imprints positioned themselves. Save Griffith, the others lost their footing completely, tumbling to the deck.

From the corridor over Adequin's shoulder, the ship's computer blared a repeat of the evacuation warning, adding to the list of affected quadrants.

Eura's gaze hardened as she picked herself up off the floor. "What's going on?"

"Sitrep later," Adequin said. "For now, we abandon ship. Everyone to the personnel air lock."

Adequin made to pick up Ivana, but Griffith pulled her back.

"I've got her, Quin," he said, and his steady tone left no room for argument.

"Okay." She eyed him as he limped toward the wounded mechanic. "Just be careful."

He knelt and lifted the small woman, his stoic visage thawing into a deep frown. His sweat-slicked brow furrowed as it became harder and harder for him to mask his pain.

Eura and Warner escorted him into the corridor, trailed shortly by Erandus and the other two oculi. Adequin helped Jackin up off the ground, keeping an arm tight around his waist until his footing seemed sure.

They worked their way back down to the main deck, then quickly donned their suits and crowded into the air lock. After confirming everyone's helmets were secure, Adequin swept the controls to depressurize. She opened the hatch door as another wave of small explosions rippled through the *Tempus's* corridors.

Adequin ordered Griffith and Eura to move the unconscious Ivana across first, along with instructions to take her directly to whatever semblance of a medbay the *Synthesis* had. Warner led Erandus and the other two *Tempus* crew members across, then Jackin climbed out next.

Adequin let him get a few meters ahead, her eyes drawing up the tall, broad side of the dark ship above her. The *Tempus* sat silent and black against the void, with only the narrow beam from the *Synthesis's* searchlight illuminating a small section of the aft.

"Coming, boss?" Jackin's voice crackled over suit comms.

She cleared her throat. "On my way."

She'd made it about halfway when Jackin pulled himself into the *Synthesis's* open air lock, then turned to look back at her. That's when she felt it, the tiniest pull—deep in her stomach, right at her core, willing her back toward the *Tempus*. Just as she'd felt on the *Argus* before having to watch Bray tumble to his death, vanishing into nothing. Her head spun and her limbs jerked on instinct to catch her, as if she was about to fall backward.

Heart racing, she stole a glance over her shoulder, and a flicker of movement caught her eye. The outline of the *Tempus* silhouetted in a flash of light that disappeared so quickly, Adequin almost thought she imagined it. Then it came again, sharp and defined—a white static flicker from somewhere outward.

With a single brilliant flash, the nose of the *Tempus* exploded. The light dissipated in an instant as the gas fully burned away.

As if in slow motion, the large ship careened aft while debris flew in all directions, radiating out from the explosion in a strangely beautiful, uniform arc. But instead of continuing the eternal trajectory as it should have, the trail of rubble slowed, reshaping into a narrow stream. The charred remnants twisted backward and outward, winding toward the Divide like the flow of water snaking through a ravine.

"Shit," Jackin swore over comms. "Rake, hurry."

Heart pounding, she refocused and continued to pull herself forward, keeping watch on the drifting ship in her periphery. The tether fluttered in her grip, like a taut string that'd been plucked.

"Rake!" Jackin shouted through suit comms. He hovered in the open air lock, reaching out, urging her forward.

She'd only made it another few meters when the tether tugged roughly under her grip. She let go so it could slide between her hands as the remaining length expended from the *Synthesis*. When it ran out, the *Tempus* would start pulling the *Synthesis* along with it.

"Jack," she shouted, "you gotta disconnect the tether."

"Uh, you're using it," he called back.

"I'll maneuver to you," she assured, letting go of the sliding line completely. "Release it!"

She flicked on her MMU. A flashing red alert in her HUD warned that the thrusters were nonresponsive. But she didn't have time to troubleshoot or belay the order.

Just as the tether snapped taut, she gripped it long enough to fling herself forward, then let go. Jackin slammed his fist into the manual release switch and the cable cut free from the *Synthesis*. It snaked lifelessly, drifting away along with the careening *Tempus*.

Thankfully Adequin's aim had been true, if not much, much too fast, and she sped feet-first toward the open hatch.

"Shit—I'm coming in hot!"

Jackin cursed, yanking himself to one side as she flew into the air lock and crashed rather unceremoniously into the far wall. Pain shot through her joints as the left side of her body crumpled into the ridged metal plating and she bounced off. She scrambled to take hold of the grab rails, but they slipped between her fingers. Floating helplessly back toward the hatch, she noted with a modicum of relief that everyone except Jackin had already left the air lock. Thankfully no one else had been forced to witness her deft display of EVA work.

"Bloody void, Rake," Jackin said as he braced himself on either side of the door frame. He caught her in both arms, stalling her before she could sail right back out the hatch again. "You do know what that rocket pack on your back is for, right?"

"It's malfunctioning. Some kind of interference."

When they were somewhat steady, he let go to grip her shoulder, tapping a palm against the side of her helmet. "You good, boss?"

Her stomach reeled and limbs ached from the impact, but she gave a quick nod. "Good."

Spinning toward the hatch, she made to close the door when another flash of light burst from behind the *Tempus*. Not the clean static white of the Divide, but another blue, domed burst. The explosion released from the outward-facing side of the ship, shifting the vessel's trajectory again, but this time pitching it slowly but certainly inward. Directly toward the *Synthesis*.

"Griff," she shouted through comms. "Tell me you're at the helm."

The comms clicked and squealed in her ear, then his staticky response came through, garbled but comprehendible. "Here, Rake—engines—response—"

Adequin cursed and punched the hatch controls, but it didn't comply, instead flashing a red warning: "Unsecured personnel." Someone was still outside the ship.

She yanked herself into the open doorway and looked back toward the *Tempus*. Halfway across, three figures floated in the void, cast in the harsh light, reaching out and pulling themselves forward, as if clinging to a nonexistent tether.

The figures' edges blurred, skittering back and forth along the path between the ships and it took Adequin a few seconds to recognize what she saw—Griffith and Eura aiding the unconscious Ivana across the expanse, exactly as they had minutes ago, their synchronized progression lit by sporadic flashes of light as the Divide grew closer. The doppelgängers seemed completely unaware of Adequin and Jackin's existence as they pulled themselves across an invisible tether toward the *Synthesis*.

Adequin glanced at Jackin, who gaped at the time ripple—the *reverse* time ripple—in total disbelief.

In a jittering flash, the three figures flickered and disappeared. The safety lockout cleared, and Adequin snapped back into the moment, punching commands into the screen. The hatch slid shut and repressurized. She and Jackin both botched their footing and fell to the ground as the ship's simulated gravity pulled down.

"Rake . . ." Jackin breathed heavily, bracing himself on his elbows. "That was the *past*."

She swallowed, nodding slowly as she met his gaze through their visors. His bloodshot eyes were full of worry, and the charred burns that ran up his face were blistering and black around the edges.

"Quin!" Griffith's deep voice cracked over the suit comms. "Cockpit—now!"

Adequin leapt to her feet and ran for the cockpit. Jackin tossed his helmet aside and followed.

Adequin hastened up the two decks to the helm of the *Synthesis*. Griffith sat strapped in the copilot's seat with a half dozen holographic screens already docked above the control terminal. Jackin limped to the defense station on Griffith's right, while Adequin made for the pilot's seat on the left.

"Shields up," she ordered, tossing her helmet aside.

"Workin' on it," Griffith rumbled as he tapped furiously at the interface.

"I'm here, Bach," Jackin said, pulling his harness over his shoulders. Griffith palmed one of the large screens and passed it along the dash. It cut out briefly as it jumped across to Jackin's starboard-facing terminal, which lit in a flurry of holographic screens as the defense station activated.

Adequin pulled the loose safety harness over her head and buckled it, yanking to tighten the straps that'd been set for the Drudger captain's much thicker torso. She spread out a slew of screens onto the dash and tried to arrange the unfamiliar layout closer to what she'd expect in an SCL vessel of similar make. She supposed their trip out *could* have been spent setting control preferences and familiarizing herself with the ship's systems, rather than just standing there, anxiously devising every terrible scenario in which she might find Griffith dead or dying.

"Where are the others?" she asked.

"Setting Ivana up in the medbay," Griffith answered. "I sent your oculi down to make sure the warp core is seated—sublights are currently off line."

"Copy. Opticals on screen."

Griffith grunted. "Exterior cams are nothin' but static."

"Perfect," she grumbled. Having to rely on sensors alone would make their withdrawal that much less fun.

A pang of shame tightened her chest at the errant thought—an instinctive reaction engrained in her long ago. She knew better. It'd been one of Lugen's many mantras: Visuals were nothing but a security blanket. A way to make your brain feel like it might be doing something right—and certainly nothing you could ever rely on. The data was all that mattered.

"Finally," Jackin said, "Shields up. At one hundred."

"Copy one hundred," Griffith said, then cursed under his breath as he continued to receive only error messages from the engines panel.

Eura's sharp voice cut in from over Adequin's shoulder. "Sirs, where do you need me?"

Adequin cleared her throat, indicating the terminal against the port-facing wall behind her, the mirror of Jackin's station. "Take sensors—they're set for ship-to-ship combat, let's get them switched to vector agility. Then prio's a read on the *Tempus*'s volatility."

"Acknowledged, sir."

"Boss," Jackin called a warning over his shoulder. "Shields are a great start—but if it crashes into us or blows up while we're still this close, they won't hold, that's a guarantee."

Adequin slid a quick glance at Griffith. "Engine report?"

"Sublights are a no-go," Griffith responded, jaw tight. "Something's interfering with the starter, but without a mechanic on deck, we're not gonna be able to troubleshoot in time."

"*Tempus* viability, sir . . ." Eura began, her tone wary. "I'm getting a lot of interference, but it's not good. We have minutes, at best."

Adequin let out a sharp breath. "All right, fuck it." She palmed the FTL screen to expand it. "Prepare for snap-warp." She grabbed Kharon's coordinates from the dock, then hastily dismissed a series of reproachful snap-warp warning messages. "Copilot, authorize."

"Authorized," Griffith replied, punching the command into his screen.

Adequin tapped to engage, but the console blurted out a casual, negative tone in response. She resent the command, and Griffith tried again. The same disproportionately docile tone rang out. And again, nothing happened.

"Shit," Adequin growled. "What's wrong? I cleared the risk warnings."

"It's not the snap-warp," Griffith said. "The drive just won't catch. Do we have eyes on the core?"

"Sirs," Eura interrupted, "I don't think it's the core. We're getting massive waves of interference across all systems. My telemetry's rough, but it looks like it's coming from the direction of the *Tempus*, though I don't see what could be causing it. We need to get farther from it before we can accelerate to warp speed."

"It's the Divide," Jackin assured. "Back at the *Argus*, the same thing happened to the *SGL*'s warp drive."

"The *SGL*?" Griffith laughed.

Jackin ignored the snickering copilot. "We didn't get warp back online till we were at least a few hundred klicks clear."

Griffith's mirth vanished, and he threw a look over his shoulder toward Jackin. "How the fuck were you only a few hundred klicks from the Divide?"

"Focus," Adequin ordered, and Griffith turned back to his screens. "Ions—?" she began, but couldn't even get the full question out before he extinguished it.

"Still a nonstarter."

"Fuck." The half-healed burns on her cheek stung as adrenaline-laced blood pumped through her veins. She'd worry later about tasking her Imprints to continue the mending process. For now, she needed to put all her energy and focus into getting them out of there before the *Tempus* either crashed into them or blew them to pieces, or both. "Any ideas?"

Jackin cleared his throat. "Short of conjuring an interference dampener around the entire warp drive . . . ?"

"That doesn't sound practical at the—"

The proximity sirens blared, drowning out the rest of Adequin's words as harsh amber light bathed the cockpit.

"Debris incoming!" Eura announced, then started shouting approximate approach vectors over the din.

Adequin barely had time to silence the grating alarms before the ship jerked and the straps of her overtightened harness dug deep into her collarbones. Griffith let out a series of staccato grunts, cradling his bruised rib cage tighter with each jostling impact.

Adequin gritted her teeth, then the onslaught finally ceased. "Report."

"Shields eighty-four," Jackin answered, tapping furiously into his console. "Recharging."

"Keep them topped off. Pull from ancillary systems if you need to."

"Copy."

"Eura?"

"Looks like that was just the *Tempus*'s anterior atmo cycler . . ." Eura replied. "Minor, compared to what's coming, sir."

"Atmo . . ." Griffith mumbled. "What the fuck is this ship we're on anyway? Feels like a Nautilus?"

"It's a lighter version," Adequin said, "but yeah, same bones."

A glint of amusement fractured his pained grimace. "Remember when we were on Palias-V, and we had to steal that armored Nautilus to get off that infernal space station?"

Adequin chuffed a laugh. "Self-extraction at its finest. But let's reminisce later, eh?"

Jackin grunted, "Seconded."

"Yeah, yeah," Griffith sighed, "super-fun war memories. What I mean is, we had to get past the orbital defenses, and they'd frozen out the guns. So Antares jury-rigged that shield atmo bubble thing so we could just ram into that satellite and take the whole grid down."

Jackin slid him a shocked look, and Adequin nodded as Griffith's point became apparent. "Because Viator systems let you override air-lock safety protocols . . ."

Griffith inclined his head. "So you should be able to vent the atmo."

"Uh, *into* the shields?" Jackin asked.

"Exactly," Griffith said. "We KO'd the satellite and bounced right out of orbit as a result. Which wasn't ideal at the time, but now . . ."

Adequin nodded slowly. Now, it was exactly what they needed.

She chewed her lip, racking her brain to try and remember how Antares had pulled that shit off. The woman had been the seniormost Titan among them, and the very definition of maverick, constantly proposing objectively dangerous ideas which—because they worked more often than not—were seen as brilliant instead of lucky.

"Void," Jackin chuffed. "Rake, are you really considering this?"

"It's sound, North, I swear," Griffith said. "It not only gives a spatial buffer—"

"At the cost of integrity," Jackin interjected.

"—but can *increase* integrity," Griffith went on. "The added tension supports the shield as a whole."

"Like pulling a piece of fabric taut," Adequin offered.

"Fuck," Jackin cursed, then mumbled, "I hate how much sense that makes."

"No harm in trying, Quin," Griffith encouraged.

"Except that it sounds ridiculously dangerous," Jackin argued. "We don't design our ships that way *for a reason*. Besides, once the *Tempus* blows, how do you know we'll ricochet off the debris field and not just plow through it?"

Adequin shook her head, the back of her throat going dry. "I'm choosing to be *optimistic*."

"Physics doesn't really give a shit about your existential disposition, Rake!"

"I know, Jack!" she shouted back. "It's all I've got, okay? If the shields hold, it'll work, I know it will. And we're at arm's length of it. We'll get hit well before the debris has a chance to disperse. It'll be like smashing into a cracked brick wall—cracked, but it's still a damn brick wall. Just trust me, okay?"

"That's a big ask at the moment, boss."

"You got another idea, North?" Griffith grunted.

"No, I just didn't realize we'd opened the table to suicidal options."

The *Synthesis* rocked with more small impacts, sending the alarms into another frenzy.

"Time to think suicidal," Griffith said.

"Fuck, all right." Adequin exhaled slowly as her thoughts reeled. Jackin was right—it was a risk. But they had zero alternatives and were already out of time. She expanded the life-support interface. "We're doing this."

"We got personnel in the back, boss," Jackin warned.

"I'll isolate them. Eura, call them to the medbay."

Eura hopped on comms.

"Griff, trigger quarantine buffers," Adequin went on. "It'll help direct the airflow. Jack, switch to banded shield mode then undock the manipulation screen and send it my way."

They voiced their acknowledgments while Adequin tapped out commands, sealing the cockpit before cordoning off smaller sections of the ship, creating a direct, sealed path from the atmospheric cycler to the dockside air lock on the posterior of the ship. At least from that direction, the force of the expulsion would propel them laterally, and not directly toward the self-destructing *Tempus* . . . not to mention the Divide.

"Crew's in the medbay," Eura confirmed.

Adequin sealed the medbay bulkhead and deactivated air cycling before sealing the vents ship-wide. Jackin's defense screen arrived in her queue, and she flicked it open, then quickly tapped in the commands to extend the shields out from the hull of the ship.

"Extending ten meters," she said.

"That might not be a big enough buffer," Griffith warned.

"Then fifteen."

Jackin blew out a harsh breath. "Too thin, we'll lose cohesion."

"Fuck—twelve and a half?"

Griffith and Jackin exchanged a look she didn't have time to analyze, and she locked the final number in.

"Pass me thrusters," she ordered, and Griffith slid her the thruster control screen.

She was getting really tired of having to move ships with fucking maneuvering thrusters. At least this time she only needed to roll them, so the belly would take the brunt of the impact. It was more thickly armored than the rest of the vessel by almost 50 percent, and devoid of any exterior systems or hatchways.

However, when she keyed in the angles and prepared to engage, the readout flashed a vehement "thruster systems off-line" warning.

"Bloody void," she growled. "Do any of the fucking systems on this ship work?"

"Uh, life support . . ." Eura responded carefully, seeming unsure if the outburst had been a legitimate question. "And uh, weapons, sir."

Adequin paused, exchanging a dubious look with Griffith. That wasn't a half-bad idea.

Griffith gave a curt nod to indicate his agreement.

Adequin undocked the useless thruster control screen. "Disengage stabilizers."

"Disengaged," Griffith responded before she'd even finished giving the order.

"Uh, guys, what?" Jackin asked, not privy to their line of thought.

"Jack, what kinda recoil-dampener system does this thing have?"

"It's thruster controlled," Jackin answered. "They automatically counter when ordnance is fired."

"Perfect," she said, gladly accepting that bit of good news. With thrusters already off-line, there'd be no need to figure out how to counter the dampener system. One less thing to worry about.

Jackin's voice creaked with alarm. "Uh, yeah, and that's perfect *how* exactly?"

The *Synthesis* shook with another round of short-lived tremors. The high-pitched vibrations rattled in Adequin's teeth as the shields incinerated waves of small debris.

"Jack, what's the armament?" Adequin asked, voice wavering in her chest.

"Uh, one sec . . ." Jackin said. "Looks like the heavy-hitters are two plasma cannons and four quad laser turrets, all dorsal. There's a dozen point-defense flaks and six railgun turrets. Here . . ."

He passed her a diagram of the ship highlighting two banks of flak guns lining the port and starboard beams. She arrowed through to see the rest of the ordnance, then spun the holographic model and took note of four other flak arrays on the dorsal bows and quarters.

"Looks like there's some aftermarket ship-to-ship missile launchers too," Jackin added. "They haven't even been tied into the primary systems. Shit—there's *twelve*."

The vibrations finally ceased and Adequin pushed out a steadying breath. "Tell me there's payloads."

"All twelve primed with seeker frags, with a second set in reserves."

"Fucking hell," Griffith said. "That's quite an array for a ship this size."

Adequin couldn't disagree, but she didn't currently have the faculties to fret over the reasons a Drudger ship might be that well-armed.

Pushing aside the unease, she mentally tallied up the firepower. She was certainly no ordnance expert, but she'd fired enough random weaponry from starfighters with busted dampeners to appreciate what kind of impact it could have. Considering their mass, it wouldn't be enough to offer any appreciable translation, but it should be enough to roll them.

"Okay, Jack, spin up those guns," she ordered.

"Uh, all of them?"

"All of them."

He cleared his throat and began to comply. "You have a vector, boss?"

She maximized the navigation screen, which continued to emit a useless mess of static and oscillating numbers. There was still no way to tell which way was which, and no time to troubleshoot.

She closed her eyes for a heartbeat, racing through the *Synthesis*'s layout in her mind's eye to orient herself. Then she hastily assembled the variables: a rough idea of the rates of fire, mass of the ballistics, a general notion of the ship's weight, and where the hell the center of mass might be. It wasn't something she could truly calculate, certainly not in her head, with a veritable powder keg about to blow next door. But she didn't have time to ask the computer to run scenarios. Her gut instincts would have to be good enough.

She cleared the hesitation from her throat. "Bearing oh-nine-five, carom three-one-zero." She clenched her teeth and sucked in a deep breath, trying not to think about how much of a total bullshit guess that was.

Jackin scoffed. "Are you *seriously* trying to use ordnance as torque right now?"

Adequin's face burned hot, and she threw a glare at him. "Just do it, Jack!"

"Void," he cursed, then reported back the bearing, voice wavering.

"We got more debris incoming," Eura warned.

"Jack, you'll need to ride them as they fire," Adequin said. "Goal is a ninety-degree roll, so counter back as needed to get that underside forward."

"Shit—yeah, I know. I'll do my best, boss. Ready on your mark."

Straps cut into Adequin's chest again as the ship jolted hard. A blazing red warning burst onto her overview screen as hull integrity predictions plummeted.

"Now or never, Rake!" Griffith yelled as Adequin called out, "Mark!"

Jackin fired, and Adequin punched the air-lock override. Her weight slammed back against the seat as the ship shifted. A cold pressure built against her eardrums, and she sucked in a shallow breath as the atmosphere seemed to lose saturation—diluting until thin and feeble like the air at the top of a mountain peak.

Though the *Synthesis*'s direction of gravity maintained the floor as "down," Adequin could sense the subtle shift as they began to reel from the recoil of the expelled weapons, turning their underside forward to face the *Tempus*.

"You got it, Jack," Adequin encouraged. "I can feel it working."

Jackin swore between calling out bursts of fire and his modified bearing adjustments.

"Sensors show a fifty-degree roll and counting," Eura confirmed.

"Holy shit, North—you're doing it," Griffith said.

"Void," Jackin grumbled. "Mind not soundin' so surprised?"

Proximity warnings overtook the small cockpit again, carpeting their temporary optimism in a din of blaring klaxons and abrasive amber light.

"That was it," Eura announced, tone hard. "The effusion cylinders went up—along with the rest of the ship. Large-scale debris and radiative impacts imminent. Incoming bearing, uh ... oh-one-zero, carom two-six-three."

"Cease fire," Adequin ordered, and Jackin complied. "Match that bearing—weapons free."

"New bearing set, firing," Jackin called as he spun the ordinance-turned-thrusters in the direction of the blast to coincide with the ricochet.

"Impact—" Eura began to call out, but her words dropped from her throat as the ship heaved.

Adequin's head snapped back against the padded headrest, sending a shock of pain down her back as the full force of the shrapnel slammed into the shield bubble, and the fractured pieces of the *Tempus* propelled them inward. Away from the Divide.

Alerts erupted across the dash: shield-impact alarms, hull-integrity warnings, evasive-maneuver advisories.

"Shields?" Adequin called out over the blaring alarms.

"Holding—forty—two." Jackin grunted each word out from behind clenched teeth.

"Dammit. The heat sinks can't keep up," Griffith said, the words wavering in his chest with the violent vibrations. He tossed a defense-systems screen up in front of Adequin.

Adequin ground her teeth as she stared at the four climbing thermal gauges. "You mean the ship's not meant to have every single one of its guns firing at once?"

The previously thin, cool air had taken on a muggy quality, warming and thickening as if the strained heat sinks were leaching warmth up through the decks.

"We gotta decrease the rate of fire," Griffith warned.

"We have to hold out until we can warp," she insisted, forcing firmness into her tone even as the temperature gauges hiked higher and higher.

The ship lurched, and the velocity readout on the dash continued its steady escalation, one of few instruments that seemed to work. Just a few more seconds.

Eura's hope-filled tone rang out seconds later. "Interference is clearing."

"The radiation burn is killin' us," Jackin said. "If we don't warp soon, shields are gonna disperse."

Adequin gripped the armrests of her chair to try and steady the unending vibrations.

"Quin, heat sinks are gonna melt down any second," Griffith said.

Unblinking, she stared at their speed as it continued to rise.

"Rake—what are you waiting for?" Jackin shouted.

The velocity meter ticked up again. She hovered her hand in front of the command, tightening a fist and digging her nails into her palm as she forced herself to wait.

Then, finally, the velocity hesitated—no longer increasing, but not decreasing either.

"Copilot—" Adequin began just as Griffith punched the snap-warp authorization.

She slammed to engage. A grating roar ripped through the ship, like the echoing wail of a thousand metal girders crumpling in half. Adequin's thrashing pulse hammered against her eardrums.

All at once the shrieking clamor silenced, the vibrations ceased, and the wash of red light extinguished, returning the cockpit to its normal, dim hue.

Adequin held her breath, eyes unblinking as she fixated on the distressingly static FTL status screen. Convinced the interface must have frozen, she reached out to wake it, but before she could reach it, it flickered, lighting with confirmation of a successful warp acceleration.

Her racing pulse steadied and cool relief flooded through her. They'd accelerated to warp speed—back to Kharon Gate.

CHAPTER TWENTY-NINE

✦

Cavalon lay on the cool metal floor and tried to concentrate on breathing. Just breathing. In and out. No pain, only oxygen. Only what he needed—air. It was all he could do to focus on it.

It'd been at least fifteen minutes since Snyder and his cronies had grown bored and left. Apparently it wasn't interesting to beat the shit out of a guy who'd completely given up trying to fight back. Now he could barely move, his weak muscles gelatinized while also managing to feel like they were literally on fire. Threads of sharp pain traced along every nerve, phantom shocks left over from the volatile interfacing.

With a squeak of boots, Cavalon's eyelids flickered. He squinted at the blinding overhead lights, his head hammering with each relentless pulse of his heart.

Emery leaned over him. Her pale features tightened in a sympathetic grimace.

Emery, who he'd wanted to leave behind to die. Emery, who'd just tried to stick up for him by threatening someone twice her size with a fucking knife.

After confirming he wasn't dead, she'd left briefly and now returned with a biotool in hand. She poked at the screen and started an internal scan. Each tiny beep the device emitted cut through Cavalon's throbbing skull like a hot needle.

"How ya feelin', boss?" she asked.

"Great," he grumbled. "How's it look?"

She held the tool up and gave him a stilted grin. "Nothin's broken . . ." she said, clearly attempting to sound optimistic, ". . . too badly. Two cracked ribs on the right side. You want a bone knit?"

"Sure," he breathed.

Emery loaded the biotool, then opened his vest and unbuttoned his shirt. She injected the cartridge below his sternum, and he grimaced with the lance of pain. He didn't like shots to start with, but shots directly into swollen, bruised flesh were a special kind of painful.

He remained on the ground for a few minutes while the medicine seeped in. When a thick warmth grew along the bottom of his rib cage, he knew it'd started working, though his entire torso continued to throb with dull, heavy pain. There wasn't much to be done about the bruising, but at least the bones would heal. Though the worst of the pain was still the residual left from the volatile interfacing. Faint echoes of the harsh, sharp pangs still twitched along the length of his nerves.

"How about some apexidone?" Emery asked hearteningly, holding up a vial of clear liquid.

Cavalon's pulse sped and cool relief washed through him even at the sight of it. Just the thought of the painkiller coursing through his veins was enough to alleviate his suffering, however briefly.

But he swallowed hard and shook his head, letting the dense pain settle back onto him like a thick, unwelcome blanket. "I can't."

She quirked an eyebrow. "Why?" Then her shoulders slumped as realization washed over her face. "Oh. As in, you *shouldn't?*" He nodded, and she gave a sympathetic grin. "There's some over-the-counter stuff back in the medbay."

Emery helped him up, then he had to pause and close his eyes to let the pain from standing upright subside. With a fraction of a modicum of relief, he realized his previously stranded royal Imprints had returned to their default formation on his right arm. Still far too tired—and far too afraid—to test them, he could at least sense their willingness to respond just under the surface, a latent sensation, queued and awaiting orders. Hopefully those few excruciating moments of volatile interfacing hadn't done any permanent damage.

"Let's not tell Mesa," he croaked, slowly buttoning his shirt and restrapping his vest.

A trace of normal Emery returned when her worried brow bent into a scowl. "That's stupid."

"It won't help, trust me. The more I get the brass to fight my battles, the harder this is going to be."

"Or the more you're going to get beat up."

He pushed down the pain long enough to give her a genuine grin. "It builds character."

She rolled her eyes. "I think you've got plenty enough of that already."

She didn't press him further, but crossed her arms and huffed. She clearly thought he was being an idiot for not reporting it, but it didn't matter. Mesa couldn't do anything anyway, whether or not she was the highest-ranking officer left on the ship. And Snyder was unhinged. Cavalon refused to put Mesa in his crosshairs as well.

Cavalon attempted to appear unaffected as he and Emery walked back to the medbay-turned-research lab, though he knew one look at his limping gait would give him away. Luckily, Mesa paid them no heed whatsoever as she hovered over the pyramid. The device sat in the middle of the table, surrounded by six small laser turrets, red beams shining onto the golden surface.

"You have returned," Mesa said, still squinting at the pyramid. "I am taking measurements. I think one facet may be *slightly* thicker than the others . . ."

"We got the, uh," Cavalon began, then tossed the bloody hand on the table. "This."

"Excellent." Mesa glanced up to smile her approval, but as her large eyes landed on Cavalon, the look quickly faded to concern. "Are you all right?"

He quickly cleared his throat. "Never better. I think this might be more what we're after, though." He produced the necklace he'd taken off the Drudger captain and held it by the chain so the golden triangle medallion dangled in front of her face. "Drudgers don't usually wear jewelry, right?"

Mesa's eyes lit up. "Indeed. That looks quite promising." She lifted both sets of thin fingers to cup the medallion delicately, and Cavalon dropped it into her waiting hands. He pulled his chair out and sat, withholding a groan of pain as his bruised organs protested the compression.

Emery appeared beside him with a canteen of water and three small tablets. He gave her a grateful nod and downed the pills along with half the water. Emery sat, and they watched as Mesa carefully swept the flat golden triangles over one side of the pyramid. She turned it over to rest on a different side, then repeated the process. When the medallion reached the peak of the pyramid, a quiet beep rang out.

"Oh," Mesa said, back straightening.

A clicking preceded a subdued hum, then a tiny panel slid open on the peak of the pyramid. Bright white, crisp holographic screens appeared in the air—the same bulging triangular panels Cavalon had seen the Drudger captain surveying.

Mesa gave a pleased shrug. "That was . . . easier than I expected."

Cavalon and Emery both slid forward in their chairs, staring at the bright screens in curiosity. Dozens of displays fanned out, some layered in stacks, some individual panels, all clustered in a tight formation just over a half meter wide.

Mesa reached out with tentative fingers to touch a screen, then swept it a few centimeters to the side. It responded, floating to the right, stopping when she let go. Exactly what they would expect from their own holographic displays—which wasn't surprising, since humans had assimilated the technology from Viators.

Mesa began experimenting with the screens, quickly discovering she could open new panels along the edges of existing ones, linking them together to create one larger image. Soon, she slid around the menus like she'd invented the tech herself. But each time she opened a new screen, the others shrank to accommodate. With a scowl, Mesa stood and discarded her chair. She pushed up the sleeves of her uniform and rubbed her hands together as she glared at the display. Cavalon grinned. Things were about to get serious.

After only a few minutes of hyperfocused trial and error, Mesa figured out how to expand the limits of the projection, so more screens could remain expanded and side by side, instead of stacked. When the whole display had become as wide as their worktable—almost two meters—Cavalon began to wonder how it was possible. The screens projected from an opening no more than two centimeters square. He had no idea how it could project an image that wide without some degree of distortion.

When he asked, Mesa's monotonous, absentminded answer was simply, "Self-refracting vectors."

Cavalon exchanged a look with Emery, who shrugged and popped a fresh piece of purple gum into her mouth.

Mesa finished expanding the screens and locked them together, revealing a handful of small, stationary dots scattered across a faint, white-lined grid. Just as he'd thought when he'd first seen the displays in the cockpit, it appeared to be some kind of blueprint or map. Though, an empty one—like a blank template that needed filling in.

"Mesa . . ." Cavalon began. "What are we looking at? Do you know what this is?"

She didn't respond at first, then with an effort she drew her gaze away, peering through the semitransparent displays to stare at him. "Maybe." She seemed awestruck, but also cautious. He thought he could sense a hint of fear behind her speculative, overlarge eyes.

"So, what is it, Mes?" Emery asked. "Spill it."

Any fear Cavalon may have sensed seemed to vanish as a smile spread across Mesa's face. An honest, unhindered, full-out grin. "I think this may be a curanulta."

Cavalon exchanged another clueless look with Emery. "And that's . . . what?" he asked.

Mesa blinked heavily, snapping out of her reverie. "Right, of course." Her tone transformed from inquisitive and quiet, to the steady and informative timbre Cavalon had grown accustomed to.

"Curanulta. It is Viator for . . . well, it is akin to 'boundless.' A fable, or so I thought."

"A fable?"

She gave a short nod. "It is a device recorded in their ancient texts, but I have never seen one, and I know of no one who has. I had thought it lost to time, if it ever existed to begin with."

"And it does what, exactly?"

"It is an atlas, of sorts, but dynamic. Fluid mapping."

Cavalon slouched and sat back, hoping she couldn't sense his utter confusion. Mesa tended to say things as if they were common knowledge, to the point where he was convinced he'd understood her, only to realize after his brain had time to chew on it a while, he had no idea what she'd just said.

To his relief, Emery took a turn at asking the next obvious question. "What the hell's 'fluid mapping'?" she grumbled.

"Well, this is all speculation, of course," Mesa began. "But it is a star map, linked to a series of beacons. The beacons send information back to the device, and the curanulta stays up to date."

"How 'up to date'?" Cavalon asked.

She raised her shoulders as she turned back to the screens. "I am . . . not sure. In many accounts, it is implied that they update almost instantly."

"Real time?" Emery asked.

Mesa's eyes narrowed. "That is the theory, but it is not practical. There would still be a lag of some kind, unless Viators had previously perfected interstellar data transfer to a degree beyond our current capabilities."

Emery crossed her arms, her tone unusually serious. "What kind of information?"

"Oh, many things," Mesa said lightly. "It could be used to monitor the status of their own ships, or enemy troop movement. There are many forms of military application. Also, simply as a record for astronomical bodies. To monitor star life cycles, system compositions, galaxy movements—a survey of the stars. It is quite fascinating."

"Galaxy movements?" Cavalon asked, incredulous. "How large of an area do these things map?"

"There are curanultas in ancient Viator texts that claim to have mapped the entire universe."

Cavalon scoffed. "How is that possible?"

Mesa shook her head slowly. "I do not know. I also do not know if there is even any truth behind the claims."

"How much does this one cover?"

"I do not know." Her mouth pinched together like the words tasted bad. She clearly didn't have to say that kind of thing very often, and never so many times in a row. She moved forward and swept the screens around, quickly scaling up a section near the top edge.

She pointed at a border of thicker white lines that ran along the top of the grid. "I would theorize that this is the outer perimeter of what this atlas has mapped." She gestured to a series of static circles spaced evenly along the edge. Some sat directly along the line, and others were a slight distance below it. "These may be a series of information beacons, sending data to the curanulta." Her lips pinched as she let out a huff. "This is all conjecture."

Cavalon rubbed the back of his neck as he let the information sink in. "If there are so many of these beacons out there, wouldn't we have seen them?"

"Certainly not," Mesa answered. "Space is quite vast, for one. Also, you would be astonished at how negligent the Legion has been in mapping the Divide. It would not surprise me if these beacons had gone unnoticed."

Cavalon's eyes grazed across the map, and he found himself looking for some kind of "you are here" indication, but saw nothing. "So, you don't know what this is a map of?"

A rueful frown pulled at Mesa's lips. "Unfortunately, no. I cannot tell if this map is showing our current area as opposed to anywhere else in the universe. From the lack of astronomical bodies, it can be presumed it is a section along the Divide. Though I possess a moderate understanding of the Viator tongue, I am unfamiliar with how to properly read a three-dimensional map, particularly a largely empty one. Someone familiar with stellar cartography who also possesses a fluency in the Viator tongue would be better suited."

"Rake knows their language," he said. "Does she know stellar cartography?"

"Better than I would, I suppose," Mesa agreed. "We will have to wait for her return and see if she can make more sense of it." Mesa rescaled the image, then let out a soft huff. "One thing that is quite odd—there seems to be three sectional overlays, each slightly different."

"How so?"

She reached up to the top row of screens that made up the edge of the map and expanded the area. "This first level shows a complete, unbroken border, which trails between these larger, outer beacons seamlessly."

She pressed both palms into the screens. They flashed once, then a full second set of maps appeared stacked just behind them. They switched places, and the first set disappeared.

"This second level is interesting." She pointed to a small symbol in the corner that had not been present on the first set, an infinity loop with three parallel slashes through it. "This more or less means 'current.'"

"As in, present?" Emery asked.

Mesa nodded. "I would theorize that this is the active state of the map. The most up-to-date information. It shows what appears to be the same area as the first level, but with an altered border. See how here, the border now skips between these two larger beacons?"

Emery leaned closer. "And all the inner beacons are now outlined in red."

"Yes."

"Maybe they're off-line?" Cavalon suggested.

"Perhaps," Mesa agreed, then pressed her palms into the map again to bring up a third set. "This third level is much the same as the second, but labeled with something akin to subsequent, or next. And it shows these . . ." She pointed to a series of slowly flashing lines that ran between the larger circles. A tiny Viator symbol labeled each one. "And all the beacons on this entire section of the map are marked red."

Cavalon chewed his lip in silence as he stared at the crisp, red circles and pulsating white lines.

He cleared his throat. "It does sort of make sense, right? That they'd be out of order? Viators have been all but gone for the last two hundred years. I doubt the holdouts in the Resurgence War prioritized running around at the Divide, repairing data beacons for their mythological atlas devices."

Mesa's brow rose and her features softened. "I suppose there is some validity to that statement."

The corner of Cavalon's mouth tugged up. That must have been Mesa's way of saying he was right.

Mesa held her palms forward again, this time pulling back instead of pushing, and the map returned to the second level. "I suppose this is the map we should work from, if it is marked as the 'active' state."

Cavalon had to wonder what that made the others. Past and future? Was this a *4D map*? He almost let out an audible laugh, but managed to hold it in.

Emery cleared her throat, leaning her chair on its back legs and feet up on the table. "So you're telling me this thing can track ship movements?"

"In theory, yes," Mesa said.

Emery gave a stilted grin. "You really don't need to give the theory disclaimer every time." Her chair banged back down to the floor, and she stood, reaching over the wide table to point at a tiny, stationary mark from the back of the map. "This guy . . ." She dragged her finger to the left. "Was here a couple minutes ago. I betcha this is our fearless EX. Only thing moving in this whole giant sea of nothin'. And if it can show ship positions, I bet this is how our Drudger friends found the *Tempus* earlier."

Mesa nodded. "Very astute, Miss Flos." Emery glared at the

name, but Mesa remained unfazed. "It may also be how they knew of your arrival aboard Kharon Gate, and our subsequent return."

Cavalon shook his head in disbelief. "This is *absurdly* powerful," he said. "If the Viators had access to this kind of tech, how did they lose the war?"

"Well," Mesa said, clearing her throat and drawing up her chin. This was clearly a topic she felt more comfortable lecturing on. "As you can see, the scale is such that it is not precise." She enlarged the screen that showed the mark Emery had pointed out. "This 'ship' will not appear to have changed positions until it has progressed into another grid of the map, which could be billions of kilometers. Also, we cannot view any details about the vessel. It could be anything from a fighter pilot, to a dreadnought . . ."

Cavalon leaned back in his chair, half listening as Mesa continued to rant about the potential faults of the impressive technology. He surveyed the expanded screens, and for the first time noticed a small stack on the top right that appeared out of place. Instead of white, they were colored a hazy amber yellow. They were muddled from being stacked atop each other, but he could tell they were filled with Viator words and numbers, along with a series of diagrams. It looked much more like a schematic than part of a map.

"So, though it may provide a general account of movement on a stellar scale," Mesa continued, "it does have its limitations. And it is unlikely many exist, or we would have salvaged them at the end of the Viator and Resurgence Wars. The few that exist must be well-guarded by the remaining Viator allies. Or simply lost."

Cavalon pushed back in his chair and his bruised stomach smarted as he stood. He ground his teeth and tried to ignore it, rounding the table to stand beside Mesa. He pointed to the yellow screens. "What's this?"

"I do not know." She swept the stack open, shoving some of the map aside in the process. Unpacking it one by one, she lined the dozen panels up in a three-by-four grid. "There was a file repository," she explained. "A submenu for storing data aside from the atlas information. This was the only file present."

Cavalon stared at the screens for a few long moments, then reached out and slid one of the panels to the side. He could sense Mesa stiffen, but she didn't say anything. Slowly, he moved the screens into a different configuration until the small diagrams, lines, and symbols matched up along the edges.

"What is it?" Mesa asked.

He stared at it, eyes racing over the unfamiliar symbols. "I don't know. Looks like schematics of some kind, but I can't read Viator."

"I may be able to translate. What would you like to know?"

He focused on an outlined section in the center of the schematic. He pointed an unsteady finger to a symbol he saw repeated many times in various forms, with a series of Viator numbers tacked onto the end after a hashed caret symbol.

"*Linu* is the symbol for chemical compounds," she answered, then pointed to one of the labels on the left side. "I am no chemist, but I believe this is Hydrogen-1. Then, these are other isotopes of hydrogen. Deuterium and tritium, I believe." She dragged her finger to a final label on the right side, larger than the rest. "And . . ." She tilted her head in contemplation.

"Helium?" he asked warily, unsure whether or not his tone reflected his growing sense of dread.

Mesa regarded the symbol placidly, then gave a curt nod. "Yes. I believe you are correct."

Cavalon's eyes raced over the information again, armed with this new understanding. Lines ran from the three hydrogen isotopes into the larger label marked "helium," and other symbols he couldn't interpret were lined up underneath each.

"What do you see?" Mesa asked, curiosity evident in her voice.

"A bomb?" He grimaced. He hadn't meant to say it out loud.

Emery's chair squeaked, followed by the light padding of boots as she crossed toward them. She stepped up beside Cavalon and stared at the schematics. "A bomb? Drudgers, building bombs?"

"I don't *know* that's what it is," Cavalon said quickly, in a futile attempt to backpedal.

Mesa looked back at the screen. "No, I think you are correct," she assured. "This reaction appears similar to that created in the fusion rifle I was telling you about the other day."

"Well, what the fuck?" Emery said. "Since when do Drudgers build fusion bombs?"

"They may not be a race of geniuses," Mesa said, her tone taking on an unexpected sharp edge, "but you are underestimating them if you think they are not capable of calculated destruction when supplied the proper motivation."

Cavalon swallowed, his eyes darting between the women, unsure of the source of the awkwardness thickening the air between them.

Emery gave a soft nod, her voice coming out strangely quiet. "Yeah, I know, Mes."

Mesa drew her neck up straight and continued, all tension gone from her voice. "Besides, *plans* for a weapon are not of consequence. I assume our inventory of the Drudgers' ship did not reveal any actual fusion bombs?"

"Not that I heard about," Emery said. "But what if these aren't the only Drudgers? What if there are others with these same plans?"

Cavalon realized then that Emery hadn't been told the whole story. She didn't know the device had come with a set of instructions from a real, live Viator. If she did, she'd sound even more right than she already did.

Emery slid in front of him and started shuffling through the menus. She pushed aside the map and schematics in favor of a panel that listed a long series of Viator numbers.

"I don't read Viator," she said, pointing at the symbols stiffly, "but these are numbers. *Coordinates.*"

Cavalon raised an eyebrow. "For what?"

"I dunno. But if this really is a map of all this," she said, sweeping her hands out to indicate their general area, "then there's nothin' out here but Sentinels. Which means these Drudgers' friends could be headed for the *Typhos* or the *Accora* or any of the other dozens of Sentinel vessels stranded out here. For all we know, they could be hopping from post to post, dropping an H-bomb on every one of our ships. And if these guys were here at Kharon, then the *Argus* was probably next."

Mesa pinched her lips together. "That seems like a leap, Miss Flos. Many leaps, actually."

"Well, *Miss Darox,*" Emery said, crossing her arms, "that might be the case. Either way, the EX needs to know about this."

"I agree," Mesa said hospitably. "We should continue to study the map and find out everything we can from it. When the excubitor returns, we will present her with only *the facts . . .*" she added pointedly, narrowing her eyes at Emery. "*Then* we will see what her decision is."

Emery sighed, but nodded her agreement, and the two set to work sifting through more screens. Cavalon sat down carefully, letting out a long breath as his bruised torso smarted and his mind chewed over the new information. He worried somewhat about what Rake's reaction would be. If she followed her original instinct when they'd first seen the Viator, she'd shrug, turn the gate on, and shuffle them all through.

Though it gave him some relief to know that even if Rake forced the rest of the crew to relay away, she would more than likely stay behind herself. Hell, she would probably blow the gate up behind them so the Viators couldn't use it to get closer to the Core. If they did find the crew of the *Tempus* alive, maybe she'd keep that other Titan with her to help fight. Maybe Jackin. But she'd make the rest of them go.

Yet in the back reaches of Cavalon's mind a strange sensation arose: that he wanted to be there too. Not that he would be overly thrilled with the idea of being thrust into a war right after the Legion had decided to withdraw from the Divide completely. But he didn't think he could live with it if he just disappeared through the gate and left it all behind.

He had no idea why he felt that way. He clearly wasn't popular with the Sentinels at the moment—he'd just gotten the shit beaten out of him as proof.

Pain twisted in his abdomen as he shifted in his seat. He braced a steadying hand on his bruised rib cage and let out a long breath. Maybe he really had deserved Snyder's wrath. But he didn't want to deserve it—not because he gave a shit about what that asswipe thought of him, but because he couldn't stomach seeing himself that way. As just another pathetic, docile, complacent pawn getting shoved around the galactic chessboard by Augustus.

He had tried to intercede, that had to count for something. Way too late, maybe, but at least he'd tried.

However, even he couldn't delude himself into believing it'd accomplished anything, not really. That day, he'd started down a path he wasn't ready for. He'd had no escape route, no way to disappear, no plan for what came after. He'd just wanted to make an aimless point with a big fucking nuclear middle finger. But what good was that to anyone?

It'd been nothing but a crime of passion enacted out of hatred and spite. He'd been trying to right a wrong that couldn't be undone. Bombs couldn't bring someone back from the dead.

He should have taken a page from Augustus's book and played the long game. Made careful, calculated decisions, called in all his favors, manipulated and bribed people, honed the weapons of his own socioeconomic arsenal. Like Rake had said, fight fire with fire.

But it was far too late for that now. The only way out would be through. If he could make it out the other side, maybe he'd have a chance to try again, to do it right this time.

To do that, he'd need to find a way to not get killed—either by nature, or the Sentinels. He needed these people to trust him. Or more importantly, to make himself feel worthy of that trust. Maybe the way to do that was to simply be fucking trustworthy—to be useful, to be needed. To become one of them.

If he made his own mark, he could disassociate himself from *fucking Augustus* once and for all. And to do any of that, he would have to see this through to the end.

CHAPTER THIRTY

The tension melted from Adequin's shoulders, and she slumped back in the pilot's seat, wiping the sweat from her brow. The *Synthesis*'s cockpit had filled with a heavy quiet, marked only by ragged breathing.

Jackin broke the silence first, letting out a noise equal parts growl and hearty laugh. "Good fucking void, Rake. How many times in one day can you save us by almost killing us?"

Griffith chuckled, but it cut off with a sharp wince as he held a hand firmly to his rib cage. "Don't make me laugh, North," he pleaded. "I think the adrenaline scrubbed all the painkillers out of my system."

Adequin sighed. In all the chaos, she'd completely forgotten about how injured both Jackin and Griffith were. She unhooked her harness and slid to the front edge of her seat, shaking out her arms, the adrenaline drop causing her muscles to tremble. "Yeah, we should get you both to the medbay. But let's run a quick systems report to be safe."

Griffith, Jackin, and Eura cycled through status screens for every system so Adequin could take stock of the total damage they'd taken. Other than some probably slightly melted heat-sink coils and completely exhausted shields, the worst outcome was the dent they'd put in the ammunition reserves. Despite the all-green propulsion diagnostic, she had Jackin add a full warp-drive assessment to the to-do list. Considering the horrific noise it'd made on activation, she wouldn't feel comfortable sending the *Synthesis* out again until it'd been looked at. Though if Puck had figured out how to get the gate turned on, they wouldn't need it.

After restoring atmosphere, she sent Griffith and Jackin ahead to the medbay, then unlocked the bulkheads, unsealed the vents, and returned the ship to its default state. She instructed Eura to hold down the cockpit, giving assurance that she'd send someone to relieve her shortly.

Adequin was disappointed but not surprised to discover the shoddy state of the *Synthesis's* poor excuse for a medbay—which the Drudgers had treated more as a storage closet. The oculi had already removed dozens of crates in an effort to unearth a narrow counter of unused supplies. Griffith stood, head low, at the foot of a filthy exam table. On which lay Ivana, unmoving, unbreathing. The blood that stained her uniform had dried to a dark crimson, a sharp contrast to her colorless skin and pale blue lips.

Warner approached Adequin with the telltale clinking of loose dog tags, and a swell of bile rose up into the back of her throat. She closed a fist around the cold metal as he passed them to her.

"Her vitals bottomed out before we even got her on board," Warner said, eyes downcast. "And we couldn't find any kind of medbot—or even just a damn transfusion kit—anywhere in this cluttered mess."

Adequin's gaze drifted across the ransacked state of the counters and cupboards. They'd clearly done their best to try and find help in time. Though plenty of cartridges and a handful of biotools lay strewn around the small room, synthesizing blood was one thing a biotool could not do.

Warner gave Griffith a wary glance, then looked back at Adequin. "I'm sorry, sir."

She shook her head and gave his shoulder a firm grip. "You did all you could." She lowered her voice. "Take a couple of others and . . . just wrap her the best you can. Make room in cold storage in the mess. We'll do a proper send-off once we're back on Kharon."

Warner nodded. "Yessir."

He motioned to Erandus and the two oculi from the *Tempus*, and together they carried Ivana out of the medbay.

Adequin cleaned up Jackin's burns, then stuck him with a pain-killer syringe and sent him and the other oculi straight back to the helm.

The door to the medbay had barely sealed behind Jackin before Griffith had his arms around her. He hugged her close, and she leaned into him, letting the embrace sieve out some of her residual tension. "I'm sorry about Ivana."

"It's not your fault," he said, then cleared his throat. "And we'd all be dead if it weren't for you. Not a ship captain, my ass—that was some damn fine captaining."

"That was just flying."

"No, that was leading. And technically there was very little actual flying."

"You helped. Which you shouldn't have."

"You'd have rather I let Eura sit copilot?"

"Jack could have done it."

"Sure, but I think it was a damn good thing we had him on weapons. I can't say I could have pulled off what he did with those guns."

"Void, tell me about it," she agreed. "Was he a gunner at some point?"

"Not that I know of." Griffith let out a quiet rasp and tried to mask a wince. He glanced down, gripping his temples between his thumb and forefinger.

"Come on," she said, taking him by the elbow. "We need to do a full scan."

His eyes flashed up, bloodshot and dry. "I'm fine. It's only a headache."

She leveled a flat look at him. "Don't think I haven't noticed all your grimacing and wheezing. You survived that deceleration against all odds, but you're still plenty hurt. You need to rest."

"Me?" he asked, eyebrows high, his gaze skimming over her cheeks. "Between that shiner and those half-healed burns, you look a wreck compared to me."

"Nice try. You've been overdoing it since the second you woke up."

"Just give me some apexidone, I'll be fine."

She set her jaw, pointing curtly to the exam table. "Scan. Now."

He scratched his chin. "Okay, okay, if it'll make you feel better. But first . . . sorry, I have to know . . ."

She quirked an eyebrow. "What?"

"Did you really name a ship the *SGL*?"

She gave a weak shrug. "I couldn't think of anything else."

"Really? Nothing else?" he said, voice high with skepticism. "'Cause I can think of a hundred different names right now just off the top of my head."

"Sorry, all I could think about at the time was *you*."

A wide grin spread across his face. "Aw, damn. You're really sweet on me, huh, Mo'acair?"

She made to smile, but her lips twitched, her amusement extinguished along with the reminder of Lace's final words. Griffith still didn't know what'd happened to her.

Heat rose to Adequin's face, and her breath caught as she looked down, kicking at the floor with the toe of her boot. She crossed her arms low and tight over her stomach as it heaved with an acidic burn.

"Uh, shit," Griffith said quietly. "What'd I do? What's wrong?"

She swallowed the sour lump forming at the back of her throat. "Lace told me what that means . . . *My anchor.*"

"Oh, she did, huh?" He tightened his arms around her back. "Well, it's apt. You're what brings me back from the Divide." She looked up and the warmth in his eyes vanished in an instant. His brow lined deep and he licked his lips slowly. "What is it?"

She swallowed more acidic phlegm. "She's gone, Griff. I'm so sorry. I tried, but . . ."

His grip on her loosened, shoulders dropping as he took a half step back.

"I'm sorry," she said again. "I know how much she meant to you."

He nodded as his vacant gaze drifted over her shoulder.

"I'm sure it doesn't help, but you should know . . . we'd never have made it off the *Argus* without her. She died saving us." Her throat burned with more swells of bile, a sharp ache tightening under her rib cage. "So many people are dead, Griff. I couldn't save . . ."

His chest swelled as he blew out a heavy breath, then pulled her into him. She clamped her eyes shut, dampening his vest as a few tears pressed out.

He stepped back, keeping hold of one of her hands. "What happened?"

Pushing out a trio of long breaths, she did her best to clear away her worry and guilt and dread long enough to explain everything that'd happened since they parted ways. He was shocked to hear about the *Argus*, and equally as shocked that someone managed to convince her to board the Hermes and escape. When she told him how *that* went down, his expression tightened—equal parts amused and resentful. She wasn't sure if he planned to thank or punch Puck later—or both. News of Augustus Mercer's cloned Drudger army, her brief and unproductive interaction with Poine Gate, and the cryptic Viator message left him looking just as bemused and fatigued as she felt about the whole thing.

"I just can't figure out what we're supposed to do next," she explained, chewing the inside of her lip as she picked at her nails. "There's no directive that even comes close to covering this situation. Except maybe the outer-colony abandonment protocols, I guess? But that doesn't even really apply—we never got an official withdrawal order, and there's certainly no 'insurmountable enemy force' to trigger it without one. So technically, as the final point of egress, we should be holding Kharon Gate until contacted. Either way, until we get that gate functional again, we're stranded out here, and the Legion has *disappeared*—"

"Fuck the Legion, Quin," Griffith said dismissively. She stood straighter, surprised by the vehemence in his tone. "We don't need them to survive this."

She swallowed down a lump in her throat, and he gripped her hand tighter.

"But you need to get this guilt-trip shit out of your system," he continued. "And you *really* gotta stop pretending like the Legion is gonna rally behind us."

Her cheeks warmed. "So that's it?" she said, aware of how desperate she sounded. "We're just on our own?"

"Has Lugen called back?"

She shook her head.

"Then yeah, we're on our own."

Her shoulders fell, and she pinched the bridge of her nose.

"Hey—" He took her hand back to force her to look at him again. "You can do this, Rake. If anyone can, it's you. I know we've lost a lot, but there's still soldiers out there depending on you. You make the call, and they'll follow you, you know that. But hundreds of their comrades have died in the last day. They need to see you steadfast. Not questioning yourself, not sitting around waiting for orders that might never come. And not wallowing in guilt."

She bit her lip. "So, what you're saying is, get the fuck over it?"

He smiled. "Basically."

"Thanks for the pep talk."

"Anytime."

Griffith wrapped an arm around her shoulders and pulled her into the crook of his neck. "Don't stress, Quin," he said into the top of her head. "We'll get back to Kharon, regroup, then figure out what's going on. Kill some Drudgers, maybe some Viators, save the fucking universe . . ." She sniffed a laugh, and he continued. "Then we'll retire to Myrdin, build a house on the beach, and everyone will leave us the fuck alone."

She scrunched up her nose. "Myrdin?"

"Wherever you want, name it."

"I was thinking Sobrius-II. Slightly more temperate."

"Sobrius-II it is."

She smiled. "Happily ever after."

"Fucking happily ever after," he agreed, then his tone softened. "Just a hiccup first, Mo'acair."

"This is quite the hiccup."

Griffith's breath hitched, and he held a firm hand to the bottom of his rib cage as he tried to hide a scowl.

"Okay, no more retirement planning," she said, tone firm. "Time to do this scan."

To her relief, he didn't argue, simply nodded with lips set in a tight, grim line, pain furrowing his sweat-drenched brow.

Adequin picked through the crates left around the room, collecting a handful of supplies that might be useful, then moved on to the cupboards where she unearthed a never-before-used disinfectant atomizer. She used it to clear the dried blood off the padded exam table, then summoned her Imprints to help Griffith get up onto it. She laid him back onto the reclined surface, then began a full internal scan with a biotool.

His headache quickly escalated into a full migraine, and when he started to dry heave into Warner's discarded EVA helmet, she grabbed a second biotool and injected him with the only above-average useful thing she'd found in the entire medbay: a multipurpose "hangover" syringe that would help with pain, nausea, and dehydration.

When the scan completed, it confirmed most of what they'd already known. The damage had been restricted to Griffith's torso, and outside of a few bruised ribs, added nothing serious to his docket of injuries. At least nothing the biotool could diagnose.

When he started to doze off, Adequin couldn't bring herself to leave him alone in the shitty room, to leave him lying where Ivana had been just minutes ago. So she called Jackin on her nexus to check in, then dragged a stool beside the table and laid her head onto Griffith's chest.

He groggily lifted a hand and ran his fingers through her hair, dragging them gently across her scalp. After a few minutes, his hand drifted to a rest and his breaths came slow and deep, synchronizing with hers.

Despite the sense of relief that sank in, her chest remained heavy with guilt. She swallowed hard. "I'm sorry, Griff."

"For what?" he rumbled.

"For sending you away again. For not warning you in time."

"No way," he said, the grogginess disappearing from his tone. "We're not doing that."

"It's my fault—"

"The fuck it is." He lifted her face to meet his gaze. The lines around his eyes ran deeper, and his dark brown skin had taken on a cool tinge. He looked tired, old. But his warm eyes shone with determination. "You didn't know what was happening before we left; there's nothing you could have done."

"It may not be *directly* my fault, but I should have seen it coming. The signs were there."

"No," he said again, tone even more adamant. "I've watched you wither from guilt over the last five years about what happened on Paxus. Like hell I'm going to let this extend that even further."

"I know you think I'm too hard on myself about that—"

"That's an understatement."

"But there's something I never told you about what happened."

His brows knit. She took a deep breath, then hesitated. He'd gone this long without knowing, what good would it do now?

But Griffith knew everything about her, except that. It'd been the only thing she'd ever kept from him, and that didn't feel right anymore. They'd come too close to death too many times in the last twenty-four hours. She didn't want either of them to die with a lie left between them.

"Why are you still beating yourself up about it?" he asked. "The targets got away, it happens. It's not your fault. It was Lugen's decision to cover it—"

"They didn't get away."

"What?" he asked, his voice a dull croak. "Yes, they did. I was with you."

"Not at the end. You were confirming the mountain pass was clear, and I was already inside."

"I think I would have noticed a bunch of corpses once I got there."

She shook her head.

"So they were never there?" he asked. "Bad intel?"

"I let them go."

He didn't respond in any perceivable way, expression blank as he stared back at her, unblinking. He cleared his throat quietly. "You . . . what?"

She just nodded slowly.

He blew out a heavy breath. "Why?"

She looked down at her hands, entwined in Griffith's thick, calloused fingers. "I . . . couldn't. That's why I'm hard on myself about it. I still can't say whether I did the right thing."

He didn't speak, but when she looked back up at him, his confusion had disappeared, replaced with serious, intent concern.

His jaw tightened. "You're not kidding, are you?"

"No."

"What do you mean you *let them go*?"

"I just . . . I couldn't do it. I was standing there with a gun to the head of the *last* breeder. And they were staring back at me, and all I could think was I would be the last thing any Viator would ever see."

"Right, which was the whole objective," he said, voice thick with bewildered disbelief. "The whole point of the campaign. Hell—of the *war*."

She cast her gaze down, unable to stomach the astonishment in his bloodshot eyes. "I know, Griff."

Unwinding his fingers from hers, he sat up, swinging his legs over the edge of the exam table. He groaned along with the too-sudden movement.

"Hey, take it easy," she warned, holding up a steadying hand.

"I'm fine," he grumbled. "In my debrief, Lugen said . . ."

"Like you said, he covered it up. He just . . . altered the details slightly for your version."

"You mean he covered up his fucking cover-up?"

"You know how bad it was before Paxus, Griff," she said, the inside of her mouth suddenly bone-dry. "Lugen didn't want to keep watching people die. Recruitment had bottomed out—the last thing he wanted was another conscription."

"You're deifying him even more than normal, Rake," he growled, his deep voice wavering with anger, a scowl lining his sweat-slicked forehead. The muscles in his neck wrung taut, and he tugged at his collar to loosen it. "Lugen may have had his reasons for lying," he went on, "but don't think for a second it's because he cared about whether we lived or died."

She took a dry swallow, trying to steady her racing pulse to keep her response even. "You're right. He knew what it meant to be a soldier; it was never about *our* lives. But it trickles down. The population was—*is*—still in decline, and only getting worse. He knew humanity couldn't afford for the Resurgence to turn into another thousand-year war."

Griffith shook his head. "That doesn't mean you just throw in the towel and give up when you're within arm's reach of victory."

"He made a hard call, but you know it was the right one," she argued. "And it's not like he had a choice. Even if he'd wanted to pursue them, they were already in the wind. It could have taken years, if not decades to find them."

"Right. Because you . . ." He glowered and his lips twisted as if he'd tasted something bitter. ". . . *let them go*."

Adequin ground her teeth. "What difference does it make whether they escaped or I let them go? They're still alive either way. You never questioned that before."

"Because now I know you had *a choice*."

The disappointment lining his tone sent a wave of nausea through her. She certainly hadn't expected a forgiving, or even empathetic response, but she hadn't expected sheer anger either. It rolled off him in palpable waves as he steadied himself and rose to standing, shoulders hunched.

"It makes a difference, Rake," he went on. "If you would have just shot the damn breeder like you were supposed to, Lugen wouldn't have had to decide whether to cover it up or not, whether to go after them or not. You held humanity's future in your hands and you . . ." He trailed off, his gaze glossing over as he broke eye contact and stared down at his boots. He tugged at his collar again, his fingernails scratching at his *Volucris* tattoo.

She cleared her throat, but her voice still came out weak. "I was trying to be merciful, Griff."

He barked out a bitter laugh. "*Why?* They were never merciful to *us*. The only reason Lugen had to worry about population decline in the first place was because the bastards spent a thousand years ruthlessly exterminating us—and when that wasn't enough— they weaponized sterility so we couldn't keep making more human fodder to throw at them."

"That was hundreds of years ago, and there's no definitive proof that was engineered."

"Bloody void," he growled, disgust pinching his brow. "Not this again."

"Think about what we saw firsthand in the Resurgence—they weren't even a *shadow* of the monsters they'd been made out to be. That could all be myth for all we know."

"You try telling that to Mesa," he fumed, and a blistering spike lanced between her ribs, stilling her breath. "Ask her how pleasant those POW camps were, and whether or not she thought the Viators might be 'misunderstood' while she watched them torture and kill her family and friends."

"Void, I know that," Adequin hissed through clenched teeth. "There's no question of how they treated the Savants. But it's a different—"

"Different?" he snapped. "No. The only 'difference' is that instead of a nuisance to be exterminated like we were, they saw the Savants as their fucking *property*. If they weren't being used like lab animals, then they were just cattle to be bartered to the SC. And all because, what? The Savants didn't want to fight—they wanted to have their own lives, their own culture, and weren't being obedient mutts coming to heel like the Drudgers."

Hot tears rose to Adequin's eyes, and she tried to shake her head, but it came out a short, rigid jerk, her muscles gone stiff with anger. "That's *not* what I meant, Griffith. There's no excuse—"

"There's no excuse for not stopping it when you had the chance!"

"It can't be that cut and dry. Not every one of them can be a monster. How would you like to be held accountable for every terrible action every other human took?"

"No. No way. They don't get the benefit of the doubt, and you certainly don't get to use it as an excuse. If you have a chance to end all that pain, you take it. After nine years of slogging through our friends' corpses, I'd think you would have understood that."

Her nails dug into her palms as her fists clenched tighter and her Imprints buzzed up the backs of her arms.

"You don't *hesitate*," he continued, "you don't question what's right or wrong when you've been fighting the same fight for a decade. You do what you were called there for, whether or not you *feel good* about it."

"That's not fair," she said. "Think about what command was asking me to do. Can you honestly say if you'd been the one in that cavern that day, you wouldn't have hesitated? Even the slightest?'

He licked his lips as he shook his head, scratching the back of his neck. "Fuck. Maybe it's my fault."

Her brow furrowed. "What? That's not what I meant."

"I thought it'd be safest to send you on. That I needed to hang back and make sure we weren't getting flanked—that we could actually escape that planet alive instead of marching straight to certain death with no escape route. Never in a million years would I have guessed I needed to be there to make sure you'd go through with it."

She scowled, letting a prickling wave of heat rekindle her anger. "You're right. Maybe if you *had* taken point, you would have been there to pull the trigger instead of me. But you let me lead the way, just like you always did."

"Because *usually* you're really fucking good at leading the way, Rake!" he shouted.

"No," she said evenly, pouring all her effort into not letting her voice rise. "That's not on me. You never led the way because you were too scared to."

His scowl loosened as his lips twitched with a response that stalled out in his throat. He seemed as shocked by her words as angry.

"It's the same reason you gave up that centurion posting with the Vanguard for the lateral ranks of the Titans," she continued. "One that meant you'd never be 'in charge.' And that's why you were so damn frustrated when everyone turned to you for guidance. You were terrified that if you were given command again, you'd fail. That it'd all been a fluke, and you'd never be able to live up to that day at Redcliff. Which is why you were so damn glad when I came along—not because I *understood* what'd happened to you, but because you knew I was someone you could push to the front while you fell behind. Whose shadow you could walk in, so you could ensure you'd never have to be more than second-in-command again."

His shoulders swelled, jaw firm as he stared back at her, seeming unable to form a response.

"So yeah, I might be caught up in something that happened five years ago," she went on, "but at least I'm not stuck *fifteen years* in the past."

Fury flashed across his eyes again, but at once it melted away, his features going slack with realization. He swallowed, wiping beads of sweat from his forehead with the back of his hand. "Shit," he breathed. "I get it. This is why . . ."

Her eyebrows pinched together, heart hammering in her chest during the heavy silence. "What?" she managed.

"This bootlicker act . . . Void."

"What are you talking about?"

"That was never the Quin I knew." His eyes narrowed. "You know, the 'person whose shadow I could walk in,'" he added bitterly. "I never understood why you'd changed so much after Paxus. Why you were suddenly so worried about being a perfect little soldier all the time."

Warmth flooded her face, stinging her partly healed burns and sending her bruised cheek throbbing.

"You think you can make up for what you did," he continued, "by acting like some exemplary commander for a bunch of criminals at the edge of the universe? Because you fucking can't. That's not how it works."

"That has nothing to do with this. I'm only trying to make the best of a shitty situation."

He shook his head, ignoring her. "I always thought Lugen had just opted to pull the plug. That he couldn't stomach another wild goose chase across the galaxy along a hundred trails of paper-thin intel, or maybe he was getting pressure from the Quorum to end it. That you were just the closest person he could point a finger at, so he'd sent you away for a few years to act as a scapegoat while the rest of the brass cooled off about it. But they don't even know, do they?"

She swallowed, shaking her head slowly. "I don't think anyone but Lugen knows."

"So this—the Sentinels, the *Argus*. This was a *real* punishment."

She nodded.

"All because you had a chance to end it, and you threw it away . . . but all eyes were on the First back then, so Lugen couldn't just disappear you. And he loved you too much to execute you outright."

His last words hung in the air, ringing harshly in her ears. She'd never been able to fully wrap her head around why Lugen had handled it the way he did. But she couldn't imagine it'd come from a sense of devotion to her, considering her current circumstances. By all rights, he'd left her out here to die.

"I don't get it, Rake," Griffith went on. "You've been a legionnaire since you were sixteen. How could you justify that level of betrayal? Outright defy an order like that?"

"It wasn't about defying orders, Griff. It's way more complicated than that—it's xenocide."

"It *was* xenocide," he corrected, the sharpness rekindling in his tone. "A *chance* at xenocide. Now it's just a mistake you can't fix."

Adequin's seething stomach turned, and only when the floor thrummed did she realize it wasn't from anger, but because they'd dropped from warp speed.

Jackin's voice came through her nexus. "We're here, boss. Cruising up to port now."

The ship gave a short jerk as the ion engines engaged. She pressed the link to respond, doing her best to steady her shaking voice. "Thanks, Jack."

She swallowed hard as a volatile mix of frustration and worry and guilt strained against her ribs and twisted in her ruined stomach.

Griffith stood with his hand over his eyes, squeezing his temples between his thumb and forefinger, his other hand braced on the edge of the exam table.

"Shit, are you okay?" she asked, her words a dry, trembling croak.

"Just this damn headache . . ." Griffith mumbled, shaking his head.

"Do you need another shot of apex?"

"It's just broken glass," he said.

She gave a cursory look around the small medbay. "What glass?"

"Not back yet."

She took a dry swallow, brow creasing. "What?"

Griffith didn't look at her. He scratched the top of his head, then let out a long breath. "Small mercies . . ."

She narrowed her eyes.

It had to be a time ripple. Maybe the real Griffith had walked away when she wasn't looking, and a doppelgänger had replaced him and started spouting nonsense.

But it took less than a glance to survey the room and confirm there was no second Griffith anywhere in sight.

"Griff, I don't know what you're—" She stopped short as his eyes closed. His knees gave way and he collapsed, head snapping hard against the metal decking.

She rushed to him, dropping to the floor and gripping his shoulders. His body had gone completely limp, head lolling to one side.

"Griffith!" He didn't stir.

His thick muscles went rigid. A vise tightened around her throat, squeezing the air from her lungs.

His shoulders twisted, then his whole body convulsed as his muscles spasmed. It lasted a few gut-wrenching seconds before he went limp again. Seconds later, his chest lifted up off the floor in another convulsion, his head hanging lifelessly. His eyelids slid open, showing only the whites of his eyes as they rolled back into his head, shocking her from her paralyzed state.

Then things began to happen very quickly.

She screamed into her nexus, and her Imprints flooded her arms. She and Warner hauled Griffith's tremoring body through the hatch and into Kharon Gate. In the medbay, someone pulled a cot away from the wall so they could set him down. She gripped Jackin's vest and yelled something at him. Mesa stood transfixed, and Cavalon ran his hands through his hair and stared at Griffith in stone-faced shock. Emery rushed up to face Cavalon, yelling at him to *do something*, then his blue eyes, terrified and confused, locked onto Adequin's.

She had no idea why she'd even looked at him. She didn't know if he could help. Three degrees, but he wasn't a doctor. But he'd been her go-to problem solver for the last twenty-four hours, so why not this too?

Cavalon finally blinked, then his pale face flushed and his doe-eyed stare hardened. He gripped Jackin's arm and said something into his ear. Jackin took her by the shoulders and dragged her toward the door.

Cavalon leaned over Griffith's twitching body, and the last thing she heard before Jackin ushered her out was Cavalon's brisk demand, "Get me a tPA cartridge."

CHAPTER THIRTY-ONE

Somehow, Cavalon got the man stabilized.

He wasn't entirely sure what he'd done to accomplish it. He'd gone into some kind of shocked, crisis state. An autopilot of sorts, where his brain filtered out every other bit of knowledge he'd ever acquired and nothing remained except anything he'd ever heard, even in passing mention, about emergency medicine.

It'd been that look Rake had given him, like he alone possessed the ability to save the man. Like he was her only hope, and if he failed, she'd be broken forever. It'd kicked his brain into motion, forced him to put aside any and all self-doubt, and just *fix it*.

Now, Griffith lay motionless on the cot, breathing steadily. He remained unconscious—probably for the best. His body needed time to heal.

Other than the unconscious Titan, Cavalon stood alone in the medbay. Mesa and Emery had taken the pyramid elsewhere to continue their study. Rake had been reluctantly pulled from Griffith's side by a concerned Jackin, insisting she needed to eat, sleep, shower, and she'd feel better in no time. From her ashen, haunted expression, Cavalon doubted she'd feel any different until Griffith woke up.

Cavalon picked up a biotool and checked the Titan's vitals again. Though he didn't know what to consider "normal" for a two-meter-tall man as burly as Griffith, the green blips next to the numbers indicated they were within healthy ranges.

He had no idea what to deduce from the man's symptoms. When they brought him in, he seemed to be suffering some kind of seizure, but according to Rake's account, he'd also exhibited symptoms of a stroke.

Cavalon's eyes flickered to the diagnostic machine processing the blood sample he'd drawn earlier. It'd give more in-depth information than the biotool could alone, but it took its sweet time delivering the results.

Though his pre-genetic engineering stint in pre-med afforded him a degree of familiarity with medical biology, he would still only have a limited understanding of the findings. Sure, he was *technically* a doctor—two of his three degrees had been doctoral level. But a doctor of genetic engineering and astromechanical engineering. Not a doctor of trying to save the EX's objectively good-looking Titan pal.

Though, Griffith appeared quite a bit older than Cavalon thought he'd be. Rake said he was forty-two—forty-five, technically, but forty-two biologically. His hair had already gone to ash at the temples, and a fair amount of gray and white flecked his thick beard. The wrinkles lining his face, however, had a depth to them Cavalon wouldn't have expected for just over forty. He'd attribute it to the hard life of a Titan, but that didn't seem to have done Rake the same disservice.

The diagnostic machine beeped, and Cavalon walked over to check the status. It only listed about half the results, none of which appeared particularly alarming, so he closed the display and shuffled to an empty cot beside the worktable. He tossed the biotool down, then cradled his bruised, aching midsection as he sat.

He gritted his teeth and wiped moisture from the corner of his eye. His body still throbbed horribly from Snyder's attack, and all the unhindered movement and panic of the last hour hadn't helped in the least.

He couldn't keep working like this, walking around acting like nothing was wrong. The bottle of banal painkillers Emery had given him sat on the edge of the table, and he palmed it open. He tossed three tabs down his throat and swallowed them dry, too sore to consider getting up again to find a water bottle. He didn't have high hopes it'd do much for his pain.

Then he remembered—Rake had come back earlier with burn scars all along one side of her face. Jackin had similar, if not far worse burns, though where his looked hours old, Rake's seemed to have been healing for days. Cavalon's royal Imprints had often helped heal a stray cut or soothe a strained muscle, but never anything like that. Then again, he'd never suffered an injury that bad before. Rake had already proved his Imprints were capable of a lot more than he realized. Maybe they could help with this too.

He took a breath and tried to task them with healing his bruised guts, but the second they kicked into motion, he immediately regretted it. The way they clawed across his skin and dug into his sore muscles only made him feel worse. Though he gained a bit of relief in seeing some proof that the volatile interfacing hadn't completely broken them.

He looked over at the stack of cartridges sitting atop one of the unopened cases of medical supplies, and bit his lip in contemplation. One option remained that he hadn't tried yet.

It'd been over three months, what could one dose hurt? Even when he'd first started on apex, he didn't get hooked for at least a week or two. He thought. Maybe. He couldn't really remember that time very clearly. It'd taken a few days, at the very least. He could take a small dose to get his pain under control, and not become addicted. He definitely could.

With a groan, he stood and hobbled over to the collection of cartridges, pulling out a single vial of apexidone. He sat back down, then loaded the dose into the side of a biotool with trembling fingers.

Switching the tool into injection mode, he pushed his sleeve up and held the tip to the inside of his elbow. He tried to steady his shaking hand as he inhaled slowly, staring at the clear liquid sloshing inside the cartridge.

He flinched at the hiss of a door sliding open and looked up. Rake stood in the doorway, her damp, lightly tangled hair swept to one side. A few of her Imprints buzzed over the skin on the un-bruised side of her face, continuing to heal her burns.

She stared at him placidly with bloodshot eyes, cheeks flushed pink. Like . . . she'd been crying. There was clear evidence, but Cavalon couldn't imagine it.

She stared at the biotool in his hand, then looked at the open case of apexidone, then back to him. "What are you doing?" she asked, her tone eerily impassive.

A wave of indignation washed over him that he couldn't quite account for. He glared and stood, tossing the tool down on the table. "Do you always have to think the worst of me?"

"Are you kidding?" she growled, marching to stand in front of him. "I've done nothing but think the best of you since you got here."

He couldn't respond at first. Anger, which he now understood to be fueled by embarrassment, continued to flood through him. The tide subsided as he processed what she'd said.

She was right. She'd done nothing but give him chances, de-spite the aggressive, snarky jerk he'd been in their first meeting. She'd put forth more effort in believing in him than he ever had himself, and even then, expected more out of him. He owed it to her to keep trying.

"It's not what it looks like," he began, taking a steadying breath to settle his temper. "I'm not taking it *recreationally.*"

"Then why?"

"I'm in pain. It fucking hurts, okay? I thought I could go without it, but it's too much."

"*What* hurts?"

He shook his head. "It doesn't matter."

"It matters. Tell me what happened."

"Just some bruises, they'll heal. I'm fine."

Rake's composed expression wavered. "Bruises from what?"

He pressed his lips together and looked down at his feet.

It'd be easy to tell her. Let her storm off and take her rage about Griffith out on Snyder and his cronies. But then he was *that guy.*

Though both his options were currently shitty, he felt better about being the silent outsider that got the shit beat out of him than the brown-nosing snitch that got the shit beat out of him. He couldn't fall back on her every time something bad happened. He had to learn to stand on his own.

"Listen," Rake said quietly. "If you're in that much pain, and you need to take it, take it."

He looked back up to meet her gaze.

"If you're worried about the repercussions," she continued, "I'll help. I'll restrict your access to it. I'll chuck the rest out the air lock if I have to. I promised to babysit you, remember?"

He blinked back at her. Void.

No one had ever offered anything like that to him before. His bouts of addiction had been met with scorn and annoyance from his family and friends, and his rehabilitations had been undertaken alone, time and time again. But here was Rake, mere days in. Willing to be there. To slap the drugs out of his hands and tell him no. To have more concern for his well-being than he did himself.

Cavalon swallowed the lump in his throat.

And now she was giving him an out—permission to use it. Alleviate the pain in the short-term, and if it went bad, she'd hobble him back together after the fact . . . but he wasn't that guy anymore. At least he didn't want to be.

He pulled up one corner of his mouth and gave her the most sincerely grateful nod he'd ever given. "Thank you, sir. But I'm not gonna take it."

Her warm eyes glistened, and her weary stoicism gave way to a hint of . . . something. The shriveled optimist in him almost wanted to say respect, but it was probably just relief.

He cleared his throat. "Can you do one thing for me, sir?"

"Maybe," she said tentatively.

"Restrict the admin controls for our Imprints?"

Her face paled as she looked down at her nexus. "Void," she grumbled as she opened a menu and tapped furiously into the screen. "I forgot I did that." She finished typing and looked back up at him, cheeks flushed again, but this time with anger.

He wet his dry lips, unsure if her rage was directed at him.

She said nothing for a few seconds, then took a deep breath. "You won't tell me who did it?"

He considered it again, for the briefest moment. He'd love to see Rake beat the shit out of someone, but getting the anti-royalists in trouble wasn't likely to endear him to the rest of the Sentinels.

Rake seemed to take note of his silence. She didn't press him further, but simply let out a sigh and said, "I'm sorry, Cavalon."

"It's not your fault," he assured. "But I think it'll be better if they don't see you protecting me all the time. You're not always going to be able to babysit me."

She nodded, then glanced over at Griffith. "Have the results come back?"

"Nothing out of the ordinary yet, but it's only about half done."

"I'm going to go check on Puck and Jack. Let me know when you find something out?"

"Of course."

Rake hovered for a few silent seconds, then turned and left.

Cavalon closed his eyes and steadied his breath.

Apex-relapse crisis averted. Time to refocus. Busy himself. Find other ways to ignore his pain.

He'd wanted a chance to gain their trust, to be useful. Rake wanted answers. He would find her answers.

So he ignored the humming diagnostic machine and went to a stack of equipment crates in the corner of the room. He dug through each until he found a cytoscope headset and a pair of interface gloves. This tech, he knew. This was Genetic Engineering 101. He would take a peek at Griffith's cells and see what was going on.

He dropped a sample of Griffith's blood into the side of the cytoscope, then pulled on the wired gloves and headset. Using the gloves to navigate, he zoomed in on the cells until they filled his range of vision. He focused inward and concentrated on the relevant

memories, shoving aside all the mechanical and theoretical knowledge that wouldn't do him any good. It was time to focus on biology.

Much to his chagrin, he'd been a natural at genetic engineering. He'd completed the degree in half the standard six-year allot-
ment, and outshone his peers, and even professors, by almost an
absurd magnitude. He didn't know if he excelled just to get it over
with as quickly as possible, or if he'd actually wanted to master the
subject—to arm himself against his grandfather by becoming more
adept than even him. Either way, Cavalon had hated every bloody
minute of it.

He supposed he should be glad for it, now. He might be able to
use it to help Rake, to save Griffith. As he processed what he saw
through the headset, however, that small solace faded.

He continued to stare at the image, unable to comprehend it.
He had no idea how a seizure or a stroke, or any other ailment for
that matter, could cause what he saw.

Lifting the headset off, he looked at Griffith. Pale, wrinkled,
tired. He'd been tremoring, seizing.

Maybe what Cavalon saw in the scope wasn't the *result* of what
happened, but the *cause*.

He collected fresh blood from Griffith's arm, put in the new
sample, and checked it. He took a small skin scraping and examined that. Then, he used the biotool to biopsy Griffith's thyroid,
and had a look at those cells. Bone marrow, next. All the same.

Pulling off the headset and gloves, he let out a resounding
sigh.

He had to tell Rake. Or rather, *someone* had to tell Rake. He saw
no reason he had to do it himself.

Cavalon lingered anxiously just around the corner from the control room. He planned to wait and pounce on Jackin when he inevitably left to use the latrine, or eat, or do whatever else optios did.

In the meantime, Cavalon picked at his fingernails, paced nervously, even ducked away into a dark corner a few times when he

heard footsteps coming up the hallway. He had zero interest in being cornered by Snyder again.

After only a few minutes, to Cavalon's intense relief, Jackin appeared, marching out the door toward base camp with a focused glower.

"Oh, uh, Optio?" Cavalon called after him. "North? Sir?"

Jackin stopped short, one eyebrow quirking up. His burns cut up the right side of his neck and had singed a path straight through his black beard. Rake had done a good job cleaning it up, but it'd definitely leave a scar—at least until they could get back inward to a real medical facility. Cavalon didn't want to think about the likelihood of that at the moment.

"Yes, Oculus?" Jackin asked, tone curt.

"I, uh, have some information about the centurion."

"Great. Let's grab Rake." Jackin turned back to the control room, but Cavalon gripped his arm to stop him. Jackin stared at Cavalon's hand, then looked back up with a heavy glare.

"I, um," Cavalon stammered, then let go. "I was thinking, I'd tell *you*, then you could tell her . . ."

Jackin scowled. "Seems much easier if you just tell her directly."

Cavalon lowered his brow, and his voice came out dry and serious. "I shouldn't be the one to tell her."

Jackin's face fell flat. "What does that mean?"

"Yeah, what does that mean?" Rake stood in the doorway, arms crossed, her now mostly dry hair pulled up into a loose bun. Eyebrows raised, she stared at Cavalon and Jackin expectantly.

Cavalon swallowed down a lump. "Well . . ."

He gave a wary glance over Rake's shoulder, where Puck and a few others hovered around terminals, working diligently. Still trying to restart the gate, most likely.

He cleared his throat. "Let's . . . talk in private."

Rake's face fell, then she nodded curtly and stepped between them to march into the hallway. They followed her back to the medbay, and when the door slid shut behind them, Rake turned to Cavalon and crossed her arms. "Out with it, Oculus."

"I decided to take a closer look at some cells," Cavalon began carefully, "just to see if I could get an idea about what's going on."

"And?"

"And, well, there's some homeostatic imbalance. Some dysplasia that implies a maturation level that I *really* don't understand. The most troubling thing is that there's an unusual amount of atrophy—"

"Okay," Rake said patiently. "Now pretend like I don't have a doctorate in genetic engineering."

"Yes, so," he said quickly, then cleared his throat. "Griffith seems to be undergoing an increased rate of cellular senescence . . ."

Rake leveled a flat look at him and shook her head slowly, back and forth.

He sighed as he realized he was pulling a Mesa. "Right. Sorry. His, uh . . . his cells appear to be *aging*."

"Aging?" she asked plainly.

Jackin's black eyebrows furrowed. "Like, abnormally so?"

"Yes . . ." Cavalon said warily.

"Why?" Jackin asked.

Cavalon swallowed. "I don't know? I'm, uh, pretty confused by what I'm seeing, to be honest. Can you tell me what happened to the *Tempus*?"

He listened intently as Jackin told him about the *Tempus*'s fate at the hands of the collapsing Divide. Rake stood in silence the whole time, arms crossed and chewing on her poor lip like she held it solely responsible for what was happening.

When Jackin finished, Cavalon took a moment to process everything, and grimaced as he realized what it could mean.

It was . . . shitty. Really, really shitty.

He looked at Rake, who stared at him with wide eyes, a narrow fragment of that same haunted look she'd had when they'd first brought Griffith in.

"What are you thinking?" she asked.

Cavalon decided to take a page from Mesa's book, and begin with a disclaimer. "This is only a theory." Rake nodded her understanding, and Cavalon went on. "If he pulled away from the gravity at the Divide, without the dampening effects of the torus chamber, and without undergoing the proper deceleration . . . then his physical presence in that space-time may have ceased, but his cells may have continued at that rate."

Rake didn't respond, continuing to stare at him, blinking slowly.

"It's like . . . time dilation, in a way," he continued, unsure if they were following his logic. "He physically left, but never slowed down. And wasn't protected from it. His body is still going that same rate. So he appears accelerated, in a sense, relatively speaking. Or to him, this gravity is 'slower' than he is. Than his cells are. I'm assuming he's *perceiving* things properly, or I imagine he'd have been acting very strange." He tore his look from Rake's dazed expression to Jackin. "Am I making any sense?"

Jackin nodded, brow creased deep.

Cavalon sighed. "Gravitational tempology, for the record." By far the most useless offshoot of his studies, but now it'd arrived in all its glory, combining with genetic engineering and his most basic understanding of medical biology to deliver Rake a punch in the gut.

"Okay," Rake said quietly, then turned to Jackin. "So, his cells are aging at an increased rate?"

The optio looked confused, seeming as unsure as Cavalon about why she chose to ask *him* the question. Jackin exchanged a wary glance with Cavalon, then looked back at Rake, his brow softening. "Sounds like it, boss."

"So . . . he's dying?" she confirmed.

"Well—" Jackin's voice caught. "I suppose so, yes."

"What can we do?" Rake asked.

Jackin frowned. "Rake, I . . ." He looked to Cavalon with wide eyes.

Cavalon cleared his throat. "Um, nothing."

She turned her doleful expression onto him, and Cavalon regretted ever answering. That look had been far less distressing when it'd been directed at Jackin.

"*Nothing?*" she asked.

"I'm not a doctor," he said quickly, "but, no. I mean, I don't even know where to begin with a cure for something like that. It's like asking for a recipe for immortality."

"Would it stop if he joined back up with the Divide?" she asked.

"Stop? No," he began, mind racing as he tried to process her train of thought. "I mean, yes, the balance might be restored, but I don't think it'd resolve itself once you left the Divide, even if he slowed down properly the next time. He'd have to ride it forever. And all that'd be doing is changing the *perception* of his life span."

"So, it's permanent?" she asked, eyes glistening.

Then he felt it, that sensation he'd been hovering on the edge of: failing her. Disappointing her. Like he'd been gutted with a white-hot iron rod.

"We can't stop or reverse the aging process," he said quietly. "It's just not possible. Just like time. Forward, never backward."

Her eyes flickered with recognition, then her tone became fervent. "Then how do you explain what we saw on the *Tempus*?"

He quirked an eyebrow. "What'd you see on the *Tempus*?"

"The *past*. A time ripple. I saw me and Griff—doing the exact same thing we'd just done moments before."

Cavalon looked to Jackin with wide eyes. Instead of the look of shock he expected, Jackin nodded.

"I saw it too," Jackin agreed.

Cavalon shook his head. "That's not . . . possible . . ." He scratched his lengthening stubble with both hands. "Not possible," he repeated firmly. "Maybe a quirk, because of how they pulled away from it? A reflection? Maybe." He filtered through his memories, all his studies, everything he thought he knew about anything. He shook his head again. "I'm sorry, I just, I don't know how that happened. Either way, I don't think that changes anything for Griffith."

The vestige of hope that'd briefly glimmered across her eyes faded away, and that iron rod buried in Cavalon's gut wrenched and took an even deeper plunge.

"Right," she said quietly.

"I'm sorry . . ." he began, but she'd already disappeared into the hallway.

CHAPTER THIRTY-TWO

Adequin shut out everything else and headed straight for Mesa. The Savant had been poring over the pyramid's screens for hours, and by now she must have had at least some idea of what information the device contained.

Mesa and Emery were alone in a small common room down the hall from the medbay. Emery paced by the door, balancing a bottle of water on the back of her hand as she marched back and forth. When Adequin approached, Emery snapped to attention, saluting to her chest with the sloshing bottle.

Mesa stood in the center of the room, shrouded in crisp, white holographic screens, which projected from the top of the burnished gold pyramid sitting on the floor at her feet. The display stretched two meters wide and just as tall, in a complete three-hundred-and-sixty-degree circle around her.

Adequin stepped in front of Mesa. The flood of light washed the Savant's warm skin in an ethereal glow. She stared up at the highest parts of the screen, then drew her gaze down to meet Adequin's.

"Excubitor," Mesa said, eyebrows high and expectant. Then all at once, her features softened and she frowned. "How is the centurion?"

Adequin cleared her throat. "Still unconscious."

"I am sorry."

"Thanks."

With a shuffle of feet and the sloshing of Emery's water bottle, Adequin turned around. Jackin stood in the doorway with Emery at attention. He gave a quick wave to put the oculus at ease, passing by to head toward Adequin.

"You okay, boss?" His eyes filled with a worry that made her breath catch and flooded her mind with the same overwhelming grief she'd just tried to march away from.

Because Griffith was dying.

Her mouth went dry, chest tightening. She never should have told him about what'd really happened on Paxus. What had she been thinking? She'd known he was weak, known he needed rest. Telling him had been selfish; he'd almost died on the *Tempus*, and she couldn't stomach the thought of having that last lie go unsaid. She'd never considered whether or not he could handle hearing it. Now those could be the last words they would ever say to each other. He very well might die hating her.

"Rake?" Jackin asked again.

"I'm fine, Jack," she managed, letting out a shallow breath as she pushed the rising tide back down. "We won't know more until he's up. Till then, we have plenty of work to do."

Jackin's eyes flickered with concern, but he said nothing more. Adequin turned back to Mesa. "Can you update us?"

"Certainly. We could use your expertise."

"Mine?" Adequin asked.

Mesa walked through the screens toward her. The images rippled in her wake, but quickly settled back into sharp lines. "I myself am rather . . . *inexperienced* with stellar cartography."

Adequin exchanged a surprised look with Jackin before looking back at Mesa. "So, it's a map?"

Mesa nodded, then gave a thorough but brisk rundown of what they'd uncovered, emphasizing what little she considered fact while qualifying any theories with heavy disclaimers, including Cavalon's speculative reading of the "schematics." When she finished, Adequin mulled over the information for a few moments, unsure of where to start.

A *fluid* map? Of this scale? It'd be like having a scanner with a multimillion light-year range. It would be unbelievable if she didn't trust Mesa so implicitly, and if she couldn't see evidence of it with her own eyes. Finally, she decided to focus on the most alarming of the possibilities.

"So," Adequin began, "is it possible there's more? That more bands of Drudgers are out there with omniscient maps and plans to build fusion bombs?"

Emery smacked her gum louder and crossed her arms, giving Mesa a smug smirk.

Mesa ignored her. "It is possible, certainly, though very unlikely."

"Because if dozens of these things existed, we would have uncovered one by now," Adequin surmised.

Mesa inclined her head. "I would like for you to survey the atlas yourself, Excubitor. Your experience reading interstellar maps may broaden our understanding."

Adequin nodded to Jackin. "Jack's your best bet for that, Mes."

"Absolutely," Mesa agreed. "He should certainly look as well. However, your fluency in the Viator tongue may make you our primary candidate. There are some phrasings I do not understand."

Adequin nodded. "Fair enough." She walked into the orb of screens. Mesa joined her, then gave a patient crash course on how to navigate before retreating to watch with Jackin and Emery. Adequin got her bearings, zooming in on a few sections to confirm the orientation. After a few minutes, she determined that most of what Mesa had surmised seemed on point. Except for one, somewhat major, difference.

"This border?" Adequin hovered her finger over the white line running between the larger, outward beacons. "The edge of the map, as you'd called it?"

Mesa's eyes lit with curiosity. "Yes?"

"It's the Divide. This is approximately where the *Argus* was." Adequin pointed to a blank section of space, then dragged her finger from blip to blip to indicate the few points of interest. "This is the *Typhos*. Here's Zelus Gate. Then Eris Gate and the *Accora*." She moved her finger farther down, well away from the line, but still not far enough for her liking. "And this is us."

Mesa nodded her understanding, squinting and tilting her head as she took in the new perspective.

"These larger beacons," Adequin continued, "are marked with symbols the Viator armed forces used the same way we use 'alpha.' They'd be considered the primary beacons. The two situated on either side of the *Argus*'s former position appear off-line, and beyond the edge of the Divide, according to this. They've likely been destroyed."

"What of the smaller beacons?" Mesa asked.

"These inward beacons have two labels—'beta' and 'redundant.' All apparently off-line, but aren't beyond the Divide."

"Of course," Mesa said. She drifted forward, peering at Adequin through the crisp white lines. "Redundancy structures. Viator technology is rife with them." She pointed a thin finger at the backside of the map. "See how there are three beta beacons positioned between every two alpha beacons?"

Adequin nodded. "So the task can get passed onto the smaller beacons if the alphas fail?"

"Correct," Mesa agreed. "However, if they are off-line, then something must have gone wrong, and the betas are not picking up the burden as they are meant to."

Jackin cleared his throat and stepped forward. "What makes you think they're not working? I mean, it's getting this much info at least, right?"

"I can't know for sure," Adequin admitted. "The readout isn't very specific. But these Divide lines that flash? They're labeled with 'approximation.' It's guessing, making an assumption about where the edge is."

"So, how do you know they haven't been destroyed by the Divide already?" he asked.

She shrugged. "We don't. But . . ." She took a moment to orient herself, then pointed to a clear spot, farther outward than the beta beacons. "We were just here, on the *Tempus*. And the Divide had yet to make it there. So assuming it's closing in with any kind of uniformity, the beta beacons should still be safe."

"Safe?" Jackin raised an eyebrow.

Adequin nodded. "Safe to travel to."

Jackin's face fell. "Travel to?"

"What is your hypothesis, Excubitor?" Mesa prompted.

"If we can bring these beta beacons back online," Adequin explained, "that would give us a play-by-play of the Divide's collapse."

Jackin crossed his arms. "You're suggesting we try to restart these beacons?"

"If we can know exactly where the Divide is at any given time," Adequin said, "it'll be a hell of a lot easier to stay away from it, if it comes to that."

Jackin sighed. "You mean if it gets here before we can figure out how to turn the gate back on."

"Right."

Emery's face went white. Mesa's visage didn't falter in the least, but she gave a curt, understanding nod.

"And until Kharon is back online," Adequin continued, "we've got nowhere to go. Eris would take weeks to reach at warp speed, and it'd more than likely be off when we got there anyway—that kid at Poine Gate said it's been abandoned as well. That's if the Divide doesn't beat us there, which at its current rate . . ."

Jackin ran a thumb along the pink scars cutting through his beard. "So, you want to see if we can *fix* the beacons?"

"I think we have to," she said.

"What about your call out to Lugen?"

She let out a sigh, and Griffith's rough assessment rang back in her head: *Fuck the Legion.* He'd wanted her to stop acting like they were going to help and to start taking action. Lead them toward *something* instead of just treading water until the Divide caught up with them. She wanted that too.

"I'm sick of waiting on the Legion," she said. "We can find out more about what's going on, right now. I don't feel particularly inclined to waste time waiting for their permission."

Jackin scratched his beard, lowering his voice even further. "I can't say I blame you, Rake, but is this really the best idea? I know you might feel like you need to be doing something . . ."

He was right, and she knew it. With an unconscious Griffith in the other room, she needed a distraction. But she also couldn't bring herself to simply lie down and wait for them all to meet their fates. At least this would be *something*.

"It's the only idea I've got," she explained, shaking her head. "What else can we do? We haven't been able to get the gate restarted, and Lugen hasn't called. What harm is it to take a few of us on the *SGL* and see if we can't get some of these beacons working?"

"The *SGL*?" Jackin scoffed. "The *Synthesis* at least has armaments."

"After the noise that snap-warp caused, I don't really trust its warp drive right now. Besides, a Hermes-class vessel's not safe to take through a relay gate on its own. The others will need the *Synthesis* once they get the gate turned back on. It should stay here, so they can escape."

He pinched his lips together and nodded ruefully. "In case we don't come back."

She gripped his shoulder. "You know the drill, Jack. It's intel on the enemy's position. Priority alpha."

"But the enemy is the collapsing edge of the universe?" he confirmed.

She gave him a weary grin. "Right."

Jackin rubbed his face with both hands. "I'm going to need coordinates."

The door slid open with a hiss, and when Adequin turned around, she found Cavalon standing in the doorway, eyes wide, face pale. "Sir, uh . . ." He gave a hasty glance around at the others before returning his look to her. "He's awake."

Adequin marched back down the hall at a brisk pace, sensing Cavalon following just over her shoulder.

"He seems to be doing well," he began. Though his tone presented itself as optimistic, she could sense the warning it carried with it. "His vitals are strong and stable, he's responding well to stimulus. Answering questions coherently."

She half listened, focusing her efforts on getting to the medbay as quickly as possible without breaking into a full-out run. As they approached the doorway, Cavalon reached out and gripped her arm.

"Rake, wait."

She stopped in her tracks, turning back to face him. "What is it?" she asked impatiently.

"I took another sample," he said, deep lines creasing his brow. "And I did some . . . estimating."

"And?"

"And his cells have already aged about six to nine months."

"Since when?"

"Since I took the last sample."

"Which was when? When we got here?"

Cavalon shook his head, and his eyes drifted to the floor. "Twenty minutes ago."

She let out a sharp breath, looking down at Cavalon's boots. Again her mind reeled with unwanted math, and she cursed the day she'd been taught basic arithmetic. Her eyes focused and unfocused a few times before she regained her breath.

She looked back up at him. "What does that mean?"

"He's got maybe . . ." he began, his voice breaking. He cleared his throat and raised his eyes back up to her. "Twenty-four hours. Thirty, at the most."

She stared at him in silence for what felt like a very long time.

After a while, he said, "I didn't say anything. I thought you should be the one to tell him . . . I'm really sorry."

She broke her gaze and turned around, and the door slid open before her.

"Griff," she breathed, whisking across the room to his cot.

Griffith's eyes opened a sliver, and his face crunched into a smile, the corners of his eyes wrinkling deeper. "Mo'acair." His low voice rumbled like churning gravel.

She knelt beside the cot and gripped his hand. "How do you feel?" She tried her hardest to maintain a steady voice despite her heart hammering up into her throat.

"Never better."

"You're so full of shit."

"I'm tired, but I feel fine, really," he said, sounding like he actually believed himself. "What happened?"

She tempered her racing pulse by reminding herself to breathe slowly. In, then out. "We're not sure. Might have been a seizure or stroke. You were unconscious for a couple of hours. How much do you remember?"

"You mean, do I remember almost getting swallowed up by the Divide, getting boarded, Drudgers killing half my crew, the *Tempus* exploding, Ivana bleeding out, and you admitting you let Viator captives go free, stayed silent while Lugen swept it under the rug, then kept it from me for five years?"

She cleared her throat. "Specific. Good to see your memory's intact."

He shook his head slowly, eyes drifting closed. "I'm sorry, Quin."

Her brow furrowed. "Why?"

He sighed, running a heavy hand down the side of his face. "Nothing like almost dying *again* to make you reevaluate a knee-jerk reaction."

A twinge of relief squeezed under her rib cage. "Knee-jerk?" she asked. "You were pretty pissed."

"Oh, don't worry, I'm still plenty pissed. I hate that you did that, I really do. I'm having a hard time even processing it. And honestly, I don't know if I'll be able to forgive you."

She gave a soft nod, that same twinge of relief turning bitter as it slid down into the pit of her stomach.

"But like you said," he continued, tone soft, "one act doesn't define someone, good or bad. I hate what you did. Not you."

A sudden chill pricked her skin, and she blinked back at him.

"Which is why, even though I can't agree with the choice you made," he went on, "I can understand it. Or try to, at least. I can see the path of logic that got you there." He let out a few short coughs, holding his side and grimacing. "It's that damn even-keeled wisdom I admire . . . that's what you used to make that decision. But I still can't say if it was the right or wrong one."

She managed a slow nod, turning his words over in her mind. It wasn't absolution, but she'd never expected that. At least he understood her perspective, could admit its validity. With time, maybe he could work toward forgiveness. But time wasn't something he had.

"Just so I know," he continued, "who else knows about what happened on Paxus?"

"The only person I ever told was Lugen. As far as I know, only him."

"Damn, Quin. Why didn't you tell me any of this before?"

She gave him a weak grin. "Caecus Level Alpha."

He scoffed. "To the void with security levels. This has been eating away at you for five years. You should have told me, let me help you."

"After that reaction, I'm kinda glad I didn't."

He gave her a flat look.

"Are you sure you don't hate me?" she asked.

"Not possible, I'm afraid," he rumbled. "But, can we put a moratorium on secrets?"

"Copy that. No more secrets," she agreed, but the last words caught in her throat. Her brow creased and she looked down.

"Shit," he sighed. "I get the distinct feeling you have more secrets?"

"Not a secret." She glanced over at the humming diagnostic machine nearby. "Just, this seizure you had . . ."

He followed her gaze, then looked back at her, taking a deep breath before letting it back out slowly. "Let me guess. Ripping the *Tempus* free of the Divide was a bad idea?"

"You saved the crew, Griffith," she said firmly. "They'd all have died if you hadn't."

"But?"

"But . . . left in the cockpit, you were exposed."

"To what?"

"We're not entirely sure. You met Cavalon?"

He tilted his chin toward the doorway across the room. "The doctor kid? Yeah."

"He ran some tests on your tissue. Your cells appear to be . . . *aging* at an accelerated rate. Something to do with how you broke free of the Divide."

"Aging?" he croaked. "Okay. How accelerated? At the same rate as the Divide? Twelve times?"

She shook her head. "I'd hoped that was the case, but no. If your cells continue at the rate they have been . . ." She trailed off, unable to find the words. It wasn't right, wasn't natural. He shouldn't have to deal with this, and she shouldn't have to tell him.

"Mo'acair," he said softly. "Just tell me, I can handle it."

She looked down and a single tear escaped the corner of her eye. He wiped it away with his thumb.

"Twenty-four hours," she managed. "Maybe a little more."

He didn't react at first, simply staring at her and continuing to breathe evenly. After a few long moments of silence, his voice returned, steady as ever. "You know why I picked Myrdin before? Over Sobrius-II?"

She looked up at him, surprised at his casual turn of topic. "Why?"

"Because they have *great* thunderstorms."

She scoffed a laugh. "Thunderstorms?"

"Yeah. I miss that about being groundside. Wind and rain and thunder and lightning. *Tangible* nature. Not this space shit with its time ripples and *relativity* and radiative flux, or what-the-fuck-ever."

"Void," she breathed, her lips turning into a pained grin. "You don't know shit about space, do you?"

He laughed, stilted and pained, but sincere. She took comfort in the soft rumble. "No. Certainly not." He rubbed his weathered face with a pale hand and sighed. "I know enough at this point to consider it bullshit, though."

She laid her head onto his chest, and he wrapped both arms around her, his beard scratching her forehead as he nestled his face into her.

"Myrdin, it is," she whispered.

CHAPTER THIRTY-THREE

Cavalon sat across from Griffith at the circular table aboard the *SGL*, drawing the Titan's blood. Again. He wasn't entirely sure why. Well, he knew why: because Rake had told him to. But he didn't know what she meant for him to accomplish.

This would make the thirteenth sample he'd tested in total, and the results remained the same. The aging didn't appear to be speeding up, slowing down, or changing in any way. His cells continued to grow larger, dividing less and less frequently, and his tissue continued to atrophy.

Cavalon figured Rake had a hard time accepting it because outwardly, Griffith seemed fine. After getting another round of fluids and noshing down a couple MREs, he'd hopped out of the cot like he hadn't just been delivered a death sentence. Then, he'd insisted on joining Rake's little adventure to restart one of the atlas's defunct beacons.

That conversation went something like: *"That's* ridiculous. *You're dying." "Exactly, I've got nothing to lose." "You're sick. You just had a stroke!" "I'm fine. Watch."* Then Griffith put Jackin in a headlock and refused to let go until Rake agreed to let him come. It was a little funny, actually.

However, even though Griffith *acted* okay—because many of the outward signs of aging that take time to manifest weren't going to affect him in the short-term, like loss of muscle mass and graying hair—he was not actually *okay*. At any point, his cellular degeneration could catch up with him, and a vital organ could be overtaxed and give out. Which accounted for his seizures earlier—the increased deterioration had met a breaking point, causing the signals in his brain to stall. And it could happen again just as suddenly.

Yet there the man sat, hurtling toward fuck-only-knows-where right along with them, as if he wasn't about to keel over at any moment. But if it was how Griffith wanted to spend his last hours, and Rake was okay with it, then who was Cavalon to argue.

Jackin had insisted on coming as well, and currently shared the cockpit with Emery. Mesa and Rake had taken up shop in the crew quarters to look through the atlas's menus for anything they may have missed about the beacon they were on their way to "repair."

Cavalon certainly hoped Mesa had prepared to go full-on Savant, because *he* didn't have the first clue how to repair Viator-tech anything. Yet Rake still brought him, maybe because he'd been able to partially read the schematics on the atlas, or simply so he could continue testing Griffith. He really hoped it wasn't because she thought he might be useful in fixing the beacon.

He dropped the newest blood sample into the side of the cystoscope, and a few moments later, took the headset off, shaking his head. "More of the same. Sorry."

"Thanks," Griffith said, his low voice an intimidating rumble. "You really don't need to keep checking, though."

"Rake wanted me to."

"I know. She can be . . . insistent. Let's forego more checks, though, if it's all the same to you. I'm not sure I want to spend my last hours being poked by a doctor."

Cavalon let out a short, breathy laugh. "Oh, don't worry, I'm not a doctor."

Griffith scratched at his thick beard and gave a half smile. "Coulda fooled me."

"Just genetic engineering. Some pre-med. Definitely not a doctor, though. I assure you."

"Wait, weren't you the astromechanic that fixed the warp drive?"

Cavalon swallowed. "Uh, yeah."

"And the same guy who figured out how to recharge that warp core?"

"Yeah."

"And you helped Quin clear those Drudgers?"

Cavalon opened his mouth to ask who "Quin" was, but caught himself as he realized the man had meant Rake. "'Helped' is a bit generous, but yeah."

Griffith's brow raised, and he seemed a little impressed. "Good man."

Cavalon blinked. He didn't know how to react to that. This guy intimidated the shit out of him, but he'd just *complimented* him. It felt weird.

Cavalon managed a feeble, "Uh, yeah. It was no problem."

"I'm gonna go talk to the optio," Griffith said, letting out a deep groan as he raised himself up from the table. He reached out a thick hand toward Cavalon. "Thanks again, doc."

"Yeah . . ." Cavalon shook Griffith's hand, cringing as the man's rugged, viselike grip crushed his fingers. From his grateful expression, it didn't seem like Griffith meant it to be harsh. He more than likely just didn't know his own strength.

Griffith nodded then turned away, disappearing into the cockpit. Moments later, Emery came out, glancing over her shoulder in curiosity before the door slid shut behind her. She sat across from Cavalon.

"He's got some 'things to say to Jackin,'" Emery said, lowering her voice to imitate Griffith's baritone rumble. "Whaddya suppose that's all about?"

Cavalon stretched his crushed hand and rubbed his palm. "No idea."

She waggled her eyebrows. "Wanna find out?"

He blinked at her. "What?"

She held out her tattooed wrist, encircled by a thin, black, Legion-issue nexus band. One she certainly did not have before.

"I got sicka not bein' told what the fuck's goin' on," she explained. "So I stole a nexus from Kharon. And I may have taken the liberty of hacking into ship comms." She flashed a grin. "We can listen in."

"No," Cavalon said, giving a fervent shake of his head. "No, no. No. That's not shit-cutting."

Her face scrunched with annoyed skepticism. "What's with you and this shit-cutting thing?" she asked as she blatantly ignored his response and opened the comms panel on the nexus.

She pushed out of her chair and slid onto the bench next to him. Cavalon buried his face in his hands.

Emery tuned her nexus to the hacked channel, dialing down the volume as Griffith's voice crackled through. "—the Rake you know is by the books, but that's not who she really is."

"You don't know that," Jackin said, his quiet words difficult to make out over the constant buzz of background static. "People change, Bach."

"You saw it back at the *Tempus*, what she was willing to risk. Literally none of that was by the book. Case in point—look at what we're doing right-the-fuck now. This definitely isn't handbook procedure. And the more that's put on her, the more she'll fall back on that instinct."

Jackin sighed.

"She'd never admit it," Griffith went on, "but she needs balance. And she'll need it more than ever moving forward. Be the pessimism to her blind optimism, and you'll come out neutral."

"Bach . . ."

"Are you gonna force me to make it my dying wish, North? All I'm asking is that you stick by her. Help her survive this—and when I say her, you know I mean just that."

"Void," Jackin grumbled. "How can you ask me to prioritize one life over another, even hers? That's pretty harsh."

"Shouldn't it be? The Legion abandoned us, Lugen's radio silent, and we're being systematically replaced by mind-controlled clones. Harsh is where we're at with this. And you think even if you survive, there'll be a welcome parade back home? You know better than anyone what going back to the Core really means."

Cavalon shifted uncomfortably on the padded bench as a chill washed down his spine. He picked at his fingernails while Emery stared at the nexus screen with focused interest, jaw slackened.

"You've had to take huge risks in your career," Griffith continued. "More than most. She's gonna need that experience on her side." He remained quiet for a few long moments, then mumbled, "Void. That kid has no idea, does he?"

"Fuck, no. And neither does Rake. Seriously—not a word." Jackin breathed out a sharp hissing noise. "I never should have told you."

Emery's gaze drifted over, and Cavalon met her questioning look with a shrug. He had no idea what they were talking about.

"Relax, North," Griffith said, "I'm dying, remember? Your secret's safe with me."

"You can't truly think she needs me," Jackin said. "That she can't do this on her own."

Griffith scoffed a laugh. "Of course she can, but that's the whole problem. She doesn't need you, so she'll push you all away, distance herself from everyone, and still find a way to die trying to save you all. But by then, you'll all be too far to reach her. She needs a stick-in-the-mud like you—"

"Eh, fuck you too," Jackin interjected grumpily.

"—to moderate her, or she'll throw her life away trying to save something that can't be saved."

Neither man spoke for a few long moments. Cavalon thought the connection had been lost, but then Griffith's deep voice cut back in.

"I know you don't owe me anything," he said, his voice softening, taking on an oddly pleading tone that Cavalon had a hard time imagining coming out of the man. "But you're the only one I trust. I've seen you two together—you already make a good team, a great one. Just don't give up on her once I'm gone."

"Shit, I won't," Jackin said, then the firmness in his tone broke. "You know I won't."

"Thank—"

A rash of heat clawed up his neck, and Cavalon reached over and swept the connection closed. The static cut out, leaving only the steady thrum of the warp engine in the silent common room. He'd already let it go on too long.

To his surprise, Emery didn't react adversely. Closing the nexus screen, she slouched as a conflicted expression tightened her lips— part pout and part sympathy.

"Well," she said. "That was a lot less juicy than I'd hoped for."

Cavalon cleared the lump from the back of his throat, but his voice still came out thick. "Juicy? What'd you think was going to happen?"

"I dunno, maybe some fraternization? They'd make a cute couple, don't you think?"

Cavalon shrugged, though he couldn't really disagree. Then again, you could put pretty much anyone on Griffith's arm and it'd turn out adorable.

Emery's sullen look thawed slightly. *The Beards of the Argus.* Could be a radio drama."

A chuckle rose in his throat, though it didn't lessen the knot of anxiety tightening in his chest. Because Bearded Protagonist #2 was right. Even if they survived, there was no way this ended with fanfare and a warm, gin-soaked welcome back at the Core. Definitely not for Cavalon.

However, something else nagged at him, something more nebulous, harder to quantify.

The sincerity of the centurion's words hung in the back of his mind, constraining his chest-knot even tighter. Griffith was a good friend, a painfully good friend—or whatever he and Rake were to each other. Good in a way Cavalon had no frame of reference for, a way he could hardly interpret as real human behavior.

After being ripped from his own space-time continuity, Griffith had earned an accelerated expiration date on life, but he wasn't spending his last hours regretting how he'd lived, or what he had or hadn't done, or worrying about what came after death, or having an existential breakdown. He was making sure the people he cared about would continue on. Be alive, be the happiest they could be, once it was out of his control to affect it otherwise.

Something about that concept settled in Cavalon's brain with surprising ease, a thought at once daunting and exhilarating. The reform he'd wanted—the reform the SC *needed*—everything he'd pitched to the Quorum before being summarily rejected by Augustus's machinations . . . He'd told himself it was all to stop his grandfather.

But there was another side to that coin—and that's what this was all about, what it *should* be all about. Making this mess better for those who came after.

"You know . . ." Emery began, letting out a long sigh. Cavalon blinked the dryness from his eyes, then twisted in his seat to face her. "I heard the EX in there talkin' to Mesa. She said something about there being Viators out here . . ." She glared at him skeptically. "You wouldn't know anything about that, would you?"

Cavalon instinctively prepared to disavow any insider knowledge on the subject. He'd been instructed to, if memory served, *"not breathe a word of this to anyone."*

But Emery had been dragged along with the rest of them to risk her life on a chance to stay a step ahead of the Divide. She deserved to know the truth, or at least whatever part of the truth they thought they knew.

"All we saw was a recorded video message," he said quietly.

"A message?" she whispered, leaning toward him, mouth agape.

"Yeah. A Viator giving that Drudger captain instructions."

"*Instructions?*" Emery squeaked. She gave an edgy glance toward the cockpit, then regained control over her voice. "For what?"

"I dunno. It wanted them to restart something. The beacons, I guess. That's what Rake claimed it said, at least. I don't speak Viator."

"Damn." Emery sat back and crossed her arms. "Just . . . *damn.*"

A few minutes later, Cavalon's stomach flopped as they decelerated from warp. Rake exited from crew quarters and Mesa followed, golden pyramid in tow, heading straight to the cockpit. Cavalon exchanged a curious look with Emery, and followed them in.

"This is . . . it . . ." Jackin said as they entered. The optio sat in the pilot's seat, Rake and Griffith standing beside him. Cavalon stepped next to Mesa, and Emery sidled up, chomping her purple gum. They all stared at the viewscreen in silence.

The *SGL's* dim searchlight shone on the side of a small structure positioned straight off the vessel's stubby nose. He found it surprising Jackin would have dropped them from warp so close to the beacon.

From the narrow portion illuminated in the beam of light, it appeared to be spherical and built of the same matte-black aerasteel as the exterior of the Apollo Gates. The hull consisted of a series of overlaid scales not unlike the ominous halls inside Kharon Gate. Unlike the gates however, each panel on this structure had a series of tiny, intricate grooves carved into the surface, similar to the perpetual, geometric designs on the outside of the atlas pyramid.

The *SGL* drifted toward it, very, very slowly. Cavalon glanced down at the terminal in front of Jackin and realized their ion engines were engaged. They were still speeding toward it.

Cavalon looked back up at the screen. His stomach stirred and his mind recomputed, shifting his perspective. It wasn't close, and small. It was still quite far away, and *quite* large. He couldn't find a way to properly determine the scope, but he could tell the "tiny" grooves recessed into the scales were in fact enormous trenches, running dozens of meters deep into the thick metal hull.

Finally, Jackin broke the silence. "That's, uh . . . quite a 'beacon.'"

Rake exchanged a concerned look with Griffith, then said, "It's definitely Viator."

"This can't be a *data beacon*," Griffith said, incredulous.

"An old operations base, maybe?" Jackin suggested.

"This far out?" Rake shook her head. "And it's nothing like their military structures. I've never seen anything like it."

Five gazes turned to Mesa. She stood staring at the sphere, eyes wide and unblinking. She licked her lips. "I, um . . ."

Cavalon gaped. The Savant was at a loss for words? Fucking great.

"Jack, can we get a read on the dimensions?" Rake asked.

Jackin slid through a few menus, and a gridded overlay appeared on the viewscreen. "Just over seventy-two kilometers in diameter."

Griffith let out a low whistle.

"No ships?" Rake asked. "Life-forms?"

"Nothing," Jackin confirmed. "On the outside, at least."

"Let's move closer."

"You got it, boss."

Jackin revved the ions, and they accelerated. The scale continued to be difficult for Cavalon to fathom, with so little visible in their dim spotlight.

As they sped closer and circled around the right side, the structure's design became more clear. The scales covering the entire inward-facing front wrapped halfway around the side. There, the slabs decreased in frequency, eventually melding into one solid piece. When the *SGL* arrived at the outward-facing side of the structure, Jackin swept the light over an expanse of smooth, matte-black metal. It carried no sheen and reflected almost no light.

"Flood it out," Rake instructed.

Jackin typed into the menus, and the beam expanded, dimming as it broadened its throw.

"Can you increase the contrast?" Rake asked.

The image flickered as Jackin arrowed through settings and the shape of the structure took form. Even through the heavy grain dancing across the image, Cavalon could tell it was a single, seamless surface.

"This whole side is just . . . solid," Jackin said in disbelief. "That's . . . seventy kilometers of solid metal."

Cavalon had never seen anything like it. Even the largest panels of the Apollo Gate hulls couldn't be more than a hundred meters wide. He had no idea Viators could construct something of this magnitude.

Mesa's voice broke through the silence. "Excubitor?"

"Yeah, Mes?"

Mesa leaned forward, peering at the viewscreen in shock. "I was absolutely wrong. This is *not* a data beacon."

Rake let out a soft sigh. "Yeah. I'm starting to get that impression."

"Or not *just* a data beacon," Cavalon pointed out.

"That is true," Mesa said. "A structure of this size could easily accommodate multiple functions. In addition to data collection and relay, it also could serve as a communications hub, a data facility, or even a biological-sample storage facility. Despite their penchant for xenocide, Viator scientists were avid in their study of alien lifeforms, so long as they did not exhibit the threat of sentience . . ."

As they returned to the inward side, things almost felt normal as Mesa exposited the potential purposes of a structure of this scale, with an occasional sidebar into less relevant topics.

Rake ordered Jackin to search for a docking port. They systematically worked their way up from the bottom of the inward side, looking for any kind of abnormality or break that might serve as an entrance. About fifteen kilometers up, almost a quarter of the way, they found it. They might have missed it if Emery hadn't perked up, insisting she saw a glint of bronze in the sea of stark black aerasteel.

Jackin refocused the light and flew toward the shimmering metallic anomaly, and it came into focus minutes later as they cruised closer to the hull.

Cavalon squinted as they approached. A gleaming triangular bronze panel sat flush with the outer face, each facet easily a hundred meters in length, outlined with a border of alternating gold, silver, and copper triangles, each no more than a meter wide.

Griffith leaned toward the screen. "What is that?" He smiled down at Rake. "Sorry, my eyesight's not what it used to be."

Rake frowned and ran a hand down her face. She didn't seem quite as ready to joke about Griffith's condition. The big man's grin faded, and he wrapped an arm around her shoulder.

Mesa cleared her throat. "That, I do recognize," she said, her voice quavering slightly. "It is a trecullis."

"A . . . what?" Rake asked.

"A type of access door. Absolutely antiquated, by all standards."

"Antiquated?" Jackin asked. "How so?"

"In theory, a trecullis will scan an incoming ship for relevant technologies to determine if it is friendly," Mesa explained. "Understaffed or decommissioned posts utilized them to allow access without requiring each vessel to obtain specific clearance."

"Why not just use a code?" Cavalon asked.

"Most did require a specific data input as well, with the technology scan as a secondary measure to ensure that the access code had not been stolen. Regardless, the Cathians discovered a way to deceive the system by lining their hulls with stolen Viator technology, and they eventually decommissioned the method."

Cavalon raised his eyebrows. They were really delving into ancient history if Mesa was talking about Cathians. They'd been the first sentient species—that they knew about, anyway—to be ushered out of existence by the Viators, over three thousand years ago, well before first contact with humans.

"There's no way it's going to scan us and think we're friendlies, right?" Emery said.

"I cannot be certain . . ." Mesa said. "However, this technology was developed and decommissioned well before Viators encountered mankind. They would not have had countermeasures in place to specifically flag human vessels. Besides, much of our modern technology derives from their own, when not simply a direct copy. The warp drive, the control system and computers, the scanners and sensor arrays, gravity control . . ." She swept a hand out toward Rake and Griffith. "Both of your Titan Imprints . . ." She turned and looked at Cavalon. "Your *original* Imprints." She held up the gold pyramid. "The curanulta. Most of our weapons. It is very possible, if it is in fact functioning, that it would judge us as Viator."

That assessment sent bile up Cavalon's throat. Another reminder of everything they owed to the creatures that'd tried so very hard, twice, to exterminate them—and maybe were about to take a third shot at it.

"Everyone okay with this?" Rake asked.

It took Cavalon a moment to realize she actually expected an answer—had called for a vote. Though to Cavalon, it sounded more or less like: "*Is it cool with everyone that we might die in a few seconds?*"

"Aye," Griffith answered immediately.

Jackin gave a reluctant nod. "If you say so, boss."

"Certainly, Excubitor," Mesa agreed.

Cavalon scratched his neck, unsure if he and Emery were to be included in this decision.

Rake answered his question, looking over at them expectantly. "Oculi?"

"Shit, yeah," Emery said, chomping a few loud smacks on her gum. She grinned at Cavalon with nervous excitement. This was likely the coolest thing that'd ever happened to her in all nineteen years of her life. Though Cavalon had to admit, it was the coolest thing that'd happened to him in all twenty-seven of his. By a long shot. It might be scary, and they might die, but the possibilities of what might be on this strange, enormous "data beacon" were too fascinating to pass up.

Cavalon gave Rake a nervous smile. "Absolutely, sir."

"Let's move forward, Jack," Rake said. "See what happens."

Jackin hunched over the controls and mumbled to himself. "*See what happens. I'm lovin' this strategy.*" Rake gave him a weak slap on the shoulder and Jackin smiled up at her. "I'm just saying, so much for our 'master tactician.'"

"Hey," Griffith rumbled. "What'd I tell you?"

"Right." Jackin gave a firm nod. "Yes, sir."

Rake gave Griffith a suspicious glare.

Jackin swept the controls and the floor shook. The SGL picked up speed, cruising toward the enormous triangular panel. At fifty meters out, the trecullis came to life. The small triangles outlining it began to glow, one by one.

"Stop here, Optio," Mesa instructed, large eyes wide with awe. Jackin slowed the ship to a stop.

The shimmering continued, dragging heavily across the metal

as if waking from an eternal sleep. The flashes accelerated, sweeping clockwise around the panel until the entire border gleamed. The triangle of light pulsed for a few brief moments before going dark.

Cavalon glanced at the others, who looked as unsure as he felt. Was that it? Had they been "scanned"?

The enormous bronze triangle glinted and split, trisecting into three equal pieces. Each panel recessed into the dark hull, revealing a gaping black entrance. No illumination came from within.

"Oh," came Mesa's soft, surprised voice. She looked down at the atlas in her hands. The grooves of the golden pyramid glowed with a subtle white light.

"That's a good sign, right?" Jackin said, sounding like he maybe half believed himself. He looked from the pyramid to Rake with raised brows. Rake looked to Mesa. Mesa shrugged.

"If this . . . *beacon* is linked to the curanulta," Mesa said, "then it may be acting as our access code."

"And if it's not?" Jackin asked.

"Well, if we did not pass the scan, it may incinerate our vessel." Mesa gave a light scoff at herself. "Although, really, it would more than likely have already done that. It is unlikely the trecullis would allow us entry, only to destroy us, a task it could have easily accomplished already."

"So . . . we're okay?" Rake asked carefully, unblinking as she stared at Mesa.

Mesa pressed her lips together, considering for a moment, then gave a curt nod.

Rake sighed and turned back to the screen. "Okay, Jack. Go ahead."

Jackin sat up straighter and slid forward on the controls, flying the *SGL* into the darkness.

Cavalon's heart thrummed violently in his chest as they stood in silence, staring at the viewscreen in unsettled awe. They were literally headed into the abyss—willingly flying *inside* an unknown Viator structure. It was an awful idea.

As they crossed the threshold, Jackin swept the searchlight around in an arc, piercing through the black before them. But it revealed nothing. "Scanners aren't getting a reading on the walls . . ." He drifted off as the blackness began to glow all around them.

From every direction, narrow bands of soft white light faded on, recessed in trench-like grooves running vertically up the length of the distant walls. Distant, as in *kilometers*. Kilometers and kilometers away. The view sent Cavalon's stomach lurching until his brain could reconcile the scale. Simple, he told himself. Just a hollow shell. A seventy-two kilometer hollow shell. But "inside" simply couldn't be this large. It didn't compute.

Strip by strip, the lights faded up as they moved deeper into the perfectly spherical chamber, revealing concave walls curving up and away in each direction.

The inward-facing facade mirrored the overlaid slabs they'd seen on the outside—slowly merging into one surface as they curved around the inside of the sphere. Unlike the outside, however, a narrow band of gleaming, dark silver metal ringed the center of the sphere—a high-walled groove at least two kilometers wide.

Cavalon's gaze fell on the only other anomaly in sight—a comparatively small bronze sphere hovering at the center of the smooth outward surface. Though too far away to judge the size properly, it couldn't have been larger than a half kilometer in diameter.

"What the . . ." Jackin suddenly grumbled under his breath, scowling down at the ship's controls.

"Looks like there's a structure across the way, Jack," Rake said. She pointed to the bronze sphere. "Let's head there."

"Sorry, boss," Jackin said, lifting his hands off the controls and holding his palms up. "I don't have control anymore."

"What?" Rake barked.

He shook his head, then continued sliding through the ship's menus. "It's bringing us in itself."

A weighty silence fell across the cockpit, and Cavalon looked to Emery. She chewed her gum slowly, a wide grin spreading across her face as she met his gaze. Of course she'd find this awesome.

Cavalon let out a deep breath. The more surprises, the more he found himself wishing he could change his vote.

"We're picking up speed," Jackin said, a hint of warning in his tone.

Rake exchanged a nervous glance with Griffith, and Mesa continued to run her eyes over every centimeter of the viewscreen, cataloging every detail. Only Emery's enthusiastic gum-chomping sounded in the nervous quiet of the cockpit as the Viator autopilot pulled the SGL across the seventy-meter expanse.

As the bronze sphere drew closer, Cavalon realized it was smaller than he'd first guessed, maybe only a quarter of a kilometer in diameter. A single triangular doorway sat flush to the outside of the sphere. Extending out from under the door, a narrow platform reached toward the SGL like a runway. As they neared, it became obvious it was far too narrow for a landing. More of a human-sized—or rather Viator-sized—walkway, with no railing of any kind.

The SGL decelerated of its own accord, coming to a stop directly above the end of the platform. Jackin swept through the controls again, but nothing happened. He even brought up the manual control levers, but the ship didn't respond.

He heaved a sigh and sat back. "Well, I guess this is it. I don't even know how to disengage us."

"Then we'll just have to check it out," Griffith said, with a hint of a grin not unlike Emery's. Cavalon had to hand it to the man. Death sentence or no, he intended to live his last moments to the fullest.

All eyes turned to Rake, but she didn't immediately respond. After a few seconds she looked up at Griffith. "You up for this?"

"Of course."

"Okay," Rake said. "Let's suit up."

✦

CHAPTER THIRTY-FOUR

Bruised midsection aching miserably, Cavalon worked his way into a space suit—yet again. He decided he would just keep it on this time. This would be the one. He'd wear it until he died, which seemed more imminent the deeper they went into this Viator monstrosity.

He stood in the *SGL*'s common room, where Rake, Griffith, and Mesa suited up along with him. Jackin and Emery had helped them prep, but would stay on board and determine how to disengage the autopilot, in case they needed to make a quick retreat—and, Cavalon supposed, just so they could leave *period*.

Cavalon sealed up his suit while Rake helped Griffith stretch his up over his broad shoulders. The pearlescent white fabric responded, glittering as it expanded to accommodate his size.

Mesa waited off to the side, clutching the atlas pyramid in both hands. She stood pristinely still, suit already sealed over her lithe frame. Hers had done the opposite of Griffith's—resizing itself smaller to accommodate her petite figure. It revealed thin legs, a narrow waist, and scrawny arms. It made her seem all the more Savant, and so much more frail than suited her presence. Her strong mind made it easy to forget the fragility of her body.

Rake and Griffith strapped their weapons belts on, and Cavalon hesitated, wondering if he should even bother taking his own. They had a two-Titan escort, after all. Then his weapons belt appeared in front of him, clutched in Emery's grip, her brows raised expectantly. He took it from her with a thankful grin and secured it around his waist.

She drew her shoulders up. "I wish you the best of luck, Mr. Mercer," she said pristinely, in a spot-on impression of Mesa.

"Actually, it's *Lord* Mercer."

She dropped the accent. "Shut up."

"Technically, *Your Royal Highness*, but I won't make you."

"You're an idiot."

He shrugged. "I don't make the rules."

"I feel like that's a good thing."

"Helmets on," Rake announced.

Emery lifted Cavalon's helmet and dropped it onto his head unceremoniously.

"Thank you, squire."

She crossed her arms and made a dramatic show of rolling her eyes.

Cavalon locked his helmet to his suit, then took in the onslaught of information shown in the HUD. His vitals sat on the left side, with the already-yellow heart-rate meter slowly picking up speed.

Emery gave him a sidelong glance, then her disgruntled look faded away. Her jaw skimmed back and forth as she rolled her gum around for a few silent seconds. "Bring me back a souvenir?"

"Not sure it's the type of locale to have a gift shop, but I'll do my best."

"Or just don't die. That'd be fine too."

Cavalon quirked an eyebrow. Emery cared if he died? Not that he thought she wanted him dead, but the sentiment still surprised him. Though, she'd probably lost people she cared about aboard the *Argus*. She might not be keen on watching more friends die, even if they were new ones.

"Copy, boss," he said with his best reassuring smile. "No dying."

Emery grinned, then turned and disappeared into the cockpit behind Jackin.

Rake's voice crackled through the comms in his suit. "Everyone ready?"

"Ready," Griffith said.

Mesa inclined her head. "Yes, Excubitor."

"Good, sir," Cavalon said.

"Depressurizing." Rake tapped the control screen and Cavalon's eardrums pulsed as the hatch cycled. Yet his feet didn't lift off the floor, which meant the structure provided some kind of artificial gravity. In his HUD, a green notification read, "Exterior oxygen levels stable."

Rake opened the hatch and a flimsy ladder unfolded to the ground. Griffith climbed down first, then Mesa shuffled forward and followed, tucking the pyramid under one arm.

Cavalon's mouth went dry, palms slicking with sweat—either from fear or excitement, or some of both. He took a few long, deliberate breaths to try and stay calm, then looked at Rake.

She tilted her head, sliding her fingers across her suit's nexus. The comms clicked, and his display indicated she'd switched to a private line.

"You okay?" she asked.

He lowered his voice. "I mean, if Jackin wants to go instead . . ."

"I need Jackin here figuring out how the hell we're going to undock," she said evenly.

Cavalon nodded fervently. "Right. I know."

"I need *you* with us." Her earnest eyes met his. The yellow heart-rate meter in his HUD slowed, then fell to green.

"Yeah. I'm with you."

She thunked her gloved hand against the side of his helmet. "You wanna go first?"

He nodded, steeled his resolve, then rung by rung, descended the swaying ladder. He hopped off the end, where Griffith stood waiting, arms out as if ready to catch him. A few meters away, Mesa stared down the platform toward the spherical bronze structure at the end of the narrow path.

Cavalon stepped out from under the *SGL* and for whatever reason, decided to look up. He instantly regretted it.

The immense curved ceiling stretched out dozens of kilometers above, sending a wave of vertigo through him. He quickly diverted his gaze down, but found much the same thing, only in a direction in which he could *fall*. He leveled out his chin, focusing on the simple bronze door at the end of the long platform. He should really just keep his eyes straight ahead for the remainder of his life. No good ever came from looking up or down.

Along with a clunk of boots, Rake appeared beside him. A click sounded in his helmet, and the readout indicated that Rake switched back to universal comms.

"Atmo reads safe," Rake said, "but let's keep helmets on just in case."

"Copy," Griffith said.

"You guys ready?" She slid past Cavalon, then Mesa, and started down the platform toward the bronze sphere. Mesa fell in directly behind her.

Cavalon startled as Griffith gave him a rough pat on the back. "Everything okay, doc?"

"Yes." Cavalon grimaced as his voice broke. One syllable. He had to croak out *one* convincing-enough word, and he couldn't even manage that.

"One foot in front of the other," Griffith prompted, tone patient.

"Right."

Cavalon willed his feet forward, focusing on the back of Mesa's head to discourage his wandering gaze. They finally arrived at the end of the walkway, where the platform fanned out wider as it melded seamlessly into the side of the bronze sphere.

"I don't see any access panels." Rake walked to the door and ran her hands over the edges of the door frame.

Mesa cleared her throat. "Might I suggest . . ." She held up the polished gold pyramid.

Rake swept her hand forward in invitation. Mesa took a few careful steps toward the door. Rake and Griffith drew their pistols.

Just as it had aboard the SGL, the pyramid began to glow. The door split down the middle, and the bronze panels slid silently into the walls on either side. They all stood frozen for a few seconds, staring into the darkness beyond the door.

One by one a series of recessed, vertical wall trenches lit, illuminating a square, open chamber slightly larger than the *SGL's* common room. The walls gleamed the same soft gold as the atlas pyramid. Terminals sat recessed into the wall on both sides. The left looked like a standard computer display, but the right appeared to be some kind of apparatus, with a strange half-cylindrical slot set into the face of the glass screen. A floor-to-ceiling, four-meter-wide piece of dark glass dominated the far wall. Cavalon couldn't tell if it was a viewscreen or a window.

Rake's voice crackled over comms. "I'm on point."

"Copy," Griffith replied.

She crossed the threshold and Griffith hovered off her shoulder. Together, they swept the room quickly and efficiently while Mesa and Cavalon waited outside the door.

"Clear." Rake lowered her aim but kept her weapon in hand.

Cavalon crossed through the doorway, and Mesa followed with the atlas. The door slid shut behind them. Sealed inside, a thick weight of silence overcame Cavalon. Hard-angled trenches of golden metal formed the walls, while a single panel of dark, ribbed aerasteel comprised the floor, yet both dampened sounds like thick carpet.

Mesa headed for the terminal on the left, but the large glass panel straight ahead grabbed Cavalon's attention. As he moved closer, it became clear that it was, in fact, a window into another area. However, the extremely thick glass heavily distorted the view. There were no lights on the other side, but from what little spilled in, he could make out an open circular chamber ten meters in diameter. Strips of coiled copper rounded up the arcing walls in unbroken rings, set between dozens of rows of reflective panels.

Rake appeared in his periphery. "What is it?"

He shook his head. "I don't know."

"Rake." Griffith stood in front of the wall to the left of the wide window. "There's a door."

Rake crossed back to Mesa, who busily swept through menus on the terminal. She passed the pyramid off to Rake without so much as a glance. Griffith raised his gun and shifted to the side.

With her pistol in one hand and the pyramid gripped in the other, Rake cautiously approached the door. It slid open, and she set the pyramid down near the threshold before moving inside with Griffith shortly behind.

Cavalon took a few cautious steps forward and peered in. The doorway led to an arched corridor made of the same smooth matte gold, curving around the outside of the empty circular chamber. Griffith and Rake disappeared down the corridor, while Cavalon hovered in the doorway and waited.

"Clear," Griffith said a few moments later.

"Cav?" Rake said.

"Coming."

He found them halfway down at what must have been the point opposite the window. The inside wall held a three-meter-wide control panel. A handful of old-school, non-holographic terminal screens, all without power, mixed with a variety of panels containing levers, switches, buttons, and gauges of all kinds.

"What do you think?" Rake asked.

Cavalon shook his head. Not a damn label in sight, even with Viator symbols. "I'm not sure."

"Cavalon?" Mesa crackled through his comms.

Rake waved him off, and he headed back out into the main room. Mesa still stood at the terminal, and he joined her, looking down at the flat, non-holographic display. She'd brought up an overhead schematic of what looked to be the chamber beyond the window.

"This technology is . . . odd," she said. "And old."

"How old?"

"I do not know. It is not the kind of design I would expect to see from Viators, ancient or otherwise. Does this look like anything to you?"

His eyes flashed over the diagram, but he couldn't make sense of most of it. Though to his surprise, he recognized a few of the Viator symbols from what he'd learned looking at the atlas menus. "Off-line" flashed in the upper corner, and symbols he'd surmised from the bomb schematics to mean "fuel" were listed below a flashing red heading, among a few others he couldn't interpret. Beside it, a bold, green symbol acted as a heading for another list full of symbols he didn't recognize.

He pointed to the first line below the green heading. "What's this mean?"

Mesa tilted her head. "The third symbol means 'aid system.' As in a support system. The first two . . ."

"'Cryonic,'" Griffith's low voice rumbled. Cavalon turned to find the tall man standing over his shoulder. "Then, 'stable.' So, 'cryostatic.'"

Cavalon looked back at the schematic, assigning that one to memory along with the few dozen others he now understood. "Is this 'divertor'?" He pointed at one listed under the red heading.

Mesa nodded. "Yes. Very astute. Specifically, 'waste diversion,' I believe. Or 'byproduct.'"

"And this last one?"

"'Plasma . . .'" Mesa said, then tilted her head back and forth a few times. "'Plasma-1.'"

"Meaning hydrogen plasma?"

"Correct."

Cavalon ran his eyes over the schematic again, trying to account for it as a whole. Fuel injection, cryostatic and waste-diversion systems, plasma, hydrogen, rings of coiled metal . . .

"This overhead only seems to include the chamber," he said. "Is there a separate one for that corridor around it?"

Mesa swept back through the menus and opened another file.

"That's it," he said, and Mesa stepped aside. Cavalon hunched over the screen, staring down at it as his mind raced. He pointed to another series of symbols. "What's this?"

"It is an alloy. Niobium and . . ."

"Tin?"

"Titanium," Mesa corrected.

He shook his head. "It's not a bomb," he mumbled.

"What?"

"Open the atlas," he instructed to no one in particular.

Rake pushed off the doorway of the curved corridor and placed the pyramid on the floor in the center of the room. Mesa knelt beside it and swept the medallion across the peak. The menus sprang to life. Cavalon stepped through the screens, then found the stack of yellow schematics and opened them.

He surveyed the information again, crossing back over to look at the terminal a few times to compare.

"This is not a bomb," he said finally. "It's a reaction *like* a hydrogen bomb, but not. It's for this."

"For what?" Rake asked.

"This." Cavalon pointed to the dark glass window. "It's a generator."

Mesa's skeptical look was apparent even through her visor. "So, this is simply a fusion reactor?"

"Yes, but no."

"Well, which is it, doc?" Griffith said.

"Sorry." Cavalon took a breath, willing his jumbled mind to calm down and organize the information in a way he could relate to the others. Or at least to Mesa. "Not a normal fusion reactor. I mean, it's just a big empty sphere. It isn't even toroidal—and I don't see any systems for plasma injection."

"Then how does it function?" Mesa asked.

"It uses this." He led Mesa back to the terminal, pointing to the circular corridor schematics. "This is not just a containment chamber. Well, it is, it's dual-purpose."

"And its additional purpose?"

"I think it's a grav generator. These coil windings? They're niobium-titanium."

"A component of superconducting magnets."

"Right," Cavalon said. "If it works the way I think it does, it'd be incredibly powerful. I'm surprised this thing doesn't suck the whole complex into it when it's on. Counteracting it must be part of the shell's design."

"What precisely is it you believe this gravity generator does?" Mesa asked.

"I think instead of plasma and an electrical charge and maintaining a magnetic field and all that crap, it just . . . takes a shit-ton of hydrogen and forces it to collapse. Then sits back and lets nature do its thing."

Mesa scoffed. "Cavalon, you are describing how a star is made."

"I know."

"It requires prodigious amounts of mass collapsing for millions of years for a star to be born."

"I know."

"Even if it were possible," she continued, "it could not be contained inside a structure. The heat and radiation generated would be astounding."

He nodded. "I know. But I swear, that's what's going on here."

Rake cleared her throat. "Okay, regardless of *how*, what about *why*? What's all this power for?"

"The beacon, right?" Griffith put in. "Is this how we fix it? Power it back up?"

"I guess, but . . ." Cavalon began, then let out a scoff. "It's kinda overkill just to collect and send out some data."

"Data across light-years," Rake pointed out.

"True, but, still . . . this thing could power a friggin' solar system."

"Mes, what's this?" Griffith pointed to a series of symbols in the highest right corner of the atlas's display, resting even above his eye level.

Cavalon realized then that even though Rake had updated Griffith on what the atlas was, he had yet to see it in person. Having him take a look probably would have been a good idea, considering he was at least as schooled as Rake in the Viator language.

"I can read most of this," Griffith continued, "but I don't recognize this word."

Mesa took a step closer, craning her neck to look up. Griffith palmed the screen and pulled it down to her height. She tilted her head as she stared at it.

"The structure of this software looks a lot like what they would use for industrial planning," Griffith continued. "I think this is part of the project name."

"Dilachia carthen . . ." Mesa's voice withered away as concern creased her brow. She shook her head. "I did not notice that before. It is the Viator word for . . . well, we call it quintessence."

"And that's what?" Rake asked.

"Dark energy," Cavalon answered.

Mesa nodded. "It is one of the fundamental forces. Such as gravity or electromagnetism."

Rake exchanged a look with Griffith, and though it was difficult to tell through their visors, Cavalon was pretty sure they had no idea what that meant.

"It's like repulsive gravity," Cavalon offered. "Sorta. Where gravity pulls things together, dark energy pushes them apart. Quintessence is a form of that. Kinda an old-school term, actually . . ." He trailed off as he looked to Mesa for help. But she faced away, staring back at the bronze door that led out to the platform.

"Repulsive gravity . . ." she mumbled.

"What's up, Mesa?" Rake asked.

Mesa still didn't turn to face them, and continued to speak low as if conversing with herself. "What if it is the opposite?"

"Uh . . ." Cavalon looked to Rake and Griffith, though they appeared just as lost as he was. "What if it's the opposite of *what*?"

"This gravity generator you theorize," Mesa said, as if she hadn't heard him at all, "which houses the containment chamber for the power source: What if that existed on a large scale? What if the outside hull . . ." She pointed to the exit door. "Was the same thing?"

"You think this whole station is a gravity generator?" he asked.

"Well, no. I mean, yes. That is what I *thought*. However, now, I think the opposite."

Cavalon gaped at her, though he knew she couldn't fully appreciate his incredulity through his visor. She'd concocted and supported a whole hypothesis, then discredited it and moved onto another, all in the same amount of time it'd taken him to figure out how to explain dark energy to Rake and Griffith.

"The opposite, but on a grand scale," Mesa continued, her tone filling out, sounding more confident than it had since they'd decelerated from warp. "And there are many of them, correct? All along the Divide? If these 'beacons' are not, in fact, beacons."

Cavalon tried to focus, tried to process her words, at least well enough to ask an informed question, but he could find nothing to grab onto.

Rake beat him to the punch, letting out a disbelieving scoff. "You think these stations are pulling in the Divide? That they weaponized the edge of the universe?"

"Well, clearly not, because it is *off*," Mesa replied frankly, "and the Divide is still collapsing."

"Wait, back up," Cavalon said. "What are we talking about here?"

Mesa drew up her posture and gave a curt nod. "I do not believe that this station is a gravity generator, but instead, a dark-energy generator."

Cavalon shook his head. He'd studied gravity generators in their many forms in great detail, but he'd never heard of anything that could create the opposing force. "Is that . . . a thing?" he asked, trying for a level tone, but it still carried with it a strong vein of skepticism.

"In the original Viator War," Mesa began, "Viator forces utilized a form of planetary defense involving the subtle manipulation of dark energy. They called them Carthen Shields."

"I've heard of those," Griffith said, exchanging a knowing look with Rake, who nodded in recognition as well. It seemed Cavalon was the one in the dark on this one. "They called them AGPs—anti-grav pulse stations," Griffith continued. "But we never encountered one in the Resurgence War, that I know of."

Mesa nodded. "It is very complex technology, on par with the Apollo Gates. We do not understand it at all."

"Anti-grav, meaning dark energy?" Cavalon asked.

"Correct. A misnomer, absolutely," Mesa said curtly, though she immediately traded in her disdain at whoever had coined the term, reverting to her cautious, yet excited state. "It would either collect or manifest dark energy, we have never been certain which, then insert it elsewhere. In the case of the planetary defense system, it would infuse the force into the upper atmosphere and create a buffer of sorts around the planet. Focused, directional versions also existed. They had made attempts at weaponizing it, though I am not aware of any success in that regard."

Cavalon rubbed the back of his neck through his suit. "What kind of buffer?"

"It'd keep enemy vessels at bay for longer," Rake answered. "It basically expanded the amount of empty space between the device and incoming ships. It couldn't produce enough to stop them entirely, but it would slow their trajectory."

"Oh," Cavalon said. It'd started to click, slowly. "So, it actually bloated space, in a sense? Made it take longer to get somewhere?"

"Correct," Mesa said. "Though as I said, on a very small scale. A ship caught in it might have taken ten or fifteen minutes longer to breach the exosphere of a planet."

"How . . ." he began, but his voice faded away. He didn't know where to start with the list of questions this concept generated.

Mesa shook her head. "We are not sure how it functioned. And it was not utilized often, only when extreme measures were called for. A 'last-ditch effort,' as they say."

"Why?" Cavalon asked.

"It took an enormous amount of energy to power," Mesa said. "So it was difficult to utilize at outposts or on planets where they did not already have a strong foothold. Also, the repercussions often outweighed the little leeway it would grant them. It interfered with ship systems, scanners, communications. Personnel reported strange accounts, both planetside and in the area of effect."

"Strange accounts?" Rake asked. "Like what?"

"Physical pressure on one's internal organs, as if being compacted or pulled apart. A myriad of psychological effects, such as feelings of complacency or unrest. Dreams that occurred out of time. Difficulty hearing—"

"Wait," Rake said. "Dreams out of time?"

Mesa nodded. "As in, dreams of the future or past. Visions, some called them. Some even claimed to have seen them when awake."

A silence fell over them as they stared at Mesa, and Cavalon's heart thudded loud in his ears. Mesa seemed unaware of the bomb she'd just dropped. Well, *aware*, but not nearly as shocked by the implication as she should have been. She'd likely already come to that conclusion, processed it, and filed her reaction away as a useless emotion.

"It makes sense," Mesa said, tone light. "Correct?"

They stared silently back at her, and Cavalon's mind reeled. She'd skipped over large swaths in the path of logic that'd led her there, but, to Cavalon's intense displeasure, he'd started to understand.

Rake managed to speak first. "Mesa, you think this structure is that same technology? A dark-energy generator?"

Mesa's eyes lit up. "Yes. You do understand." She smiled and nodded. "But on a far grander scale. Clearly it would take a *great deal* more power to create the amount of dark energy needed to overcome the gravitational imbalance of the universe—"

Griffith let out a sharp scoff. "Okay, what the fuck are we talking about here?"

Rake stared down at the floor for a beat before looking back up. "Can you walk us through this a little more, Mes?"

"Of course. Let me start at the beginning." Mesa cleared her throat and laid her hands together. "After its creation, the universe expanded. This was due to an abundance of dark energy. It pushed the confines of space outward, at an ever-accelerating rate. However, after a time—many billions of years—the amount of dark energy present began to underperform the gravity created by the mass of the universe. The expansion slowed and eventually ceased. Now, the theory had been that it would eventually begin to collapse. But, it never did. It held still, achieving a balance, a stasis. But what if that was not a natural equilibrium?"

In the midst of the resulting long, heavy silence, Cavalon found himself nodding. He finally fully understood it. And he didn't like it one bit.

"Without us, you will perish . . ." It took Cavalon a moment to register that Rake had spoken, under her breath, barely audible.

"Rake . . ." Griffith said, tone heavy.

"I think Mesa's right," Rake intoned, her expression flat, gaze distant.

"Uh, back up. What'd you say?" Cavalon looked between the two Titans. Griffith stared at Rake, who stared at the floor.

"That's what they told you, right?" Griffith asked. "The breeder?"

Rake nodded. Cavalon's mind reeled. He was way out of the loop on this one, but too shocked to form a proper response.

"A breeder spoke to you?" Mesa asked, tone inquisitive.

"You think they knew," Griffith said. "About these stations."

"Then we killed them all off." Rake gave a rueful shake of her head. "And now the stations are falling apart."

"Except we didn't kill them," Griffith said. "Not all of them."

Cavalon gaped. "Wait, we didn't?"

Rake leveled a flat look at him. "You saw the Viator on the video yourself."

"Right, but, you said . . ." Cavalon let out a short sigh. He had no idea what they were talking about, but he knew it didn't matter. The gist was: There were Viators left, and one had said some shit to Rake, and that somehow translated into her believing this *ludicrous* hypothesis of Mesa's.

But the trouble was, Cavalon found himself believing it too. As much as he wanted to find a way to refute her, it actually made a lot of sense. The science was unsettlingly solid. Why gravity got so dense and strange at the Divide. Why comms and other systems started to break down, even when millions of kilometers away. And the time ripples. If these stations had sat around for thousands of years pumping out tremendous amounts of dark energy, it would wreak havoc on the natural order of things.

That, however, didn't even skim the surface of the implications this hypothesis presented. If these stations had been active since the universe stopped expanding, that would put Viators in this part of the universe well before they arrived at mankind's doorstep in the Core.

"Mesa, I get where you're coming from," Cavalon said, "I really do. But come on. The implication of that?"

"Correct," Mesa said, her voice steady as ever. "The implication being that the Viators stopped the collapse of the universe by building these stations."

Griffith let out a heavy breath.

"But then what?" Cavalon said. "They just battened up this side of it and left it at that? What about the rest of the *entire* edge? They can't possibly have traveled the entire universe."

"No," Mesa said. "Only the perimeter."

Cavalon scoffed. "Right, but still . . ."

"Think about what we do know," Mesa prompted. "They traveled the Divide for millennia before they found mankind. They may have come from the other side of the universe. There could be trillions upon trillions of Viators still alive wherever they came from. The Viators we know could be a small sampling, sent for the express purpose of building these stations in this sector of the universe."

Cavalon shook his head. "I thought they traveled here *on* the Divide. They can't have if they built it."

Mesa shrugged. "That was the assumption, but we had no outposts anywhere near the Divide at that point. We have no direct accounts of their origin."

"So, what," Griffith said, "they finished building the stations and decided to stick around awhile and pillage mankind?"

"Right," Cavalon agreed. "I mean, even once they were losing, they never tried to leave. Or get reinforcements."

"Maybe they couldn't go home," Rake said, tone heavy.

Mesa's face suddenly went blank, and she stared up and off into the distance.

Cavalon cleared his throat. "Mesa . . ."

Her consciousness seemed to snap back to her in an instant, and her eyes refocused onto him. "There is an ancient Viator phrase," she began. "Part of a series of verses. Not from two centuries ago, but their history, very old, some of the earliest chronicles we have from them. It does not translate well, but part of it essentially says, 'the shunned will build the edge.' It has long been interpreted to imply the expectation of inclusion. As you know, Viators did not segregate within their species."

Rake hung her head. "You think it's literal?"

"Maybe," Mesa said. "There is more to the saying than that, but I have not committed it to memory. It was actually the basis for the Sentinel nursery rhyme, you know the one, 'Sentinel, Sentinel, at the black—'"

"Yeah, we know the one," Rake grumbled. "Fuck, Mesa."

"Indeed," Mesa agreed with a curt nod.

Griffith leaned against the wall. "So you think ancient, far, far away Viators sent their shunned troops to stop the collapse? And they had to circle the universe to create all these stations?"

Mesa inclined her head. "That is my hypothesis, yes."

"All right . . ." Rake drew in a long breath. "Reconstructing Viator history right now is way off point."

Griffith nodded his agreement. "So the 'data beacons' we see here . . ." He moved away from the wall to point to the crisp white holographic map. "They are actually all dark-energy generators?"

"If my hypothesis is correct, yes," Mesa said. "It is likely that the alpha stations began to break down, but the redundant beta stations, being inactive, have failed to pick up the load. It is possible their power sources failed, as it appears this one has. And with no, or . . ." She eyed Rake and Griffith warily. ". . . with *so few* Viators remaining, they were not able to maintain the generators properly."

"So, that's what the one in the message meant by 'restart the station'?" Cavalon asked, turning to look at Rake. "And why there are so many chemicals and strange supplies aboard the Drudger ship? They were recruited to restart the reactors and fix the stations?"

"Right," Rake said dryly. "And we killed them."

Cavalon sighed. That was . . . great. Just fucking perfect.

"Rake." Jackin's voice came over the comms.

"Go for Rake."

"We figured it out. Had to delve into the secondary control permissions, simple little data lock, old-school stuff. We're good to head out whenever you're done."

"Great, Jack. Thanks. We'll be in—"

"We figured it out," Jackin said again. "Had to delve into the—"

"Jack? What?"

"—secondary control—oh, fuck." Jackin crackled away.

Rake put her hands on her hips and looked straight down at her boots. "Jack."

A few moments later, he came back on. "Yeah, boss. So, *little* bit of a time ripple thing going on in here—Emery!" He cut away again, then came back a few seconds later. "Okay, I got them split up. Take your time, boss—hey, what did I *just* say!"

"She started—!" was all the comms caught of Emery's high-pitched voice in the background before cutting away.

Rake let out a long sigh. "Shit."

Cavalon swept his gaze from Rake, to Griffith, then to Mesa, but no one seemed sure what to say.

Rake finally spoke up, turning to Cavalon. "There's nothing we can do right now, correct? There's no restarting this generator without the supplies from the *Synthesis*?"

"I doubt it. Unless there's a large amount of hydrogen just lying around somewhere."

"Okay," Rake said. "Then we head back to Kharon. We'll come up with a plan after that."

✦

CHAPTER THIRTY-FIVE

Adequin tasked Mesa and Cavalon with updating Jackin and Emery, then sat next to Griffith on the circular bench for the short trip back to Kharon Gate. They quietly discussed their discovery, but Adequin couldn't find a way to focus her full mental efforts on it. It was ridiculous and unbelievable and daunting. But Griffith was dying, and somehow, that overshadowed even this.

He still claimed he felt fine. Tired, but fine. She could hardly believe he had so little time left, but she trusted Cavalon's diagnosis—which somehow wasn't difficult. He had no reason to lie, and he clearly understood what was going on. She didn't like it, but she believed it. And it was killing her.

When they decelerated from warp and cruised up to the gate, they hadn't even docked before Adequin's nexus lit up.

"EX?" Puck's voice crackled in, thin and staticky. "You guys reading us yet?"

"Go for Rake."

"We, uh, just got a mayday from the *Typhos*."

"What?" she barked. The *Typhos*—the next closest Sentinel ship, and the next in danger of being wiped out by the Divide.

"I lost the connection," Puck said, "But I recorded it."

"I'll be right there," Adequin said. She waited for the gravity to flip, then headed straight up the ladder and out the hatch. Griffith and the others followed close behind.

In the control room, Warner and Puck stood at the terminal next to the one that still held an open comm link to Poine Gate.

Puck glanced over as she approached. "Find anything useful?"

"You could say that," she sighed. "What's going on with the *Typhos?*"

Puck brought up a recording on the terminal and pressed play. The brassy audio came with a great deal of crackling, cursing, and a few back-and-forth grumbles. Puck gave her a nervous grin, then fast-forwarded and pressed play again.

Puck's voice played first. "*Typhos,* this is Kharon, we read you."

"Oh, fucking finally," the gruff voice on the other end crackled through. "Kharon this is Optio Beckar—SCS *Typhos,* we—mayday—"

"Optio?" Puck said. There were a few seconds of hissing static.

"—hear us?"

"Yes, hearing you again, sir."

"We need to abandon ship immediately—send vessels—"

"Sir, be advised, we cannot relay to you. Both Zelus Gate and Kharon have been turned off and abandoned."

"Kharon's been abandoned too?"

"Yes, sir."

"Then who the fuck are you?"

"We're, uh . . . we're what remains of the crew of the *Argus,* sir. The same thing happened to us, we retreated to here."

"We—" The man's voice cut away, and Adequin grimaced as a loud squeal rang out, drowning the rest of his sentence in static. "—Divide is contracting toward us."

"It is, sir."

"Fuck."

"Do you have any warp cores?"

"Void. No."

"You need to get as many of your people as you can aboard your away vessels and start flying inward."

"Away vessels? We have a thousand fucking people. We could only fit . . . maybe thirty . . ."

Puck stayed silent for a few long seconds, then his voice came back low and apologetic. "You'll just have to do the best you can, sir. Fly straight inward. Try to make it here—or Zelus Gate."

"How can we—" Another peal of static overtook the recording, and Puck slid his finger across the screen to close the playback menu.

"That's when we lost them," he said quietly.

Adequin rubbed the back of her neck. Puck looked down, and she gripped his shoulder. "You did good, Circitor. It'd take us weeks to warp to them, and by that time the Divide would be so far in, we'd all be done for. It's all you could do."

He let out a soft sigh, then gave a furtive glance at Griffith and Jackin standing behind her, speaking quietly. "Sir," Puck said, "can I talk with you in private for a moment?"

She nodded, and he followed as she crossed to an empty corner of the room. "What is it?"

Puck lowered his voice. "I didn't want to announce it in front of everyone because I wasn't sure what you'd want to do. But I dug deep into the code, and I found a restart fail-safe. It's what's been keeping us from getting the gate turned back on."

Her heart skipped a beat. "You can turn it on?"

He nodded.

"Rake!" Jackin called suddenly. She looked back over to find Jackin hovered over the main terminal. "It's . . . Lugen."

Adequin's breath stalled in her throat, and she hesitated only a second before jogging across the room and sliding into the seat. It'd taken fucking long enough. He'd probably been sunning himself on some Outer Core tropical beach. But she was relieved. If anyone could do something to help them, it was Lugen.

She let out a heavy breath, then pressed the link. "Go for Rake."

"Prius statute, Rake?" Lugen's gravelly voice rang through—thin, tinny, and distant.

"Sorry, sir," Adequin began. "Protocol calls for delta clearance or higher when reporting matters relating to SC security. I wasn't sure what this would be classified as—"

"It's fine, Excubitor. What's this all about?"

Adequin hesitated. She'd run this conversation through her mind dozens of times, but now, she had no idea where to start. She cleared her throat and pressed the link. Might as well hit him with it up front.

"Sir, the Divide is collapsing, and moving inward at an increasing rate."

"What?" he said, incredulous. "Who gave you that report?"

"No report, sir. I saw it with my own eyes."

"You're still out there?"

"Yes, sir. And the *Argus* . . ." She cleared her throat. "It's gone, sir."

"Where are you?"

"Kharon Gate, which has been abandoned. Sir, have we withdrawn from the Divide?"

Lugen hesitated. "That happened weeks ago."

Adequin clenched her teeth. She already knew it was true, all the signs pointed to it. It was another thing to hear it confirmed. She took a steadying breath. "Why weren't we informed?"

His tone grew disconcerted. "I don't know, Rake."

"And the Apollo Gates too? That oculus at Poine claimed Eris and Zelus have been decommissioned as well. Why? What's going on?"

"I wish I had answers for you, I really do. But none of this is my jurisdiction."

"Have the other Sentinels been informed? We just heard from the *Typhos*, they didn't know either."

"Shit, Rake . . ." Lugen clicked off for a few long seconds, then came back on. "Something's not right. Get Kharon operational and come back here, directly to me. We'll sort this mess out on this end."

"Wait, sir," she said quickly, "we found something out here. Viator technology. We might be able to use it to stop the collapse, but we need soldiers, resources. Backup."

"That's not your responsibility, Excubitor. You and your crew need to return to Legion HQ."

"But, sir, there are dozens of other Sentinel ships still stranded—thousands of soldiers. They'll need arks, and that could take weeks.

The crew of the *Typhos* has *hours*. If a rescue's not already incoming, we might be the only ones left that can help."

"I . . . I'll look into it. I'll try to get a hold of Praetor Teign, confirm ships have been sent."

Adequin let off the link and sat back, digging her fingers into her scalp.

Jackin scoffed. "Like hell they're sending anyone."

She nodded slowly. He was right. Like hell they were.

Whispers rose up behind her, but her addled mind ignored them. This was what she'd wanted, what she'd been waiting for—a definitive course of action, an *order*. But she'd barely been able to save twenty of her own soldiers. And there were over a thousand people on the *Typhos*.

"Rake, you still there?" Lugen asked.

"Sir, I . . ." She swallowed a lump in her throat and leaned forward. "Sir, I have to go."

"What? Rake, wait. What's going on? Is your gate operational?"

"It will be shortly, sir."

"So you're returning to the Core?"

"No, sir."

Lugen didn't speak for a long time, then his weary voice crackled back on. "Excubitor—"

"The majority of my crew will be coming through on a Drudger vessel, call sign . . ." Jackin swept open a file on his nexus and held it out in front of her. "VCF-840115."

"Fine, if you're going to make me," Lugen growled. "Excubitor, I *order* you to return to the Core."

"I can't, sir."

"Rake . . ." His serious tone carried a heavy warning that instantly made her second-guess herself.

She swallowed and steeled her nerves. "I have to fix it, sir. Or at least stop it from getting worse."

"There's protocol for this kind of thing."

"For the universe collapsing, sir? I'm not sure there is."

"You have to trust me on this. We'll send assistance."

"That'll take too long. We can't keep waiting for the Legion."

He stayed silent for a few tense seconds. "Do not do this to me again, Adequin," he breathed, his tone furtive. "I don't know if I can protect you this time."

Adequin disconnected the call. She sat in silence and stared at the dead link.

"Rake?" Jackin's voice broke through, low and full of worry. "What are you doing?"

She stood and turned around. Jackin, Griffith, Mesa, Cavalon, Emery, Warner, and Puck all stood eyeing her in various degrees of shock and discomfort.

"Rake?" Jackin said again.

She shook her head. "We can't just go back to the Core."

"But it'll stop, right? The Divide? Once it settles between the alpha stations that are still working? It's just . . . squaring off, sort of? It won't just keep collapsing and wipe out *everything* . . ."

"If those stations don't fail as well," Adequin said. "Even if they do stay on, it would still take out every Sentinel ship between the two. And what if it starts wiping out Apollo Gates? Then any Sentinels that manage to flee the Divide will still be stranded out here, with no way home."

"She's right," Griffith said. "If the gates at the Divide are taken out, it's over. It'd take a lifetime or longer to warp to the next closest gates."

Adequin nodded. "We *have* to get that beacon restarted. Stop the collapse."

"Sorry . . ." Puck said suddenly, hovering behind Mesa and Cavalon, eyes wide in disbelief. "What does that mean exactly? Stop the collapse?"

Thankfully, Mesa turned to him and made brief work of it. "The data beacons are not data beacons, but dark-energy generators. Their cessation seems to be the cause of the Divide's collapse."

Puck gaped at her, mouth open. Warner ran a hand down his face.

Adequin looked to Cavalon. "So, we have to restart the power source. Correct?"

"Right," Cavalon said, face fixed in shock.

"By that, I mean *you* have to restart the power source."

He didn't move. "I know."

"Which is . . . what?" Puck asked warily.

"A star, apparently," Griffith said.

"A contained fusion reaction," Cavalon clarified, scratching his stubble with both hands. "It's not *really* a star. Just sort of."

"So, you're saying we have to restart a star?" Puck asked.

"Well, no," Mesa corrected pleasantly. "We have to *make* a star. Or, primarily, Cavalon does."

Cavalon pinched the bridge of his nose. "I think I get the theory behind it, guys, but . . ."

Adequin took a step toward him, lowering her voice. "That's all any of this has been," she said, trying to sound encouraging. "Just putting theory into practice. You've built hydrogen bombs— it's similar, right?"

Jackin's eyes went wide in alarm. "I'm sorry—what?"

"Bombs?" Puck croaked.

"Really . . ." Mesa's large eyes narrowed.

Cavalon shook his head. "Similar, maybe . . . but I mean, you're asking me to jury-rig a star. *Inside* of something else. With ancient alien technology I can't even begin to understand."

Adequin nodded. "Yeah, I am."

He stared back at her, unmoving.

"Can you do it?" she asked.

He let out an extremely long breath that went from his nose to his throat in a crackling grumble. "Yeah, I think I can."

She shook her head. It wasn't good enough. To risk their lives at a chance to stop this, she needed him to be sure. "I can't accept that. Can you do it or not?"

Cavalon's resigned stare flickered into worry. Then his features flattened out, eyes narrowing. "Yes. I can do it."

Adequin swept her look to Mesa. "Mesa, I would like you to be there to help, but I only want you to go if you feel comf—"

"Excubitor, please," Mesa scoffed. "I will be going."

"Jack—"

"Come on, boss."

Adequin sighed, knowing the futility of trying to talk him out of it. She looked at Griffith next, and her heart sank. "Griff, I think you should stick with the crew. They could use your guidance, and a couple relays inward, you might be able to find a doctor."

He rolled his eyes and crossed his arms. Adequin swallowed the lump in her throat. Arguing with him would be beyond pointless. Of course, he'd be coming. He literally had nothing left to lose. Hours of life left.

"Fine," she said, voice weak. She cleared her throat, then turned to Emery and Warner.

"Sir," Emery said, back straight. "I'm there if you need me, sir."

Warner nodded. "Me too, EX."

"Thank you both for all you've done," Adequin said, "but I need you to help out with things here. Report directly to Circitor Eura."

"Yes, sir," Emery said.

Warner saluted, fist to chest. "Yes, sir."

"And me, sir?" Puck asked.

"You need to get the gate turned on, then help Eura get everyone aboard the *Synthesis* and ready to go through the second we're back."

"Excubitor," Mesa began, then gave a hesitant glance at Puck. "His expertise may be useful. We do not know what kind of issues we may encounter with the generator's mainframe."

Adequin wrung her hands. She didn't want to risk anyone else, but Mesa was right. If they ran into issues with the computers, Puck would be their best shot. She locked eyes with him. "Puck? You up for it?"

"Yes, sir." His back straightened. "Of course, sir."

"You understand the risks?"

"As in—suicide mission?"

She swallowed back bile. "Yeah."

"Sounds great," he said pleasantly. He glanced at Mesa, and his tone fell serious. "I mean, yes, sir. Understood, sir."

432 ◄ J. S. DEWES

"Okay. Then you're with us," Adequin agreed. "But get the gate back on first, and make sure Eura or someone else feels comfortable piloting the *Synthesis*."

He saluted. "Yes, sir."

"Jack?"

"Boss."

"Take Cavalon and Mesa and however many others you need to unload the supplies off the *Synthesis* and onto the *SGL*."

"You got it," Jackin said.

"Why not just take the *Synthesis* ourselves?" Griffith asked. "It's already loaded up with everything we need."

Adequin shook her head. "We can't—we need to leave them a vessel that's safe to take through the gate, in case we . . ." She swallowed. "In case we don't make it back in time."

Griffith's brow furrowed, and he gave a short nod. Jackin patted him on the back, then gripped Cavalon's shoulder and led him out of the control room. Mesa, Puck, Emery, and Warner followed.

Griffith waited for the others to disappear around the corner, then turned to face her. "I'm proud of you, Quin."

"Why?"

"You all but told Lugen to go fuck himself."

She let out a pained laugh. "Yeah, I'm really screwed this time."

"Nah, Mo'acair," he said, warm eyes glistening. "You're better than ever."

She pushed up on her toes and kissed him.

Griffith winced, cradling his rib cage with one arm.

"Void," she said. "I'm sorry. You need more apexidone?"

"No, I'll be fine. You know there's such a thing as being too apologetic? Especially when it's for things that aren't your fault."

"I mean, your whole situation is *objectively* my fault," she said. "I asked you to captain the *Tempus* to begin with, and I insisted you go on one last trip. Not to mention you're stationed out here to start with because of what I did."

"What are you talking about?" he asked, seeming honestly confused.

"You were sent to the Divide because of what I did."

He shook his head. "No, I wasn't. I asked to be stationed here."

She stared, unblinking. "You asked?"

"Of course."

Her chest warmed, but with it came a tinge of anger. All she could manage in response was a feeble, "Why would you do that?"

"Because I didn't want to be a hundred million light-years away from you."

"But you're here, now, like this," she said, her voice fervent. "You could be safe at some boring post in the Core."

He quirked an eyebrow. "You think I'd be happy at some boring post in the Core?"

"Well, no," she muttered. "But here? Why?"

"Because I love you, Quin."

She stared at him, unblinking, completely unsure of what to say. She'd known it for so long, voicing it almost seemed superfluous. Yet something about actually hearing the words come out of his mouth consoled her. Validated something she'd hid—even from herself—for so long. Griffith loved her.

She wound her fingers into his, his skin warm, almost hot. "I love you," she said.

He leaned in, lips locking onto hers. He pulled her closer as the kiss deepened.

He let out a wistful sigh. "I should probably help load the SGL," he said quietly, taking a step back.

She scowled. "You're hurt. You should let the others take care of it."

He flashed a grin and ignored her as he started for the door. "'Cause, ya know, the strength of ten men. And that's without Imprints."

She rolled her eyes as he disappeared around the corner. His playful smile warmed her heart, but too quickly the feeling grew tainted. She was well aware of his impending fate, and that she could do nothing to stop it.

434 ◄ J. S. DEWES

She took a breath, steeling her resolve and deciding to focus on what she still had a chance to stop: the Divide.

She started down the hall toward their makeshift base camp, wanting to confirm they had every warp core they'd collected aboard the *SGL*, just in case. She stopped partway to wait as a line of soldiers passed toward the air lock, on their way to help transfer supplies. A flicker of recognition had her sticking her arm out to bar the last from continuing on. Seconds later, they were alone in the narrow hallway.

"Snyder," she said.

The man stared at her arm, watching warily as her Imprints re-arranged themselves. He stepped back and snapped to attention. "Sir."

She crossed her arms. "Got anything you wanna say to me?"

"No, sir."

She stared back at him. His eyes flitted to the ground, but he remained impassive.

"He wouldn't say anything," she said. "But I'm not blind."

"Sir?"

She gave a pointed look down at his hands. He rubbed his red, bruised knuckles and his face flushed. "Er, that's just—"

"Rake," Jackin's voice called over her nexus.

Adequin ground her teeth. As much as she wanted to put this guy's head through a wall, she was in fact trying to *save* the Sentinels, so murdering one felt like a step in the wrong direction. It wouldn't do much for morale to start executing people.

She leaned in and lowered her voice. "If you lay a hand on one of my soldiers ever again, I will personally end you."

Snyder's face paled and he nodded quickly.

"Tell me you understand."

"I understand," he managed.

"Get the fuck out of my sight."

He backed away, then scurried down the hall after the others.

She opened the comm link on her nexus. "Go for Rake."

"Uh, meet me in the control room," Jackin said.

"Copy."

Adequin headed back to the control room and a few seconds later, Jackin appeared. He pushed a stiff hand through his hair. "I saw a ripple."

Her eyebrows shot up. "Just now?"

"Yeah."

"How can it be that far in already?"

"I . . . don't . . ." he said distantly, then sat at the terminal. She sat next to him as he slid through menus. Finally, he grumbled, "Shit."

"What?"

"Gate sensors are picking up a gravitational pull like what we were getting on the *Argus*. It's still far away, but it's starting."

"Already?" she breathed. "What does that mean for the beta beacon?"

"I don't know. We're gonna be pressed for time, for sure."

"We can check the atlas on the way, see if it looks like it's updating or not. But we should leave ASAP."

"They're on-loading the supplies now," Jackin assured. "Shouldn't be more than fifteen minutes."

"Good."

Jackin grimaced, rubbing his fingers gingerly over the healing burn marks that'd cut a path through his beard.

"How's it feel?" she asked.

"Better. Starting to itch, is all." He scratched at the unmarred half of his beard. "I should probably shave it, huh?"

She tilted her head. "Nah. I kinda like the asymmetry."

He quirked a brow.

"Makes you seem edgy."

A grin twitched on his lips for a brief moment before being overtaken by a frown. "Rake?"

"Yeah, Jack."

"We haven't had a chance to talk about Bach."

Her eyes fluttered down to the terminal screen. "I know."

"Are you okay?"

"As okay as I can be."

"I know you like to blame yourself for things. Just . . . don't. It's not your fault."

She continued to stare down at the terminal. "I don't blame myself," she said. "I blame the Legion."

He grinned. "About time you joined the party."

She smiled back. "I think my invite got lost in transit."

"Probably. You know how well comms work out here."

She let out a heavy breath, then stood. "Ready for this, Jack?"

He stood as well. "Ready, boss."

CHAPTER THIRTY-SIX

Adequin could do nothing, and it drove her fucking mad.

She'd helped off-load the supplies along with Griffith and Puck, then gone into detail with Jackin about the Divide's position, checking the atlas to determine its approximate location and speed. They had an hour, maybe less—but they couldn't be sure. The atlas appeared to be updating, but they didn't know the severity of the delay.

But as they'd flown the SGL back toward the enormous structure, Adequin had seen the telltale static sparks flashing as the various debris, stray gases, and random stardust that lay outward were extinguished from existence. So she knew it was close, and growing closer every minute.

Once they were inside, she could only stand there as Cavalon and Mesa fluttered around within the enormous bronze sphere—apparently an extremely powerful fusion reactor—and *watch*. Wait for them to figure it out. Try to interpret their rushed requests if they called out for things. But mostly it'd been a two-person operation, and she could do little but stand back and wait to be summoned.

After a time, she'd taken up post outside the door to the curved corridor and deemed herself responsible for running interference between doppelgängers and the real Mesa and Cavalon. It'd been a bit of a time-ripple nightmare, exacerbated by the fact that approximately every three seconds, Mesa or Cavalon changed their mind about something. That sent their duplicates into rippling, confused choruses of possibilities, and they were not quiet about it.

The Mesas were enraged that their work had been hindered, and the Cavalons immediately became flustered and unsure of what to do with themselves.

Griffith had offered some sage advice—apparently approaching a duplicate with a bit of a paradox could expedite its disappearance. If you informed it that it was not in fact real, pointed out the present version of itself, or better yet, did something to the present version of itself that it couldn't have recalled happening, because you'd just decided to do it, it would vanish much quicker.

However, she'd pinched Cavalon a half dozen times already, and she was pretty sure he'd started to get annoyed. So she sat back and tried to think of another approach to fielding the duplicates. Jackin had suggested leading them straight out the door and off the edge of the platform. But real or no, that was a little too disturbing for her to seriously consider.

Thankfully, none of the strange *past* time ripples had occurred, at least not yet. She wasn't sure if they'd show up as the Divide grew closer, or if they were an anomaly specific to whatever had happened to the *Tempus*. The future ones were causing enough of a problem all on their own.

As Cavalon and Mesa's work began to wind down, the duplicates grew less and less frequent. They made fewer snap decisions, changed their minds less often. It wouldn't stop the far-off futures from showing up, but it lessened the likelihood of the near-future ones considerably.

"We're ready for the hydrogen," Cavalon's voice called through the comms.

Adequin exhaled a sigh of relief. She summoned her Imprints and picked up one of the four dozen, meter-and-a-half-tall compressed-hydrogen tanks. Griffith grabbed another, and together, Jackin and Puck lifted a third, and they filed down the curved corridor.

Adequin rounded the bend to find Cavalon and Mesa hovered in front of the wall-sized panel of gauges and screens.

"I don't know, max grav sounds pretty good," Cavalon said.

"But how can we be sure that is the proper setting?" Mesa argued.

"Well, we can't, but I don't think there's an instruction manual lying around, do you?"

Mesa crossed her arms. "Certainly not."

"Then I say we go big or go home."

"That is a *ridiculous* statement."

"Hey, you two," Griffith said, hefting the tank up onto his hip. "In the market for some hydrogen?"

"Yes, please," Mesa replied. "Thank you, Centurion."

Cavalon took Adequin's tank from her and marched it over to the far side of the bank of panels. Griffith set his nearby, and Puck and Jackin followed suit, then the three men disappeared down the hall to grab another round.

Adequin turned back to Mesa. "Hey, Mes?" She tilted her head down the hall, and Mesa took the hint, following her a few meters around the bend.

"Yes, Excubitor?"

Adequin switched to a direct comm link and lowered her voice. "Listen, I don't wanna get Cav all worked up, but we might need to pick up the pace a little bit."

"I understand." Mesa inclined her head. "I will . . ."

"Light a fire under his ass?" Adequin offered.

Mesa's disdain at the crude turn of phrase was apparent, but she nodded her agreement.

"But, gentle," Adequin warned. "Don't get him all freaked out. Tell him a story or something. Keeps him focused."

Mesa gave an amused smirk. "I understand."

Less than thirty minutes later, Mesa was three tales deep into her harrowing chronicle of experiences as a prisoner of war during the Resurgence—delivered of course with the utmost dispassion, as if reading a bland passage from an ancient historical account—when Cavalon finally finished. He emptied the last of the hydrogen into the vacuum-sealed chamber, then Mesa said something about checking the schematics one last time and disappeared down the

440 ◄ J. S. DEWES

hall, leaving Adequin alone with Cavalon as he detached the last tank and rolled it aside.

"That's all of it." He stepped back, hands on his hips. Sweat glistened on his forehead, visible even through the visor.

She switched to direct comms. "You okay? Your heart rate's still high. Thought you were pretty distracted by Mesa's stories."

"I was," he admitted. "That's some shit, huh?"

"Yeah," she agreed, letting out a heavy breath. It'd managed to dredge up some memories of the war she could have done without at the moment.

"Hydrogen's just extremely explosive," Cavalon said. "And that injection valve's seen better days. Probably one of the least-safe things I've ever done. And that's saying a lot, honestly."

She turned a glare onto him. "Void, why didn't you tell us?"

"Why, so we can *all* be freaked out? Plus, it's not like we would've had time to replace it."

Adequin shook her head, but decided to let it be. It was over now, and no one had exploded.

She gestured to the pile of empty tanks strewn all over the corridor. "Doesn't seem like much." Not that she had the first clue what star-building entailed. But it didn't seem like someone should be able to make one from four dozen tanks of compressed hydrogen. "Will it be enough?"

Cavalon shrugged. "No idea." He crossed his arms and stared at the panels for a few seconds. "Can I, uh, be frank with you, Rake?"

Adequin swallowed. This was it. When he tells her this is foolish and it'll never work, and all she'd done was bring them here to die in the wake of the Divide aboard an overlarge, dead data beacon.

"Go ahead," she said.

"There's an apparatus on those schematics. It's marked as a primary system. We had to feed it some freaking teracene—you know, the metamaterial that runs the gates? I have no idea what the system is. But I'll tell you what I *hope* it is."

"And what's that?"

"Some kind of . . . hydrogen duplication machine."

"That sounds made up."

"Yeah. It would be. That doesn't exist. Then again, none of this does."

"Fair enough."

"I *also* hope, there's some kind of . . . spacial compression that's going to happen, even once it's burning. I just can't see how the mass is going to be enough to sustain itself in a chamber only ten meters in diameter."

"This really isn't bolstering my confidence that this is going to work."

"No," he said, shaking his head. "Me either. I mean, we're putting in the right amount—the amount the atlas schematics call for. So in theory, this should all work, assuming the Viators didn't give shitty instructions." He looked to Adequin and grinned. "We'll find out, I guess."

"So we're ready?"

"Yes, sir," he said, with too much forced cheer.

"How do we start it?"

He pointed to an inconsequential, small rectangular button near the center of the control panel, enclosed in a glass casing. "The schematics say this is the guy. Press button, make star." He swung his look back toward her. "You wanna do it?"

"Not in the least. This is your baby, you do the honors."

"I get it," he grumbled. "You want *me* to be the one to kill us all."

She scoffed a laugh, then took in a deep, calming breath. He stared back at her expectantly. She sighed. "You want us to push it together, don't you?"

"Looks like a tough button," he said with a grin. "Might take two of us, even with the aid of Imprints."

She rolled her eyes and switched back to universal comms. "Fine. Everyone ready out there? Mesa?"

"Ready, Excubitor."

"We're good," Jackin called back.

Cavalon flipped open the glass casing and hovered his finger above the button, and Adequin lifted her hand as well.

Cavalon cleared his throat. "Do we need to have one of those conversations about what 'on three' means?"

"Bloody void," she cursed, then grabbed his hand and pressed it into the button.

A light below the casing flickered on, but otherwise, nothing perceivable happened. She exchanged an expectant glance with Cavalon, who shrugged.

"Rake," Griffith's weathered tone crackled through. "It's doing . . . something, out here."

Adequin headed back to the main room, Cavalon on her heel. Griffith, Mesa, Jackin, and Puck stood a ways in front of the long, dark glass window. The metallic panels that lined the inside of the sphere shimmered with a blue-white, almost iridescent glow.

"If this happens," Cavalon warned, "it's gonna be, er . . . *bright.*"

Adequin nodded, stepping up beside Griffith. "Guys, switch on your visor's advanced light shielding."

The others complied, but Cavalon just looked down at his suit's nexus in confusion. "Uh," he mumbled. "How . . ."

Adequin took his forearm and slid through the menus to turn his on, then did the same for her own. A gridded overlay flashed over her vision before fading away. A readout in the corner indicated the automated shielding was currently at zero percent.

"And maybe just don't look at it," Cavalon warned. But they all kept staring at the chamber, even Cavalon. Adequin could already tell it was going to be one of those things you just couldn't look away from.

It began slowly, with tiny dots of concentrated light sparking throughout the chamber, like the tiny stars of a tiny universe. They hovered perfectly still, wavering in intensity as they flickered into existence. The floor rumbled lightly.

A sharp, chalky crack thundered through the chamber. Adequin's breath caught along with a dense thud in her chest that pressed into her heart and throat and eardrums.

She looked to Cavalon beside her.

"The grav generator," he explained. Though the comms crackled with static, his voice came through surprisingly steady and reassuring.

She gave him a short nod, then looked back at the sparkling field of minuscule stars. Dozens more, then hundreds flickered to life, the number growing exponentially by the second.

In an instant, the visor's shielding flashed to a hundred, and Adequin's entire display shorted out. A sonorous, hollow *whoosh* preceded a wave of intense heat billowing from the glass.

Sweat beaded on her skin. Griffith turned and pulled her into him, eclipsing her from the wave of heat, though she could still feel it burning through the side of her suit. Her comms crackled and her HUD flickered with static and blackness, interspersed with flashes of blinding white. She kept her eyes shut.

Moments later, the flashes ceased in favor of a steady stream of white. She opened her eyes, staring down at Griffith's boots and the dark aerasteel floor while her vision adjusted to the new, incredibly bright light level. She drew her gaze up slowly as Griffith let go and turned along with her to stare at the wide window.

A five-meter-wide, perfect sphere of colorless light sat hovering in the center of the containment chamber. Tiny flares of white and faded magenta licked up off the edges as it churned. The window's glass had taken on a dark film, shading the view to make the reaction visible, though the intensity of the filtered light remained almost blinding.

Adequin looked to Cavalon. He still stood beside her but had faced away, arms hovering to his sides. He looked back over his shoulder to stare at the churning ball of gas, his face awash in the bright light, his stunned blue eyes exhilarated.

He turned his beaming look to meet her gaze. "Is it a bit toasty in here?"

She couldn't help but smile back.

While Puck tried to get Mesa to give him a high five, Jackin crossed over to give Cavalon an exuberant handshake. Griffith gripped the side of Adequin's arm and peered down at her. Inside his visor, sweat dripped down his forehead, wrinkles deeper than when they'd arrived. He was fading fast.

"Quite a thing, Mo'acair," he said.

"Still think space nature is bullshit?"

"Bullshit can still be awesome."

She laughed, and he wrapped his arms around her.

"Oh, man," Cavalon said with a breathy chuckle, rubbing his hands together and seeming quite pleased with himself. "If we could recreate this tech, stick it on a ship? Feed a jump drive? Holy shit. You could have unlimited jumps."

"Shit, yeah . . ." Jackin agreed, turning back to gape at their mini-star.

"Well, the power source is certainly on," Puck said. "But what about the station?"

Mesa crossed over to the terminal and tapped on the screen for a few seconds.

Jackin grabbed the atlas and walked over to the doorway that led back out into the main structure, then returned moments later. "Nothin' new happenin' out there."

"Reactor stability is excellent," Mesa announced. "Energy levels are at optimal output." She slid through a few more menus, then pointed over her shoulder. "That appears to be the control switch for station activation."

"This?" Puck asked. He stood across the room near a terminal set in the opposite wall, which lacked any kind of screen or visible control system. At chest height sat an angled glass panel with a half-cylindrical slot recessed into the face.

Mesa inclined her head. "Yes, I believe so."

"Looks like an arm slot to me," Puck said, then laid his arm into the opening.

"Puck!" Mesa barked. Her harsh, uncharacteristically loud tone caused Adequin's heart to skip a beat.

Puck waved Mesa off as the face of the machine glowed white, then buzzed, enclosing his arm in a cylindrical sleeve of metal.

Moments later it gave a negative beep, then the sheath reopened as the light faded away.

"Huh . . ." He rubbed his forearm. "I don't think anything happened."

Mesa stormed across the room and pulled him away with a sharp, annoyed grimace. "Please do not *stick your appendages* into things when you do not know what they do."

Puck's cheeks flushed, though his lips pulled up into a small grin. "Sorry."

"You are lucky that did not kill you," she snapped. "With your imitative Sentinel Imprints, who knows what kind of reaction that machine could have had?"

Cavalon nodded, staring at the churning ball of hydrogen. "Volatile interfacing."

Mesa looked back to Puck. "It probably could not sense them through your suit. But *do not* do that again."

Puck nodded, though he still seemed more amused, or even pleased, than remorseful.

"Wait, Mes," Adequin said. "You know how this thing works?"

"Yes," Mesa said brusquely, still reeling with irritation at Puck. "It is an interface method for complex industrial structures, network systems management, large-scale database searching, et cetera." She swept a disdainful look over the apparatus. "This appears to be a somewhat crude version, likely one of the earliest iterations of the technology."

"And it does what, exactly?" Adequin asked.

"It functions in conjunction with Viator Imprint technology to allow the user neural access to a mainframe."

"Looks like an arm slot to me," Puck said.

Adequin looked back to find a new Puck standing beside the apparatus again. He laid his arm down into the slot.

"Fucking void," Jackin cursed.

Mesa crossed her arms and watched in irritation as the duplicate Puck disobeyed her orders. Real Puck pressed his hand to his visor and sighed.

Adequin found it quite amusing for a half second prior to re-alizing what it meant. Reverse time ripples. Future *and* past shit mingling in the present to create glorious chaos. As well as a very pronounced, visceral reminder that the Divide rushed closer every second.

Adequin walked over to real Puck and punched him in the chest.

"Ow, boss, what . . . ?" Puck trailed off, watching in surprise as his duplicate flickered and faded away.

"Wait . . ." Adequin's brow creased in confusion. She'd reacted on instinct, but that made no sense. She looked to Griffith. "Why did that work?"

Griffith's eyes were wide, and he gave a weighty shrug. "No idea."

She shook it off, then checked the readout in her HUD, con-firming that the exterior oxygen levels and temperature remained safe. Gripping the sides of her helmet, she released the lock and pulled it off her head. An immediate onslaught of oppressive heat greeted her along with a wash of blinding light as her eyes adjusted to the unshielded brightness of the room.

"Rake!" Jackin barked.

"Quin, what are you doing?" Griffith asked, voice low and dis-tressed.

Tossing her helmet aside, she began to peel off her suit from the neck down, skin slick with sweat. She hadn't realized how much her suit had dampened the heat.

"We're short on time, guys," she said. "We need to get this thing turned on. Now. It wants real Viator Imprints?" She shouldered out of the sleeves of her suit and tied them around her waist, then held up her arm. The silver and copper Imprint squares flashed brilliantly in the intense light. "How do I control it, Mes?"

"I . . ." Mesa began, face slack. "I am not sure, Excubitor."

Adequin nodded, decided she didn't care, then turned and laid her forearm in the slot. The glass glowed white as the cylinder en-circled her arm and the cool metal clamped down.

Her skin tingled and a brief pang of horror spiked in her chest as her Imprints sprung to life of their own accord. She'd never not had control over them before, never seen them act other than under her urgings or instincts. She watched in awe as they folded and unfolded in a glittering cascade down her bicep and onto her forearm, disappearing under the metal sleeve.

Then she realized what was really happening, because it started to hurt. Hurt like it had when she'd gotten them, but instead of scorching metal burning into flesh, it was the opposite. Like the squares infused into her were being torn off, carved out of her skin and muscles one by one as they transferred into the machine.

She ground her teeth as the Imprints continued to flood from the rest of her body, up her back and chest and into her arm, disappearing into the metal cuff. She let out an involuntary, guttural growl, and though she bit the pain back down, it quickly became all-consuming.

"Shit, Quin," Griffith's low voice hissed as he hovered in her periphery.

Then in an instant, the pain ceased, the tension left her muscles, and her eyelids dropped closed. The awareness of her physical presence withered as her mind disconnected and faded into the machine.

She instinctively knew what to do, how to interface with it. Just like her Imprints—will thought into action simply with intent. The Imprints would translate.

So she got right to the point and asked them to turn the structure on. They faltered. They couldn't do it. They wanted to obey her, but a barrier stood in their way. She asked to see what blocked them, and she knew it was only data, but she could *feel* the answer as much as know it, and it felt real, like a perfectly recorded memory playing back in exhaustive detail.

She confirmed she had all the information she needed, then asked to be released.

In a shorter but equally intense rush of pain, her Imprints flew out of the machine and up her arm, returning to their default formation. The metal sleeve opened and she stumbled back.

Griffith caught her, keeping her upright until she found her footing. He turned her around, gripping her arms. "Adequin."

She blinked the watery haze from her eyes and focused onto him. "I'm okay," she assured, though her voice came out haggard.

"What happened?"

She breathed heavily, letting her mind catch up and process what she'd learned. Of *course* it wouldn't be as simple as building a star.

"The station can't connect to the power source," she said, turning away from Griffith to face the others. "An expulsion system overloaded when the last power source collapsed."

Cavalon stared, eyes wide. "Collapsed, like . . . supernova'd?"

Adequin shrugged. "I guess. It exploded, and the mass had to be expelled or it would've taken out the entire structure. There's a fail-safe for that exact purpose, but it was damaged during the emission. The vent is still open, and until it's properly sealed again, the station can't turn on."

"Where is this 'vent' located?" Mesa asked.

"On the hull."

Oddly, Cavalon immediately sat on the ground, legs crossed under him. Adequin turned a confused look onto him, but he didn't seem to notice.

She looked back at Mesa. "Can you bring up the schematic labeled 'imens ma'ertis'?"

"How—" Mesa began, but then cut herself short, seeming to dismiss her curiosity with an effort. Adequin followed as the Savant marched to the terminal. She brought up the main structure's schematic, and Adequin recognized the layout from what she'd seen inside the mainframe.

"There, that's where it is." She pointed to the spot and Mesa enlarged the area. Adequin tilted her head to get her bearings. "That's the . . ."

"Outward-facing side," Mesa said.

"Do we have to fly out there to reach it?"

"I don't believe so." Mesa zoomed in even farther, narrowing in on the corridor that arced around the power source. "There is an access hatch here, which leads outside the hull."

"Right, I remember now." She nodded as the details of the information she'd collected from the mainframe solidified. "I can get us there."

She walked over to Cavalon, still sitting on the ground in the middle of the room, both arms wrapped around his midsection.

"Cav?"

He looked up at her, the weight of his helmet lolling his head back with a light bounce. "Hey, sir."

"Just having a bit of a sit?"

"I figured I'd rest while I could," he said dolefully. "We're going on another EVA, aren't we?"

"Yeah."

"Okay." He looked back down, nodding slowly.

She offered her hand and he gripped her forearm, then she pulled him to his feet. "Can you tell me what we need to make the repair?" she asked.

He turned to stare at the Imprint apparatus with wide eyes. "You want me to do that thing?"

"No. It may not be safe, since you also have Sentinel Imprints. But I have all the information," she assured. "I don't understand it, but I've got the details."

"Okay," he said. "What's broken?"

"There's a purge valve located on the outer hull, where the mass ejected after the explosion. The emission blew off the outlet cowl. It doesn't have to be replaced, but it does need to be hermetically sealed."

"What's it made of? The valve?"

"Aerasteel."

"And how large is the vent?"

"Point eight two meters in diameter."

"Okay . . . I can take the recoil paneling off the *SGL*'s warp drive. Fuse it on with a plasma torch. Unless it'll cold weld, but it's probably coated . . ."

"The recoil paneling won't affect our ability to, uh—" She cut herself short, but her reeling mind couldn't come up with a more subtle word. "Escape?"

"No, sir," he assured. "Might make accelerating and decelerating a little rougher, but it's perfectly safe."

"Let me take him, sir," Puck said.

"No, you're too inexperienced," she said. "This is going to be a dangerous walk."

"Then I'll go," Jackin said. "We can't risk you."

"I need you to have the *SGL* locked and loaded. If we fail out there, you need to be ready to get the others back to Kharon before the Divide's too close."

"Did you even hear what I said?" he asked, brow creasing.

"Yes. Thank you both, really," she said sincerely. "But I saw the layout in the mainframe. I know where this thing is, how we get there, and how to fix it. It has to be me."

Puck nodded slowly. Jackin crossed his arms and exchanged a wary look with Griffith.

Finally, Jackin let out a relenting breath. "All right, Rake." He turned to Puck. "Take Cavalon and run back to the *SGL*, get whatever he needs. Bring back two MMUs, harnesses and tethers, and every zero-g tool we have."

"Copy that, Optio." Puck led Cavalon out the door toward the *SGL*.

"Rake . . ." Jackin took a step closer, expression tight. "Can I get a minute?"

She followed him as he walked to the far side of the room.

"I know what you're going to say," she said, crossing her arms. "This is a risk, I shouldn't be going—"

"Actually," he said, flexing his jaw, "for once, no. I wanted to say I'm proud of you."

The tightness in her shoulders loosened as she uncrossed her arms. "Oh . . ."

"This whole thing's been one tough call after another. But you've made all the right ones." He stared down at her bare arms.

"And putting your damn arm in that thing . . ." He shook his head. "I wish I could be half as fearless as you."

She gave a grateful nod, surprised at how much his words loosened the caustic strain that'd taken root in her chest.

"You like to say you're not a ship captain," he continued, "but command isn't about knowing how to run a ship. It's about people. Being an example. And you're damn good at that."

She swallowed the lump at the back of her throat. "Thanks, Jack."

"And . . ." He ran a hand over the top of his helmet. "I'm sorry for questioning your orders. On the *Argus*, Kharon, the *Synthesis*. It's not my place, not only because you're my CO, but because . . ." He paused to clear the hesitation from his throat, and his tone came revived, unyielding. "You've earned my trust. You earned it a long time ago. I never should have questioned that."

A smile tugged at her lips. "Hate to break it to you, Optio," she said. "But you're wrong."

Beneath his visor, his eyes flickered with unease. "I'm tryin' to apologize here, boss."

"I know, and I appreciate that. But it *is* your place to question me—it's exactly your place. You think I want a second that's just going to blindly follow me, no questions asked? I need you to be you. And you're the only one I trust to get the others safe if this goes lateral."

He let out a long breath. "We've had enough lateral for one day."

"I agree." She gripped his hand and squeezed, and he pulled her forward, wrapping his arms around her. He let out a long, heavy sigh.

"Don't die, please," he said. "I want to be able to continue judging all your decisions."

"Copy that."

Jackin's arms dropped away as he stepped back. "I'll go help Puck and the kid."

She nodded. "Thanks, Jack."

Jackin disappeared out the door toward the SGL.

452 ◄ J. S. DEWES

"Excubitor?" Mesa called from across the room. "May I have a moment of your time?"

Adequin crossed to where Mesa and Griffith stood beside the station activation controls.

"What's up, Mes?"

The Savant cleared her throat. "We have been discussing it, and, well, if we get . . . low on time, in regards to the Divide, and you are still out on the hull . . . Well, we will need Viator Imprints in order to start the station."

Adequin's stomach turned at the implication, but she quickly tamped it back down. No one had real Viator Imprints except her and Cavalon . . . and Griffith. But she couldn't ask that of him.

"We'll be fast enough," Adequin said, tone firm. "We'll get the repair done and get back in to start it."

"Are you kidding, Quin?" Griffith scoffed. "I'll do it."

She shook her head. "Griff, it was extremely painful. I'm not sure you could handle it in your state."

"What state?" His expression remained impassive, eyes glinting playfully.

She pushed her sweaty hair out of her face and sighed. Mesa gave a light smile and walked away toward the primary computer terminal across the room.

"Are you calling me old?" he asked.

"Griff . . ."

He reached up and released his helmet.

"Don't—"

"Fuck, it's hot," he grumbled, then dropped his helmet at his feet. He peeled off the top of his suit and tied it around his waist, then faced her squarely. "Listen. If you make it back in time, great. If you don't, then it's gotta be me."

"Griff, I don't think you understand. It was like getting the Imprints all over again, but way, way worse."

"What's it gonna do, kill me twelve hours earlier?" he said dryly, then his tone fell serious again, low and haggard. "I'm too young to die of old age anyway, Quin."

She forced a swallow, though her throat had gone bone-dry.

"I'm not long for this world," he said quietly. "Let me do this."

She bobbed her head slowly. He pulled her into a hug, and she let a couple of tears get lost in the sweat of his shirt. "I love you, Griff," she murmured.

"Love you too, Mo'acair."

CHAPTER THIRTY-SEVEN

Cavalon sighed as he looked out across the black void. Static light sparked in thin lines in the not-distant-enough distance, illuminating the matte-black hull of the station in flashes of sharp white light. It was weirdly peaceful. Like watching lightning flash across thunderheads as a storm rolled in off the sea. Except it was nothing quite so tedious as a thunderstorm.

One good thing about being out on the hull with Rake was that he no longer sweat buckets out every pore. Instead, the sweat had chilled into a viscous film all over his bruised, aching, tired, beaten body, and his icy, wet clothes stuck to every part of him. Life was good.

The discomfort proved a solid distraction from the fact that Rake had to pull him thirty meters to their destination, and the only thing they could tether to was each other.

Though, the whole excursion had yet to feel the proper amount of dire. Rake had been the picture of cool, calm, and collected as she palmed her way carefully across the surface toward the purge valve, making small, expert adjustments with her MMU, lugging him behind like a weightless anchor.

The whole time she'd been telling him all about Titan hazing rituals—he assumed for his benefit, but now he wasn't so sure. Wistful sighs and heavy silences cluttered her words, and she'd lost her place and repeated the same bit a few times.

Cavalon had just realized she might be the one who needed a distraction, and intended to take over the task of storyteller, when she let out a particularly resounding sigh and said, "This is it."

He looked up to where she hovered three meters above . . . or, to the left. He cursed to himself as he realized he'd completely lost track of which way was up—or which way had been up when they'd exited through the access hatch. Though he supposed it didn't really matter, so long as Rake knew where they were.

Rake looked down at him, and the spotlight on her helmet blinded him briefly as it flashed across his face. She tugged on the tether and his bruised stomach smarted as she pulled him toward her.

The stupid harness hit in all the wrong places, and though it had hooks in a multitude of spots—along the back and shoulders and chest, and lots of less-bruised places—Rake had insisted it needed to be as close to his center of gravity as possible.

He'd moaned, "*But there* is no *gravity*," like a petulant child, and she'd glared and grumbled back, "*Well, you still have* mass," and he'd scowled and said, "*Oh, you think you're a scientist now?*" Then Jackin had hushed them, reminded them the Divide sped toward them at thousands of kilometers a second, and could they be bothered to please shut up and go stop the universe from collapsing.

Rake finished pulling him toward her, and Cavalon found himself hovering in front of a less-than-one-meter-wide circular breach in the otherwise pristine hull. He turned his helmet to aim his suit's light down the vent shaft, which descended deep into the structure, no end in sight. Charred and scorched metal lined the lip of the vent, the tubing within melted and warped.

A bracket of sorts encircled the breach: a raised rectangle of thick bars around the vent's opening. Likely the mounting that had once held the outlet cowl in place. Now, it made a perfectly acceptable anchor point, and Rake busied herself unhooking and rehooking their long tethers until they each linked to the bracket, and no longer to each other.

Cavalon watched in silence—his heart-rate meter a golden yellow.

A flash of static light illuminated Rake's face as she turned to stare at him through her visor, amber eyes expectant. "Ready?"

A particularly violent bout of flashes made his pulse spike to red. Panic took over again, and it made him feel like an idiot.

He'd wanted this—to be needed, to matter. And what he was about to do couldn't matter more. Saving-the-universe-level shit. So why did he want to be anywhere but here right now?

He took a breath and told himself it was a natural reaction. Utter annihilation from space and time rolled toward him, a slow wave of ultimate destruction. Who wouldn't be flustered?

But what scared him even more was what it probably really was— weakness. He wasn't cut out for this kind of shit. He could have an all but perfect memory, a ridiculous capacity to learn, maybe even some creative ingenuity, but that didn't give him any guts.

Thoughts of guts made his real guts throb in pain, reminding him yet again of his bruised and beaten midsection. He'd been too weak to fight against that too.

Another onslaught of flashes startled him, and he craned his neck to look outward. They were getting closer. *It* was getting closer. He could feel it in his core.

"I did flirt with that recruitment officer," Rake said suddenly.

Cavalon turned to gape at her.

"*Nothing happened,*" she assured. "But I did flirt. A little."

He scoffed a laugh. "I knew it. How'd that go? I want details."

"It was incredibly awkward, actually." She turned away, and he carefully removed the recoil paneling strapped to her back.

"Really? Kid Rake wasn't a smooth talker?"

"Well, no, not really. But it wasn't that." She turned back around, and he passed her one panel, then laid the other down across half of the vent opening. "He just wasn't interested in flirting with a beat-up kid."

"But he helped you anyway?" he asked as Rake passed him the plasma torch. "Despite the awkwardness?"

"Yeah. We became friends, actually."

She kept the panel in place while Cavalon held the plasma torch to the seam, then clicked the ignition to light it. The arc caught in a rush of blue flame.

"We kept in touch for a long time," she continued, "but he went MIA in the Resurgence."

"Oh. Sorry to hear that." He began to drag the tool along the first seam. "What was his name?"

She let out a heavy breath. "Circitor Hudson Rake. Though, he eventually became a centurion."

"Uh . . . wait, what?"

"It was the only way it could work."

"To get married?"

She laughed. "Void, Mercer. No. He told them I was his niece. 'My papers got lost when my refugee ship got hijacked by Drudgers on its way from the IE.' I don't even know all the details of the story he told."

Holy shit. He couldn't believe she was telling him this.

Rake passed him the second panel, and he lined it up beside the first.

"You're not just making all this up, right?" he asked, then started welding again. "You're being for real?"

"I'm being for real."

"So what's your actual—" But he could no longer form words. His chest constricted, his throat closed, his bruised gut heaved. Without moving a centimeter, he felt like he'd been thrown off a three-meter ledge and slammed into the ground. His head spun from lack of air, then in an instant, the wave ebbed and the pressure ceased. His vision reeled as he gasped for breath to fill his lungs again.

"Cav?" Rake breathed, voice weak.

"What, the fuck, was that?" he managed, breath equally labored.

Rake stayed silent for a few long moments. "I don't know. Let's hurry."

Cavalon forced his trembling hand to remain steady as he dragged the plasma torch along the seam. He had to be quick, but he also had to be careful. Had to hold the flame long enough to form a solid bond, or it wouldn't be enough, and it wouldn't be a hermetic seal, and the station wouldn't start, and they'd die, and a lot of fucking other people would as well. This was one of those low-pressure situations in which he thrived.

But this had to be it, right? The last leg on this ridiculous journey? Had to be. The only way out was through. Might as well focus it all into this moment, or it could really be his last.

Suddenly, all the stupid shit he'd gotten all worked up about the last two days felt even stupider—dumping acium out of warheads and cutting it out of fuel lines, throwing doors at Drudgers, and a walk-in-the-park EVA—compared to this one. Those were the days. Hours. Whatever. Fuck, it'd been a long day.

He inhaled a wavering breath as he finished the seam between the two and moved on to the top. Three edges down, two to go.

"Griffith, you read me?" Rake asked.

Griffith's low rumble crackled on the comms. "Go for Bach."

"You ready to do this?"

"Ready on your mark. Just let me know when you're back inside and the hatch is sealed."

Rake didn't respond for a few long seconds, and from his periphery, Cavalon could see her looking outward toward the static flashes. "We're not going to be able to wait for that," she said.

"Rake, what?" Jackin's voice cut through. "We can't turn it on while you're still on the hull."

Rake's haggard voice came back weirdly calm. "I think you're gonna have to."

Strangely, a sense of warm serenity flushed through Cavalon. His heartbeat steadied, so smooth it was almost imperceptible. Maybe he'd finally learned to control it. Or maybe it'd started going so fast, it'd melded into a singular, unending beat.

He moved on to the last seam.

For the next few seconds, he was vaguely aware of argument in the comms. Jackin and Griffith didn't want to start it while they were still on the hull. Too dangerous, who knew what could happen? Mesa said it might be fine, might be safe. What did Cavalon think?

Cavalon thought nothing, because Cavalon's world was fifty

centimeters long, built of aerasteel and plasmic fire. He knew nothing else.

A moment later dread overwhelmed him, a wrong, empty feeling, painful and dark. It was too familiar—a heavy, weighted heart, like when your dad dies—the fucking worst, a *physical* pain. How could a force of nature make him feel this way? That was all this was, right? The edge of the universe? Just science?

Fuck that. It was here. He had to focus.

His world was thirty centimeters.

Then that first breathless feeling came again, like the air had been punched out of him. He could sense it pulling him away. No, not pulling. Falling.

Forward started to become up, and he began to fall away, anchored at that pesky center of gravity, off the hull and outward, into the Divide.

He stretched forward, keeping the torch close to the metal, but he couldn't hold the tool steady *and* keep himself in place; he didn't have enough hands.

However, he didn't need to ask for help, because Rake had already started moving. She kept hold of the bracket with one arm, then swung out behind him. She pressed her chest to his back and grabbed onto the other side of the bracket with her other hand, trapping him against the hull. He could continue.

Ten centimeters.

A shower of static light flooded his vision, and he had to squint to keep his place with the arc of the torch. On either side of him, Rake's hands vibrated. Or the whole hull did. Or Cavalon's head did. No, it was her.

Her grip loosened, and one by one, her fingers peeled away from the bar. The force of his whole body pressed against her, but she grunted and roared and somehow kept her grip.

"Done." He let off the plasma torch, which fell away over his shoulder. He immediately grabbed the bracket with both hands, using his Imprints to pull himself forward—upward—and take the pressure off Rake.

"Do it now, Griffith," Rake barked.

"Are you in—?"

"That's an order!"

"Shit—"

The comms cut away, and for an infinitesimal moment—peace. Silence. Just nothing. His world was zero.

A nanosecond later, his heart fell into his gut. A horrifically loud noise tolled, one he knew couldn't exist in the vacuum of space, so he must have been making it up, must have. Like the hollow twang of an enormous metal string being plucked. He could feel it as much as hear it.

Then the outside rushed in and expanded, like a thousand tiny balloons inflating inside him. It tried to diffuse him, pull him apart, cell by cell, atom by atom.

His breath fogged his visor, and though he couldn't hear it, he knew he'd started yelling, screaming, really. He thought Rake did too. Her hands still held the bracket on either side of him, keeping him tucked into the hull. He held on, Imprints clamping into his muscles to keep his grip, but he was suddenly unsure whether he was getting pulled away or pushed back in. The two forces battled, struggling against each other.

The notifications in his visor had gone haywire, flashing every awful warning that'd normally make his pulse race faster. But his heart-rate monitor had disappeared—he figured it'd moved past orange, into red, then cruised right into infrared. So fast, it was no longer in the visible light spectrum.

Every other possible warning remained active: breach imminent, loss of pressure, scrubbers off-line, oxygen levels dropping, a dozen more. The suit's fleet of nanites had fully deployed—repairing apparent blunt force damage.

Cavalon refocused his attention from the pointless slur of suit activity onto Rake's vibrating hands. Because they were slowly being wrenched open. She was going to lose her grip.

He kept an Imprint-assisted iron hold on the bracket and craned his neck to look over his shoulder as the static light ceased and the pressure began to lift. Because the Divide had started to move back outward.

It should have been a relief, but it wasn't, not in the least, because Rake was floating away along with it. Falling. Whether he turned too late or it happened too fast to react to, he wasn't sure. He blamed himself either way.

Her harness had ripped. He had no idea how. It floated off her back, torn at the shoulders. She twisted to grab it, but she'd gotten ahead of it somehow, and she couldn't reach it. She swiped at her MMU controls, but nothing happened.

She was moving away faster than the tether. Free-falling. *Careening.*

Cavalon spared the briefest moment to confirm his harness remained intact, then checked his own MMU. Nothing, no response.

His visor's display still flickered in chaos, but his suit couldn't listen to him in its schizophrenic state. It'd have laughed at him if it could. Stupid request, stupid mortal.

So he threw "no sudden movements" out the window and yanked Rake's empty tether and harness toward him. He pulled the broken harness free from the tether, then hooked it to his hip. Double the tethers, double the chance of this working.

Cavalon counted to himself as Rake floated away, then did the quickest math he'd ever done to calculate the force he'd need. Not too slow, because, well, that would be the most pathetic way to fail her ever. But not too fast, or it could break his harness when the tethers ran out.

He turned and pressed his feet to the hull, then launched himself toward Rake.

He felt pleasantly surprised with his apparent ability to translate math into real, physical force, because it soon became apparent that he was slowly gaining on Rake. At least it'd been fast enough. Maybe too fast, but only slightly so. A handful of terrifying seconds later, he caught up with her. He reached out and closed his arms around her shoulders as he clunked into her. She sped up along with him.

"Can you read me, sir?"

"Fucking void, Mercer," she cursed.

"Is that a yes? Listen—"

"What did you do *that* for?"

"Rake, fuck, just let me save you!"

"Void—"

"You need to have a good hold on me," he insisted. "All the strength your Imprints can muster."

She let out a sharp breath.

"I'll use mine too," he continued. "But when these tethers run out, we're gonna snap back pretty hard. The Divide's pulling us and the generator's pushing us. We're riding a wave. There'll be quite a bit of force at the end of the line. If we don't have a good hold on each other, I might lose you."

"If the tethers don't break and we don't *both* go careening off into the Divide?"

"Right."

Rake sighed, then shifted to wrap her arms loosely around his chest. They stared back at the impressive, looming station as they drifted away. The edges glowed, as if the opposite side had lit up, basked in a soft, white light.

"How long are these tethers?" he asked.

"Fifty meters."

He swallowed hard.

For a few silent seconds, they watched the expanse between them and the station slowly grow. Again, it felt weirdly peaceful. He could do nothing but wait.

The slower Cavalon's pulse became, the more his body began to ache. Not only his already-injured guts, but everything. Everywhere. Organs, skin, muscles, hair. His head throbbed, and a constant, onerous thrum reverberated in his ears. His stomach roiled with that same unnerving nausea that'd launched him into his vomiting episode on his last EVA. However, this time, he wasn't sure he'd be throwing up the contents of his stomach. Any organ from the neck down felt like fair game.

"Rake?"

"Cav."

"Can I ask you something?"

"Go ahead."

"Do . . ." He took a long, deep breath. "Do you think that gave us superpowers?"

Rake let out a breathy scoff and didn't respond at first. After a few seconds, she said, "Probably."

"I always thought X-ray vision would be great. How about you?"

"Invisibility."

"Oh, good one."

"Although, teleportation would be great about now."

He gave a short laugh, heartier than he thought he had in him. The station continued to drift away, and the slack in the tethers started to disappear. "I think my eardrums are bleeding," he said.

"Mine too."

"And maybe most of my internal organs."

"Cav . . ."

"I know." He watched as the snaking tethers grew tauter.

"This is going to hurt you."

He shook his head, clunking his helmet awkwardly into hers. "Don't worry about that, I'll be fine. Hold on as tight as you can."

She didn't respond, and his stomach churned with unease. He could see it now: The tethers seconds from running out, and Rake lets go to save him. She waves goodbye and wishes him luck and tells him to take care of Griffith and Jackin as she floats back into the Divide. Fucking typical.

"Rake, I can handle it," he said seriously. "Promise me you'll hold on." He craned his neck until he could see through the side of his visor and into hers.

Her eyes were cast down, sweat beading on her forehead, cheeks flushed.

"Or I'm never building a star for you again," he threatened.

The muscles in her jaw flexed a few times before she responded. "Yeah, okay. I promise."

Cavalon looked up as the tethers drew straighter, then summoned his Imprints to strengthen his grip and protect his stomach. He locked his arms around Rake's back, and she closed hers tightly around his torso.

And that hurt, sure. Sent lances of pain throughout his whole body. Yet it was nothing compared to what came next.

The tethers snapped taut and the harness yanked hard on his midsection as their full weight tugged back against it. Every muscle in his torso seized in reaction, clamping down on his internal organs in a surge of agonizing torment. As his stomach drew forward, the momentum flung Rake, slinging her around on his back. She managed to keep hold of him, arms locked around his chest.

The pain quickly proved too much. His head swam, thick and murky. A bile-heavy lump grew in his throat and his vision faltered. The star-strewn inward view smeared into muddy gray as his eyes welled with hot tears.

He could barely make out the hull lights of the *SGL* rounding the side of the station before he passed out.

CHAPTER THIRTY-EIGHT

Adequin laid Cavalon's unconscious body on the floor just inside the doors of the bronze-sphere chamber. She knelt beside him, then tore off her helmet and tossed it aside. A rush of heat baked her clammy, chilled skin.

She pulled his helmet off and pressed her fingers under his jaw, searching for a pulse. Her suit's HUD had begun to function again on their short jaunt back on the *SGL*, and it'd promised her he was fine. Breathing steady, pulse strong, so she told herself he would be okay. He had to be. He was tougher than he thought he was.

But he looked downright *awful*—his pallid skin slick with sweat, the color gone from his cheeks. Dark bags hung below his eyes and, even unconscious, he looked utterly exhausted.

Adequin, on the other hand, felt strangely . . . great. Her heart beat fast but light. Refreshed, invigorated. Every part of her throbbed horribly, but her chest felt airy, like she could finally take a breath again after being underwater for so long. A weight had been lifted that she hadn't realized was crushing her. She'd met the edge of the universe head-on and survived. They'd mounted a defense, the enemy had retreated, and they'd won the day.

Puck knelt on the other side of Cavalon. "What happened?"

"He just passed out from pain." Adequin breathed a groan as she stood. "He should be fine."

Jackin handed Puck a biotool, and the circitor injected it into Cavalon's neck. Moments later, his eyes slid open. He tried to sit up, but Puck laid a hand on his chest to stop him.

"You did it, boss," Jackin said quietly, gripping Adequin's shoulder.

She leveled a flat look at him, and he raised his hands in submission. "Sorry. *We* did it."

"What *did* we do, exactly?" she asked. "Did you check the atlas?"

"Yeah, it's better than we thought. It not only stopped it from getting closer, but pushed back. Seems to have settled about five hundred thousand kilometers outward. Other sections are still moving inward, but they've slowed. They won't get nearly as far as quickly now that this one's active."

"And the *Typhos*?"

"They should be safe," he assured. "For now."

"Excubitor . . ." Mesa's voice cut through, so heavy with anguish that Adequin's chest seized. She looked across the room toward the Savant, who sat crouched beside Griffith, lying on the ground beside the mainframe interface terminal.

Everything else fell away, vacating her mind completely as she crossed the room and slid to her knees beside him. He grimaced, eyes clamped shut, breaths coming in shallow gasps. His brown skin glistened with sweat, wrinkles deeper than ever. Silver and copper Imprints flickered around his arms of their own accord, seeming unsure of what to do. Mesa disappeared from her periphery.

"Griff?"

"Hey . . ." He peeled his eyes open. The color of his irises had faded to a muted brown. "It worked, huh?"

She nodded. "Yeah, it worked."

He let out a short burst of breath, then with an effort, found his voice again. "You were right. That thing fucking hurt."

"You'll be okay."

He grimaced, his voice a crackling, dry rumble. "This is it, Quin."

"No."

"Yes."

She shook her head. "I can't do this without you."

He gave her a weary, half grin and the corners of his eyes wrinkled. "You've been doing it without me for years."

She laid her head into the crook of his neck, and he wrapped his arms around her. His Imprints buzzed lightly as they trembled along his skin.

"I'm sorry for that, by the way," he rumbled. "I should have been there for you."

She opened her mouth to refute it—he shouldn't have regrets—but the words caught in her throat.

"I know it might not feel important right now," he said, "but I do forgive you for what happened on Paxus."

A hard pressure grew in her chest.

"You did what you thought was right," he continued. "You always do, and I've always trusted that wisdom as a matter of course. Relied on it, even. It'll have been the right call, in the end, I know it. It's what you do."

She squeezed his hand harder, but his grip on her continued to slacken.

He hacked out a few short, weak coughs, wheezing as he drew in a constrained breath. "You said one act doesn't define us . . . and you're right. One doesn't. But *this* choice you made, to stay here, to save the *Typhos* . . . it's decisive, Quin. And where you decide to go from here will matter just as much."

With every word, his voice grew thinner, each syllable requiring a force of will.

"So do me a favor," he continued, "and go make a fucking ton more of these decisions, so it does define you, so it *has* to. Be the Quin whose shadow I couldn't escape, even all the way out to the edge of the collapsing universe."

She nodded as a tear trailed to the tip of her nose.

Griffith wiped it away with a trembling thumb. "I'm sorry, Quin. I guess you're gonna have to grow old without me after all."

A jolt of pain fired under her ribs, stifling her breath. More hot tears stained her cheeks.

"Promise me you will, though," he breathed. "Grow old, I mean. Wherever this leads. Just . . . find a way to live."

She swallowed, nodding as she looked back up.

"One more favor?" he asked.

468 ◄ J. S. DEWES

"Anything."

"Punch Lugen for me?"

She let out an effusive, pained laugh. "Gladly."

His tone fell serious again. "And maybe find a thunderstorm."

She managed a nod. "Copy that, Centurion." Salty sweat and tears mingled as she pressed her lips into his, then breathed, "Aevitas fortis."

He let out a withering sigh. "Aevitas fortis, Mo'acair."

Griffith's eyes closed. The Imprints jittering on his arms slowed, then shuddered before coming to a rest. Adequin laid her forehead on his chest and closed her eyes.

She waited for his chest to rise again. Waited to hear his breath catch, waited to feel his heart thud against his rib cage. Just waited.

Because this wasn't it, it couldn't be. They had a lifetime ahead of them. That's how she'd justified it all—not telling him how she felt, letting him captain the *Tempus*, all the time apart that could have been together. Something better would come after the *Argus*, and they'd do it together. They just had to be patient.

So she kept her eyes clamped shut and waited; she didn't know for how long. Seconds that could have been minutes that could have been eons, she waited.

Soon it'd been too long, and she knew it was over, but the grief she'd thought would overwhelm her never came.

Because how fucking long had she been *waiting*?

Waiting for orders, waiting for permission, waiting for requests. Waiting for the Divide to swallow them whole.

And waiting since Paxus for that other fucking shoe to drop, because it was never going to be *that* easy, she'd known that from day one. She'd defied an order, didn't pull the trigger, didn't tie a nice tidy bow on their war and pass them their consummate victory on a silver platter.

A promotion and a safe, easy post wasn't a punishment. For five years she'd waited for the real one—the one *she* needed, so she could rectify her guilt.

With sharp, bittersweet relief, she realized it'd finally come. It was over. She'd found the real punishment and could move on. If she could find a way.

She opened her eyes and lifted her head. Sweat dripped down her temples. She had a vague awareness of Jackin in her periphery, crouched beside her. She found Griffith's dog tags tucked between his shirt and chest. A chest that didn't raise or lower, didn't move. Just sat perfectly still.

She ran her fingers along the etched metal and glass pendants. Antiquated, like everything else issued to the Sentinels. Too much effort or expense to maintain a chip database for soldiers they'd already written off as dead.

She unhooked the chain, then closed the clasp around her own neck, tucking them under her sweaty shirt along with her own. She turned to look at Jackin, his brow creased deep with worry.

He laid a hand on her shoulder. "Rake . . . I'm so sorry."

She stood and passed him to stand in front of the wide glass window. Crossing her arms, she watched their mini-star churn and spin, reflecting brilliantly off the metallic panels lining the interior sphere.

Jackin approached, hovering off her shoulder. "Rake . . ." he began, then cleared the hesitation from his throat. "Are you okay?"

She didn't respond; she couldn't yet. Her mind reeled, searching for an explanation—for the point of it all.

Why was she here, now, like this? That same thought had gnawed at the back of her mind for years. She was as far removed as one could get, lingering on the edge of the universe—a universe that had tried its very hardest to end its own existence despite them. There had to be a reason. Griffith didn't die for nothing.

Maybe that day on Paxus, she'd been part of something bigger than she'd realized. When the Legion's best, most trustworthy, most brainwashed soldiers started to recognize they could make decisions for themselves, what do you do? You cut it off at the head. You make a new plan. Out with the old. Find a new army, one that'll listen, one that *has* to listen.

The Legion brass could have been playing ahead of it for years— quashing a rebellion that hadn't even happened yet. Some of the "offenses" she'd seen on intake paperwork had been flimsy at best. Warner, when stationed in a remote system in the Perimeter Veil, had worked off-duty hours helping a settlement install shield walls to keep out the ravenous local fauna. Puck's little thruster hack aboard the SCS *Somnium* had been in an attempt to catch up to a Drudger cruiser that'd taken a half dozen Core-bound IE refugee ships hostage. Technically, they'd defied orders, but come on.

Maybe they weren't just sending the Sentinels all their criminals and miscreants, but those most likely to rebel. Those that had proven themselves capable of defiance. If the SC truly had started the Resurgence to silence a fledgling uprising from the citizenry, why not this too?

There was more to it than that, though, and she couldn't shake the feeling it was all related, connected. It had to be. She could already see the headlines that'd roll in from the Core: "Legion Tragedy at the Divide. Sentinel Forces Lost in Horrific Accident. New Legion Personnel Welfare Act Proves Worth. Thank the Void for Augustus Mercer's Amazing Fucking Foresight."

Cavalon was right. The more one man consolidated power, the less the SC looked like the republic it was intended to be. That it should be, that humanity deserved. This was all part of that "longer game," and even out on the fringes of nothing, they were pawns in it.

Despite the exhaustive list of implications, the part that made her stomach churn and bile creep up her throat, was the possibility that *they knew*. That the Legion or the Quorum or the Allied Monarchies or all of the above, knew. Knew these stations were the Viator's responsibility, knew they'd fall into disrepair once they were gone. That they'd been counting on the Sentinels to die, so they could use it as part of their propaganda.

And the worst of it—what if *Lugen* knew? He hadn't been able to look her in the eye when she'd left his office that day. Did he know about it, even then? He had Omega clearance, he should have known everything there was to know about the Legion and the SC. He'd have known about the LPWA and the cloned Drudger army and how easy it'd be to sacrifice the Sentinels to make a point. Who knew what dark secrets he'd shared over teatime with fucking Augustus Mercer.

Her face heated, and she took a deep breath that quavered in her throat. She knew she was spiraling, that she'd thrown logic out the window. She had no proof of any of this.

Except that sinking feeling in her gut that'd always told her when she was right. *That* was the recruitment officer that would finally help her. She'd thrive if she joined the Titans. Paxus was the right planet. Let the breeder go. Fix the "beacon."

She might be wrong, or she might be right, but it didn't matter anymore. What was done was done. Griffith was gone, and it was time to stop waiting.

After a few silent minutes, Jackin spoke up again, his voice quiet and worried. "What are you thinking, boss?"

Adequin continued to stare at the blinding ball of gas. "That there are still thousands of Sentinels that need saving."

He said nothing for a long time, then stepped up beside her, arms crossed, shoulders hunched. "Rake," he whispered. "What about Lugen's orders?"

She glared. "You think we're going to relay back to the Core, get a round of honorable discharges, and go home? They clearly wanted us gone, Jack. Our survival will be considered, at best, a nuisance."

Jackin scoffed. "I can't really disagree with you there. But what can they really do once we're back—court-martial us? Again? Send us *back out* to the Divide?"

She shook her head. "No."

His scowl drifted to Griffith. The ire left his voice and his tone became serious as he looked back at her. "You really don't think it's safe to go back to the Core?"

"Not yet." Adequin looked over her shoulder toward the doorway, where Puck helped Cavalon stand. His brow furrowed with pain, but his face had flushed with color. He leaned on Puck's arm as he found his footing, then looked up and locked eyes with Adequin.

She inclined her head. "They might have a dictator on their hands, sooner rather than later. One who's already trying to replace us."

Cavalon slicked his sweaty hair out of his face and he nodded his agreement. "That's . . . very true."

Jackin let out a sharp sigh. "Okay, fine. You want to muster a force? Gather the Sentinels? How the hell are we even gonna begin to do that? All the gates at the Divide are *off*, except Kharon. We can't go anywhere but inward."

"Puck fixed Kharon," Adequin said. "So we help the *Typhos* fix Zelus. Then the *Accora* with Eris. And so on . . ."

Jackin flexed his jaw but gave a short nod. "Okay, so let's say that works, then what? We'd only have a handful of Hermes between us—which we can't even take through the gates. And regardless, the second we try to take a single ship through, the Legion will know we're still alive and come after us. How're we gonna get everyone to safety without showing our hand?"

"Mesa?" Adequin turned to the Savant.

She stood beside Puck, wringing her thin hands nervously. "Yes, Excubitor?"

"Can you reverse engineer this technology? The reactor, I mean."

Mesa's brow raised. "Yes, well, I would need some . . ." She turned her look to Cavalon. After staring down at his boots for a few long seconds, he gave a quick nod. Mesa inclined her head, then turned back to Adequin. "Yes, Excubitor."

"Jack?"

"Yeah, boss."

"What's the *Typhos*'s maximum personnel capacity?"

He blew out a long breath. "I don't remember its make, but it was a capital ship. Maybe ten thousand?"

"Does it still have its jump drive?"

His exasperated grimace softened, then he exchanged a questioning glance with Puck. "It's at least a hundred years older than the *Argus*, so, yeah. I don't think they would have repurposed it. But it'd still need solar power to charge . . ." His words died in his throat as his gaze fell on the window, onto the collapsing mass they'd created, and his face fell slack.

"Cav?" Adequin asked.

"Yeah."

"Are you with us?"

"Yeah, I'm with you."

She raised an eyebrow, surprised by his lack of hesitation. He stood unaided, clutching his stomach in one arm, trying to hide his pain under a look of steadfast determination.

"Were you serious when you suggested putting this thing on a ship?" she asked.

He blinked in surprise. "Well, not just *any* ship. Not the *SGL* or the *Synthesis*, if that's what you mean."

"Could you build one into a capital ship?"

His mouth gaped open. "Uh . . ."

He stared past her, through the glass into the containment chamber, then threw a look to the terminal, then the atlas, then Mesa. He scratched the back of his neck.

A few moments later, he looked up, swallowed hard, and nodded. "I'll need resources . . ."

"Of course."

"And man power."

"Certainly."

"And time."

She waited.

The corner of his mouth pulled up. "I can do it."

She tried to give him a grateful smile, but her face wouldn't listen. It wanted her to scowl, to grit her teeth, to glower in defiance. Cavalon grinned in response.

Adequin turned to face Jackin. His worry had faded, his brow smooth, dark brown eyes wide and clear. He now looked . . . anxiously impressed.

"What do you think, Jack?" she asked quietly. "Want to be a CNO again?"

He didn't respond at first, pressing a hand to his forehead.

She lowered her voice to a whisper. "I don't know what's going on with you and the Mercers . . . but if you have some vengeance to pay the king, this could be your chance."

"Rake, void," he breathed. "That's *mutiny*."

"I know."

He turned to stare back at where Griffith lay, and his hardened features softened.

She swallowed down a lump, praying to the void that Jackin would be on board. She needed him.

After a minute, his hand dropped away and he gave a deep sigh. "Just tell me the plan, boss."

"First, we save the Sentinels." Adequin let out a long, heavy breath. "Then we take the fight to the Core."

ACKNOWLEDGMENTS

Thank you . . .
(In order of appearance-ish)

★ **Mom** and **Dad**, for instilling in me a love of books and science fiction, respectively.

★ **Jessie**, for being the most supportive sister ever, and **DJ**, **Skyler**, **Dawson**, and **Lincoln**.

★ **Matt Olson**, who acted as a sounding board for this story in its infancy, and who has always blindly believed in my creative endeavors more than I ever could myself.

And for introducing me to *Battlestar Galactica*.

And for showing me what a true friend is. I have been changed for good.

★ My husband, best friend, and all-around favorite human, **Dave Dewes**, who encouraged my initial interest in fiction writing by challenging me to tackle a short story—because when I couldn't figure it out, I tried a novel instead.

And for being the only person to have inspired a character in this book, whether I realized it at the time or not.

And for being able to make words rhyme, because void knows I can't.

★ **Ember**, **Arya**, and **Sylvanas**, for keeping me sane.

★ All my critique partners and beta readers on Scribophile and Beta-Books, for their invaluable feedback and support. Especially . . .

★ **Dave Hollis**, aka **Hollis-bot**, for his impressive ability to mimic human emotion and generate an endless trove of thoughtful, constructive, spot-on feedback. He's impacted this book and my writing more than he knows.

- ★ **Tullio Pontecorvo**, who made me realize how hard I'd channeled my inner Commander Shepard, and reminded me how that's never, ever, a bad thing.
- ★ **Tina Chan**, for her keen ability to search-and-destroy my gratuitous prose flaws, and for studying engineering so she can be my Cavalon during the AI uprising.
- ★ **Rebecca Schaeffer**, who first introduced me to the Big Scary World of Publishing, and has been a steadfast beacon of advice and sanity ever since.
- ★ **The Landing Eagles**, Marco Frassetto, and Francesca Tacchi.
- ★ **Margaret Bail**, for believing in this book, and somehow delivering it into the hands of my dream publisher.
- ★ **Tricia Skinner**, a tremendous cheerleader, advocate, and most venerated Sith Lord.
- ★ My editor, **Jen Gunnels**, whose keen insight not only made this story light-years stronger, but has made me a better writer.
- ★ Everyone at **Tor** for their hard work on making this book a reality; I could not be more thrilled with the final product.

And finally, thank you, **readers**, for making this all possible. May you always find wonder in the vastness of space.

ABOUT THE AUTHOR

J. S. Dewes has a bachelor of arts in film from Columbia College Chicago, and has written scripts for award-winning films, which have screened at San Diego Comic-Con and dozens of film festivals across the nation.